Cowboys Dream Too

MORGAN Q. O'REILLY

Cowboys Dream Too
Author's Print Edition

Copyright 2013 Morgan Quinn O'Reilly

Cover Art by: HotDamn Designs 2013

This book was previously digitally published with the same name by Lyrical Press, Inc. 2009. It was re-edited by the author and published independently in 2012 by Morgan Quinn O'Reilly.
morgan@morganqoreilly.com

ISBN-13: 978-0578119441
ISBN-10: 0578119447

Warning
Contains explicit situations, carnal massages,
and inventive riding lessons.

A Few Kind Words for Morgan O'Reilly

ONE

"One of my mother's fondest memories, or so she says, is toddler-me clinging to the hand of an old, bowlegged, grizzled cowboy as he walked me down the hill to the barn where my brothers were messing around at the time." Reed O'Brien leaned back in her lounge chair and sipped her iced tea. A half dozen feet in front of her, kids and beautiful people played in the cool blue water of the hotel pool.

Her best friend, Sam don't-you-dare-call-me-Samantha Bond, listened raptly.

"Paint me a picture, Reed. You do real good with words," Sam ordered.

Reed ignored Sam's lazy grammar and closed her eyes to draw upon those too-distant memories. It had been so long ago--twenty-five, twenty-seven years?--and she'd been so very young...with only one visit since then for a weekend when she was in college. The luxurious Las Vegas setting around her faded as she sank deeper into the past.

"The main house was uphill from the barn. By no means at the top of the hill." Digging into her memories, she couldn't recall the exact outline of the house, but knew it had a long, deep, covered porch perfect for rocking chairs. At least two had been there. There may have been more, but she couldn't see them in her mind.

Craggy rocks rose sharply behind the house. Rocks where her brothers had often found snakes and tarantulas to bring home as pets. Dubious pets that had always died by mysterious means after a day or so. Mom had later confessed to leaving them in the hot sun or getting chloroform from the local vet. The chloroform worked particularly well with rattlesnakes.

"That's why he had to walk me down. The hill was too steep for me. When I went back about nine years ago it was really just a gentle slope. I guess I was about two, maybe two-and-a-half at the time. Mom says I took my first steps on that very porch." Reed lazily swirled the ice in her glass. "Anyhow, the way Mom tells the story, my brothers took off down to the barn--I don't know where my sister was at the time--and I howled because they didn't take me with them. Well, old Ernie, as genuine a cowboy as there ever was, stood up from his rocking chair. Must have been all of sixty at the time, but he looked much older in the few photos we have of him. He said, 'What's the matter, honey? Won't those mean ol' boys walk you down the hill?' Then he reached for my hand, and keeping pace with my baby legs, walked me down the steps of the porch and down the hill. Mom says she can still see it. Ernie in his cowboy hat and faded plaid flannel shirt, worn jeans over bowed legs, wearing his cowboy boots, slowly ambling down the hill with a tiny mop-headed princess clinging to his fingers."

"Where was this?"

"Hmm? Oh, back up behind Livermore. Hidden in those lovely California hills. On the other side of the hill from the reservoir. The road veers off to the left and hugs the side of the hills, about halfway up. Barely wide enough for one car in spots. Mom hated that road. Just like she still hates vertical drops of any kind. You drive about, oh, I don't know, four or five miles, or it might have been only two or three, back along the road until the hills start to flatten out a little. That's where the ranch buildings were, in the bowl of the little valley where the road ends."

Reed sipped her iced tea again. Just the memory of the dusty ranch made her throat dry. As clearly as if she stood there, she could smell the arid dirt, sweet hay, and animals of the ranch where her parents boarded a horse. Snowy, so named because he was white. Fading photographs provided proof she'd ridden the huge beast. Usually with one of her three older brothers or sister, safely snugged in the shelter of their arms. Mom liked to say her girls were the Alpha and Omega of the brood with the three boys in the middle.

When had the family stopped going up there? At some point Ernie had died and his wife, Cora, had moved into town, turning the ranch over to her nephew. How old had Reed been? Four? Five?

"So, why don't you like cowboys?" Sam asked, then tipped her glass of iced tea and drank the rest of it down.

Reed waved her hand and set her glass, now empty but for the ice, on the low table between them. "I never said I didn't like them, they just don't...do it for me. Despite that silly t-shirt you made me buy."

"You're missing out, strumpet," Sam said, and exchanged her glass for a bottle of tanning oil.

"Perhaps, but keep in mind the whole town was overrun by cowboy types. Each one with a pick-up truck and a pick-up line. Hell, even the high school mascot was a cowboy."

"So tell me about your dream last night." Sam's abrupt change of topic took Reed by surprise.

"Dream?" Reed adjusted the cloth over her legs.

"Yeah. Dream. You were muttering in your sleep. Who's Carrick?"

"That dream." Did Sam have to mention it now?

"Is it the same dream from college?"

"Yes." Reed sighed. "It always starts the same, but I can barely remember any of it when I wake up. It never feels complete, that much I remember. I always wake up feeling if only I slept a little longer I'd reach the end. It's like getting three quarters of the way through a book and finding the rest of it missing."

"But romantic, right?" Sam snickered. "At least I'd assume so based on the way you thrashed and moaned." Sam waggled her brows and popped open the top on her oil bottle.

"Give me a break." Reed groaned and leaned back against her cushions. "If I could remember the dream I'd tell you every juicy detail, but it fades as soon as I wake up."

"Maybe I'll sit up and listen tonight." Sam smirked at her. "Then I'll tell you exactly who Carrick is. Maybe he's a hot cowboy."

"Right." Reed snorted as she looked over at her friend and felt a familiar pang of envy.

Sam was long and leggy with the looks of a supermodel. Thick, long, dark brown hair was accented by natural auburn highlights glinting like copper pennies in the sun. At a confident five-feet-nine, with a perfect 36C bust and size eight waist and hips, she towered over Reed, which was one of life's little ironies.

Sam was also bait for every red-blooded male ever born. From infant to senile codger, all men turned to stare with their tongues hanging out when she walked past. Or like today, when they walked past her. Reed had never seen so many men sucking in their paunchy guts while thrusting out their chests. It was only a matter of time before one fell into the pool or walked into a palm tree.

Reed's envy never lasted, though. Hating Sam just wasn't possible. She was too nice, too funny, too wicked and just too good a friend. Reed wrinkled her nose and pulled her large-brimmed straw hat more securely down over her face.

"You know me," Reed said. "I like those suit types. They only get sweaty in the gym and in bed. The rest of the time they smell like expensive leather." Oh yeah, she went for wool suits, primo cotton or silk shirts, and ties. Groomed hair, manicured hands and nails that never injured tender skin, and arms that knew how to hold a woman when dancing--that did it for Reed.

A man who could carry her to bed would be asking too much. Men who tried to carry girls like her ended up with ruptured disks or hernias. She shifted against the raised back of her padded teak lounge carefully covered by the shade of a poolside umbrella and a large potted palm. Idly she watched the beautiful, and a few not-so-beautiful, people move around the pool.

"So why, pray tell, are we going to a dude ranch tomorrow?"

Out of the corner of her eye, Reed saw Sam begin smoothing tanning oil over her already bronzed body. Her friend never hid from the sun. Everyone else was slapping on layers of SPF 70 sunscreen while Sam rubbed some exotic banana-coconut-pineapple-scented oil on her skin. Most likely SPF 2, if Reed wasn't mistaken.

"I didn't choose the location, so you can't pin this one on me." Reed watched from under the cover of her mirrored sunglasses. One of those businessman-types she so adored, turned in his chair to unabashedly watch Sam apply the oil first on her legs, followed by her stomach, then between the cups and strings of her bikini top before covering her arms. When Sam lifted her chin to oil her throat, the man dropped his beer can on the concrete apron of the pool deck.

"Stop showing off," Reed growled.

"Hmm?"

Sam looked around with genuine confusion on her face, her chocolate-brown eyes hidden behind fashionable, tiny-lensed sunglasses.

Reed dipped her fingers into her glass, snatched out an ice cube and flung it at her friend.

"Hey! What's that for?" Sam brushed the rapidly melting ice cube away.

"Pass it on to your boyfriend over there to cool him off." Reed adjusted the length of black linen she used as a sarong to cover her pale legs. The shade of the umbrella wasn't enough to protect her from the glaring mid-August sun, and she didn't care for sunscreen. No one had ever convinced her the chemicals didn't cause skin cancer any less than UV rays.

A diaphanous, sun-blocking long-sleeved black

shirt protected her arms and shoulders. Sunlight reflected from the windows of the tall, sleek hotel surrounding them was enough to burn her uncovered milky skin in less than thirty minutes. Covering up didn't bother her, really. Self-conscious about her curvy body, she often hid behind layers anyway. While Sam called her voluptuous, Reed and her brothers had another word for it--fat.

"My boyfriend?" Sam looked around then laughed out loud. "He's not my boyfriend. He's more your type."

Sam was right, but Mr. Business didn't seem to agree. His tongue nearly swept the pool deck. No, he wasn't quite Reed's type after all. She liked her brain-boys with a sense of style and decorum. This one apparently had neither going for him, although he tried to cover up his major fashion faux pas with a towel across his lap. He needed to lose twenty pounds and do about a million crunches to fix that error. Honestly, men should have to gain the written approval of ten women, not relatives, before wearing bikini swim suits. It should be a law. Especially in Vegas.

Reed hid her disgust by trying to coax an ice cube from the glass into her mouth. Predictably, the ice clung to the bottom of the glass no matter how much she rattled it. She tried one last time only to have the entire mass let loose and spill across her face, over her chest and down inside her suit.

Typical, Reed snarled internally while Sam hooted with laughter. Reed didn't dare look up as she brushed the rogue cubes away. *How humiliating.*

"May I offer you a towel?"

The smooth deep voice and an undeniably male presence made Reed notice the man holding out a towel. Black hair, eyes hidden behind the mandatory sunglasses, bronzed skin, lean but bulging muscles and six-pack abs sliding into baggy swim trunks. Hideous swim trunks. Bright red with a white hibiscus pattern. Strong looking legs, also bronzed. Hawaiian? Italian? Hard to tell without seeing his eyes and the rest of his face. No wedding ring and no band of white showing where one might have been. Overall, quite drool worthy. *He* could have worn a Speedo--and how.

"Thanks," Reed said, as pleasantly as she could, and took the offering. She looked away to pat her chest and ignored the ice cubes that had slipped down her cleavage to melt against her stomach under the one piece black suit she wore. Blessed with a more impressive cleavage than Sam, it was her one point of pride. 36DD, fortunately still firm. "All better now." She smiled up at her hero of the moment.

"My pleasure," he replied with a smile bordering on a leer as he stared at her chest.

Reed was tempted to point at her eyes and say, 'Up here, bud, my eyes are up here.' Instead, she bit her lip and let him stare at her nipples hardening from the shock of the ice as much as from his regard.

This was the only man to ogle her since their arrival yesterday morning. All other eyes had been glued on Sam. Ogles like this were few and far between--Sam or no Sam. Better to enjoy the few directed her way because all too soon the time would come when no one ogled her at all.

"Allow me to get you another drink," Mr. Sexy Body said.

"It was just the dregs of iced tea, but thanks anyway," Reed replied sweetly and gave him a sassy smile. Maybe he'd be in the casino later tonight. Which game did he play? Poker? Black Jack? Craps? Most likely wouldn't see him in the nickel slots.

He waved for a waiter, then pulled a wooden chair close, laid another towel over it and sat down beside her. "My name is Gray."

"Hello, Gray, I'm Reed." She shook the hand he extended. Large and warm, it swallowed hers, making her feel petite and delicate. "This is my friend, Sam."

"Sam." Acknowledging the other woman to be polite, Gray nodded toward the brunette.

She was pretty enough, but it was the redhead who'd caught his eye. At least, he thought she was a redhead. Hard to tell with the huge hat she wore. Since most of the men nearby were focused on the brunette, he'd have an open field to the smaller, more curvaceous woman. Which suited him fine, as she was just his style anyway. He'd watched the two women long enough to see that as long as she sat next to her friend, she had no clue of her value. He could show her.

Acknowledging the waiter with a nod, he turned his attention back to Reed. "Iced tea? Or something a little stronger?"

"Is it after five yet?" Reed quipped without missing a beat.

Gray had his reply ready. "It is in New York."

"Well then," Reed paused, then glanced at her friend. "What say you, wench?"

"Oh, by all means, Long Island or Cape Codder at least," Sam agreed with a toothy grin.

"Three Long Islands," he told the waiter and turned back to the women. "I believe the sun is well over the yardarm."

"Thanks." Reed gifted him with a dazzling smile.

"My pleasure. What are you lovely ladies doing in Las Vegas this fine day? Did I overhear you discussing cowboys?" He bit back a laugh when Reed ducked her head to hide her face under the large hat she wore.

Watching as she fussed with the towel he'd given her, Gray figured she was trying to find words to cover her embarrassment. At least she hadn't wrapped the see-through shirt back over her chest after wiping up the spill. The very fact she swathed herself in tantalizing fabrics made her sexier than the women strutting by in their string bikinis.

Her pampered, pale skin enhanced her resemblance to a Celtic queen of mystic legend. She belonged in a forest primeval with a pool of clear water at her feet and a wreath of wild flowers circling her head. Just like the woman in his dream.

The talk of dude ranches had been a convenient excuse for him to approach them, but the true hook in his gut had been the discussion of her dream and the name "Carrick."

Pulling his attention back from his musings, he noticed Sam wasn't prone to embarrassment. He smiled when she cast an affectionate glance at her oblivious friend.

"We're just catching our breath before

moseying on to our dude ranch retreat tomorrow," Sam told him, and settled back in her lounge, a sleek goddess, bronzed and oiled in her tiny yellow suit.

Gray sat so he was turned toward them yet could still see most of the pool. It also allowed him to take advantage of the shade from Reed's umbrella. From there he could easily converse with both women who looked to be around thirty. Without seeing their eyes it was hard to tell. No wedding rings. Again, not very helpful. Reed's hat just made it worse.

All he could see was her chest, her almost pointy chin, and bow-shaped lips. It seemed likely she had a heart-shaped face to match the heart-shaped backside and hourglass figure he'd seen when they arrived. With her milk-white skin, she was most likely a true redhead, but until she removed the wide-brimmed hat, he could only guess. While it was smart of her to cover up in the harsh sun, he felt deprived. He wanted to see more of her. All of her.

"Forgive me for saying so, but you two don't look like the dude ranch sort," he said to keep the conversation from stalling.

Reed snorted. "You don't say." She laughed and glanced at her friend before looking back at him.

She had a million-watt smile with a show-stopping laugh, and probably didn't know it. The music of it stroked his heartstrings. Gray felt the stirring he'd been trying to ignore for the last hour rise up again, and he lifted a foot to rest an ankle on the opposite knee. Thankfully, he wore loose swim trunks.

Aside from their conversation, her laugh had drawn him over as much as the ice down her magnificent cleavage. The smile alone would keep him attached to her hip--and any place else she'd let him latch on to.

Gray nearly snatched the towel from her when she curled her legs to the side and turned slightly in his direction. If she separated her knees a little and let the wrap open a tad more, he'd have a raging hard-on that would be damn near impossible to hide. Better she remained coy for the moment.

"Which ranch?" he asked while the waiter handed out drinks. Making sure the ladies had theirs first, Gray signed the ticket before taking a deep sip and savoring the icy refreshment. Not too sweet, good. Two of these ought to break down her resistance.

"Oh, somewhere not far from Denver." Reed waved her hand dismissively and sipped her drink. "Well, the sun *must* be over the yardarm. Why didn't we get drinks like this last night?" She tossed the question to her friend.

"Nobody was trying to hit on us last night." Sam lowered her sunglasses enough to wink at Gray. "So, we got the watered down version."

"Hey, who says I'm hitting on you?" He laughed.

Reed lowered her sunglasses enough to give him a disbelieving once over.

Green eyes. Eyes he'd seen before in only one place. Gray smiled to cover the lurch of his heart. Heavily lashed, large, and open, these were not just any average emerald, hazel or blue eyes, but an exquisite, deep, smoky, jade green--like the stone he favored. He'd have to wait until they were in better light to confirm the exact shade, but the tightening of his stomach said he was right. These were the eyes he'd been searching for.

Stunned, he sat and stared like a pubescent teen seeing a supermodel in the flesh.

Like the sigh of the faintest summer breeze, he felt the caress of those beautiful eyes on his skin before she pushed the concealing glasses back into place. Feeling like he'd been hit by lightning, he covered his reaction by nearly finishing his drink in one long gulp.

"Right. Did you hear that, Sam? He's not hitting on us."

Reed's musical laugh acted like a hand wrapping around his heart and Gray longed to feel her wrapping around another part of him. The part stealing all the blood from his brain. Much more torture like this and he could forget about impressing her with intelligence. Send over the towel boy to wipe up the drool.

Gray's grin widened as he lowered his glass. "Actually, not that your friend isn't attractive, but I can't handle two beauties and your attraction is far stronger. I'm really just hitting on you." He chuckled at Reed's mock gasp of outrage.

This one had a healthy sense of humor. That was a relief. Had she been humorless it would have been a disappointment. A challenge, but a disappointment nonetheless. No, not her. Humor was one of her gifts.

"Shameless ploy, Mr. Gray." Reed tsked, then wrapped her luscious lips around the thin straw in her drink.

"Honest. I'm a sucker for milk-skinned

maidens. I appreciate a bronzed goddess as well, but I mean no disrespect when I say your friend doesn't hold a candle to you." *Oh, Reed of the luscious red lips.* What would her lips feel like?

The perfect O of surprise they made right now nearly ruined his plan to look cool and sophisticated. To leap onto her lounge chair and start kissing her might result in an assault charge he really didn't need.

"Ha! See?" Sam exclaimed. "Just what I've been telling you for years, trollop! I think I might like this guy you picked up." She threw a brilliant smile his direction and raised her glass to him.

Raising his own glass in response, Gray returned the grin while Reed spluttered and had to use the towel to again dry her beautiful skin. How refreshing for someone as attractive as Sam to know the value of her friend. Integrity and loyalty such as hers were precious commodities.

"Do you two always call each other such names?" While it was undoubtedly another sign of mutual deep affection, he found it curious they used antiquated English insults. He was tempted to grab the towel and wipe away the drool close to dribbling down his chin. After licking the drops off Reed's skin, of course.

"Trollop, wench, hussy, baggage, strumpet, shrew...slut." Reed shrugged. "Whatever suits the moment." Did she really think the coy tilt of her head would cover a blush? "But that's between us. Anyone else tries it..."

Gray's body shook as he laughed at her glower. "I get it. Anyone else who tries is toast. So, what's with the ranch?" He didn't dare ask about the dream now. Later, once she knew him better. In his dreams he'd listen for himself. The thought very nearly made him groan. To get Reed into his bed--

"Back to that are we?" Reed's brow wrinkled. "Not vacation at all. A work thing. Team building. Sam and I took an extra few days off to stop here. We're not really driving on to Denver. We'll catch a flight tomorrow, then drive up to the ranch. Somewhere in the Rockies, an hour or two from the airport. Or so they say."

The back of Gray's neck tingled with what he recognized as anticipation. "You don't seem impressed even though it sounds like you grew up around ranches."

"Boy, you really were eavesdropping, weren't you?"

He had the impression she rolled her eyes. "Sorry, the subject of horses catches my attention." That, and the name Carrick associated with a dream.

"Oh? Why is that?"

The tingling at his neck increased as he sensed sharp eyes peering at him from behind the mirrored lenses. Damn, he couldn't tell exactly where she looked. Unsettled by an odd twinge of nervousness, he rested his cold glass on his thigh to disguise his attraction indicator. Might be time to jump in the pool. One end was nearly shaded, maybe he could talk her into the water. "I hang out with horses from time to time," he answered casually.

"Well, other than once riding behind a friend, in junior high, and galloping through the vineyards, I haven't been around horses since I was three or four. I'm a city girl." Reed slipped the straw between her lips again and spoke around it. "From whence do you hail, Mr. Gray?"

He grinned at the quicksilver change of her mood. Playful and flirtatious. This might work out better than he hoped since he was ready to play with something other than numbers and merchants.

Playtime was the very reason he'd stopped here the night before last. Another couple of hours and he could have landed in Vail, but he wasn't ready to face the family yet. *And if she's the one...so much the better.* Cosmic forces at play? Bring it on.

He was doubly glad he'd stopped. The feeling of anticipation grew stronger.

Fresh from a long month scouring the Far East markets for just the right crystals and innovative physicists, he and Roger had both been due for a layover and necessary rest.

Not only his pilot but right hand man, Roger had been pleased with the unplanned stop in Vegas. After two nights and a day of blowing off steam, Roger now slept off the excess pleasure in a lounge chair across the pool.

"I'm from no place in particular, but the family homestead is high in the legendary Rockies."

"Ah, therefore the question about the dude ranch." Reed nodded and he watched her relax in her lounger, idly pushing the towel aside.

That was part of what he wanted. Her skin fairly glowed against the severe black she wore.

Why did curvy women lean toward black? Did they think it made them less visible? He wanted to see her in electric blue, maybe with a swirling design in the fabric to emphasize her melon-shaped breasts. A little smaller than cantaloupes, he bet they tasted just as sweet as ripe fruit.

"Yes, the question about the ranch," Gray answered her. "I was raised on one. Was lucky to escape to college. My brother got the business."

"Still, you're some sort of cowboy." With a wave of her hand he knew she had him neatly categorized. Funny, since he'd never considered himself a cowboy. "I can't remember the name of where we're going. I'm told it isn't far from Vail or some hot springs. Supposed to be pretty swank. All I really care about are the hot springs." Reed rolled her neck and he could hear the vertebrae pop. "They tell me there's a masseuse on staff. I doubt I'll even touch a horse, though Sam made me pack jeans and cowboy boots. But just to be proper, I did indulge in a Stetson."

"Tell me you didn't pack the obligatory snap shirt," he teased.

"Of course I did. For the evening campfire I'm sure they'll drag me to." Reed snorted. "They told me it was a requirement, just in case one needed to shed a shirt quickly, like if it got caught by a horn or branch."

Or caught in his hands. Gray smiled into his ice cubes. He'd count as something horny. The thought sobered him almost immediately. Getting caught by a bull's horn was no teasing matter, as his brother Dustin would no doubt confirm right now. Damn, that's why he should have just kept flying. He'd hear about it, for sure, when they arrived. Too late, now. Roger was in no condition to fly until morning.

"How many from your company will be there? And what company is it?" he asked casually, wanting to verify the funny feeling they were headed for his family ranch. There were only a few in the vicinity, and the others couldn't be described as swank. Budget-minded would describe them better.

He glanced across the pool to where Roger lazily stirred. Tomorrow, for sure. Better let Roger know they'd be heading out so he wouldn't be in violation of FAA flight rules about drinking.

"Sam? Do you remember the name of the place?"

Gray was treated to a glimpse of lovely neck when Reed swiveled her head to look at her friend.

"Eagle Mountain," Sam said.

Reed looked back at him. "Sound familiar?"

"Yes." He couldn't hold back the grin. "Which cabin are you bunked in? Or are you in one of the multiple unit lodges?"

"The one with the outdoor hot tub." Reed rubbed her neck again.

"There are two." He could ease those tense and aching muscles. Funny, he had a few himself that she could ease.

"Sounds like we'll be on your turf, then."

"Yes, ma'am." He gave them his best cowboy drawl. Where was his hat? He had a sudden mad urge to tip it.

Two

"There, doesn't the water feel good?" Gray held Reed's hand as he coaxed her down the steps into the pool. Using his best manners, he resisted the urge to grab her around the waist and pull her up against him. A flash fantasy of trapping her against the side, her legs wrapped around his hips, head thrown back to let him kiss her neck, made it especially difficult to behave. A vampire could go centuries without seeing a neck so beautiful.

Okay, Roger had him watching too many vamp movies.

"Yes," she agreed. "The water feels great."

Gray grinned. Not only did her lovely nipples react to the cool water, she'd shed the hat, sunglasses and all her layers to reveal a figure-enhancing suit.

Auburn hair and eyes just the shade of smoky jade he'd known they'd be, made her white skin seem all the more pure against the severe black of the one-piece suit embracing every curve. She may have barely reached his shoulder, but she was flawlessly proportioned from her little toes to her softly rounded stomach and generous breasts. Not stick thin, no, but rather a perfect luscious handful, she'd be soft and sweet in his arms. He wanted a taste, just one little lick and nibble. To start with, anyway.

"And I'm trying to figure out why we stopped

in Vegas in the summer." She laughed, then moaned with happiness as she sank into the water up to her neck. "I'm not a sun girl."

"I noticed." He reluctantly released her hand and watched her hair float on the surface of the water.

"You don't have a problem with the sun."

"Never been a problem. I grew up in the mountains and spent practically every day outside."

"Right, wrangling horses and herding cattle."

"Exactly, and at eight or nine thousand feet the sun is even more intense."

"Oh. I hadn't thought about that." She frowned even as she eased into a graceful, slow breast stroke across the narrow end of the huge pool.

He swam beside her, leisurely dodging a pair of kids tossing a ball back and forth. Without warning she dove beneath the surface, her curvy rear breaking the surface like a dolphin. Tiny white feet, pedicured toes perfectly pointed, were the last part of her to slip beneath the water.

Obviously an experienced swimmer.

Gray dove to watch her swim with the grace of a mermaid, long hair streaming behind her like a silken flag.

Following, he surfaced at her side and watched the water flow down her face and hair, leaving glistening drops clinging to her lashes. Still crouched low in the water, her hair floated out behind her, just begging his hands to gather it up and bury his fingers in it.

He'd watched in amazement when it had tumbled down from where she'd had it tucked into her hat. Her hair fell to the middle of her back, thick and wavy as if she kept it coiled and pinned up most of the time. Just like the dream.

He'd caught the movement when Sam's lips twitched with amusement. She'd seen him swallow his lust even if Reed hadn't.

"Over here." He took her hand. "This corner seems relatively quiet. Enough shade?"

"Uh huh." Reed lifted her feet and let him pull her along. As an antidote to the heat, the water was heavenly. She rolled to her back and looked up at the hot, cloudless sky. What the hell were she and Sam doing here? The casinos were fun, but this wasn't the kind of place she really liked.

Wine country and mineral spas--that was her idea of a good vacation. Vine-covered stone cottages or an elegant Victorian bed and breakfast dripping with romance to slow things down, that would work. Then again, with Sam at her side, they had excellent poolside service from the gorgeous young waiters, not to mention plenty of eye candy strolling by.

Gray's smiling face drifted into her line of sight. Without the sunglasses, he was truly beautiful. High cheek bones and a slight tilt to his eyes indicated anything from Asian to Islander to Native American heritage. Strong jaw, squared chin, full lips and white teeth. Thick black hair cut close enough she couldn't tell if it would be curly or straight when grown out a little. Eyes so dark brown they appeared black, virtually blending with his pupils. He even had manners and charm.

Reed dunked her head back to cool her face, before pushing her feet to the bottom.

"There's a built-in bench," he said, and drew her to sit beside him.

An unaccustomed blush burned across her cheeks when his thigh pressed against hers. She scooted away, putting at least six inches between them. "Slow down there, mister," she warned.

"Why? Isn't this Vegas? And if I heard correctly, you're leaving in the morning. Doesn't give me much time to woo you properly."

"Woo?" Reed laughed and looked into his teasing eyes.

Sense of humor. Very sexy.

"If I told you I loved you and wanted to marry you right now, you'd walk away from me, wouldn't you?" He sighed dramatically.

"You're right, I would. And then I'd call for the men in the white jackets to take you away."

"Why? I'm not insane."

She gave him a long steady look. He *looked* sane enough. Maybe he was hoping by paying attention to her, he could get close to Sam faster. It'd happened often enough.

Take Jerry the Rat, for example. Just the latest proof of her point, he'd dated Reed three times before suggesting a double date with his best friend. The next thing she'd known, Sam was sandwiched between the two men, while Reed sat by herself. Sam had sized up the situation fast and hauled Reed out of the restaurant.

At least Reed had gotten the last laugh. Two months ago, word had come down from Troy Spearman that budgets needed cutting. He'd also noticed Jerry's Marketing Department was over-staffed and its people seemed to have a great deal of leisure time. Not only had it been pure logic, it had been sweet revenge.

"What's that evil smile?" Gray asked.

"Sorry, I was just thinking about the last guy who *wooed* me to get close to Sam."

"Although that isn't my motivation, I'm curious. What happened to him?"

"Got whacked off at the knees, not literally or physically, but in the corporate sense. It wasn't my fault the CEO took a hatchet to the guy's budget, but he blamed me anyway. I didn't mind. It was actually one of the few times I was tempted to kiss my boss for being ruthless."

"Ah, corporate warrior. What department are you in?"

"Finance. I play with numbers. What do you do?"

"A little of this, a little of that. I dabble," he said, clearly evading the question.

"Hmm, either a jet setter or a corporate raider. Guess we're done talking business. What do you do for fun?"

"I play with gemstones. Are you aware your eyes are a nearly perfect match for the deepest Imperial jade? An emerald color so dark it's almost forest green, with a hint of smokiness."

Her cheeks heated again and she looked away. "No, they're just plain green." Damn, this man was getting to her in a way no else ever had.

Gray's finger caught her chin and gently turned her face back to his.

Reed saw no sign of teasing in his eyes, only sincerity.

"Your eyes are not plain, nor are they ordinary. I've never seen prettier eyes, and I've seen plenty of green ones."

Unable to look away, Reed found herself mesmerized by his intense gaze. Almost visible, it seemed as if a beam of light connected them. Her breath caught in her throat and her heart skipped a beat. Trying again for a bit of oxygen, she drew in an unsteady breath. "Th-thank you."

Instead of releasing her chin, Gray drew his thumb across her lower lip and lifted one corner of his mouth. "You're welcome, beautiful Reed," he said softly.

Finding the tiniest bit of free will, Reed made herself smile and give a weak laugh. If the truth be known, she didn't have the strength for more, and it looked as if he intended to kiss her. Her heart now beat so wildly, if he'd looked down he would have seen it leaping under her skin.

His gaze did drop but only to her lips.

Her eyes stared at his. Generous lips, neither too thick nor too thin, but rather--

It happened so fast she found herself confused. Reed blinked, trying to process the fleeting touch against her temple.

What?

She shook her head and caught a flash of annoyance in Gray's eyes before he released her chin and reached for the soft beach ball floating nearby. Had that bounced off her head?

"Sorry, lady!" A boy, about nine, small and skinny, all bony arms and freckles called out the apology.

Reed laughed and watched Gray toss the ball back.

"Be careful there," he advised the kid.

Reed saw the crooked, rueful smile on his face. Although certainly frustrated, he wasn't the type to yell at kids for being kids.

"Yes, sir. Sorry!"

The kid turned away and lobbed the ball toward another, slightly older boy. A woman on the far side of the pool waved her arms from her lounge chair.

"Timmy! How many times have I told you to watch out for other people? Pay attention and don't make me take that ball away!"

"Yes, Mom!" Timmy promised, though Reed was sure he'd never be able to keep it.

"You all right?"

Reed turned back to Gray.

He'd asked the question low, with concern in his voice.

"The day I can't take a beach ball to the head without injury is the day they scatter my ashes." Shaking her head, she laughed. "Looks like the kid did me a favor. I do believe my virtue was in danger for a moment there."

Oh God, had she really batted her eyelashes? *Virtue? What virtue?* She cleared her throat and looked away. Time to pack away the Regency romances for a while.

Gray's eyes twinkled. "I don't know about doing you a favor. He certainly didn't do one for me, unless you think a kiss might cure the bump on your head?" he asked hopefully, sliding closer to her again.

"Whoa there, mister. I've heard cowboys were friendly, but this is kind of fast, don't you think?"

"Okay, okay. I'll slow down." He grinned and held up his hands. "Why is it I never seem to find the fast, loose women?"

"Why is it I get the feeling you're telling tall stories?" she countered, then looked away as the ball came flying back. Thankfully it missed her by a few feet this time.

Ow. There was that pinch again.

Reed grimaced and tried to slowly rotate her head to ease the numbness creeping down her right arm. Usually a day or two away from her computer was enough to make it go away. Flexing her hand, she chased off the prickly tingles caused by an irritated nerve.

"Here." Gray's hands settled on her shoulders and turned her. It felt as if his hands completely covered her upper back as he began to massage her shoulders. "I know a thing or two about tight muscles."

Did he ever. Reed let her body relax under the gentle kneading.

"Where, exactly, does it hurt?" he asked.

"My neck is stiff, but that isn't the real problem. There's a knot in my shoulder..." She held her breath while his fingers traveled down, just to the left of her spine. "Just a little more to the left... There!"

His fingers prodded the knotted muscles.

"Nobody seems to be able to find it or get rid of it." She grunted as he traced the area.

"They must be blind or not know what they're doing. Right where I thought it would be. Try to relax. It's pretty big."

"Ugh." Reed grunted again and let her head drop forward. "Yeah," she gasped as his fingers probed the extent of the knot. "What I call my computer shoulder." *Oh, that hurt.* She also knew it was necessary or she'd never sleep tonight. Like she'd slept well in weeks? Months?

She had to give Gray full marks for knowing what he was doing.

He didn't dig right in with all his strength but worked at the knot, applying pressure then soothing the muscle. As the knot eased, she relaxed to the point of feeling boneless. Several minutes later, he worked his way back to her neck and shoulders causing her to nearly slide into an orgasmic swoon.

Had they been tucked away in a private room, she was sure she'd have passed out from the sheer pleasure of his touch and relief from the pain. "Ummm, that feels good," she purred, her head lolling to the side.

"Yes, it does." His soft voice was suspiciously close to her ear.

Oh God, she was practically in his lap, her head dropping back to rest on his shoulder. The smooth skin of his broad chest was warm against her back, even in the water.

"Relax," he said. "You must work very hard to get a knot like that."

"Mmm." She didn't work any harder than anyone else. Okay, so maybe the rest of the world didn't work fourteen to sixteen hour days. It was also true most people didn't sleep on the sofas in their offices or keep a rotating wardrobe there for the times they were just too tired to drive home.

When Troy started noticing she'd worn the same outfit twice in one week it usually meant it was time to go home for a night or two to the small house she shared with Sam. Maybe it wasn't such a good thing the drycleaners picked up and delivered to the office.

Reed felt Gray's cheek rest against her head, his lips brushing the edge of her ear. *Too fast*, she told herself.

But I feel so good, the other half of her whined.

Great, the good girl and the bad girl are about to get into it.

"That was a heavy sigh," Gray whispered, his breath teasing her ear and sending shivers of heat spearing through her body.

"I should be running from you, right now. I should. I just feel too damned good to move. Almost like I've been drugged."

"Nothing more than your natural endorphins whisking away all those nasty toxins locked up in that knot. Rest, and let your body do its thing."

She laughed weakly. "Right. While I melt into the arms of a stranger." Where was Sam when she needed a protector?

"You're safe. I won't take advantage of you. Yet," he murmured.

Reed's lashes fluttered as she tried to open her eyes.

His strong hands moved to the edge of her shoulders and started working her upper arms.

Endorphins, right. Good one. She had another word for it, *hormones.* And hers were beginning to sizzle. She didn't have to look down to know her nipples stabbed against the thin, stretchy material covering her. The surface of the water undulated right at nipple level, teasing them unmercifully into aching buds.

"Where do you go numb first? The right hand ring finger?"

"Uh huh." The barely coherent response sounded more like a grunt to her.

"I'll work down to it. More on the right side than the left?"

"Uh huh."

"You're right handed, then. That's why the knot in your shoulder is on the left. Ever try moving your mouse to the other side?"

"Hopeless. Didn't work." Did he have a camera in her office?

"And I suppose you've done all the ergonomic things possible."

"Even had a professional consultant come in and arrange me. Helped a little."

"Then the problem would be the number of hours you spend at your computer, and your bed."

"What are you? A chiropractor? Osteopath?"

He sounded like he wanted to fix the problem in her bed. The particular problem he had in mind most likely being the extreme level of inactivity. Hard to have activity there when she spent more time sleeping at the office, usually in front of her computer when she failed to crawl to the sofa.

"I dabble in natural healing. Spent a few hours with various massage experts learning a few of their secrets. Did you know jade is believed to have healing properties?"

"I thought crystals were healing stones?"

"They are as well. Fascinating subject, all the uses for the hard minerals found on the earth. I could finish putting you to sleep right here, just by telling you everything I know about jade alone. It's used to soothe everything from chakras to heart and stomach ailments and even help improve sleep."

"I get the feeling you like jade," Reed murmured. Her eyes didn't want to open. Sleep improvement wouldn't be a bad thing.

"I do. Which is one reason I notice green eyes."

His lips brushed her temple and the jolt of

energy shocking her system popped Reed's eyes open.

"Hey there," she said softly. "No fair."

His chuckle was warm in her ear. "Couldn't resist. You looked so peaceful."

"I feel peaceful, or did." She laughed as a splash of water landed on her face. Another kid had jumped into the water a few feet away.

Using the opportunity to escape, she straightened and turned away from him. "You're dangerous, mister," she playfully scolded him. "I practically forgot where we were."

"I have a solution, then. Come have dinner in my suite tonight. I have a hot tub in the middle of the living room. Then you won't have to worry about location."

Reed eased away from him with another laugh. "Tempting, cowboy, but I'm not going there. I already have a date tonight."

She looked toward Sam and saw her talking with what looked like a Swedish weight lifter. Yup, that was more Sam's type. All muscles, no brains.

Gray followed her gaze and grinned. "Looks like your date may stand you up." Leave it to Roger to find the leggy ones. This might be fun.

"And if she does, then I may actually get some sleep tonight."

Not if he had anything to say about it.

Reed looked back at her friend before glancing at him with a mischievous half smile that transformed her face from beautiful to exquisite. "A lane just opened up. Race you back!"

He barely had a chance to see what she meant before launching off the wall to follow her. Nice strokes. Reminded him of one who'd spent long hours swimming laps. Swim team in high school? College? Pushing a little, he caught up to her as she touched the far wall.

"Let's see, you're an overworked financial expert who used to swim, I'd say on a school sports team. Am I starting to narrow in on your character?" He pushed a strand of hair from her face as she caught her breath.

"I'm an out-of-shape former swimmer. Then again, I never was fast. Always too... well, I displaced too much water to get through it efficiently." She gave him that sexy half grin again. The one that said she didn't take herself too seriously.

An odd contrast, since most financial types he knew lacked discernible humor.

"Long distance races?"

"Yep. Who are you? Mister Know-It-All?"

Gray laughed. "Hardly. But I do make a point of learning people. I have to."

"Why is that?"

"I need to predict, as close as I can, how my opponent will act or react before I make my moves."

"You sound like a chess player."

"Just so."

"You've piqued my curiosity. Which are you? Cowboy, jet setter, jeweler, massage therapist, or corporate raider?"

She looked cute with her head cocked to the side, an eyebrow raised inquisitively. The urge to kiss her quadrupled.

"A bit of all, I suppose. Come on. Have dinner with me tonight." He softened his voice in the way that usually worked. Tougher than most women he'd seduced, she was melting, he could sense it. He also had her loosely trapped against the side of the pool, a hand on either side of her head. A good start to his earlier fantasy.

Straight white teeth caught her lower lip and tugged it in indecision.

He cupped her cheek with one hand, and his thumb gently pulled her lip free. "You won't be sorry. I'll tell you all about the ranch so you'll know what to expect. I can even make sure you get the best masseuse when you get there." Or masseur, as the case may be.

"Okay." She gave in gracefully. "But not in your suite. Somewhere public."

"Your suite?"

"That's not public," she softly chastised him. "And we only have a room."

He let his thumb slide down her throat to rest in the pulsing hollow at its base. Her breath still came fast, but he didn't think it was because of the swim.

"Sir, you grow bold. I'm not a witless *ingénue* to fall to the charms of a handsome stranger."

Damn, she was adorable when she dropped her chin and playfully batted her eyelashes at him. Put her in a gown of velvet with a gold crown on her head and she could be medieval princess flirting with a suitor.

"Forgive me. I find you exquisite and am eager to taste your charms."

How she swallowed and blushed... such a turn on. Her increasing pulse rate said he was getting through her defenses.

"I doubt you'll experience much more than the sharp edge of my tongue if you keep going down this path. Not to mention I have a pretty mean right hook. And three older brothers who taught me how to defend myself quite well."

Getting the message to back off, Gray eased away until his arms were straight, grasping the edge of the pool on either side of her. "Is this far enough?"

"It's a good start."

"Where would you like to eat?" he asked.

"I'm in the mood for steak and maybe seafood. Where's a good place? And don't say your suite."

"Foiled again. What room are you in? I'll pick you up. I want it to be a surprise."

"How should I dress? Are you the type to wear a suit, a sports coat or a polo shirt?"

"If I wear a suit, will you wear a dress that shows off your legs?"

"My legs? That's a new one," she muttered.

"And put your hair up so I can fantasize about taking it down and kissing your throat."

"Well, you seem to have this all worked out."

"I have a vision of you, elegant and cool on the surface, sizzling and unrestrained underneath. Am I wrong?"

"I don't know..." Her teeth worried her lip again. "I think I'm rather boring, actually. I can do uptight and cool quite well. Strict hair style, severe glasses, basic black."

"No, no, not the librarian look." He groaned and bowed his head, pulling himself closer to her again. His forehead was bare inches from hers. "I won't last five minutes if you dress like that tonight. In college, I nearly flunked out because I kept fantasizing about taming the snooty librarian in the stacks."

"I think I'm more the old-woman-in-the-shoe type than the hot librarian."

"Well, let me put it this way, if you aren't dressed in your absolute most sexy manner then it's dinner in my suite, just the two of us and room service. No swim suit required and clothes won't matter. Deal?" Ah, she got the message judging by her blush. *Damn.*

Reed extended her hand, forcing him to open one side of her loose prison. "Room six-fourteen. Eight o'clock."

"Seven," he countered and held her hand. So tiny and delicate, the nails perfectly shaped and polished a sexy blood red.

"Seven forty-five."

"Seven fifteen."

"Seven forty."

Time to throw her a curve. "Seven ten."

"No fair! You're not supposed to go backwards." The protest burst from her lips as her flashing eyes stared at him accusingly.

"Why do you need so much time? It's not quite three-forty now, and I suspect you're going to run away as soon as I let you out of the pool."

"I have a massage in twenty minutes and then I'll need time to rest and dress. The sort of transformation you expect can't be rushed."

"Okay, seven-thirty. That's my final offer. If you don't like that one, we go back to seven."

She gave him a narrow eyed glare. "Fine. Seven-thirty."

"Or you can cancel your masseuse and let me give you a massage. I'm most thorough." *And she blushes so prettily.*

"I'm sure you are, but I have a therapeutic

massage in mind, not an erotic one."

"Touché, but I'm very good at deep tissue massage." *And the other too.* Just the thought made him smile, and her eyes widened ever so slightly.

"I'm sure you are," she murmured as her pulse leapt under his thumb. "Now, I really must go. I want to shower off the chlorine before my massage."

Stepping back, he took her hand and led her up the steps.

THREE

Gray glanced at his watch for the hundredth time before straightening his tie in the mirror. Seven ten. It would only take five minutes to get to her room. He was tempted to stroll down to the bar, toss back a whiskey to steady his nerves, then meander to her room. No good. Better not to arrive with alcohol already on his breath.

"You look beautiful, dear." Roger's mocking voice came from the door of the bedroom.

"Why thank you, honey. Where are you going? You look stunning too."

Roger was dressed much like Gray, in a good suit, only Roger had chosen all black with the no-tie approach.

Gray took one last look at his charcoal, summer-weight wool suit, light gray shirt and matching silk tie. Remembering the conversation he'd overheard, he couldn't help smiling.

Reed liked men in suits who smelled of expensive leather. She also liked them to sweat in bed. Easily accomplished while exploring each and every one of her delectable curves.

"I have a dinner date with the brunette, Sam. I believe she's a friend of your date."

Gray caught the wicked twinkle in Roger's eye. Roger knew damn well the two women were friends. Sam would look good on Roger's arm. "Where are you taking her?"

"Haven't decided yet. She was more interested in taking care of her friend. We'll figure it out when I pick her up. How about you?"

"Half the reason we chose this hotel was the food. I have an intimate table booked for two."

"Complete with champagne and roses?"

"Am I that predictable?" Gray took the stairs down to the living room of the luxury suite. He actually felt a little silly in this room with the two-story windows and the circular hot tub in the floor nearby. It was a suite for either honeymooners or wild parties with lots of scantily clad women, as Roger had proven the night before last.

"It's been a while since you've had to work for a woman. Might want to change your technique."

"Why? The classics are always a safe bet." Gray headed for the mini bar.

"From what little Sam said about her friend, safe may not be the right thing."

Gray opened a small bottle of carbonated water and eyed Roger. "What did she tell you?"

"Keep in mind I wasn't thinking about spying for you, but it seems her friend lives something of a regimented and predictable life. Something unusual and special might catch her attention faster, unless a one night stand is all you want."

"Hmm. Which reminds me, we'll take off in the morning. The girls are headed for Eagle Mountain tomorrow."

"Going to offer them a ride?" Roger's smile was a little too wise.

"Absolutely. Much better than driving from Denver. I'm sure they won't resist."

"What time do you want to take off?"

"Not too early. Ten? Eleven? That will get us in

at a reasonable time."

"Reasonable enough for what? The third degree from your mother?"

"Don't remind me." Gray grimaced and chugged his water in a few large swallows. "If we're at the ranch by three, we should be fine. There're a couple corporate groups coming in. You may get pressed into playing wrangler."

"Sure." Roger grinned. "I can hardly wait to see Sam in jeans. Watching her ride a horse will give me all kinds of ideas. Think I can commandeer the teepee for a night or two?"

"How long has it been since you were last on a horse all day? Two years? Three? You'll be too saddle sore." Gray glanced at his watch. "Plan on being ready to leave for the airport by nine."

"Aye, sir." Roger gave him a sarcastic salute. "What time are you picking up?"

"Five minutes. I'm outta here."

"I'm right behind you."

~ * ~

"Stop fidgeting," Sam scolded Reed.

"I feel like I'm going to burst out of the dress," Reed grumbled.

"You won't. It's gorgeous."

"It better be." For four hundred dollars it had better get her a damn good dinner. Starting with a four-hundred-dollar bottle of bubbly. What was she doing spending four hundred dollars dressing for a date? Especially after spending only a little more than that on a week's wardrobe for the visit to the dude ranch.

Insane. She was insane.

"Stand up straight," Sam nagged her. "Taller, shoulders back a little more...good. There's the prow view he's looking for."

"Thanks." Reed resisted the urge to tug the short, stretchy, hunter-green dress down. Tugging it down would only expose more of the creamy white skin he'd already spent so much time admiring.

She felt like she was wearing a large rubber band with a spaghetti-strap choker barely holding the cut-out halter around her neck. One large teardrop-shaped center cut-out showed the swell of her cleavage, two smaller ovals showed more white skin. With no room for a bra, it was a good thing she was firm and the dress was tight.

The slightly flared skirt was too short for stockings, and pantyhose waistbands had a tendency to roll, so Reed only wore a thong, leaving her feeling exposed. One stiff breeze and the world would see her version of pasty white globes. Thankfully she'd had a pedicure and manicure just that morning.

Reed raised a hand to pat her hair. The curling tendrils hanging down her neck tickled. Sam had helped there as well, pinning her hair up in a loose, but secure, chignon, a curling iron taking care of the strays artfully arranged around the edges.

Thank God for Sam. Her friend had dashed down to the shops for the dress, shoes and hair pins with crystals. The two of them had shopped together often enough they could buy clothes for each other in an emergency, and Reed was thankful for Sam's fashion sense. If Reed's wardrobe were left up to her, she'd wear slacks and sweater sets most of the time. Sam talked her into dressing better.

Then again, left to her own devices, Sam would wear jeans and Hawaiian shirts with biker boots. Reed had the reverse influence on her friend. Too bad they couldn't share clothes. The hairpins they could, which was why, Sam had explained, she'd splurged on them. Better not lose them.

Right. And how would she lose them? Only by removing them in someone else's bedroom. If Gray had his way tonight... Damn, she wanted it, too, but... there's that four-date rule, the good-girl voice reminded her.

Screw it! The bad-girl voice shouted. We're in Vegas and you only live once!

Lord knew she hadn't been living at all lately. This was not the time to think about why they'd stopped in Vegas for a couple days before joining the guys at the dude ranch. The topic, along with the credit card receipt for the new outfit, would only make her hyperventilate.

Not for the first, or last, time did Reed look at her friend with a twinge of envy. Sam had just tossed on a little black tank dress, brushed her hair, dabbed on a touch of makeup and perfume, slid into high heeled pumps and had been ready in ten minutes. Fini, and devastatingly beautiful to boot.

Sam's body could give Jamie Lee Curtis from True Lies a run for her money. Reed, on the other hand, felt she could compete well against Janeane Garofalo.

God help her, Reed knew she was better padded and not as cute as Janeane. Certainly not as witty.

Once again Reed wondered if her mother had been hoping the name Reed would inspire her body to grow long and beautiful despite the short squat people they came from. No luck there.

"What's in your purse?" Sam quizzed her.

"Cash, room key, ID, perfume, lipstick, condom, cell phone," Reed recited the list.

"No mints?"

"I'm out." Reed held her purse open while Sam dumped in a few mints from the roll she had in her purse. Reed snapped it shut then slung the long narrow strap over her head so the purse crossed her body. More secure, even if it did draw more attention to her top half. This was not the night to get distracted and leave her purse lying around.

"Wrap?"

"Right here." She lifted the length of fringed velvet Sam had picked out to go with the dress. Slipping into the black strappy sandals with three inch heels, Reed felt instantly taller. "Five nothing to five-three in three seconds," she joked.

"You're so gorgeous." Sam stood back to smile. "I wish I had your hair."

"I wish I had your body, so we're even."

They shared a giggle from the familiar envy exchange that broke off when a knock came at the door.

Reed glanced at the gold watch on her wrist, a Christmas present from her boss, Troy. She'd tried to give it back but he'd insisted she keep it. She was always running just a minute or two late, and he'd wanted her to make it to meetings on time.

He'd said the Rolex had the best chance of keeping her on schedule by reminding her time was money and he'd spent plenty of money to keep her on time. Still, she had to admit it was accurate. Seven-thirty on the dot.

Troy had even checked it against the Boulder Atomic Clock and confirmed it to the second after she was five minutes late for a meeting just three days ago. His next threat was to set it five minutes fast for her. Then, maybe, she'd be a minute early for a change, he'd said.

Sam reached the door first and smiled at the two men on the other side. "Welcome, gentlemen. We're ready."

Reed drew in a breath and steeled herself to look at Gray. She expected his eyes to be drinking in Sam and was surprised to see him staring at her. God, why did she have to blush?

His dark gaze raked her from head to toe and back again, stopping at her eyes and not her cleavage as was usual for most men.

Okay, knock a hundred dollars off the first bottle of champagne. Besides, he looked damn good in a suit. Better than any other man she'd seen in the flesh. Dressed in this manner, he also looked a little familiar. Where had she seen him before? The image of him as a cowboy didn't jive with the chairman of the board standing before her, and it left her feeling a little confused.

"Reed." Sam called her attention back to the moment at hand.

"Right." Reed patted her purse then stepped into the hall.

Gray took the wrap and carefully draped it around her shoulders. "Beautiful, beyond my wildest dreams," he said quietly.

"Thank you." She ducked her head a little. The man made her feel breathless. She took the arm he offered as much to have something solid to hold onto as from polite convention. "You're not so bad yourself," she told him with a smile.

And he smelled even better. What was that cologne? Leather, sandalwood and something savory she couldn't identify. Exactly how a cowboy should smell. Outdoorsy and clean. Fresh.

He escorted her to the elevator and pressed the up button. Good. They weren't traveling far from home, or was he pulling a fast one? No, there was a restaurant up top, she remembered before returning his smile. A chuckle and a soft laugh behind her made her jump. She'd completely spaced Sam and her date.

Reed turned around. "I'm sorry," she started to apologize.

"Are you following us?" Gray asked the blond man he'd briefly introduced to her at the pool this afternoon.

"No, we're going down." Roger reached past her to press the down button. "Wouldn't want to cramp your style or make the ladies feel uncomfortable."

"Oh, I thought we were doubling..." Reed glanced at Gray and blushed at his slow head shake. "I see." She ducked her head again.

"I hope you do," he murmured, then grinned when her gaze flew back to his.

The elevator came and Gray led her on.

Reed turned back and gave Sam a tiny wave that was answered with a double thumbs-up. Reed nearly choked on the laugh she tried to stifle as the doors closed.

Gray pushed the button for the top floor, a small engraved brass plaque next to it confirming the restaurant, then turned to her and lifted her hand to his lips.

"I meant what I said. You were beautiful at the pool, and you're exquisite beyond compare now."

"Th-thank you." She could barely speak, the intensity of his gaze stealing her voice. His lips, warm and supple against her knuckles, nearly melted her into a puddle at his feet right there. "You'd better pace yourself or I'll swoon in your arms before the first glass of wine."

He grinned and took a half step back. "Didn't you realize that was my plan?"

"I guessed as much, but I'm starving after all the work it took to get dressed," she joked.

"Oh, of course, we must restore your strength. You might need it later."

"Are we going dancing then?" One step back and her shoulders touched the wall of the elevator.

"Possibly."

There was nowhere to run as he stepped closer, a predatory gleam in his eye, and she could only watch as he lifted her hand and pressed the back of it against his cheek.

"I can't wait, Reed, I have this overwhelming urge to kiss you." The gruffly spoken words served as a magic spell, rooting her to the spot.

Ensnared as much by her own traitorous body as his powerful one, Reed found herself watching his lips descend toward hers. She had to tilt her head back to look up at him. Six one? Six two? He made her feel small and delicate. It was a nice contrast to feeling like a round puff ball.

Just a breath away from her lips, he stopped. "Reed?" he whispered.

His eyes, held a hint of vulnerability. It tempered the burning desire that heated his intense gaze and weakened her resolve to hold him at arm's length. As natural as breathing, she answered by lifting her lips to his.

Did he think she was fragile? That she'd break or melt at his slightest touch? Moving with agonizing deliberation, he rested her hand on his chest then moved his to stroke her jaw, moving lightly and slowly to her ear. He brushed his lips across hers then slowly licked her bottom lip with a feathery touch.

Aching for more, Reed pressed closer and he took advantage, using his lips and tongue to open her mouth. Still, he didn't attack, but slowly, gently, explored just inside her lip, his tongue running over her teeth.

Reed gasped at the absolute sensuality of the unhurried kiss, and her patience ran out. Gripping the lapels of his suit coat, she pulled him to her and he came willingly, cornering her, a hand at her waist, his thigh pinning her in place.

The kiss grew hot in the space of a racing heartbeat. Reed completely forgot where they were and ignored the rush of air from the opening of the elevator door. The repeated sound of a clearing throat snapped her attention back to their location at the same moment Gray broke the kiss.

As if his coat had turned to fire, she released Gray and he stepped back, his breath as ragged as hers, dark eyes burning with a fire of pure want. He paused a moment then took her hand and led her past the people waiting in the elevator alcove. Reed turned her gaze to the floor after a grinning man patted Gray on the shoulder and another gave her a wink.

Just past one of the many potted palms in the hotel, he pulled her aside and into his arms, hugging her to his chest, which was still rapidly rising and falling from short breath and racing heart.

A small thrill of triumph filled Reed as she felt both against her cheek even as she fought to control her own body.

"Reed..." Her name on his lips was almost too sweet to bear, not to mention the fact that words failed him.

"Wow," she whispered.

His soft laugh rumbling under her cheek made her smile. "So simple a statement, and yet so profound," he murmured. "I don't think we'd better do that again before dessert."

Reed leaned back to look into his eyes that still burned like hot coals. She could only stare back. What did he see in her eyes? She certainly didn't feel hungry for food anymore. Damn the champagne.

"Did I hear that properly?"

"Hmm?" She stared up at him.

"Did you just say 'damn the champagne'?"

Reed cleared her throat and stepped back, trying to ignore his wide grin. "I couldn't have."

Gray took her elbow and steered her to where the *maître d'* waited. "We'd better get some food and take a break. Otherwise you'll seduce me before we make it to my suite."

"Who says we're going to your suite?" she whispered.

Amusement twinkled in his eyes, belying her weak denial. He knew as well as she did where the night would end.

"*Bon soir*, Monsieur Dunbar, Mademoiselle, this way please."

FOUR

"Dunbar?" Reed choked on his name. "Gray Dunbar? Gray*son* Dunbar? *The* Grayson Dunbar?"

"You've heard my name before?" He glanced down at her, tempted to pat her on the back as she stared up at him with wide eyes. *Why did her face go pale?*

"Once or twice. Usually with some colorful metaphor thrown in for emphasis," she said through barely moving lips.

At the discreet cough of *maître d'*, they followed him, dodging linen-draped tables. Gray wasn't surprised to see more than one man do a double-take to follow Reed's graceful walk across the dining room.

Watching the gentle sway of her hips temporarily distracted him from her reaction to his name. For the first time ever, he found himself wishing a woman wore more clothing. She was his to savor. His unprecedented jealous thoughts were almost enough to make him laugh out loud before he decided they were just another sign Reed was The One.

They were led to a secluded window table, all but hidden by more potted palm trees, with a view of Las Vegas spread below. As darkness fell, the lights would look like a jeweled blanket. Gray seated her, before taking his own chair across the small table. A table between them would give them both a chance to catch their breath. Hard and primed, he ached to lay her across the table and devour her for dinner.

However, there was this problem with his name. Well known in one small scientific community, only casually known in a few others, he didn't have household name status like Bill Gates. So how did she know his name and not his face?

With champagne already waiting in an ice bucket, they had another few moments before the need for conversation would set in. Gray could almost see the gears whirling in her head. What had she meant by she'd heard his name usually associated with colorful metaphors? He had several business rivals, any one of whom would likely curse his name. Some with more heat than others. It depended on the industry.

While their waiter poured the wine, he watched Reed take in the elegantly set table. Her gaze seemed approving as she noticed the label on the bottle. She recognized good wine? That was promising.

Between them, a low vase held a bouquet of pink roses surrounding a long tapered ivory candle topped with a golden flame. Silver and crystal reflected the light. Music, light and airy, seemed to weave around them in their private bower, reminding him of another, more intimate, setting. Her hand shook slightly as she laid the linen napkin in her lap. Was it his name or the kiss that had shaken her up?

All that aside, he couldn't stop looking at her. When he'd said she was beautiful beyond his dreams, he hadn't lied, and he had pretty good dreams. One in particular that she starred in--he was certain of it now.

Across the table from him, she fairly glowed, the green of her dress deepening the already deep green of her eyes. Her skin was flawless, well-applied makeup covering the few freckles she'd acquired that afternoon at the pool. And her hair--a more magnificent flaming crown he'd never seen.

Multiple shades of auburn red with streaks of gold brought life to tresses he'd bet his plane were softer than baby goose down. Her artful curls sparkled nearly as much as the tiny crystals twinkling like stars each time she moved her head.

The only jewelry she wore, other than her very expensive watch, were two pairs of earrings. Classic and elegant, diamonds, a little larger than fifty points, set in gold, graced the upper piercings. In the lower set, she wore gold earrings hanging from wires. Fourteen karat, it wasn't the gold, but the design, that caught his attention.

Celtic in nature, the weaving strands twisted in an elongated teardrop pattern an inch and a half long. He'd seen similar modern interpretations of traditional Celtic knot work the last time he was in Ireland. Could it mean...? Another confirmation?

The waiter stepped away and Gray lifted his fluted glass, waiting until she lifted hers as well and met his gaze.

"To the beginning of an extraordinary new friendship," he said and touched his glass to hers.

"*Slainte*," she replied then delicately sipped from her glass, averting her eyes.

Why did the response in Irish surprise him? It shouldn't have, he thought, sipping from his own glass, more to take a moment to gather his thoughts than from thirst.

"So, you've heard my name spoken in less than favorable terms?" he asked lightly. Might as well get over that point. He set the glass down and ran his finger around the base.

"You could say so." She laughed softly. "I'm sorry, I should have asked your full name earlier. I didn't realize your reach extended to the dude ranch as well. I wonder if Troy knows?" She murmured the last question to herself but he still heard it.

"Troy? Troy Spearman?" That explained a few things. His sigh was mental. The very worst of his competitors. How much of Troy's venom would he have to overcome?

She looked up at him with startled eyes.

"Troy Spearman is one who would attach many colorful metaphors, none flattering, to my name. You wonder if Troy knows what?"

She cleared her throat. "I wonder if he knows you're associated with the ranch we're going to."

"You work for Troy." And her company executives were gathering at the ranch. For a retreat. She didn't know enough of the history between him and Troy to know of their original association. *Interesting.* "And he is the boss you wanted to kiss?"

Troy definitely knew of Gray's association with the ranch. The thought of Reed wanting to kiss Troy was like a punch in the gut. Not going to happen again. Thoughts of ever kissing Troy would evaporate from her mind after tonight.

"Not really, but he did allow me to smack a jerk around, budget-wise anyway."

"You admire him?"

"Troy? Oh, he's okay. I don't want to sleep with him, if that's what you mean. Still, he hasn't given me too many reasons to hate him either. I've worked for him for several years, and he treats me well enough." She lifted a shoulder delicately, her wrap sliding down to rest in the crook of her elbow.

Just like he wanted to slide his hands down her body.

When she lowered her shoulder the flesh above her neckline jiggled so enticingly. Natural. Somehow he'd figured as much.

He lifted his glass to sip the wine so his drooling wasn't obvious. Good, she didn't want to sleep with Troy. One worry gone. Next piece of the puzzle...

"You work for Troy. You deal in numbers. Your name is Reed...O'Brien, right? Of course, how many Reeds are there in one company, much less one so small? So, that would make you..." Gray narrowed his eyes, sorting through information. "You're his CFO, aren't you?"

"Are you saying you've heard *my* name?"

He almost laughed at the shock on her face, but his mind was moving too swiftly through the facts falling into place. "Sure, I've heard of you. You're virtually a legend in the laser research community."

"For what?" she gasped, her mouth hanging open for just a moment before she snapped it shut.

"For keeping the company afloat. Rumor has it no one can figure out how Troy makes his money."

He watched her lips clamp tighter and a window slam shut in her eyes. There was something interesting there. She wouldn't spill the beans though.

Gray carefully formulated his next words. "He treats you well enough? Is that why you have a knot the size of a baseball in your shoulder and a crick in your neck?"

Her eyes widened.

Damn, he hadn't meant to sound angry. Why did Troy have to be such a bastard? Why had it never mattered quite like this before? Because he couldn't stand the thought of that son of a bitch anywhere near Reed, much less working her into the ground.

"I take it, then, you usually have a few colorful metaphors of your own when discussing Troy?"

Gray laughed. "If only you knew. I think we should change the subject. That way you can tell Spearman you didn't spill any company secrets."

"No, I'm curious. I sense it's something a little deeper than industrial competition between you two. What started it all? Rumor has it you two were once partners."

Despite the look of curiosity in her eyes, urging him to confide, Gray shrugged as if her statement had no basis in fact. If Troy hadn't told her, he wasn't about to either. Troy had started it, but Gray wasn't going to continue it.

"Nothing. Just business. He once got an account I wanted. Later I got one he wanted. We've been at war ever since." Troy was no longer welcome on this date. "What do you want to know about dude ranching?"

"Do I have to ride a horse?" With a twist of those luscious lips, she accepted his change of subject. For now.

He knew he'd have to answer her later, but he'd just as soon put it off as long as possible. "That depends. I assume your company has booked an overnight riding and camping trip?"

"Two nights."

Ah, she wasn't pleased. Though he did like the way she stuck out her lower lip as if nibbling on her upper lip. He wanted another taste of both.

"Will we have to do cow stuff?"

Gray laughed out loud at the question as much as the adorable way she wrinkled her nose. "No, no cattle drives. At least not from what I recall. The next cattle drive isn't for another month, so you're safe. Just riding from one tent camp to the next and then back to the ranch. Lots of beautiful scenery. Are you staying the whole week?"

She'd mentioned a Stetson earlier, and he could just see her now, perched on a horse, her little legs squeezing the animal... Damn! Now he was feeling jealous of a horse she hadn't even ridden yet.

"Yes. I don't think Troy is staying the entire time, but the rest of us are supposed to. We're supposed to find divine inspiration to solve our latest dilemma."

"Which is?" Gray raised a brow.

"I can't tell you." She lifted her glass. "That could get me fired. Besides, I don't know how to solve it. I'm just going along for the camaraderie and to tell them whether or not it's financially feasible to complete the project. Sam hates to crunch numbers when it comes to finances."

"What does Sam do? Wait, Sam--Samantha Bond? Doctor Samantha Bond?"

"You've heard of her too?"

Damn, that put a guarded look on her face. What was the real connection between her and Sam? "I've heard of her work. She seems to be the brains behind the research." *Tread carefully.* "She's quite well respected in the world of physics."

Now that he thought about it, he should have recognized Sam, but she looked very different in a bikini or skimpy dress with her hair down. The first time she'd been pointed out to him at a conference, she'd worn shapeless slacks and a baggy sweater with her hair coiled in a tight bun, strict glasses perched on her nose and not a spot of makeup. The perfect picture of a nerdy female scientist with not one curve in evidence.

Completely unlike the supermodel she'd resembled today. And Sam hadn't recognized him in swim trunks and sunglasses either, though now he thought about it, she'd given him a curious look when she'd opened the door this evening.

"She's got more brains in her little pinky than ten Rhodes Scholars put together. It isn't her fault God also blessed her with the physique of a goddess." Reed's voice warmed with great affection for her friend.

"You weren't skipped when they handed out beauty."

That made her laugh.

He frowned. She shouldn't be putting herself down.

"I've spent too many years near Sam to believe you. Men want a willowy goddess, not a pasty white, bland dumpling. I get her leftovers from time to time. It's okay, she's tossed off some pretty cute guys. Then again, she usually discards them because they aren't nice to me, or it's obvious they're being nice to me to get close to her. She's a good friend," Reed finished quietly and turned to gaze out the window.

He could see that slightly envious admission hurt her on a level so deep she rarely acknowledged it. A hurt so much a part of her she wasn't even aware how it was revealed in her eyes. Gray filled her glass again. "The smart ones look at you first. Sam's great, but it's time for you to come out of her shadow and shine on your own. You do realize she adores you, right?"

"And I adore her." Reed turned back to him. The soft smile agreed with her statement. "She's the best. We balance each other. Where I'm weak she's strong and vice versa. Where we're both weak, we fake our way through it or tell the world to kiss off." She laughed.

"And where you're both strong, you kick ass and take names later."

"Exactly."

God, what a smile. "What are you hungry for? You mentioned steak earlier."

"Red meat, medium rare. I don't much care about the rest. I'm sure it will be delicious."

"Ah, a challenge. Will you let me order for you?"

"Certainly."

His eyes never left hers as he signaled for the waiter. The sparkle of green was more intoxicating than the fine bubbles of the wine.

~ * ~

"Divinely delicious." Reed moaned over the last bite of her dessert. Chocolate, of course. She lifted her coffee cup and held it with two hands, elbows resting on the table. So much for Mother and her rules of etiquette. At least Reed had made it through dinner without slopping anything down the front of herself. Damn near miraculous. Slowly sipping her coffee, she tried to stop smiling into Gray's hypnotizing dark eyes.

"What does that look mean, I wonder?" he asked playfully, one long finger stroking the rim of the saucer that held his coffee cup.

He'd been teasing her all night and once the work tension had disappeared, the sexual tension had soared. While telling stories of growing up on the ranch, he'd found ways to slip in a never-ending supply of innuendos.

Reed could almost see him roping a calf in her mind's eye. Even clearer was the image of him roping her. A shiver of raging desire created a tiny wave pattern in her coffee.

Eagle Mountain was a working ranch, he'd told her. The guests were a sideline to even out the cash flow.

She'd shared her scattered and vague memories of the ranch in California. A few details about growing up east of San Francisco in a little valley just shy of the great Central Valley. The topic of work was carefully avoided.

Not only did the man have impeccable manners and conversational skills, he had a sense of humor. And that kiss on the elevator--it had been like nothing she'd ever experienced.

That kiss blew all the rest clear out of the water, and her lips tingled from wanting more. The way he stared at her, his eyes half closed as he studied her with a look of carnal hunger, warmed the arousal that had been simmering since his first words this afternoon.

"You're killing me with that look, Reed. You've got me thinking of four poster beds and long sexy baths. I want to test my fantasy of soap bubbles sliding down your body for accuracy."

She grinned and lowered her gaze to the table. Either she was transparent as glass or he could read minds. After another long drink of the rich coffee she set down the cup. "What are we going to do, Mr. Dunbar?"

"I know what I want to do. Something tells me you want to, but are reluctant."

"You're a smart man. More of that figuring out your opponent stuff?" Lord, she must be tipsy to slaughter the language that way. Then again, a bottle of champagne, two bottles of red, and now coffee with a shot of brandy over a three-hour dinner would do that to a girl. How the hell was she supposed to walk out of here? Dancing the night away was seriously out.

"It pays to pay attention to people," he said.

"You have to stop smiling at me like that."

"Like what?"

Damn his knowing smile. "Like you have a secret. Like you know you're going to get exactly what you want."

"What do you want?"

"The same thing you do, but it isn't wise. I believe it would be seen as fraternizing with the enemy by certain people."

"Considering I planned this seduction before I knew where you worked, I don't think it counts."

"You would justify it that way." Her accusation was halfhearted at best.

"I'm good at that. Shall we go?"

Reed hadn't seen him take care of the bill. Most likely he'd arranged it in advance. She'd bet they knew him quite well here. "By all means." She waited for him to come around and assist her from her seat.

Gray plucked a rose from the center piece and offered it to her, along with his hand. "Steady there," he murmured in her ear when she swayed against him.

"I believe you got me in...tox...in...eeee-bri... smashed. No fair, sir." She lifted the bud and inhaled the sweet scent. It reminded her of her garden at home. Pink roses she could deal with.

Reed didn't like red roses. White ones were nice, but the best were the huge, overblown old fashioned roses, white with delicate, barely pink centers. But her all-time-favorite out-in-the-garden flowers were ripe voluptuous double-petal peonies. In fact, most of the flowers she planted were voluptuous varieties in all their rich colors. Yup, she liked fat flowers. Just like her.

"All part of my master plan." He settled her wrap around her shoulders, followed by his arm about her waist.

Reed felt as if she floated out of the restaurant. "Where's your room?" she asked.

"Roger and I have a suite a couple floors down."

"Ah, then we should go for a walk."

"We aren't far from the fountains at the Bellagio. Would you like to see them?"

"I don't know if I can walk that far. 'Sides, Sam and I took a gander last night between casinos."

"Do you want to go to the casino?"

"Probably not a good idea." Reed let him guide

her onto the elevator and watched him push a button. Not her floor.

"We'll just stop by and see if the suite is occupied. If it isn't, we'll sit a spell. It has a spectacular view. How's that sound?"

"Much better than it should," she whispered. His mouth looked very tasty. She was tempted to caress his lips with the rose.

"Wait until we get to the room. Otherwise we'll embarrass the other guests." The heat in his eyes just about singed her.

Reed shamelessly leaned against him and savored the feeling of his arm around her. Oh, this was a very bad idea. She never had sex on the first date. Fourth date at least. Not to mention, Troy would have a fit. If there was one person in the world Troy despised, it was Gray Dunbar.

The elevator opened and he guided her down the hall.

Reed stepped past the foyer when Gray ushered her through the door of the suite with a warm hand on the small of her back, and slowly walked toward the double high wall of glass, taking in the luxury. Considering the few facts she knew about him, it was all too much.

Not that he was often a topic of discussion, but over the years there'd been hints of him getting one or two particularly lucrative contracts Spearman had wanted. Everything about Gray said big money. Not that she wasn't used to Troy's displays of wealth, but she also considered Troy untouchable and not just because of his money.

"I get the feeling you're way out of my league, Mr. Dunbar," she said quietly. Funny, now she felt stone cold sober as she wrapped her arms around her waist.

The window made a nearly perfect mirror, and she used it to watch Gray shrug off his jacket, and drop it over a chair. He loosened his tie and collar as his reflection stepped up behind hers, his hand reaching for her waist.

"I get the feeling you're too modest." He spoke softly, his mouth hovering tantalizingly near her cheek. "You hang with Spearman. Wealth doesn't intimidate you."

How wrong he was, but there wasn't time to think of it now. Heat from his body pressed against her back, and his arms wrapped around her, burning away the slight chill from the air conditioning. Their eyes met in the reflection, his gaze hot enough to sear her heart. The dream-like image looked so right...

A tingle of *déjà vu* shimmered down her spine, the very rightness of this image--had she seen this, felt this very embrace, somewhere, sometime, before?

"Reed," he murmured then kissed her temple.

Thought, speech, movement--all fled. Capable only of standing and breathing, she waited for his next move. Senses, fine tuned to him, screamed for his caress. The force of her desire would have scared her, if she'd stopped to think about it.

Gray took the rose from her hand. With their gazes locked in the reflection, he stroked the tender petals down her temple and cheek, along her jaw line to her pointy chin, his eyes taking in the evidence of her wildly beating heart.

"A heart-shaped face."

His voice should be registered as a lethal weapon. Come to think of it, so should the rose now traveling to her ear.

Unable to stop her body from succumbing to the seductive lure, she laid her head back against his shoulder, propped against his neck. It felt as if that curve of his body was sculpted just to provide support for her. Even in her heels, the top of her head barely cleared his chin. In her bare feet or flats he'd be able to easily rest his chin on her head. Cozy. Perfect. Home?

The rose slowly skimmed down the side of her neck and she lifted her chin. Too weak to fight the feelings swamping her, she gave up the battle with her heavy eyelids, letting them close.

Sweetly scented, the rose traveled across her shoulder and down her arm. Delicious shivers coursed through her and she felt his practically silent rumble of want. Her eyes fluttered open for just a moment to meet his gaze in the reflection again.

"That look in your eyes steals my every thought," he whispered.

"That look in yours steals my will to resist," she replied as lightly as she could.

"Then we have a situation."

Reed turned her face to his lips. "What do we do?"

"Don't fight it. We'll both be much happier if we follow the course nature has in store for us."

Like a branding iron, his lips left their imprint on skin that felt too hot.

"What?" Was he trying to tell her this was a predestined meeting? Things like that only happened in Hollywood or between the covers of a book. The man was obviously well versed in temptation. An expert at the well-executed, carefully choreographed love scene.

"Our souls are meant to be together," he said.

So that's all this was. Not a bad line, but still carefully scripted. While his lips hovered over hers, disappointment plunged her heart into her stomach. "Have much success with that line?"

Gray stiffened and the rose dropped from her arm. Barely making sure she stood firmly on her feet, he stepped back and paced to the bar. Cold chills raced across her skin and she pulled her shawl up around her shoulders. "I'm... I'm... Gray?"

"Would you like a water?" He held up a small bottle he'd pulled from the fridge under the counter.

"Sure." Feeling helpless, she watched him pour the water into a glass from the bar. Her comment had actually hurt him. But his comments had been part of an act, hadn't they? She walked to him and rested a hand on his arm. "I'm sorry."

It wasn't like her to hurt someone. Most of the people around her would have laughed off the comment and tossed one back. It was banter. Had she underestimated Gray so badly?

He gave her a small half smile. "We don't know each other all that well, do we?" Turning back to the bar, he put the rose in the small bottle where there was just enough water left to reach the bottom of the stem. With the next breath he turned and held out a cut crystal tumbler to her. "Here."

"Thank you."

Selecting another small bottle for himself, he escorted her to the sofa. "Let's sit and catch our breath."

Reed wanted to cry at the closed look on his face. Did he really believe they were meant to have something special together? The thought threw her for a loop. Men were the ones who didn't want commitments. Men were the ones who ran at the first sign a woman was thinking of houses with white picket fences. They only wanted a warm body to share their beds and then it was off to the next adventure. Right?

Was it the thought of something more than a one night stand that scared her? She shrugged off her shawl and sank down to the sofa, leaning forward to rest her head in a hand, elbow propped on her knee. *Think, brain, think!* What was she missing?

Gray's hand warm hand on her bare back comforted her.

"I'm sorry if you think I was acting like an ass."

"No." Reed leaned back against the soft cushions of the sofa and drank the water. "You've been a gentleman all the way. Courteous, attentive--if a little bold about your intentions, but still very much a gentleman." His arm fit so very nicely around her waist.

"I've rushed you." Gray took the empty glass from her hand and set it on a side table.

"I accepted your invitation knowing very well you wanted to sleep with me tonight."

"I don't want you to think that's all I want. That that's all this is about."

She turned to look at him and the fierce expression in his eyes made her bite back the smart ass retort on her lips. The man was serious. Deadly serious. He cared very deeply about whatever it was hovering between them, a sensation of something so palpable she could nearly see the air shimmer from it.

"I am beginning to think you see this as more than a simple one night stand."

"You're a smart lady." His hand tightened around her waist and he pulled her against him.

Reed melted when his lips kissed her temple. "Gray, you're messing with my mind. I want your touch but I don't know why. Is it, as you say, that we have strong chemistry? Or is it because it's just been so long since I've been touched? I don't know." Anguish added a hint of anxiety to her whisper.

"Does it matter?" His soothing voice, as much as his warm lips placing gentle kisses on her face, calmed her fears.

"Until I knew you were Gray Dunbar, no, it didn't."

"Ah. Because of who we are, we have complications."

"Yes, and it cuts both ways. I can see Troy going ballistic. On the one hand, he'd love for me to pump you for information. On the other, he'd be terrified of what information I might pass on to you. Surely you can see the conflict." Pulling away, Reed looked up into his eyes, now nearly black and fathomless.

"I can. Does Troy figure so prominently in your life?"

"My work is my life. I have no other life. And since I report to Troy, I'd have to say yes, he does figure prominently in my life."

"Do you date him?"

Reed moved away so she could stare at Gray. "No. I do not date him." Defensiveness rose up like the hackles on a dog. Date Troy? Never. He'd blown his chance.

"You've never had dinner with him?"

"Sure we have dinner on occasion--to discuss business."

"Has he ever given you gifts? I don't mean the usual promotional job-well-done fluff."

Reed looked down at the eighteen-karat gold watch on her wrist. It was beautiful and it worked, but it was over the top, in true Troy fashion. It certainly wasn't fluff.

"Nice gift. Birthday? Promotion? Christmas?"

"Christmas," she whispered.

"Anybody else get one like it?"

She closed her eyes trying to remember. Others in the company wore Rolex watches, but they'd bought them for themselves. Had Troy ever given anyone else a comparable gift? She couldn't remember.

Dinners out, sure, good ones, but not thousand dollar dinners. Expensive bottles of wine were common. Though she'd never bragged about her watch, others had bragged about their gifts from Troy. Not to mention she saw the expense reports, credit card statements, and bills. As much as she'd never wanted to think about the motive behind the gift, she wore it constantly.

Leaving it lying around and the possibility of losing it scared her more than wearing it. In a way, she realized suddenly, it was a pretty and expensive shackle tying her to Troy.

Reed shook her head. No, no one else's gifts compared with the watch. Not by several thousand dollars. She'd checked the price online, and she hadn't seen the charge for it, which meant it had been a personal gift. Her heart sank. No use trying to deny what had been in her face for months. And now she was here, with Gray. This was so not good.

She'd turned Troy down more times than she could count over the last few years. She owed him a good day's work, but her nights and her body belonged to her. To do with as she pleased. She had a right to think of herself.

Gray's caress was slow as he brushed her cheek with the back of his fingers. She leaned toward him. Strong and warm, his fingers wrapped around the back of her neck and drew her to him.

"Reed," he said. "I don't give a damn about Troy Spearman, and he has nothing to do with the energy between us. I felt this way before I knew who you worked for. Your employer, your work, has nothing to do with my feelings. Can you set it aside and just be with me?"

His eyes were intent on hers and she could taste his breath, his lips were so close. Against all logic, all common sense, she felt her body sway. No good could come from this.

FIVE

Gray's heart, his entire being, stopped in that one moment, and the whole world paused, waiting for her answer. This tiny woman held the fate of his very happiness in her exquisite little hands and didn't even recognize it. Just one word and she could inflict a severe wound and never know the depth of it.

"Yes."

Soft as butterfly wings, her answer brushed his lips.

Downstairs, jackpots and black jacks were ringing out, but this was the real thing--this was what truly mattered. Between one breath and the next, with one word, she'd gifted him the winning hand.

His fingers curled around her neck, his lips possessed hers. His. She was his. She had to be, or too many years had been wasted in reaching this point.

Dragging her to half lie across his lap, he pulled her close. The perfect armful, soft and warm, he gathered her in, pliable breasts pressing against his chest. Her arm snaked around his shoulder, clinging to him. Strong. She made him feel invincible.

Heat, fast and urgent, assaulted him just as it had in the elevator. More prepared this time for the overwhelming rush, he controlled the kiss, taking his time to thoroughly taste her. How sweet she was. Her lips fit perfectly to his, her tongue, small and supple, entwined with his.

Aching for more, he slid his hand over her curves from shoulder to waist, his thumb teasing the side of her breast on the way past. The quiver running through her body would have made him smile had his lips not been otherwise engaged.

Teasing not only her, but himself as well, he stopped his hand at her waist. Under the tight fabric of her dress he thought he felt the barest slip of fabric. A thong? What would he find under it? Did she trim, shave, or wax?

Cupping a hand around her firm derriere, he pulled her even closer with a growl he didn't recognize. His hand had itched to hold her this way from the moment he'd watched her walk across the pool deck.

She and Sam had exuded a confidence and natural grace far more alluring than any blatant display of female flesh in sight. The fact that Reed's figure bore a resemblance to the woman in his dreams had merely cemented his decision to approach her.

As she responded to him now, he knew she wasn't thinking about the power of the forces whirling around them, but she was responding to them. Now to convince her theirs was the mystical union of soul mates.

Craving the softness of her skin, Gray's hand slid down her thigh to where her dress ended, baring her leg. He groaned with raging hunger, his body hard and ready for her. Knowing they'd be smooth and silky, he wanted to feel her legs wrapped around him. It was a need unlike any he'd ever known. His hand traveled down her leg to her tiny foot wearing its sexy shoe. Slipping the sandal off, his thumb brushed along the bottom of her foot. Shaking, she broke the kiss on a giggle.

"Gray! Please! Don't..." She moaned as he grasped her foot.

"Ticklish are you?" He kissed her cheek.

"I won't...be...responsible..." She kissed his chin. "For injuries...if you...keep it up."

"I won't tickle on purpose," he murmured near her ear. Releasing the one foot he removed the shoe from the other and grasped the warm appendage in his hand. "So tiny."

"The only thing about me that is." She rested her head on his shoulder.

"Hush," he told her, his hand returning to cup her cheek and turn her face to look up at him. "You're beautiful. Just the perfect size."

He didn't like the many shadows of doubts in her eyes. "Reed, you're the sexiest woman I've ever known. Your curves are made for long nights of erotic exploration. I want to spend all night tasting and touching every inch of you. I want to bury myself in your lush embrace and drink your sweetness."

There, that was the look he wanted to see in her eyes. Full desire. Now, to completely sweep her off her feet.

He slid his arm under her knees and lifted her in his arms. "But not here. The bedroom." Grinning at her astonished face, he rose with her and carried her up the stairs to the loft bedroom.

"Wait! You'll hurt your back," she protested weakly.

"Not a chance." He shifted her higher in his

arms, loving her squeak of surprise.

~ * ~

When Gray gently set her on her feet beside the bed, Reed saw raw desire like she'd never seen before in his face. Instead of feeling weak or frightened, she felt empowered. Most surprising, he wasn't even winded from carrying her. It took a moment for her legs to agree to hold her.

She helped when he lifted her purse from around her neck and set it on the nightstand. Rising on tiptoe, she slid her arms around his neck as their lips met.

His mouth did wonderful things to her as his hands grasped her ribs, thumbs rubbing the sides of her breasts, trying not to tickle. Need stole her breath and she broke the kiss to keep from losing herself.

His hands stilled on her hips when she reached for his tie. The fine silk made it easy to loosen the knot completely. Wanting to feel the smooth skin of his chest, she started on the buttons of his shirt, each brush of her fingers against his skin sending a prickle of heat up her arms.

She risked a glance at his face, and the heat in his eyes stole her breath. Greedy for him, she tugged his shirt from his pants. The fine silk of his shirt flowed like soft silver in her hands.

Chuckling, he pulled her close, and she inhaled his scent while he removed the links from his cuffs behind her back. Kissing his chest, she let her hands slide up the warm taut skin of his back. Muscles flexed and bunched under her fingers. She grinned when he groaned and together they pushed his shirt off. Cuff links clinked on the surface of the night table.

"Ree," he murmured and gathered her close again.

Ree, the nickname of her childhood. Only her family and Sam called her Ree. She lifted her face and he swooped down to capture her mouth with a hungry growl. He stole her mind, that's what he did, leaving not a single intelligent thought in her head. She clung to him, barely noticing him untying the string holding up the front of her dress and lowering the zipper.

A rush of cool air touched her skin, but only for a moment, then she was warm again, his hands splayed across her back, pressing her body to his. Warm skin to warm skin, the contact was better, more intimate, stirring a feeling of familiarity. Rightness. It was almost as if she remembered...

His hands only stayed a moment to explore her skin before he buried his fingers in her hair. The expensive crystal-tipped pins were pulled and dropped beside his cuff links on the nightstand. Such a simple gesture, yet she found it incredibly sexy, more intimate in its own way than the deepest kiss.

Despite Sam's teasing over the years, she'd never thought her hair particularly wonderful or beautiful. Until now. With reverence, Gray ran his fingers through her locks as they tumbled to the middle of her back.

"I knew it," he said. "Softer than baby goose down. Finer than silk. Living flame that burns and soothes at the same time."

"It's just hair," she said dryly.

"Bite your tongue, woman," he scolded her before doing just that himself.

"Mmm!" she protested.

"I'll bite harder if you don't stop saying nasty things about yourself," he said, when he let her go at last. "If I say you're beautiful, then beautiful you are."

"Yes, sir." She leaned against his chest with a sigh. "I feel beautiful in your arms." The surprise at realizing just how much she meant it was disturbing.

"Then this is where you belong."

His eyes were hot with excitement as he looked into hers. A rush of emotion too strong for words poured through her body, and her only thought was to get as close as possible.

Gray's arms were strong, lifting her against him. How he managed to sweep an arm under her legs and deposit her on the bed, she wasn't sure. Leaving her just long enough to skim off the rest of his clothes, he used the time to look her over from head to toe.

"Ree," he said. "You're more than beautiful."

In an invitation older than Jezebel, she reached out a hand and he joined her on the bed. Hot skin and solid muscle, his body was a wonder to her fingers. He felt huge and hard against her thigh. Wanting to touch and learn the feel of him, she protested when he pinned her wrists to the bed and kissed her throat.

"I've been dreaming of this since I first saw you," he murmured.

"My neck?" She gasped as his tongue, licking up and around her ear, sent spikes of need through her. Her blood, normally not noticed as a moving, living part of her, suddenly felt like sun-heated honey.

"A vampire's wet dream." He released her

hands and moved his to her side.

"That's a new one." She clutched his shoulders. He was the only secure thing in her world at the moment. A solid, stable presence in a world turned upside down. "What about to a cowboy?"

"Oh darlin', you're purdier than a palomino galloping across a meadow at sunrise."

Reed laughed weakly as his lips worked across her collarbone to the base of her throat. His thumbs brushing over her breasts made her skin tingle and nipples ache.

"A business man?"

"Better than a billion-dollar contract."

"Why do you get to have all the fun?" She could barely speak. His hair was soft between her fingers. Taking in all the sensations of him and what he stirred in her was overwhelming. Pure sensuality swamped her.

"You'll get your turn. I've wanted you longer." His tongue slowly circled her areola, making her squirm before drawing a nipple into his mouth, lips holding her as his tongue teased the needy flesh.

Reed arched her back, pressing her head into a pillow. This was heaven.

No, she was wrong. Heaven was when he pulled her thong down with his teeth then worked his way back up her legs with hot, wet kisses. She melted into the soft bed and writhed under his mouth. Every time she thought he'd give her the relief she craved, he veered away, leaving her wanting.

"Gray!" She didn't recognize her own husky voice pleading for satisfaction.

He laughed.

Couldn't he get to the point? She wiggled her hips trying to encourage him to take care of her burning need. Strong hands pushed her legs open wider, his thumbs pulling her labia open as well. She'd never felt so exposed. And still he wouldn't satisfy her. He kissed and licked every inch of her now pulsing cleft, his tongue dipping inside, teasing her.

Grabbing his head, she tried to guide him.

Wickedly, he countered by pulling her hands away and pinning them to the bed.

"Gray! Don't tease," she begged on a moan.

He chuckled. "You taste so good."

"I don't care!"

She whimpered when he gave her one long slow lick, sending her higher yet. Holding her breath, she waited in suspense until at long last he circled her clit. Wrapping his lips around her, he suckled, his tongue flicking over the sensitive flesh.

Set free at last, Reed's universe exploded in a shower of stars, her body taken by the onslaught of bliss beyond her control.

Gray watched, his fingers stroking her while she came apart, back arching to thrust her breasts into the air. *Stunning.* Her pale skin infused with a pink blush, her sweet voice whimpering as she called out his name. Once more he dipped his tongue into her and lapped up the juices flowing like manna from heaven.

She shouted his name again as her body shuddered.

Unable to hold back, he pushed up on his hands and knees to cover her, and, with one strong thrust, buried himself in her sweet body.

She arched back, legs coming up to wrap around his waist instinctively.

Tight. Lord, she fit like a glove made just for him. This was right. She was made just for him, as he'd been made for her. This was the missing piece of his soul. Without a doubt, the two of them belonged together.

"Yessss!" she hissed and clenched her soft legs tight around him.

Still throbbing from her release, she massaged him, every warm, soft, wet luscious inch undulating around him as he began to slowly move within her. Braced on his arms, he watched her face as he thrust deep. The feel of her, slick and hot, was meant to be savored, but he wouldn't last long. Ree wasn't helping.

She pulled him in and her sexy whimpers drove him on. Incredibly, she began to quiver again, an orgasmic flush once more blossoming across her skin. Gritting his teeth, he held back the orgasm screaming to rip from his taut body. If he could only last...

Once more she shouted his name, her cry followed by a burst of heat deep inside.

The rush of moisture erupting from her tore away his restraint as she clamped down on him so hard he could barely move. It was as if his body transformed into a hot mass of pure energy as he emptied his very soul into her.

Two slow thrusts were all he could manage before his arms collapsed. Carefully, he braced himself on his elbows and rested his head on her shoulder, lips at the curve of her neck. "Sweet Jesus," was all the prayer of thanks he could muster.

Reed's arms embraced his shoulders and she pulled him down onto her. Too weak to fight, he nuzzled her neck while warm lips kissed his temple. Her legs still held him and he flexed his hips just a tiny bit. He felt her groan vibrating through her body, as she contracted those wonderful muscles, making him groan in response.

"Enchantress," he murmured.

"Would that make you wizard or warlock?"

"Shaman."

"Magic man?"

"Just so." His lips brushed over her tender skin, finding the spot behind her ear that made her giggle softly. "And your devoted servant, my queen," he added with a soft murmur.

"Give me a minute."

"You?" He shook his head in disbelief. "I did all the work."

"Only because you insisted."

He loved the feel of her small hands following the contours of his body, slow-dancing across his back, breasts pressed against his chest and legs around his hips. Best of all, her body encased his, gently squeezing. The oil used to massage her, combined with her natural fragrance, made an intoxicating perfume he wanted to carry with him always.

Feeling a small measure of strength returning, he rolled, taking her along to snuggle on top of him, still fused together. It was several long moments before either had calm breaths and normal heartbeats. Even longer still for her body to relax around his, letting him slip from her.

How could she deny it now? Heaven and Earth

had both moved. Forever altered, his future, their future, stretched out as one long, loving adventure. Nothing would be right ever again without her. Not that anything had been perfect to this point. His whole life, every ounce of energy and drive for success, had been focused on this very moment.

Thirty-six years. Twenty-four years since he'd first dreamed of those jade eyes. For twenty years he'd worked hard to have wealth to offer her a life fit for his queen. Each time he had the dream of her and felt the warmth of love shining from her eyes, her value and his need for her grew.

The dream of her had fueled the dreams of his accomplishments. To meet her now, did it mean he'd accomplished all he'd set out to do? Or did it mean he could do more with her help?

From his first paying job he'd saved like a mad man, putting aside money, studying hard to be better than just top of the class. Overachiever, his parents had called him while shaking their heads.

His father had scoffed at his dream. "It isn't pretty eyes that get you through life, boy. It's a strong woman who works at your side without complaining. One who can match you with brains and strength. Your physical strength matched by her strength of character. Life is work. Find yourself a woman who will share your work and not expect you to cater to her. There's the secret to a happy marriage."

His mother's words were similar. It had always struck him as odd, as if he'd expected more from his mother. At times he could swear he saw touches of sadness in her eyes, as if she'd missed out on a great romance. Then she would roll up her sleeves and bend to the task at hand whether it be baking bread or helping with the delivery of a colt or calf.

Now, the burden of those years weighed heavily on the shoulders of his mother. Especially the ten years since his father had died. Any softness she'd once had was long gone, beaten out of her by the grind of running a ranch and catering to spoiled rich people. His elder brother, Dustin, now served as president of the family corporation that owned and operated the ranch, but the true backbone was his mother. Tomorrow, for the first time, he'd bring his girl home to meet her.

~ * ~

"That was an interesting laugh," Reed said.

Gray had snorted softly from beneath her, the rise and fall of his chest and the air from his nose both quite palpable.

"Hmm?"

"Penny for your thoughts."

Did she really want to know? Strangely enough, she did. Was she forever damned to worry about what people thought of her? Was he regretting this already?

"Just thinking about taking you home with me tomorrow."

"Oh. The ranch. That's right. I guess we'll be meeting you there, won't we?" Home? As in, to meet his family? That put a new twist on the screw. *Um. Not the right thought.* A new knot in the rope? *Oh hell.*

"Meet me there? Not on your life. You and Sam will fly with Roger and me straight into the airport near Vail."

Reed pushed up and braced her arms so she

could gaze down at him, her hair forming a curtain enclosing them. "Excuse me?"

"We leave for the airport at nine. Or ten. Or whenever we decide to get out of bed," he said with a grin and folded his arms behind his head.

His grin and sigh of satisfaction were a tad arrogant, she decided.

"You have such a flexible departure time?" She gave him the raised eyebrow that sent underlings running for their backup notes.

"Just one of many advantages to having your own plane."

"Really?" Not quite sure how to react, she let the word hang in the air between them. Okay, she knew the guy was loaded, but had never stopped to think about how rich he might be. Troy was rich, but he didn't own, or even use--often--a private jet. At least not lately. And usually not with company money.

"Yes, ma'am. A nice little jet, comfortably appointed, and best of all, no ticket counters, no checked luggage and no lines. Oh, and drinks are free."

"I see. And you invited us when?"

"I meant to mention it earlier. Must have got side-tracked. Can't imagine how that happened." He raised a finger to caress her face. "Will you let me whisk you away in luxury?"

"Well, I don't know." Reed drew out the words. It took a bite on the inside of her lip to keep from grinning. "There was that assumption of acceptance... hmm."

Her eyes widened when his hands traveled down her sides, thumbs stopping to rub her nipples. Ooh, that wickedly wonderful cascade of heat rippled down her body again.

"We can spend more time playing like this," he said.

"Well... I suppose..." She gave in with a whimper.

His large hands closed around her breasts and lightly massaged. "Is that a yes?" His eyes twinkled with victory at her moan.

"Tweaking my nipples is unfair, but...ooh... Yes, that's a yes," she said on a moan.

"Good."

"I need to confer with my colleague, but I'm sure she'll agree."

"Undoubtedly, Roger has already passed on the invitation."

She didn't resist when he pulled her down for a kiss. The man was a kissing genius. What would it be like to make love in a private jet? And no three-hour drive from Denver.

"Oh shit." Reed braced her hands on the mattress and pushed herself up. A toss of her head flung her hair to one side.

"Excuse me?" Gray's startled face would have been funny if not for the thought that had struck her.

"Sorry, but I need to call Troy." She winced. Bad form to mention another man, particularly a business rival, just after mind-blowing sex. Not to mention she was still damp with sweat from the encounter.

"We're supposed to meet him at DIA and share a rental car to the ranch. I'll have to let him know not to wait for us." She watched Gray's eyes go from shocked amusement to resignation and back to a wicked twinkle. Unable to resist, she touched her fingers to his lips.

"What time is your flight due in?" He kissed her fingertips and she felt that fabulous searing heat soaring up her arm.

"Around one, I think. Twelve-forty or something thereabouts. I just know we're supposed to be at the airport here no later than eight."

"So, leave Denver by car by one-thirty, make it to the ranch by four-thirty or five?"

"Right. There are six of us so he's renting two cars to drive up. Sam and I are supposed to ride with him." Reed wondered at the growing look of wickedness in his eyes. "What?"

"Instead of getting up at five in the morning, you get to sleep in until at least seven, still have an hour to make love and get dressed, an hour to check out and have breakfast, then meander to the airport. It takes Roger about an hour to do the flight plan and preflight checks so we'll take off about ten. Allowing for the time change, we'll land at the Eagle Airport about one and be at the ranch no later than two. Or three, if we take two hours to make love and get dressed. Depends on whether or not we want to save energy to make love on the plane."

He looked mighty pleased with himself, she decided.

For some reason she felt annoyed. "You have this down pat. Do it often?" Good God, she was thirty and no virgin. The man had wealth and his own plane. Of course he'd had women on it. Without a doubt, he'd played out this scenario more times than he could count.

Is that why it annoyed her? After implying he

wanted a long term relationship, why did it bother her that he may have had other relationships? Casual or serious? Since she wasn't buying the happily-ever-after line, it shouldn't matter. This didn't make sense. Not one little bit.

"Sorry." Pushing off him, she rolled to the side of the bed. "That was ungracious and catty of me. I didn't mean it." Sitting up, she ran her fingers through her hair. What was with her? That was the second time tonight she'd accused him of being a player. She had no basis, much less room, for the complaint. *Time to get a grip.*

She didn't expect him to reach for her, but was inexplicably grateful when he rolled and curled around her hips, an arm around her waist.

"I don't expect you to believe me, but I'm still going to swear to you I've never once made love to a woman in the plane, either on or off the ground," he said quietly.

Reed dropped her head and tears filled her eyes. "I'm so sorry, Gray. I believe you. I shouldn't have said it. It isn't any of my business anyway." She buried her face in her hands. "I don't understand what's wrong with me."

Jealousy wasn't her bag, not her thing at all. Why did it burn so strongly in her gut? Was it fear? Could he be right about this being real? It felt real, so why did it scare her?

She didn't resist when he rolled backward and pulled her down into his arms.

"Shh, sweetheart. I'll never lie to you, however, if I tell you why, I'm afraid you'll give me strange looks again. Will you just trust me for now? Give yourself time to know me? Time for me to know you better? Time to believe in us?"

Reed nodded against his chest. More than anything, she wanted to believe him with her whole heart. A small part of her wanted to give in fully to the strange and wonderful things she felt in his presence. That tiny piece of her heart, the part where the hope of dreams still resided, throbbed in agreement.

"So, do you want to call Troy now and ruin his whole night, or wait until tomorrow when he's standing at the airport waiting for you to meet him?" he asked, sounding entirely too gleeful.

"I'd better do it tonight and get it over with. Oh God, what do I tell him?"

Gray's warm hand cupped her cheek and tilted her head back so she could see his eyes. The twinkle looked unholy to her.

"Tell him you've met your prince and he's taking you home to meet his mother. That will blow his mind."

Reed laughed and kissed his chin. "I will tell him no such thing. Why don't you go start a bubble bath or something, and let me make this phone call?"

"Your wish is my command," he said before kissing her breathless.

Six

"Troy, I didn't do this to annoy you." Reed let him hear her exasperation. "I got an offer I just can't refuse."

Leave it to Troy to not accept the simple statement that she and Sam had made other arrangements to get to the ranch. Why did he always play the guilt card on her? Probably because it usually worked.

"Reed, I was looking forward to a few hours of conversation with just you and Sam. It's her project we need to figure out, and the time was meant to be spent planning without the others making a fuss."

"We can do that Sunday morning. The three of us. We can saddle up some horses and wander off into the mountains where no one will hear us talk. Sunday morning is free anyway, right? That will leave plenty of time for you to relax with the troops before we get down to the serious work of learning how to rope calves or ride bulls."

"Very funny, Reed. I know you're looking forward to horseback riding about as much as you'd look forward to a root canal. Who is this guy anyway? It isn't like you to throw yourself into the hands of just any old guy with a private jet. You don't do one night stands, remember?"

She flinched at the undercurrent of bitterness lacing his words.

"Um, well, see, here's the thing, Troy..." Lying had never worked for her and Troy knew it.

"Reed? I'm not going to like the answer, am I?"

A grimace twisted her face as she looked up to see Gray standing in the doorway of the bathroom, arms folded while he casually leaned against the jamb. Damn that smile on his face. Then there was his body, gloriously nude, sculpted muscles under bronzed skin. Gray's smile just widened as her gaze returned to his face.

"Go ahead, tell him," Gray said softly.

"Reed?" Troy sounded impatient on the phone.

"I... I... Oh hell. I met Gray Dunbar and I didn't realize who he was until we were sitting down to dinner." She let the words rush out.

Silence fairly screamed at her from the other end of the phone.

"Troy? Are you still there?"

"Yes." His answer was curt. "How could you not know who he was?"

"You never introduced me, and I've only ever seen a photo of him in a magazine. Of course I didn't recognize him in the flesh."

Oh lordy, what flesh. She licked her lips, thinking of Gray at the pool that afternoon and all that delicious skin in front of her right now.

"Sleeping with the enemy, Reed?" The cold disapproval in Troy's voice made her flinch again and the rising lust faded.

"This has nothing to do with you or the company, Troy. I... I like him. He's nice," she said lamely.

"And he knows who you are and who you work for?"

"He didn't know, either, until we were already

seated at the table. We haven't discussed business at all, and I have no intention of doing so."

"So. You called me at midnight to tell me you're having sex with my worst enemy. Classy, Reed. I never suspected you had such a cruel streak. Then again, there was a certain light of triumph in your eye when you told Jerry his budget was cut in half. Should have seen it then."

"Troy! How can you say such things about me?" Reed poured as much indignation into her voice as she could. It didn't help that he was technically right. "This has nothing to do with you or the company," she repeated. "I hate airports, and I hate long car trips. You know that. I'm side-stepping both. My shoulder and neck still hurt, and the less time I spend hauling my laptop and luggage through airports, and the sooner I get up there and relax, the easier it will be for me to think. And if I can think, I'll be better able to help you and Sam figure out whatever it is we need to figure out."

Like she knew what needed fixing. She did money numbers. The others did the inventing thing. The invention needed to work before the money would follow. Things had to happen in the proper order and the invention needed to be in production pronto. Reed's stomach clenched and a familiar dull throb took up its rhythm in her temples.

"I'm sorry. I know how much you've been hurting. Has the time in Las Vegas helped at all?" Thankfully, Troy's tone softened.

"I've had massages both days here. I'm assured the masseuse at the ranch is top notch. I just hope she's on duty tomorrow. Please, Troy, don't assume the worst. You can trust me. I won't betray the company."

"Reed." Troy heaved a gusty sigh. "I'd hoped for the time alone with you. I'm hoping this week you and I can reignite our mutual attraction and make it work. We have both chemistry and history on our side. If Dunbar has already put his big foot in the door it rather puts a crimp in those plans. I don't want your attention divided."

Reignite their mutual attraction? Reed pulled the phone away from her ear and stared at it in disbelief. How many times had she told him to take a hike?

"Reed? Are you there?" Troy's voice was faint and she put the phone back to her ear.

"Yes... Yes, I'm here. Sorry, you just surprised me. I was under the impression you'd given up on that whole line of thinking."

"Why?" Troy's chuckle was low. "We have a connection. It's long since past time for you to stop putting me off. I've made how I feel clear, Reed. I know you feel it too. We just got sidetracked by our misunderstanding. It's time to fix it, now."

Ugh, not the smooth sexy voice. It annoyed the hell out of her when he used that voice. "Troy, it's late. I've had a fair amount of wine, and the heat has been draining. I need to get some sleep. Can we talk about this in a day or so?" Reed rubbed her temples. She wasn't entirely surprised when the bed next to her dipped and Gray's arm wrapped around her.

"Will Dunbar be at the ranch this week? Is that why he's flying to Vail?"

"You knew? I mean, you knew his family owned the ranch?"

"Of course." Troy snorted.

"I'm shocked. I'm amazed you'd give his family the business."

"I have my reasons. Okay, keep your mouth shut and your ears open. If you pick up any interesting tidbits store them away until we can talk."

"Troy, I will not participate in any form of industrial espionage, in either direction," she snapped at him.

"Oh come on, Reed, stop pretending to be a prude. Look, I need to get up in a few hours. Since you'll be there long before the rest of us, I expect you to sort out the rooms when you get there. Put mine next to yours. That will make it easier for us to get together and...talk things over. Okay?"

Talk. Right. There was no mistaking that not-so-subtle inflection of his voice. Had Troy not been listening for the last eighteen months?

"See you tomorrow, Troy." She growled, hung up, then tossed her phone to the bedside table next to Gray's. "I'm such an idiot." She moaned into the hand she buried her face in.

"I take it Spearman wasn't pleased."

"You knew he wouldn't be. I should have waited until morning to call. I should just climb on that damn nine forty-five flight and do my damn job," she groused and tried to twist away from him.

Gray's arm held her tight against his side.

"No. As you pointed out to him, your body will have a better chance of relaxing and healing if you go with me. Carrying luggage is the last thing you need."

Too tired to fight, Reed rested her head in the

crook of his neck and shoulder. "Brains. I actually had them before meeting you this afternoon. You sucked them right out of my head. An IQ of one hundred and fifty-two just flew right out my ears when you sat down next to me. I thought I heard something at the time. I just didn't know what it was."

"That wasn't your brains leaving. It was the sound of Destiny calling to you. And you answered. Beautifully." Gray cupped her chin and lifted it until she faced him. "Your feet are on the path to true happiness. Don't let old ties hold you back."

"You're speaking like a mystic again. Strange occupation for a businessman."

"Business is a sideline to who I am. My mission in life has been to find you. Nothing else is important anymore."

"You're scaring me again."

"Trust me," he murmured against her lips.

Funny how his kisses made everything he said make sense. Reed wrapped her arms around his neck and let him carry her to the tub filled with fragrant bubbles.

~ * ~

Gray held her, watching her face while she slept smelling of wildflowers from the bath gel, her hair fanned out across the pillow. The scent of their bath and loving clung to both of them. He only had a few hours to imprint himself on her, impress upon her their paths were destined to merge.

Troy was just enough of a bastard he'd try to convince Reed that Gray had sought her out with the express purpose of revenge.

Egotistical idiot. Taking Tiffany hadn't hurt as Troy had thought it would. Gray had merely let Troy think he'd gotten one over. Again. Compared to Troy's first betrayal, Tiffany was nothing.

Taking Reed, turning her against him, now that would hurt. That wound would be far more malicious than the initial knife in the back. It would be an axe through the heart--twisted, fatal and to be avoided at all costs.

Reed smiled in her sleep and rolled toward him, nuzzling his chest. Afraid of losing her before they had a chance, Gray held her close. He'd searched so long. Troy would not mess this up. Gray wouldn't allow it

Unable to stop himself, Gray pressed his lips to her forehead, then her eyelids followed by her cheek and lips. With a sleepy, breathy sigh she responded. For the fourth time in as many hours, he made love to her, slow and sweet, her cry of satisfaction the ultimate song from heaven.

~ * ~

Could she, for once, not wake up to the ringing of her cell phone? Yesterday morning it had been Troy looking for a file at the office. The ringtone bleeped out Godsmack's *Voodoo*--Sam's tone--while Reed mentally pushed away the thick blanket of dreams holding her securely on a comfortable bed that felt just like... she blinked and rubbed her cheek against warm male flesh.

It hadn't been a dream, or at least not everything had been a dream, but the interruption was very real. Her phone stopped ringing, only to start again a few seconds later. She watched a deeply tanned male arm reach for the phone and snatch it off the nightstand.

"It's yours. Want me to answer it?" he asked.

"I'll take it." Without moving off her comfortable Gray couch, she touched the screen and lifted the phone to her ear.

"Ugh," she grunted into the phone. Closing her eyes, she enjoyed the feel of Gray's hand stroking her hair.

"Good morning to you too, Mary Sunshine. Did you accept the offer of a private plane ride?"

"Yup."

"Good, I'm resetting the alarm for eight. Talk to you later. Oh--are you going to tell Troy or do you want me to?"

If only she'd thought of that the night before. "Already done," she grumbled.

"Oh?"

"By the way, did you know he was Gray *Dunbar*?"

"I thought so after seeing him in a suit. I thought you knew."

"I do now. We'll talk later. I should be back at the room by nine."

"Thanks for the warning." Sam giggled. Translation: Roger spent the night.

"You too?"

"Kiss now, tell later." Sam laughed again, then made a loud smooching sound into the phone and hung up.

Reed tossed the phone back to the nightstand.

"Hmm," Gray's chest rumbled under her, "where were we?"

"Sleeping," she muttered, sliding down to snuggle up against his side. "How could you sleep with me crushing you?"

"No burden at all." He kissed her forehead.

"Set the alarm for eight?"

"Please," she answered with a yawn.

A glance at the clock had told her it was just after five. Three more hours of sleep sounded like a great idea. She moaned with contentment when Gray wrapped himself around her. There were a few things she could get used to, she decided.

~ * ~

With a soul satisfying sigh, Reed stretched and opened her eyes. Above, green leaves fluttered in a gentle breeze. Staring at the leafy roof, she tested the surface beneath her and discovered a cushion of moss and fragrant leaves covered by a length of soft cloth she'd woven herself for this very purpose. Sunlight filtered through the branches curved overhead, forming a haven for fairy folk. Her long hair was unbound save for a circlet of small flowers she felt when she raised a hand to her head. Cool and sweetly fragranced, the shelter was familiar and comfortable.

She'd been here before. Many times.

A perfect place to tryst with her lover.

A thrill of excitement coursed through her. *He would come today*.

Turning her head, she spied a golden goblet sitting nearby. The shelf it rested on had been carved from a large rock forming one wall. A thin, clear rivulet of water sprang from the rock and fell to a small pool only inches below. The pool drained to a trickling stream that flowed under the branches of the living haven.

She rolled to her stomach and reached for the goblet. She sipped, and deep red wine rich with the essence of berries and a touch of chocolate, teased her palate. Perfect. Just the way he liked it.

Only the best wine for him. The tip of her tongue caught and savored a stray droplet.

Looking around, she set the goblet down and took in every perfect and ready aspect. Vines dotted with small white flowers twined around the branches arched over the bed wide enough to share.

Slowly more details became clear as she mentally reviewed her checklist to confirm all was ready. Bracelets of thick gold, wide and intricately engraved, embraced her wrists. Small chains of exquisite workmanship linked to rings on her middle fingers, also made of gold and engraved.

As she shifted to sit, long loose sleeves slid down her arms. Like delicate cobwebs, the finely woven fabric was thin. She raised an arm and admired the diaphanous quality of the ivory gown. Her lover would like that. Anticipation of his admiration heightened her physical awareness. Already her body warmed for his touch, longing for him to hurry and arrive soon.

Standing on cool springy moss, she felt the weight of delicate gold chains about her bare feet. Bands enclosed her ankles attached to toe rings similar to those on her fingers. Three chains for each hand and foot.

Looking down she saw a girdle of gold resting comfortably about her waist. Again, three lengths of finely crafted links encircled her. Just as his hands would soon do.

Continuing her exploration, she touched the neckline of the gown as she looked down her body. Barely covered, the full roundness of her breasts held up the dress. Hands traveled up and encountered a necklace, also of gold, she assumed.

More a collar, it was as solid as the bracelets, and a large stone inset in the center that lay over the hollow at the base of her throat. Her fingers caressed the smooth, cool disc. What kind of stone was it?

Hoping to see, she leaned over the pool. She saw her face, the same face she saw each morning in the mirror. But not Reed. That name didn't fit this world. The flowers around her hair were the same as those on the vines.

A scene out of a Celtic dream, she thought with a small smile. Had a fairy chosen to perch on her shoulder at that moment, she wouldn't have been surprised.

The necklace caught her eye. Engraved like the bracelets and ankle bands, the design was intricate and she recognized the twisting cables of Celtic knots representing ley lines, mystical threads of energy, crisscrossing the earth. Sleek dragon heads of gold formed the connection that held the stone in place. But it was the stone that caught her attention.

A little larger than a quarter, it was deep green. Jade. She'd seen jade this color before. One couldn't live near San Francisco and not see jade of all kinds. Round and rounded, a cabochon cut. The mirror qualities of the little pool weren't adequate for examining the stone properly. Bemused, she sat back on the cushion of moss. By what magic had she traveled here? And where was here?

Without a map to follow, she listened to the woods, and let her thoughts flow. Here, was where she'd meet her lover, as she instinctively knew from memories of many such visits, she understood it was a dream, but the why remained a mystery. Why here? Why him? Would the dream finally progress further this time? Would she at last see a familiar face? So far the features of her lover had remained unfocused, the dream always stopping as their lips met for their first kiss.

She lay back and stared up at the intricately woven branches, the pattern interesting and familiar. Curious, she raised a hand to look at one of the bracelets. The engraving was very similar to the pattern of the branches. Smiling, she lowered her hand and lounged, enjoying the sweet air, listening to the forest around her.

Yes, she'd been here before. Remembering it from the other world was difficult, but now she was here, it felt like home, a blanket that obscured the other time. Only one thing was missing--her lover.

Birds chirped and called out to one another. Their shadows flew over the bower, briefly blocking the small shafts of sunlight streaming through the leafy twig roof. The spring added its quiet, melodious tune to the music of nature. Leaves rustled overhead and she breathed in the scent of flowers, green leaves and the rich loam of the forest floor.

He would come soon.

How she knew was a mystery; she just knew. The time was appointed and he would be there. Thinking of her lover brought a smile to her face. Though she couldn't recall the details, there were memories of times they'd been together before.

She could feel his body moving against hers, his hands in her hair, lips on her neck. Stretching once more, she raised her arms and the gown's fabric caressed her hardened nipples. Soft, like his touch when they first came together. Touches that alternated between rough and gentle as they loved. She moved restlessly now, running her hands down her body, longing for him.

A new sound entered the forest. Or rather, all sound left. A hush of excited expectancy fell. He was near!

With a pulse leaping in anticipation, she moved to the center of the bed and raised a knee hoping to present an enticing picture. Raising her arms over her head, she reached for the goblet, thinking to hold it, the better to offer him refreshment.

A jingle of horse tack. A soft snort, the sound of hooves. Slowly and steadily, he approached.

Unable to stay still upon the lounge, she rose to her feet and lifted the goblet. She stood, waiting breathlessly, heart pounding. How long it had been since she'd seen him last! She ached for him, her body ready, the scent of arousal perceptible in the secluded space.

Through the leaves and branches she saw him approach. How tall he sat on his horse, both man and beast dark and dangerous looking. Pride and desire filled her heart to overflowing and she wanted to sing from the joy of it. He liked her singing.

A haunting tune filled her head as her champion drew closer. She watched as he stopped just outside her hiding place and swung down from his black stallion. A proud beauty, the perfect mount for his master. Her lover patted his friend, spoke a quiet word, and was answered with a nod and nicker as he turned and ducked to enter through the low entrance.

Through lowered lashes, she watched as he straightened, his head of shoulder-length black hair just missing the top curve of the branches. Holding her breath, she raised her eyes to his and knew for certain, her heart hitching in recognition--this man was hers for all time.

Their love started here, but their souls had met in other worlds and at other times. His eyes, a brown so dark they were nearly black, smiled at her with love and desire. He'd missed her too.

Gray? But not Gray. Another name came to mind. *Carrick.* That was the more familiar name. Gray was a new name, but the man was the same.

"Carrick." She said his name slowly, savoring the syllables, then raised the goblet to him.

With one hand he took it while the other curled around her waist and pulled her close. Without taking his gaze from hers, he drank, desire making his eyes look darker, more liquid.

"*Liadan.*" The name rolled off his tongue as if he spoke it every day.

Breath shortening, she smiled at him. That's who she was. Liadan. Carrick's beloved Liadan.

A sinful smile curved his lips as he lowered the cup and held it to her lips.

She drank, gaze locked with his, pulse leaping with excitement. This time she saw his face, clear, strong and handsome. Looking away from such perfect male beauty was a feat beyond her powers.

A long, deep sip later, he lifted the goblet from her and drank again, draining it, before letting the cup slip to the ground.

Raising her hand, she touched his cheek where dark stubble stained his jaw. He'd traveled long to be with her.

A gleam lit his eyes a moment before he lowered his mouth to hers.

Eager, she leaned into him and met his lips with a soft whimper and sigh.

Anticipation dried her mouth as she removed his clothes, forgetting to go slow, before he lifted her to the bed. Lying beside her, he rolled into her arms, obeying as she tugged on his shoulders until he lay cradled between her legs. Savoring the feel of him, she slid her hands down his back to his hips, drawing him in.

"Carrick..." Liadan shifted to better feel her dream lover. Oh, this was just too wonderful.

A hand, large and warm, held her breast, gently squeezing and molding the pliant flesh. Her nipple pushed against the palm. Warm lips nibbled the length of her neck and with a shiver she rose to sleepy consciousness.

Not a dream. In the flesh, a sleep-tousled, warm, and aroused man.

"Gray," she murmured.

"Ree, beautiful Ree." He swallowed her sigh with his kiss, his body filling hers, completing her yet again.

~ * ~

"What's wrong?" Gray bit back his grin. Luscious Ree--God, she was a morsel--clutched a towel around her body and glared at the dress she held in the other hand. Personally, he wasn't sure he'd let her keep the dress on if she wiggled back into it.

"I need to put that back on and get back to my room. I can't zip it up by myself. You'll have to help me." She glared at the offending garment.

"I have an idea."

"I'm listening."

"How about if I dash downstairs and grab your suitcase?"

He watched her mull the suggestion over.

"I... I guess that would work. It's mostly packed anyway. I just have toiletries scattered around the bathroom. Let me call Sam and make sure she's cool with that."

"She should be. Roger came back ten minutes ago."

"Oh."

A woman who could still blush. It must be her pale skin. Smooth as white silk. Sweet as fresh milk. *Stop.* Gray felt himself growing hard again. He hadn't had such a sex-fest since college. Even then, with the stamina of youth, it hadn't been this good.

Not wanting to eavesdrop while she made the call--well he did, but chose not to--he reached for his own clothes. By the time she hung up she wore a bemused look.

"What's up?" he asked, zipping his jeans. No need to dress up for the ranch. Chinos or slacks would only earn him scorn. He selected a short-sleeve casual cotton shirt and pulled it on without buttoning it, while walking across the bedroom to stand in front of her.

"Apparently Roger brought my suitcase up with him and Sam will be up in a few minutes for breakfast."

"I'll go check in a minute. First, I want to give you this." He opened his hand to show her the necklace he'd pulled from his briefcase. One of his more recent purchases, planned for the day he met her. He was excited to be giving it to her now.

"Oh." Reed barely breathed the word as she stared at the jade disk resting on his palm. "It's beautiful."

About the size of a silver dollar, the shape of a dragon's head had been carved in relief upon it.

"It's actually a Celtic dragon, rather than a Chinese one," Gray explained, as he opened the clasp on the chain of twisted gold. Twenty inches long, the chain was the perfect length for the disk to nestle at the top of her cleavage. Directly over her heart.

"Thank you, it's lovely." She stared up at him, her small hand covering the green stone. "What made you think I liked dragons? I mean, I do like them, but how...?"

He grinned. "How do I know so many things about you? I just do. I'm glad you like it."

"More of that scary mystic talk."

They'd have to talk soon.

He leaned down to kiss her and tugged on the towel. "You look too good to get dressed. Maybe I'll whisk you to the plane in a towel."

"Gray! Stop playing." She laughed and clutched the towel tighter.

"Who says I'm playing?"

The towel opened enough for him to slip a hand inside and cup soft, rounded flesh.

"I can barely walk as it is," she said against his lips.

"Okay, I'll get your suitcase. Gonna wear a skirt?" he asked hopefully.

"Incorrigible."

And that wasn't a no.

SEVEN

"Gray!" Reed whispered furiously. "Behave!"

"Sam, your friend is no fun at all." Highly exaggerated, his sigh sounded anything but real to her.

Reed held his hand to keep him from pulling her skirt up. Thankfully, Roger was ready to take off. She settled into her seat and ignored Sam's laugh from across the small table. Gray sat in the seat next to Reed in the grouping of four leather chairs, two facing two, over a well lacquered table.

Outfitted in dark wood and trimmed with brass, soft dark-gray leather upholstery and carpet, the interior of the jet was luxurious by anyone's standards. Galley in the front where they'd entered, lavatory at the rear, there was also a sofa and seating for nine in the cabin. During the tour, Gray had made sure she knew the sofa could be made into a cozy bed for two, complete with a hopeful suggestive look. She was beginning to question the vow that he'd never tested it.

After a word from Roger, they buckled their seatbelts and settled back to enjoy the ride. Before the plane left the ground, Reed was sold on the concept of private flying. She hadn't missed the line to check in, the shuffling through security, waiting at the gate, jockeying to board the plane, or fighting her way down a narrow aisle. In fact, she hadn't handled a single piece of luggage other than her purse. Roger and Gray had done it all. She could easily fall in love with the plane. Gray, she was still thinking about.

Once in the air, Reed toed off her boots, curled her legs at her side, and leaned against Gray's shoulder, a luxury she rarely had on a commercial flight. As wide as a first class seat without the consol in the middle, these were made for cuddling. He seemed to think so, as well. Reed caught Sam looking on with amusement before her friend pulled out her laptop.

"What did Himself say when you called?" Sam asked her.

"You don't want to know," Reed grumbled. "He wasn't pleased. The fact that it was around midnight didn't help much."

Sam's snort fell far short of ladylike. "I bet." The added glance from her to Gray and back again didn't make Reed feel any more comfortable.

"He accused me of being a traitor," Reed confessed.

"I'm not surprised. He's been trying to get you on his office sofa since practically the day we started. I suspect that's why he hired us in the first place."

Reed gave her friend a good scowl. "That isn't true."

Sam returned her look with a level stare. "Why is it you're so brilliant in some areas, but in others you're completely oblivious?"

"I'm not oblivious." Reed looked from Sam to Gray when both of them choked on their laughter.

"May I get you ladies a beverage?" Gray kissed her forehead then stood.

"What do you have cold?" Reed chose to ignore

Sam's last comment. After all, Sam spent too much time in the lab to notice anything outside of it.

"Soda, water, champagne, wine, beer and assorted juices. For the more dedicated drinker, scotch, rum and gin. There might be something else. I haven't seriously looked lately."

"Water's good for me," Reed said.

"No champagne?" He teased her with a grin.

"I need to rehydrate." She gave him her best droll stare.

"Yes, ma'am. Dr. Sam?"

"Diet Coke?"

"Sure thing."

"Any chance I can ride in the cockpit for a bit?" Sam asked Gray.

"That's up to Roger. I may pay for this toy, but it belongs to him." He nodded toward the cockpit. "I only tell him when I want to fly. He tells me if it's feasible."

"Who's the boss?" Reed asked.

"I know when to let go of control and let my people do what they do best. In return they do their damndest to please me," Gray replied with a half shrug. "I get good results. All Roger asks is that I give him as much notice as possible. Also, when I declare time off, I give him at least thirty-six hours. He usually gets more. The downside is if he's bored and wants to fly, he makes me schedule a meeting somewhere."

"Softy," Reed accused him with a small smile.

"Shh. Don't let that get out. Remember, you promised not to get involved in industrial espionage. If I hear that one get around, we'll have words," he warned her with a long sexy stare.

She couldn't help giggling and bit her lip to

stop when Sam gave her a look with lifted brow.

"I can't remember the last time you giggled," Sam commented.

Reed cleared her throat and took the glass of water Gray held out to her.

"Funny," Gray said, "she giggled most of last night."

"I did not!" Reed declared.

"That's right, she didn't." He sat down next to her again. "She moaned, whimpered and screamed. *Then* she giggled."

Reed rolled her eyes and looked out the window. "What are you working on, Sam?" Maybe a change of subject was in order.

"I can tell you, but if he overhears I'll have to kill him," her friend joked.

"Right. Let me know when you want me to look over your numbers." Reed sipped her water and rested her head on Gray's shoulder. Utterly sated, a nap sounded wonderful.

"Ah, c'mon, Sam," Gray complained with a teasing grin. "Is that any way to treat your host? Besides, sometimes fresh eyes help solve a problem."

"Sorry, Mr. Competition, it isn't worth my life to share this information with you. Now if you want to tell me how your engineers are solving the transmitter problem I'd be willing to listen."

Reed snorted into her glass.

"And just what transmitter are we talking about?" Gray's fluttering eyelashes were so overly dramatic it was actually cute.

"Right. Thought you might see it that way." Sam shook her head, a tiny smile ruining her complaint. "Actually, the problem isn't in the transmitter. I was just curious to see if you'd fall for it."

"You're right, the problem is in the processors and how the data is analyzed."

Reed watched as Sam rolled her eyes. "We are so *not* having this conversation."

"Actually, I'm considering giving up the project," Gray said casually, his eyes on his bottle of water.

"Not falling for that trick," Sam declared and bent over her computer, tapping at the keys.

"What trick?" Reed wanted to know.

"He's trying to get me to let my guard down. I know his people want to know where we are in development of the project. They're working on the same thing and the first one to bring it to market stands to make a fair amount of money."

"Which is why Troy is hauling you out of the lab for this week-long team-building experience?" Reed thought Troy was an idiot for taking Sam away from her lab. It was best just to let Sam work, tossing food and drink at her each time she emerged to find the bathroom or stretch her legs in the company gym. The fact she could go several hours without looking at the door was often a blessing and a curse.

"Troy has his reasons," Sam muttered. "Still, I'm not about to reveal the true status of the project to our main competitor."

"Fair enough." Gray laughed. "I don't really want to talk business anyway. These next few weeks I'm a rancher and a wrangler anyway."

"Why is that?" Reed was intrigued. He still hadn't explained why he was headed to the family homestead.

"My brother, Dustin, who runs the ranch, got injured a few days ago. I was on my way home when I had this mad urge to stop in Vegas. I'm glad I did." The warm smile in his eyes said it all.

"You stopped in Vegas while your brother was hurt?" Reed's eyebrows felt as if they'd hit her hairline. Playing while his brother lay in the hospital?

"It's not like he's alone there." A hint of defensiveness entered Gray's posture. "My mother manages the lodge side and the books--the General Manager, if you will. Dustin is the CEO and, between the two of them, they manage some twenty to thirty employees. Not to mention, my sister and her husband are there along with our baby brother and a few nieces and nephews. I'm not really needed. He's not dying and there are plenty to carry on the work. They just haven't seen me in a while and are using this as leverage to remind me of family obligations."

"'Tell us how you really feel," she retorted. "You sound a little bitter and resentful."

"What is your experience with family obligations?"

Family obligations she had down pat. Funny, work obligations seemed the same to her. "I'm the youngest of five. Five very independent people who rarely see each other all together, even more rarely individually. But, illness, injury or death will always draw us together. We even get together for the odd life celebration as well. Case in point, my grandmother's one hundredth birthday coming up in a couple months. Or when we found out my dad had cancer, we were all there at the hospital while he had his surgery. We casually rotated being there to care for him and give Mom a break. No organization, just being on hand and filling in when a gap came up." Same thing with his last weeks of life. Some wounds were too fresh even after a few years. She pushed that one deep again.

"You get along with your siblings?"

That made her laugh. "I didn't say that. Most of the time, I ignore them completely. Is that it? You don't get along with your family?"

Gray shook his head. "We get along okay, but this will sound trite. They don't understand me. My drive, my dreams, have very little to do with developing and running the best guest ranch in the west. They think I've stepped too far away from my roots." He paused to shrug. "Maybe I have, but there was a good reason for it. Now my search is over, maybe it's time to go home and reconnect."

Reed leaned away and eyed him carefully. The back of her neck itched and a funny, goose-bumpy kind of feeling crawled over her skin. "I don't want to know what ended your search, do I?"

Gray's grin confirmed her suspicions. "I found you."

For a very long moment, the only sound was the muted hum of the engines and the faint sound of air rushing over the wings. Reed abstractly knew Sam had stopped typing and now watched the small drama taking place.

As Reed stared at Gray and he stared back at her, she found it best to concentrate on simple things. Like breathing and listening to the beat of her heart. Yep, the body still functioned. Higher brain level activities had ceased, but the basics kept right on chugging away.

"So," Reed finally found her voice. "That's your

story and you're sticking to it?"

"It's the only story," Gray said gently. "And I'll keep saying it. Until you believe me, and then long after, so you never forget. My whole focus in life narrowed down to yesterday afternoon and last night. From here on out, life begins anew. Today is the beginning."

Reed dropped her feet to the floor and leaned back in her seat. Yesterday, she'd been enjoying a break from work, dreading the coming week, but there'd been nothing really scary on her horizon. Well, nothing scarier than keeping the company afloat until the new invention was working.

Now, it seemed a cowboy had ambushed her and trussed her like a calf. Metaphorically speaking. How long before he put his metaphorical brand on her? She touched the necklace and wondered if he already had. How long before she thanked him for doing it? Good or bad didn't even figure in at this point. She had a situation to deal with and needed time and space to think things over. Apparently Gray had her--their--future mapped out, and she hadn't thought much beyond surviving the coming week followed by the fourth quarter. It was daunting.

"Gray, don't you think you're moving a little fast? How can you be sure I'm the owner of the green eyes you've been searching for?"

He reached out and touched her cheek.

It was all Reed could do to hold still. The decision on whether to run to or from him was still in the air. In any case it was a moot point for the foreseeable future. There wasn't room to run on the plane and he'd be at the ranch. Short of a parachute jump over Utah, she was stuck.

"I've had this dream off and on for nearly as long as I can remember. From the first time I dreamed it, I've never known peace and love like I feel when the dream visits me. Until yesterday. You're the woman in my dream, and we're meant to be together."

Gray's dark eyes were liquid soft with emotion, and his hand cupping her cheek felt warm and strong even as he gently held her.

Reed felt a shift deep inside. The kind of shift felt when the San Andreas Fault decided to ease a little pressure. Something akin to the shaking of the 1906 San Francisco Earthquake.

She didn't know what to say. Didn't know what to do. An odd mixture of feelings fought a fierce battle inside her. One voice screamed in rapturous joy--*there is a love for me!* Another voice screamed in panic--*this is insane!* Love at first sight was nothing more than a cruel fairytale. Wasn't it?

Gray's thumb caressed her cheek before sliding down to rest over the pulse she felt jumping in her neck. "Be brave, Reed. Open your heart and mind to the possibility. The rewards will be greater than you could ever imagine."

Yeah, her heart was so open it was practically falling into his hand. She drew in a steadying breath though it didn't help much. Maybe if she had more information. "I guess, then, you'd better tell me about this dream."

"I will, but not right now. You won't believe me just yet. Just open your mind to the possibility of a new future and we'll go from there, okay?"

Reed searched his face. She didn't know him well enough to know if he was a good actor or not.

Was this a test?

"I'll try."

"Good, now come here and cuddle. You look tired. I'll be your pillow."

Reed blinked and realized her eyes were heavy. A short nap wouldn't go astray. Giving in to temptation, she curled her legs up beside her again, and leaned into his arms. He did make a very nice pillow.

~ * ~

Lanterns and fireflies lit the forest surrounding the dim pool. In summer time, the sun was high quite late, the night never entirely dark as the brilliant orb slid into the dusky between-time. The soft sounds of the waterfall provided a musical backdrop to the birds calling out through the warm air.

"My lady," Carrick teased, his lips reaching for the tender spot behind her ear.

"Hush, you." Liadan playfully pushed him away. Shaving him was a careful business anyway, to accomplish it while he was kissing her was downright impossible. "Your beard has scratched me enough for one night. Hold still, lest I accidentally slice your throat."

With a mock look of terror, Carrick complied as she brandished the knife before using it to scrape the last rough stubble of his beard away.

"There, all smooth again." She reached for a cloth, wet it and wiped the last of the soap from his face. "And handsome enough to gaze upon once more."

"Smooth enough to do this..." He bent his head to her throat, his arms holding her hostage. This time she didn't fight. As tired as she was, she still craved his lovemaking. One night was all they had in which to satisfy themselves. She'd sleep tomorrow when he left.

Carrick's hands possessed her body as surely as he possessed her heart and soul.

Liadan couldn't get enough of him touching and kissing her. Letting him direct their lovemaking, she found herself floating on her back in the pool as his hands and lips worshipped her. Resting on the surface, she found the water a soft bed on which she had no purchase and he moved her at his will.

The supple cloth was used now to tease and torment her, gliding from her sensitized nipples to her swollen cleft. Carrick washed her gently, slowly attending to each and every fold, just as she'd washed him, his fingers every bit as arousing as she'd made hers just a little while ago.

"Is my face smooth enough to avoid causing injury here?" He murmured the question against her nether lips, the warm air of his breath a stark contrast to the cool water.

"Yes," Liadan said on a needy sigh.

In answer to her impatient wiggle, he merely laughed quietly and teased her with his tongue. Slow strokes, long, from top to bottom and back again, he tortured her. Even though her legs locked themselves over his shoulders, he held her hips, containing and controlling the movement of her body.

"Thrash all you like. I'm already wet."

She felt his laughter all through her body. His mouth settled against her, lips working with tongue, the vibration of his vocalizations adding depth to her excitement.

"Don't talk, don't tease," she ordered harshly as his lips wrapped around her tender flesh and suckled. Threading her fingers into his hair, she attempted to control him.

Not giving in to her, he pulled her hands away and trapped them under his, holding her hips, as she groaned. Taking his time, he played her, slowly building her orgasm, one lick, one suckle, one pinch, one stroke at a time.

Writhing as best she could, she urged him on, the water adding to the caresses. Her nipples, taut and straining in the air as the soft liquid lapped around the base of her breasts.

Unbearably needy, she moaned, begging, "Carrick..."

~ * ~

"Reed."

A softly spoken male voice said her name. Reed moved against the hand cradling her head. His voice...but the name he called her, the accent, it wasn't right, the name wasn't right...and, yet...it was. Confused, she frowned.

"Wake up, my love."

"Mmm?" She wanted the release. It couldn't be over. *Not yet!* She moaned and nuzzled against the warm body under her cheek. The covering was soft, but not as soft as the water that had been kissing her a moment before. What happened to the cool green scent of their secret place? The pool? Shaking her head, she sought to push away the hand and voice intruding on her dream.

Warm lips brushed over hers and strong arms held her.

"Sweetheart, we're landing soon. You need to wake up and buckle in."

"No!" Her protest was hardly more than a mumbled whimper.

"As much as I'd love to let you sleep on, Roger will have my hide if I don't get you buckled in." It was Gray who murmured against her lips and gave her a gentle peck, telling her the dream was over, leaving her sad even as she opened to his kiss.

"Gray." Reed moaned. Carrick had faded into the mists of dreams again. But he was here, in the flesh. It was too much. She wanted the dream and the reality together instead of this eternally split existence.

"Yes, love, I'm here."

"I dreamed... so sweet...hidden in the forest..."

"Yes, love, I want to hear about it, but now isn't the time."

"Remember... I want to go back...to the pool..." The sooner the better. The aching familiarity of unfulfilled emptiness overwhelmed her, and she wanted to cry.

"You will. I promise. Now sit up."

"Yes, Gray." Reed sighed, still mostly asleep, and let him push her into a sitting position. The plane began to descend as she reached for her seatbelt, another layer of sleep drifting away. Blearily, she opened her eyes and looked out the window to see the ground coming up. Mountains rose steeply into the sky, more barren than she'd expected. "Where are we?"

"Eagle, Colorado. Just west of Vail. The car is waiting for us. We'll be at the ranch in about an hour."

"Hmm." Reed leaned against Gray's shoulder. The dream. Twice in twenty-four hours and this time she'd seen the face of her lover, the look in his eyes. Tears clogged her throat. How unfair to have the moment interrupted. Would she ever learn the meaning of the dream?

Could Gray be right? Was he her one true love? How closely tied were they?

EIGHT

"Reed? You okay?"

She turned to look at Sam. They stood on the tarmac, taking in the view of the mountains framing a wide valley, while the plane was unloaded and squared away--however planes were squared away when not in use.

"I don't know who I am anymore, but other than that I'm just fine."

"What do you mean?" Sam's eyes looked worried.

That joke fell flat. Reed reached out and touched her friend's arm with a small smile. "I'm fine. Just trying to figure out what's happening to me. Gray has turned my secure, routine, little world upside down in under twenty-four hours."

"Love at first sight?"

"So he says. I don't know." Reed turned to watch Gray stow luggage in the back of an SUV. A pale gold Suburban, she noticed, with the name *Eagle Mountain Guest Ranch* painted on the side. Beside him, a man introduced as Blake, younger than Gray, but unmistakably related, tossed the last bag in the back and shut the doors.

"How's Roger?" Reed asked.

Sam smiled. "I like him. He's fun. He let me fly the plane for a bit, too."

Reed knew that smile. "That good, eh?"

"He's da bomb," her friend confirmed. "We

went through an entire box of condoms last night." Sam's sigh and expression uncharacteristically dreamy.

Despite Sam's satisfied purr, Reed felt the blood drain from her face. "Oh shit."

"What?" Sam's smile disappeared into a frown.

"Condoms," Reed whispered, a hand covering her mouth. "We didn't use any."

Sam grabbed her shoulders and turned to face her. "What?"

Reed dropped her head to Sam's shoulder. "The subject never came up. We didn't use any. Not one."

"How many times...?"

"I don't know...four? Five? Six? I'm exhausted. I can't remember."

Sam wrapped her arms around Reed. "Okay. No problem. You just had your period last week, right?"

Reed nodded.

"You're lucky. But no excuses from here on out, hear?"

"You're right. I won't forget."

"Ladies?"

Reed stepped back at the sound of Gray's voice.

"Ready?" His dark eyes scanned her face. "Everything okay?"

Reed grabbed his arm and pulled him away from the car and the others.

"What?" Gray asked.

"We need to talk, and now," she said through clenched teeth. "I swear, you're turning me into a mindless idiot. Did it occur to you that neither one of us mentioned birth control--forget about disease protection--last night or this morning?

Condoms? Are you familiar with these simple but useful items?"

Reed wasn't amused when Gray grinned.

"Honestly, I once had a fleeting thought, but then we felt so good together, I forgot all about them. However, since we'll be married soon, it's a moot point. I'm glad to hear you aren't on the pill. Messing around with hormones like that isn't a good idea."

"You assume a lot, Mr. Dunbar." *Arrogant son of a bitch!* Reed gave him her best cold glare. Too bad it didn't seem to faze him in the least.

The man had enough confidence for ten men. Or was it just plain conceit? Was it the dream? Would slapping him knock some of the arrogance down a peg or two? Fingernails dug into her palms as she curled them into fists to stop herself from hitting him. With her brothers she wouldn't have hesitated. Then again, her brothers knew better than to dismiss her out of hand.

"Ree, relax. If it's that important to you, we'll use them from now on. Better?" His hand on her arm was gentle as he lowered his forehead to hers. "I realize this is moving so fast, but you'll see. It will all work out just fine. Even if you get pregnant and have to make an honest man out of me, I won't mind, really."

Pregnant? "Stop. Just stop." She stepped back from him, a hand on his chest holding him at arm's length. "I'm here to do a job, so please, stop trying to twist my mind, okay? I'm not ready for long term and I don't know you well enough to make those kinds of decisions anyway."

"Yes, Ree. Will you have dinner with me tonight?"

"I don't know." She exhaled in exasperation. The man was pure frustration. Dealing with him felt like dealing with a slightly more grown-up version of Troy. "I need to deal with my coworkers first and...well... Troy may want to have dinner with Sam and me tonight since we cheated him out of the car ride. We need to make up some of the points we lost."

"Okay, we'll take it one step at a time. Shall we go? The others are waiting."

~ * ~

Gray stared out the window from the front passenger seat. He'd rather be in the back with Reed, but his brother wanted to talk. Blake had a lot of news. Gray already knew most of it. Dustin and Mom kept him up to date. Email was a wonderful thing for keeping connected to the family.

"You know we have a small corporate group this week, right?" Blake gave him a sideways glance

"Yes, I know." Gray glanced over his shoulder to Reed and Sam. "Meet the CFO and the Principal Investigator."

"You're with Spearman?" Blake's voice cracked a little.

Gray saw Blake's eyes glance into the back seat in the rearview mirror.

"Yes, Blake. We met up in Vegas yesterday and I offered them a ride."

"But, they're with Spearman," Blake's voice trailed off in confusion.

"It's okay, Blake. Troy and I won't duel with revolvers at dawn if that's what you're worried about. iPhones, maybe."

The snort of laughter from the back seat made him smile. With a well-timed email Gray could do some damage to Troy's company if he wanted. Troy could probably get in a matching blow. Maybe. Unlikely. Gray was far more diversified than Troy.

"But, I thought...green..."

Gray resisted the urge to pop his brother upside the head. Blake didn't get the joke. "Yes, Blake, Reed has green eyes." The boy was being dense. "How's Dustin?"

"He's cranky as all hell." Blake's short laugh sounded relieved.

"I can imagine," Gray replied mildly. Their older brother was as dour and rigid as their father had been. Practically Dad's clone, Dustin had a set path and knew exactly where he was going, what was required of him to get there and he steadily plodded along it. Being laid up would annoy him greatly. "How did it happen?"

"A kid wandered into the wrong corral. The Old Man is feeling his age these days and didn't take kindly to it. Dustin got the kid out, but the Old Man's horn caught him up. Poked him through the leg. Good thing the helicopter was handy. We got him to the hospital fast enough he didn't lose too much blood. We brought him back this morning. I think the doctor was ready to kick him out--Dustin was waiting at the curb when we drove up."

Gray glanced back at Reed and saw she was avidly listening. "The Old Man is an ornery old bull," he told her. "He was ornery ten years ago. Should have been made into stew then."

Blake laughed. "He might be there, now, but

119

Dustin has a soft spot for him. Ordered us to not shoot the beast before he got hauled off."

Gray snorted and looked out the window as they followed the two lane road, slowly climbing in altitude. He extended his arm along the back of the seat. How was he going to make this work? He needed time with Reed, but the family expected him to step in and run things. Reed needed to participate in her company gathering. There was going to be precious little time to get together. Breakfast and dinner were about it. Unless...

"Who's slated to guide the pack trip?" Gray asked.

"Jim and Hank are taking Spearman's group. They're heading out Tuesday morning."

"Dustin wasn't going to take it?"

"Not that I know of."

Blake glanced in the rearview mirror again. Gray could tell his brother was dying to ask questions. The kid could keep wondering.

Gray looked over his shoulder again at Reed. She watched him while trying to ignore Sam and Roger sitting to her right. Reed met his gaze for a moment before she turned away to look out the window. Her eyes still held a haunted look from the dream.

He allowed himself a small smile thinking of the thin slice of jade Reed wore over her heart, and wondering if it had enhanced her reception of the dream. Mentally scanning the cases still stored on the plane, he couldn't think of one more piece he could readily give her. The pendant had been the best of the lot. Why hadn't he bought any of the jade rings he'd seen? Earrings, even? Those accessories would have to wait until they got back to civilization.

Gray remembered watching Reed's face on the plane. So peaceful and lovely. Curiosity to learn just what she'd experienced burned inside him. He knew the dream from his side, and always felt the thrill of anticipation, savoring that moment when his horse approached the sylvan rendezvous.

In the early days, the dream had started farther away as he rode across a verdant land. Scenery he recognized as the land around the ranch transitioned into what he'd come to believe was ancient Ireland or, possibly, England. It had been years before the dream had moved beyond the moment when their eyes first met.

Later, toward the end of high school, the dream had always ended with drinking from the goblet, leading Gray to search far and wide for a vintage that came close to the one she had waiting for him. Finally, a few years ago, he'd bought a winery just to make a wine comparable to that in the dream.

Cases of *Clocha Lomhara's* respected bottling were stored in caves, ready to ship at his whim. A few were sold to collectors each year, but most he hoarded for himself, especially the vintage just produced. He could hardly wait to share it with her. A case was in the back of the Suburban even now. It would go quite well with a good steak.

Gray had the feeling Reed had awoken from the dream in the middle of lovemaking. Did she remember the taste of the wine? The taste of their kisses? These days, for him, the dream went much further, the dress slipping from her shoulders, the gold girdle removed long enough to let the gown pool on the ground. Lying on the soft bed, urgent kisses speaking of their longing, he usually woke, hard and aching, just before joining with her.

An erotic vision of the gold jewelry draped around her body sent a shaft of need through him. What stood out most of all was the collar of gold with the perfect cabochon. Searching the jewelry markets for years hadn't turned up its equal anywhere.

Until one day, a chance encounter in Hong Kong had led him to study the properties of jade, following the trail until he found the perfect stone in Burma, where a craftsman had willingly shaped it to his specifications. Then, on a trip to Ireland, he found an innovative jeweler and together they designed the collar of carved and engraved gold that now held the jade stone matching her eyes perfectly. The necklace, along with matching girdle, bracelets and ankle bands, was locked away in a safe in his California home.

Last night, or rather this morning, as he'd slept, the dream had taken a new leap forward. At one point he hadn't been sure what was dream and what was real as he'd slowly thrust into her sweet, welcoming body. Making love to her was everything the dream promised and more.

Her soft limbs and lush body wrapped around him was a feeling beyond any he'd ever hoped for. Her kisses far sweeter than the wine. Her scent more intoxicating than the flowers decorating their hideaway. Even now, his body ached for her touch and his mouth hungered for hers. Somehow he suspected he'd never get enough of her, would never feel completely sated unless joined with her on the spiritual level as well as the physical.

Wanting her, Gray glanced back over the seat

and found her mysterious eyes watching him. He smiled and was pleased she smiled back.

Blake slowed the vehicle and turned. When the road became smoothed gravel Gray knew they were almost there. Now all he had to do was deal with Mother and Dustin.

~ * ~

Reed nervously looked out the window at the passing land. It reminded her of childhood camping trips into the Sierra Nevada Mountains.

Tall wooden poles forming the ranch's main gate came into view. The initials of the ranch, in the shape of mountains, formed the apex of the rough trellised arch. Hanging from a pole beside the gate was a sign painted with the head of a Texas Longhorn. No wonder the brother had been seriously hurt. Those were sharp and pointy horns.

Blake turned left into a large circular drive and stopped in front of the rustic-looking lodge. The woman who stepped out onto the long covered porch had to be a relative of Gray's. The sister most likely. Her black hair was long and straight. There must be a strain of Native American in their ancestry. It fit with Gray's use of the word 'Shaman' and his ready belief in mystical things.

Reed settled her sunglasses in place and accepted Blake's help out of the tall SUV. Stepping down onto the gravel, she regretted the denim skirt she wore. She also felt silly in her boots as she reluctantly put the tan Stetson on her head. Gray hadn't been kidding about the sun's intensity in the thinner air. Already she felt it pricking at her exposed skin like small needles.

"Easy there," Blake said kindly. "The altitude can knock you for a loop the first day or so."

"Thanks." Reed managed a small smile.

"Drinking lots of water will help, and keep your sunscreen handy," he advised.

"Water, yes, but I don't use sunscreen," she replied absently.

Reed followed Blake to the back of the vehicle to help with luggage.

"Hey there." Gray intercepted the bag Reed reached for. "No carrying the luggage." He tucked her under his arm. "Come meet my sister. Have I mentioned how adorable you look?"

"Only once or twice." Reed still wasn't sure if he was teasing her or not. Before leaving the hotel, he'd walked around her and murmured words of approval with a silly grin on his face.

Now, compared to the woman wearing jeans and a polo shirt with the ranch logo, she felt ridiculously over dressed. At least her boots and hat were plain tan.

The A-line, calf length, denim skirt, tank and retro western styled shirt were enough to make her look like a bad ad for western wear though not as flashy as some of the clothes she'd seen and passed by. The western shirt, white with a black yoke accented by turquoise-colored flowers, cute in the store, was completely impractical for the ranch, unless she was spending an evening in the saloon. It would do for tonight, but she had plain jeans and more practical shirts for the rest of the week.

"Kiri." Gray let go of Reed and hugged the younger woman. He'd been missed, judging by the way she hugged him back. Gray released her and pulled Reed forward. "This is Reed O'Brien. Ree, my sister Kirima. It's just easier to call her Kiri."

Reed slid her sunglasses down so they perched on the end of her nose and shook Kiri's extended hand. "Pleased to meet you," she said forcing a smile to fill the silence as Kiri stared at her.

"Reed is part of Spearman's group," Gray explained.

That seemed to shake Kiri up. "Oh, speaking of which, Troy is here. He's inside with Mother," she blurted out.

Reed felt a prickle of annoyance. Why was Troy there? He wasn't due for a couple more hours yet.

"Oh, sorry, pleased to meet you, Reed. Troy is just sorting out the room assignments. Why don't you go in and see if you need to straighten him out."

Reed wondered at Kiri's smile. Friendly enough, it hinted at something and she felt her stomach flip. What was Troy up to now?

Reed glanced over her shoulder at Sam behind her and they shared a look.

Sam raised a brow and shrugged as if to say, 'I told you so.'

Urged forward by Gray's hand on the small of her back, Reed mounted the wide steps to the planked porch, which was covered by an upper balcony. Stepping into the cool interior of the lobby, she removed her sunglasses in order to see in the dim light.

"Well, we can put you in one studio, the ladies in the other and then the rest of your party in one of the rooms with a loft. They can toss for who gets the private room. Does that work for you, Troy?" The older woman behind the polished wood reception desk looked over her reading glasses at the man casually leaning against the counter. An older version of Kiri, her black hair liberally streaked with white, this could only be Gray's mother.

"That will work great," Troy said, turning to watch Reed approach with Gray. "Thank you, Sora. Ah, here's my wayward crew, now. Gray, you should know better than to steal my senior staff."

Reed didn't care much for the cold expression in Troy's blue eyes, despite his mild, familiar tone. Like Gray he had black hair, but he'd let it grow long. Loose, thick curls fell in waves to the collar of his denim jacket. Troy looked like a city boy in his stiff new jeans, though the hat dangling from his fingers was as worn as his scuffed boots. Troy's eyes softened as he took in her appearance from head toe. A small, crooked smile she recognized as patronizing touched his lips. So he thought her new look was cute, too. Great.

"Troy. You should take better care of your staff."

Reed noticed that while Gray extended a hand to Troy for a short, hard handshake, he kept an arm securely wrapped around her waist.

"Mother."

Gray reached a hand across the counter and the older woman gripped it briefly, her eyes barely touching her son's face before lingering on Reed's.

"Mrs. Dunbar," Reed said with a warm smile. Better to greet the mother first. "Thank you for having us."

"Mother, this is Miss Reed O'Brien. Troy's money keeper."

Reed ignored the two men suddenly fidgeting like her eight year old nephew. "Did Troy mess up our room reservations?" She asked the question with what she hoped was an indulgent smile. *Would humor work?*

Gray's mother seemed to shake herself awake. She'd been staring intensely at Reed. "No, no, Troy was just confirming the arrangements. We have your group in the upper lodge. The views are superior from there. We're pleased to have you. It's been many years since we've seen Troy."

Reed caught the look Gray's mother sent her son and wondered at the older woman's wrinkled brow and pinched lips. Apparently, the history between Troy and this family went deep. The look only lasted a second before Gray's mother was back staring at Reed.

It was so very tempting to put her sunglasses on again. She'd never thought her eyes unusual before. Now she felt as if she were from outer space.

The sound of footsteps came from the door and Mrs. Dunbar's glance swung beyond her and Gray. With a quick look over her shoulder, Reed confirmed Roger and Blake were carrying in the luggage. Sam followed with both laptop bags over her shoulder. As her friend approached the counter, Reed reached for hers only to have Sam shake her head.

"I have it, Ree."

"Thanks, babe." Reed turned back to see Gray's mother staring at her again.

"If you ladies will sign in," the older woman said briskly, pushing registration cards and pens across the counter. "Blake will see your bags make it to your room."

She gave each woman a map of the property with the location of their lodge highlighted. "Your studio is in here. Troy can show you the way, his room is next to yours. He assured me you ladies wouldn't mind sharing."

The last was said with a barely raised brow.

"Oh no, we've been roommates for years. Nothing new about sharing," Sam said cheerfully, doing a fine job of ignoring the not-so-subtle implication.

Reed glanced at Troy. His steady gaze indicated exactly where he expected her to sleep. *Great.* Had he been making hints the last few weeks? Had she been too tired to notice? Gray's arm snaking around her neck, hand dangling down between her breasts, sent a different message and Reed wanted to slink off into the woods to avoid them all.

Instead, Reed glanced at Sam. "Shall we go find our room?"

"By all means."

Gray turned Reed to face him and lifted her chin. "Dinner, here at five-thirty, if I can't come for you. Roger and I have to check in with the boss."

"Fine." Reed bit off the word.

Gray grinned and kissed her nose. "I'll try not to be long."

Reed ducked out of his arms and headed for the door leading out to the covered porch.

"Oh, Ree? We'll take care of your massage after dinner," Gray called after her.

Intent on stomping down the steps, she didn't even stop to acknowledge it.

NINE

"Reed! Sam! Wait up."

Reed kept walking. She really didn't want to talk to Troy right now. Rapid footsteps told her he was catching up anyway. Her short-legged march was no match for the longer strides of her companions. Sam strolled easily at her side.

"You'll have to face him sooner or later," Sam said.

"Later works for me. What about you?"

"I don't think you'll get your wish."

Reed knew Sam was right, and her friend's prediction was confirmed a moment later when Troy reached her side.

"You can't run, you know," he said, huffing in the thin air.

"Lost your altitude conditioning, Troy?" Reed asked, her tone a little sharper than intended. Come to think of it, she felt a little lightheaded and winded herself.

"Slow down, you're puffing like a steam locomotive," Troy said as his hand fell on her arm.

Reed stopped, shook him off, and turned to face him, hands on hips. She knew he couldn't see her eyes behind the dark glasses, but he could damn well see the frown, and tried to head her off.

"Reed, don't take that tone with me," Troy started.

Ignoring his attempt to stop the tirade before it

began, she lit into him. "I've only just arrived and already I've about had it with you. How dare you change the room assignments?"

"What do you mean?"

"You downgraded Sam and me into a studio. Why do we have to share a bed?"

She didn't like Troy's smile.

"Why, Reed, I figured it would be more discreet this way."

Reed slapped away the hand he reached out to her. "Is that why I'm here? Well, I've got a newsflash for you, Troy Spearman. I'm not crawling into your room after hours. Not even in daylight hours. I have enough man trouble at the moment without you suddenly deciding to renew your pursuit."

"Oh yes," Troy drawled, his eyes narrowing as a sneer curled his lips. He shoved his hands into his pockets. "Gray. Is he your new main squeeze? What was that comment about the massage later? Are you crawling off to his quarters?"

Reed clenched a fist around the shoulder strap of her purse, turned and marched off to catch Sam who'd tactfully moved up the trail a few yards. She heard Troy's footsteps behind her but didn't slow. Grabbing the room key from Sam's hand, she stomped up the steps of their lodge.

"It's a good thing you don't snore," Reed muttered before throwing the door open. Snatching her sunglasses off, she tossed them and her hat onto the small coffee table.

"But you do," Sam laughed.

"Very funny." Reed snorted as she dropped her purse on the sofa. "One bed. Don't even think about hogging it."

"Hump me like Roger and it won't matter how much of the bed you take up."

"Too much information," Reed muttered. Out of the corner of her eye she saw the door open and she turned to her friend. "But Sammiekins, you know I always sleep better on the bottom." Reed reached out a hand and stroked a finger down Sam's arm as a lover would. "Just wear me out tonight and it won't matter," she said with a sultry glare.

"I've always wondered." Troy's amused voice came from the door where he lounged. "Is this why you two have been roommates since college?"

"We'll never confess." Grinning wickedly, Sam slipped an arm around Reed. "But if you want to watch, it will cost you. Big." She ran her fingers through Reed's hair, idly twisting a lock around one long finger.

"Might be worth it." Troy's gaze raked them slowly.

"You'll pay, whether you watch or not." Reed blew out her exasperation and stepped away from Sam. "And you'll never know. Now get out." She pushed him back and slammed the door in his face.

~ * ~

Gray watched from the window of the second floor office. He smiled when Reed slapped Troy's hand away. Good. She wasn't amenable to his rival's advances. Once Reed had turned and stomped away, Gray turned back to the room. His mother watched him silently.

"Did you really have the two women in a studio?" he asked and paced around the room tastefully decorated in a western theme.

Horseshoes, framed cowboy prints and log furniture were heavily featured. A large hand-woven Navajo rug warmed the polished planks of wooden floor. Nothing had changed. Not a piece of furniture had moved. Time stood still here.

"Troy requested the change. He implied one would stay with him."

"Over my dead body," Gray muttered, moving to the mini bar in the corner. He found a bottle of spring water in the bar's small fridge.

"What is the woman to you?" his mother asked sharply.

"She's my soul mate."

"How can you be sure of this? Because of her eyes? Plenty of women have green eyes."

"I know." Gray twisted off the top to the bottle and tossed it in the trash. "If anyone knows, it's me. But she's the one. She had the same dream and the dream went further than ever last night. She's the one."

"What is Troy's claim on her?"

Gray watched as his mother sat on the sofa. She didn't move as gracefully as she once had. Funny, she'd always seemed ageless to him. It was unsettling to notice she wasn't, and he glanced around the room again.

"She works for him," he answered her question.

"And why is he here?"

"I don't know. How is Dustin? Why am I needed?"

"He's home from the hospital. We put him here in the lodge so he's easier to look after. Fortunately they sent him home with plenty of painkillers. Rachel is caring for him, so in effect, we've lost two hands. The pills should keep him asleep most of the week and out of our hair. You can see him in a bit."

Gray drank his water, returning his gaze to his mother. It'd been nearly two years since he'd last been home. Business had taken him overseas during the holidays when he normally would've come back.

His mother didn't look much different. A few more lines on her weathered face, more streaks of gray in her long black hair. Overall she'd aged fairly well, if a little early. He had her darker skin that tanned deeply, a lingering trace of the native heritage she brought to the family. Fourth generation Cheyenne with a touch of Castilian Spaniard accounted for the black hair and nearly black eyes. Strong genes had passed the traits on to her children.

She looked back at him with those deep eyes, reading glasses hanging from a chain around her neck. Those were new. She still wore the ranch uniform of jeans and a flannel shirt over a polo with embroidered logo. Soft moccasins encased her feet. The familiar silver and turquoise necklace passed down from her grandmother was around her neck as if she never removed it.

Gray had a running disagreement with her over which stone's powers were stronger: jade or turquoise. He believed in the power of jade because of his dream. She believed in turquoise because of her grandmother's teachings. It was a friendly rivalry.

"So, you're two hands down. Roger and I will both fill in. What do you need from me?"

"We have a livestock sale coming up. I need

you up to speed."

"Blake knows the livestock. Kiri and Jim know the livestock. I haven't been here." Any of the three he mentioned could easily handle the negotiations. Kiri had never left the ranch and her husband, Jim, had come to them as a ranch hand fifteen years earlier.

"They know the livestock. You're the better businessman and will get the best prices. You're the better negotiator."

Gray paced the roomy office. Once two guest rooms, the office had been expanded following construction of the guest lodges and cabins. Domestic staff lived in the old lodge rooms. Wranglers and ranch hands shared a bunk house.

"Where are Roger and I bunking?" He finished the water and tossed the plastic bottle into a recycling bin.

His mother's heavy sigh drew Gray's gaze.

"What does that mean?" he asked.

"Since we put Dustin in the room meant for you two, it means you and Roger will get the fourth unit in the upper lodge. Get that grin off your face," she muttered. "Blake is taking your luggage over." She frowned at him before shaking her head. "What do you know of her?"

"All I need to know." At his mother's deepening frown he relented. "I did a cursory background check this morning. No arrests. No speeding tickets. And her credit score is excellent. My head of security is doing a deeper check." He hated it, but such measures had proven necessary in the past. One reason he hadn't been terribly upset over Tiffany's defection.

As much a gold digger as he'd ever come

across, Tiffany had shown up when he was feeling lonely and discouraged about ever finding Reed. Just another point of contention between him and Troy. At six months tops, it had been his longest relationship. All the others he'd considered as practice for pleasing his dream lady.

"Don't leap too fast," his mother advised.

"Too late." He grinned and winked at her. "I'm head over heels. I just need time to sweep her off her feet." *Like last night*. All he needed was time to do it over and over again until he was completely imprinted on her senses.

"You have work to do while you're here."

"I know, but I'm going on the pack trip. I'm not sending her out there for two nights with Troy. After that I'll get serious."

"You don't have time to play around. You need to come up to date with the business end and study the market. You also need to attend the stockman's meeting."

"I'm not that out of date. You have the day-to-day operations under control, I won't mess around there."

"Why didn't you come right away?"

"Mad about that, are you?"

"You should have been here as soon as I called."

"Ma, I had to follow my heart. Because I listened to my heart, I found my soul. Roger and I were also exhausted. It's a long trip back from Asia. Had we arrived sooner we'd have been sleeping the last few days."

"I hope you're right." Sora pushed to her feet, and Gray noticed once again her stiff movement.

"It's the age. Sixty is a bitch," she muttered.

"Come. Dustin wants to see you. The Spearman pack trip leaves Tuesday morning. I'll give you tonight to settle in, but tomorrow and Monday you need to concentrate on business. Do that and I won't complain about you going out with them."

"Thanks, Mom." Gray pulled her into a hug and kissed the top of her head. She was barely taller than Reed. It felt good, familiar and comforting, when she briefly hugged him back.

"My bad boy. Why couldn't you be more steady? We need your business sense here."

"I had to follow my dream. Now that my dream is within my grasp, let me capture her and then we'll see what fate has in store for us. It may be time to come home."

He smiled into the solemn dark eyes that stared up at him with a touch of sadness.

"You'll see, Mom. She's the one."

"Hmm."

Gray followed her from the office.

TEN

"This is perfect. We'll flip a coin and one of us will trade places with one of you." Gray wrapped an arm around Reed's shoulder and used the opportunity to peek down her shirt. The fork he held out for her held a healthy portion of apple cinnamon crisp. He smiled when Reed opened her cute little mouth and let him slip the fork in. With the exception of a few other lingering guests, they had the dining room to themselves. Almost.

Roger and Sam sat on the other side of the table for four. Troy and three other men Reed had identified as co-workers sat at the next table over. Reed had expressed surprise when Gray greeted Ian and Dennis by name. Stuart was too fresh from college to be known in the physics community. The other table was close enough for Troy to sit at Reed's right, just twelve inches away. Gray was sure Troy had picked that table just to be annoying.

It had taken Gray the first half of the meal to win a smile from Reed. Whatever had happened up at her room had put her in a foul mood, and with Troy sitting so close, it hadn't readily improved. A little wine, teasing, lots of touching and a few stories about growing up on the ranch had helped everyone relax.

Reed's annoyance with Troy he understood, but Gray wondered at the wary looks Ian and

Dennis directed Reed's way. Maybe he could get the story out of her at some point. What was it about the two men that put a sad and wary light in her eyes?

Gray took advantage of sitting thigh to thigh with her, kissing and caressing her often. Very slowly she relaxed against his side. Too bad they hadn't sat like this the previous night when they'd dined alone. Just the thought of her little hot body close, with no one else around, was enough to make his head spin.

Reed swallowed the bite and he saw her glance toward Sam's expression of amusement.

"Are you actually encouraging this?" Reed asked her friend. "You want to swap roommates?"

Gray's grin felt triumphant as Sam nodded, her eyes sparkling while Roger slipped an arm around her.

"See? You're outvoted, the three of us agree," Gray whispered in Reed's ear.

"Okay, okay." Knowing when to give in, she threw up her hands in defeat.

"We'll wait until we're outside." Gray kissed the tender spot behind her ear, pleased by her giggle.

"Stop!" She half-heartedly tried to push him away, but Gray knew it was more for show so he kissed her again.

"Reed." Troy's voice was sharp. "Are we going to have a serious business discussion or not?"

"Troy," Gray looked over Reed's head, "give it up for tonight. She needs a massage. Her shoulder is still sore. Save it for the morning."

"Since when is it your business?" Troy asked.

"Since yesterday. She's my concern now, and

I'm not going to let you abuse her. Tonight is for relaxing. Both ladies will have clearer heads in the morning."

"Hold on there," Reed interrupted and held up her hand. "I will make the decisions concerning me." She looked from him to the other man. "I agree about needing a clear head, and yes, I need a massage. However, this isn't just about me. We've all traveled today and none of us are used to the altitude. Why don't we have a social evening? Hang out at the saloon, chill, meet in the hot tub later and just get relaxed. Is that reasonable?"

Gray saw everyone but Troy nod in agreement.

"There, Troy." Gray reinforced Reed's suggestions, but they wouldn't be socializing with the group. Other plans had already been made. "Done deal. Relax. Visit with Kiri and Mom. Blake will be in the saloon tending bar. There's a small contingent of travel agents and a group of women up from Boulder here this week. Have some good conversation and if we run into you in the hot tub, then great. Otherwise, breakfast is at eight-thirty after grooming and feeding the horses. You should remember the routine. Talk to Mom and she'll set aside a room for you to meet in private once breakfast is over. Fair enough?"

Troy agreed, but with reluctance.

"Great." Gray picked up his napkin and wiped his mouth. "Let's get out of here," he said to Reed. Standing, he helped her from her seat. "We'll see the rest of you later."

Roger and Sam followed. On the porch, Gray pulled a quarter from his front pocket. "Who wants to call it?"

"Heads she moves, tails I move," Reed said and

glanced at Sam who shrugged.

It seemed as good a plan as any. Gray balanced the coin on his thumbnail and flicked it into the air. Catching it, he slapped it down on his wrist, praying for tails. First of all it would mean they were over Troy rather than next to him, and second, they'd have the larger room.

"Ready?" he asked, his hand over the coin.

"Just show the damn coin," Reed said.

He lifted his hand carefully.

"Tails." Sam laughed. "I'll help you move, Reed."

"Good thing I didn't unpack," Reed replied.

Gray loved her pale blush. "The massage table and oil have been delivered. I've already set things up." He settled Reed's hat onto her head, wrapped an arm around her shoulders, and sauntered down the wide steps.

"You're doing my massage?"

"I told you I was qualified."

"I thought you were feeding me a line."

"Well, that too, but in this case, I do know how to give a good full-body massage."

"Without the funny stuff?"

"Well..."

"I knew it." Reed playfully slapped his chest.

Gray stopped and pulled her up against his body. "I know how to deal with you," he said. Staring into her eyes, he smiled. The light of anticipation made the jade depths sparkle. Passion was beginning to simmer. He slipped the fingers of one hand into her hair, the other around her waist.

Hours. Lowering his head he breathed in her breath. Sweet. It had been hours since he'd tasted her. Apples and cinnamon. Coffee and cream. And best of all, Reed.

He brushed his lips over hers, trying not to smile when her hand slid up his arm, gripping and releasing as she felt his muscles. Teasing her lips, he waited until she whimpered in frustration. Unable to hold back, he pulled her close. She responded, reaching back to hold her hat on. He was going to knock a lot more than her hat off.

Sam's cough only served to remind them to take it inside.

"Time to get naked," Gray said once he closed the door to their room.

The wary look on Reed's face was cute as she stood looking at the massage table in the middle of the sitting room. The furniture had been moved out of the way to make room for the table which was covered by soft flannel sheets.

"You're enjoying this too much," she accused him.

"And your point would be?" He moved to stand in front of her. "Come on, I can't give you a good massage through all those clothes." Slipping his hands under the loose shirt she wore like a jacket, he gently pushed it off her shoulders.

"You just want to get me naked," she said, her eyes deepening with a smoky passion.

"True. I like you naked. I also want to make you feel good."

"Put a smile on my face?"

"Uh huh." He tugged her tank top from the waistband of her skirt.

"I should take a shower first. I'm sure my feet are stinky." She shifted from one foot to the other.

Gray smiled. "I think we can arrange a shower. Nice and long, with lots of good smelly soap and hot water. I want to run the soap bubble experiment again."

Her skin felt like soft chamois as he slid the tank top up and over her head to uncover her flesh-colored bra. He let the top drop to the floor.

"Is this when we talk about my dream last night and on the plane?"

"Now would be good." He reached behind her and released the hooks of her bra.

"Are we going to close the curtains?"

"Nobody can see in." The bra joined the other clothes on the floor. "You wore an awful lot of clothes today."

Reed smiled at him and raised her arms, linking her hands behind his neck. "I can't always wear a cocktail dress and thong."

"Why not? I like that dress." His hands searched the waistband of her skirt until he found the button and zipper.

"You gonna help me with my boots?"

"Uh huh."

Her skirt made soft sound when it fell to the floor.

"I do believe I'm still wearing my boots." Her warm lips pressed against his chin.

"Uh huh." He hooked his thumbs in the waistband of her panties. Flesh-colored, stretchy fabric. His lips found the soft skin of her neck. "Mmm. You taste good."

"You keep saying that."

"It's true," he murmured. "In my dream, you cling to me, just like now."

"Your dream?"

Her breathy responses tickled all the way down his spine. He trailed his lips down her neck to her collar bone. "My half of the dream."

"Do you...see me...in a leafy glade?"

"Uh huh." He bent to suckle a nipple and smiled as her body quivered under his touch.

"With flowers in my hair?"

Gray sank to his knees and kissed her stomach. The musky scent rising from her made it hard to go slow. Unique to her, he'd recognize her aroma in a dark crowded room. That scent stayed with him and fueled his fantasies. "A pagan queen, with a crown of little white flowers."

"With gold jewelry?"

"Bracelets, with chains linked to rings." He lowered her panties over her hips. "Ankle bands, toe rings, more chains."

"Oh!" She gasped as the fabric continued down her thighs.

"White gown, long sleeves. Gold torc around your neck," he murmured, kissing a wet trail from her stomach over her lower abdomen. Smooth muscles rippled under his lips. Ticklish. "Gold chains around your waist."

"Goblet?"

"The best red wine. Deep red," he told her.

"Yes," she gasped.

Gray hovered, his breath caressing her skin as he drew out the moment and took his time just looking at her. Not shaved, just nicely trimmed auburn curls. The scent of her growing arousal made his head swim.

"Gray?" she moaned.

"Yes?" He eased her panties over her boots. "Nice boots."

Reed laughed weakly, her fingers digging into his shoulders. "Glad you like them."

He kissed her upper thighs, hip bones, the soft swell over her womb. Was she pregnant yet? Little did she know how much he wanted her to be.

"Gray." She moaned his name again.

Hard and hungry for her, he rose to his feet and lifted her in his arms. "Your boots are made for riding, sweetheart."

"Yeah? What am I going to ride?"

A few strides and they were in the bedroom. He lowered her to her feet, near the bed. "I think you should ride your cowboy first. You can ride horses later."

Reed's hands reached for the waistband of his jeans.

"What about your boots?" Her hand slipped inside, soft gentle fingers wrapping around him.

"Sweetheart, my pants aren't going to make it off in time." He grunted and pulled his shirt over his head. Two pairs of hands pushed his jeans down his hips. He fell backwards on the bed and pulled her up on top of him. Gripping her hips, he lifted, then lowered her down as he thrust up.

Her gasp matched his. Once again he was surprised at her tight grip.

"Gray!" she whimpered. "Oh God! You feel so good! So...big!"

"Oh baby, you've got motivation down," he said on a groan and thrust up, lifting her. He felt the leather of her boots against his thighs. "Ride me," he ordered.

And did she. Gray's eyes crossed as she took over the rhythm. Starting slow she lifted herself, the softness of her body sliding up him, until just the very tip remained inside her tender folds. God, he loved that feeling. Hot, wet, flesh wrapped around him. Damn, forgot the condom again.

"Reed...? Condom? I forgot, baby."

"Next time." The way she growled the words was cute. Less cute was the way she pressed him down into the mattress, hands on his shoulders as she proceeded to tease him. Making small movements with her hips, she took only an inch of him in before rising.

With the grip of an iron will, Gray held his patience. His gaze met hers, and he saw a teasing light in the green depths or her eyes. Her luscious lips curved into a small, sexy smile. For now, his hands rested on her hips and she slid down his length with excruciating precision. He let her play with him, feeling the pressure building in his body, the heat in hers. Slick wetness eased the way for him. Passion building, she began to move faster, sliding up and down, sighing each time he filled her completely.

It wasn't fast enough for his growing need, so Gray reached for her breasts to encourage her to move faster. Rounded and firm, they filled his large hands. Her skin, pale and soft, the areola surrounding her sensitive nipples so delicate a pink he could hardly tell by color where the nipple left off and the white of her breast began. As her arousal grew, she flushed to a dusky pink where her nipples hardened to peaks reaching for his touch.

"Beautiful Ree," he whispered. It spurred her on, her booted legs gripping his. "Ride me...harder," he ordered and pinched her nipples.

Reed fell forward to rest on hands planted on either side of his head. Gaze locked on his, he saw a look of deep concentration on her face as she began to grind her body against him.

"Yes!" he urged her on.

Her eyes closed as she rocked, her breathing rapid and short.

He felt her heartbeat racing and picking up more speed. "Take us home, sweetheart," he encouraged and felt her spike of excitement. Moisture flowed from her, the scent of their loving thick and sweet. He breathed it in and thrust up.

Reed's breath caught and her face screwed up into the mask of ecstasy he recognized from the night before.

"Yes, baby!" He pulled on her nipples and she let out a cry as a rosy flush blossomed across her skin, her whole body infused with an orgasmic glow.

Reed cried out his name as pleasure took over her body. Hands sliding down to grip her hips, Gray drove upward hard, his own climax starting deep and pulsing through him and into her. For one long, glorious moment the world paused, and Gray swore in that very instant their souls merged.

She rocked against him, slowing with each pulsing wave until she lay on his chest, legs still clamped against his hips and thighs. He cradled her, savoring the afterglow, the sheer lack of desire to move, her weight resting on him, and pressed his lips against her forehead.

Gray couldn't guess how long it was before she spoke. "How did I do for my first riding lesson?"

"Cowgirl, you can ride me anytime, anywhere," he murmured into her hair.

~ * ~

"Aren't massages supposed to start on the back?" The suspicion Reed harbored bled into her voice. Every massage she'd ever had started with her lying on her face.

Gray held up the soft sheet while Reed rolled over onto her back.

She noticed he didn't look away like other massage technicians.

"Sometimes, but since your back is your problem, I want to start on your front."

With a small sigh of what she took to be regret, Gray laid the soft flannel sheet over her. "A pillow for under your knees?" he asked.

"Please. Let's keep the lower back from going out too."

"See? All the more reason to do it this way."

He lifted her legs and slipped a thick king-sized pillow under her knees, then readjusted the sheet to keep her warm.

"Comfy?"

"Yes." Or as comfortable as she could be when naked under a sheet in the same room as an incredibly sexy and handsome man. The fact he was also still naked from their shower only added to the eroticism.

Music, soft and ethereal, came from a small stereo system. Harp, pipes and flutes. New age with a Celtic influence. Restful and soothing.

"Just breathe naturally and relax. Let me do the work," he said close to her ear before kissing the center of her forehead.

Reed looked up to see him standing at the head of the table. "*Oui, Monsieur.*"

The oil he used had a light floral fragrance. She breathed deeply. It seemed familiar in a haunting way.

"I love this oil," she murmured, as his fingers

stroked her face and worked her neck and scalp.

"Shh. Don't talk. It's a special oil, non greasy so you won't slide off the bed or break out. Now relax."

"Hmm." Reed subsided again, eyes closed.

Once she got over her initial nervousness, Reed found it easy to relax. He'd staged the mood as well as any therapist she'd ever visited. Thick pillar candles around the room provided a golden glow and soft vanilla fragrance. Everything about the experience was soft, except his hands and fingers working her muscles, encouraging them to naturally align her bones.

She tipped her head backward, arching into his hands when he leaned over her head, his hands, slick with the oil, slid over her chest and under the sheet. His wrists skimmed over her nipples and sent a delicious zing of heat down her body.

"Mmm," she moaned. She'd never had a therapist massage below the top swell of her breasts.

"Relax," he said and kissed her nose. "This is legitimate."

With a sigh she once again subsided.

"First, I'm oiling your skin," he said softly.

Using steady strokes he covered each inch of skin with an even coating of warm oil. It felt wonderful on her breasts, but he didn't linger around her nipples like she wanted him to.

"Here we go."

His hands rested on her shoulders, fingers aimed toward the center of her body. They easily covered all but a few inches of her upper chest. Gliding toward her stomach, his fingers followed her sternum down the valley between her breasts.

Once he reached the bottom, his fingers traveled outward, the heel of his hands tracing her lower ribs until they wrapped around her sides, fingers meeting at the center of her back.

"Breathe in, slow and deep," he told her.

Gently, Gray lifted her body a few inches, strong fingers massaging along her spine, working up her back. Thumbs dragging along her sides, he kept lifting and massaging until he reached her armpits. He gently set her down and she let her breath out in a long sigh while his hands smoothly glided back to her shoulders.

"You like that." His laugh was low and soft, especially when she turned her head and kissed his arm. "None of that now. Breathe..."

After repeating the sequence twice more he took her arms and folded them behind her head.

"This will help release the tension in your neck," he told her.

The pain was exquisite as he lifted her elbows and gently pulled them back toward him. With a deep moan, she felt an ecstasy, nearly as deep as her recent orgasm, roll her eyes back in their sockets. The man was seriously good. Another level of wariness melted away as his hands continued to work down her body.

Every part of her received attention as he slowly moved around the table, even her stomach which she never let anyone touch. Too ticklish, she'd always been afraid of ruining the experience by bursting into laughter. Not tonight. Gray was even able to massage her feet without causing a twitch. Her eyes fluttered open enough to see him grin at her moan of happiness. Only the girl at the nail salon had ever been able to give her a foot massage before. Reed was becoming more convinced with each stroke--Gray was a serious keeper.

Working up her leg, he lifted it. Ever the helpful soul, she lifted too.

"Let me do it," he growled.

"I always do that." She never wanted her weight to hurt the tiny women who worked on her. *Gray is strong*, she told herself and consciously let go.

"Good," he praised her and rested her foot against his shoulder.

First one leg then the other, he set them down in turn and with ease returned to the center of the table, hands smoothing more oil on her lower abdomen and upper thighs.

Reed no longer paid attention to the exact location of his hands. She felt wonderful. A part of her mind was aware of the moisture seeping from her, the warm scent blending with the fragrances of the oil and candles. Her senses were surrounded in soothing experiences aided by the music continuing to weave a soft and dreamy magic spell.

More moisture pooled in her center. Oil started at her mound and flowed downward. Had it been anyone but Gray touching her, she'd have come off the table. Instead, she only tensed in anticipation, and gentle fingers massaged her mound until she relaxed again.

Slowly, ever so slowly, the fingers moved down between her slightly parted legs, spreading the oil over her labia. Taking his time, Gray never faltered, never rushed. Gently squeezing her swelling outer lips, he slid down and up the entire length of her, top to bottom, then slowly up again. Over and over.

Reed opened her eyes and found him watching her face. Not wanting to shut out the look in his eyes, she kept hers half open. The expression, as much as his hands, touched her somewhere very deep inside, right in the center of her heart. Step by slow step her body began to feel excitement on a level far more profound than ever before.

"Breathe slowly," he reminded her.

Sure. Breathe slowly. Tell her heart to beat slowly. She focused on her breathing, counting to five with each measured breath. He was taking her someplace she'd never been with either masseuse or lover.

Almost imperceptibly his hands moved to her delicate inner lips, the same motions, the same rhythm. How did he do it? So calm, so in control. Her heart rate picked up again. Reed whimpered with pleasure and he smiled.

What? Almost disconnected from her body, she noticed his finger stroking her most sensitive bundle of nerves. His touch, so gentle as he moved from one side to the other, circling around and over, he'd made the transition seamlessly. She shifted her hips a little.

"Relax, breathe," Gray said gently. "Enjoy."

Slowly he inserted what felt like the middle finger of his right hand into her. With extreme care he gently explored and massaged the inside of her with his long finger.

"I don't remember this part." This she would have remembered.

"*Yoni* massage. Tantric," he explained.

"As in the Kama Sutra?"

"Um hmm." He continued to rub her clit as he internally massaged her, moving up and down, side to side, varying the pressure and speed just a little. Driving her higher.

Reed felt his finger flexing, pressing, stroking the upper wall of her inner passage, his palm resting against her. Heat infused every cell of her body. How did he draw her out like this?

"Oh...my... God." She moaned. "What...are... you..."

"That would be your G-Spot." She could hear the smile in his voice.

"It exists?" she gasped.

"*The sacred spot,*" he murmured.

He slipped another finger in and she felt the pressure of his little finger pressing lower. Waves of unknown emotion threatened to overtake her and she tensed, a little frightened of the feelings he evoked in her. She wanted more, but at the same time it was too much. Her heart pounded against her breastbone as reality spun out of her control.

"Breathe," he reminded her. "Relax."

"I... I..." She felt tears well up in her eyes.

"It's okay," he assured her. "Let it out. Let yourself feel."

His hands moved against her. Right thumb over her clit, his left hand drifting across her body until he massaged her breasts.

She barely heard his next comment. "I'm now holding one of the mysteries of the universe in my hand," he said with reverence, his speed and pressure increasing with her rising emotions.

Tears continued to fill her eyes and the nameless feelings overtook her, pleasure and pain bursting from the center of her body, rippling outward to her extremities in a consuming rush. Her entire body pulsed, muscles contracted to arch her body, as with head thrown back, she cried out, the tears spilling over and sliding down her temples into her hair.

"Breathe, sweetheart, breathe." Gray's gentle voice told her she'd been holding her breath and she drew in a deep and shuddering rush of air.

His hands slowed and gentled, but didn't stop. Twice more he massaged her to climaxes with ever increasing power. When she openly sobbed with emotions far stronger and complex than she'd ever experienced, Gray slowed and gentled his touch, slowly moving away from her center as she calmed and the tears trickled away. Her head rolled to the side and she drifted in a plane apart from her body. His lips brushed hers in the sweetest of tender kisses.

"Gray," she whispered.

"Shh."

Drained and feeling boneless, Reed didn't resist when he rolled her over and helped her settle face down over the headrest. The warm sheet settled over her like a cloud.

How he had the energy to continue on she didn't know. In a dreamlike state she drifted with the music, Celtic harp and pipes weaving intricate mysteries around her, his hands working the remaining traces of the knot in her shoulder out of the muscles. She felt her neck settle into perfect alignment with her spine, and eased the rest of the way into a trance.

~*~

Gray grinned as he finished the serious part of her massage. *Limp as a noodle.* He doubted she'd ever been so relaxed. She hadn't even noticed the music had come to an end and started over. Using long strokes, he rubbed oil into her skin, covering the entire length of her body, shoulders to toes, softening his touch.

With more oil, he started bringing her back to consciousness. If she was able to respond, he'd take her even further down the path of bliss than he'd taken her with the *yoni* massage.

Gliding over her gleaming skin, his hands seeking out her pleasure points, he tried to pinpoint what was different tonight.

While he'd sought to perfect his technique with previous partners, and they had enjoyed the massages, they'd never reacted with such intensity, shaking his own emotions. The profound emotional connection had to be what made it a deeper, more intense, experience. Surely it was an indication of their spiritual bonding?

So beautiful. He'd never seen anything more magnificent than her complete release. The power to bring her such pleasure was soul satisfying for him. If she was spent for the night he could happily call it a day and hold her. If she had one more orgasm in her, he'd be happy with that as well. Either way, he wanted only to be close to her.

Reed shifted under his hands when he massaged her rear curves. Such a beautiful behind, round and full, curving into her waist, she was the epitome of a classic hourglass figure. Her heart-shaped ass reminded him of the polished, puffed, heart-shaped gemstones he had at home. Jade, turquoise, malachite, and so many more, he had a complete collection just waiting for her. Everything waited and he wanted to show it all to her.

Slowly, move slowly. Too much, too soon would scare her. Had it only been twenty-four hours since they'd first kissed? She was already wary enough.

Reed moaned and moved against his hands. One more? She had one more in her? He bent and kissed the small of her back, hands and lips conveying his admiration and love for her. This was just one night. So many more nights of wonder stretched out before them and he didn't want to miss a single one.

"Gray."

Her moan reached into his heart.

"I'm here, Ree." His lips moved up her spine.

"I... I...want..."

"Just tell me. Say it and it's yours." He kissed her shoulder.

"You."

Reed's whisper made his heart soar. It was the first time she'd actually voiced her desire for him. Not wanting to waste a moment, he lifted her in his arms and carried her to the bedroom.

ELEVEN

Dim light filtered through the window, softened by the trees surrounding the lodge, when Gray rolled to his side. Attracted by her warmth, his arm settled over the indent of a feminine waist and he rolled closer, molding himself tight against the curved form trying to hide her face from the light.

He agreed with her. It was too soon for the night to end. Burying his face in her soft hair, he inhaled the mix of many sexy scents. Together they were far more intoxicating than any one on its own, and yet, ultimately her. Them. He liked that part best.

With a deep moan Reed melted back against his body, and pulled his arm tight around her.

"Gray," she whispered.

Music sweeter than any other, her voice filled his heart to overflowing.

"Ree, my beautiful Ree." He gathered her close, just enjoying the feel of her. She had to be exhausted.

"I need to get up," she whispered.

"Hmm?"

"Personal business."

Gray sighed and reluctantly released her. "Hurry back."

"I will," she promised.

He smiled as he watched her shuffle off to the

bathroom. He'd practically forced a quart of water down her before letting her fall asleep. Another quart when she woke in the night. And yet another waited on the nightstand. She wouldn't be able to function today if she didn't flush her system. A massage that intense released a serious load of toxins.

A few minutes later, she returned and glared at the water bottle. Guarded and assessing, her eyes slid to him and he grinned. Small white teeth tugged at the corner of her lower lip before she grimaced in resignation and climbed onto the bed. Vigorous punches plumped up the pillows she used to lean against the log-and-stick headboard. Gray shifted and rested his head on her lap.

"Drink your water," he said.

"I know," she grumbled. "Who knew you were such a nag?"

Gray chuckled. "I just want you to feel the best you can feel."

"I appreciate that," she said softly and threaded her fingers through his hair, raking her nails lightly over his scalp. Delicious chills danced across his skin all the way down to his toes.

"Oh, baby, I'm yours. Don't stop."

She snorted as she tilted the bottle up and drank.

"I could do a better job with two hands," she said after lowering the bottle.

"When you finish."

"Meanie."

"How do you feel?"

"I feel wonderful." She sighed. "Gray..."

"There are no words to describe last night, Ree. I tried to find them. They just don't exist." He rolled just enough to look up at her. *Hmm, had to remember this angle. Nice view.* Almost on its own, his hand reached up to caress her. *Very nice.* He grinned at her puckering nipple.

"Oh Gray." She giggled. "Where do you get the energy?"

"Clean living and an unquenchable thirst for you."

"Water?" She held the bottle out, offering him a drink.

"Drink at least half and then I'll have some."

She knew how to sigh. Took his eyes right back to that fabulous view.

"There were times, last night, I couldn't tell if I were dreaming or living it live." Reed smiled down at him. "What's different about you?"

"I love you," he said simply. "Like no one has ever loved you before."

"Is that it? But you don't know me. How can you love me?"

"Keep drinking." He grinned when she stuck her tongue out at him. There were a few ways he could interpret the gesture. The best one involved her mouth and a certain body part of his. "Promise?"

"Later." She laughed at the innuendo and tipped the water bottle to her mouth.

Instantly hard at her pledge, he suppressed the urge to roll her under him. Such a talented tongue in a hot sweet mouth, so unlike any he'd encountered before. It was hard not to curse the family obligations waiting for him.

He watched the movement of her lovely throat as she swallowed. "Your skin is so... luminescent."

Small drops of water splattered on his face

when she choked.

"Excuse me?" she said around a cough.

"Your skin, it's smooth and pale. Do you burn easily? Is that why you guard against the sun so zealously?"

"My dad had skin cancer ten years ago. I decided I didn't want to go that way. He actually died from another cancer, but the skin cancer seemed easiest to prevent."

"Then why don't you wear sunscreen?"

"I don't like the feel of it, nor am I convinced the chemicals don't cause their own harm."

For a moment he looked as if he wanted to argue, but then he let it go. "It's so rare to see such white skin these days. You're beautiful."

"Okay." Reed laughed. "Stop with the beautiful talk. It's difficult for me to swallow to begin with and to hear it fifty times a day doesn't help."

"As you wish. I'll take it slow. Monumentally difficult as that is to do."

"You don't seem like the overly impulsive sort. You wouldn't succeed in business that way."

He turned his face into her hand resting against his cheek. Morning stubble rasped across her palm. A shower would be nice. "Not usually. I can't help it with you."

"Now's a good time to exercise whatever self control led to the legend of Grayson Dunbar."

Reed looked down into his eyes and he saw the questions in hers.

"Grayson Dunbar. Boy Wonder of the laser world. What on earth are you doing with me?" she asked softly.

Boy Wonder. It sounded so different coming from her. He'd long since learned to ignore the term when spoken by others. It had nothing, and yet everything, to do with finding her. "You had the dream."

"Yes, I remember. Tell me about your half of the dream."

"My oldest friend. That dream has been with me longer than anyone, not counting family. The earliest I can pinpoint the start is about age twelve." Settling his head more comfortably in her lap, he told her every detail of the dream and how it had changed over the years. Wariness filled her eyes, then questions, followed by wonder as he told her how it had progressed in the last thirty-six hours. "Last night we made love in the dream as many times as we had in this world. Each world seemed to enhance the other. I think the only reason you understand what I'm talking about is because you experienced both as well. Right?"

Reed slowly nodded, as if still working it all out. "So you're convinced I'm your soul mate?"

"I am. You had the dream. If you weren't my soul mate you wouldn't have known, you wouldn't have had the dream." To him it was perfectly logical. "Can we get married and head out on the honeymoon? There's so much I want to show you."

"Whoa there, cowboy. We need a little *getting-to-know-you* period, don't you think? You think you know me from the dream, but that isn't who I am today. I don't routinely hang out in forest clearings waiting for a man on a black stallion. In fact, this is the closest I've been to a forest in, oh, fifteen or twenty years? People count on me to get their paychecks to them and track the money side of their projects. Troy counts on me to keep him informed of the financial state of the company and let him know if we're heading into trouble." She gently tapped him on the forehead. "You paint a pretty picture, but that's all it is right now--a picture. I'm a little more pragmatic than that."

"You just had to be a bean counter this time around, didn't you?" He sighed with exasperation then grinned. "You do know bean counters drive CEOs crazy, right?"

"Yup."

Her grin was far too smug for his comfort. She held the half-full water bottle over his face.

"Do you want some water now?"

"Let me sit up first." He made a show of rolling over. For a moment there he'd been afraid she'd pour the water on his face.

One second. He let go of her for one second and she escaped from the bed. She stood to the side holding the water bottle. That little smug smile still on her face.

Crouched on hands and knees, he stared at her. Wanted to play did she? Waiting for her to move, he froze, sizing up his options. She stood closer to the door. Once out of the bedroom she could duck into the bathroom or dash up the spiral stairs to the loft. He didn't think she'd run bare-assed for the hot tub or the pond. A game.

His gaze never left her and yet, one moment she was there, the next she was gone and he was trying to catch the bottle of water. With a shout, he deflected the bottle and leaped from the bed. Footsteps on the stairs told him she was headed for the loft.

As he neared the top of the wrought-iron spiral, the first pillow bounced off his head. Knocking it aside he cleared the last step and was hit by a barrage of pillows from the beds. Catching one, he stopped.

She was cornered.

Grinning, he advanced a step.

She giggled, making her breasts bounce so very nicely.

"What's on your mind, little girl?" he asked.

"My, what big teeth you have." She laughed, clearly enjoying the game and still plotting her next move.

Another step took him closer to her.

She stepped sideways, toward one of the three beds in the loft.

"You want to make love up here?" He didn't mind. He'd make love with her anywhere.

She glanced downward and he felt himself grow instantly stiff. Eyes widening, she licked her lips.

"Keep that up and you may get it a little rough," he warned her.

With a hand behind her back, she lifted a finger to her mouth, biting it with her little white teeth.

"Rough?" she asked with an air of innocence.

"You like it rough?"

"Aren't some cowboys called 'rough riders'?"

"That would have been Teddy Roosevelt and the First U.S. Calvary. There's also a minor league baseball team by the name."

"Ah." She took another step toward the bed. "Do you like it...rough?"

Big green eyes looked up at him from under thick lashes. Innocent. False? Definitely. With nipples that aroused? Most definitely false.

"What do you have behind your back?"

"*Moi*?"

"You. What are you up to?"

"I don't know what you're talking about."

"Oh darlin', I'm bigger than you. I can catch you."

"Can you now? What would you say if I said I could catch you?"

"You can try." He grinned.

Playing her game, he watched until she made a feint toward the stairs. Taking the bait, he lunged for her. She jumped back and he fell on the bed.

Sucker, he thought as she pounced on his back and pinned him to the mattress. Then again, there were worse things to fall for. He reached behind and tickled where his hands landed. A shriek followed her laughter and she pushed away from him. Making a quick roll, he caught her wrist and reeled her back into his arms. The momentum made them both fall back on the bed.

Neither was prepared for the bed frame to collapse beneath them, the mattress and box spring crashing to the floor.

"Oh!" she squeaked and he rolled her under him.

"Oops." Laughter burst from them at the same moment.

Reed shrieked again when the apartment door burst open to shouts from her co-workers.

"Anyone hurt?"

"What's going on over here?"

"Hello?"

Troy's voice cut through the shouts from below. "What the bloody hell is going on up here?"

"Oh God!" Reed whispered and pulled Gray down over her like a blanket.

Footsteps started up the stairs, heavy enough she felt them as the thick metal vibrated the floor of the loft.

"Anyone alive up here?"

"Stop him!" she hissed at Gray.

"Troy, it's okay," Gray called out. "The bed just collapsed, but no one's hurt."

"Sounded like a war going on up here." Troy kept coming up the stairs.

Reed squeaked and pulled at the comforter to cover herself. *This was so bad.* She tried to stop the giggle and had to use a corner of the quilt to muffle it.

"Troy, stop right there," Gray said as Reed peeked from under the quilt to see Troy's head clearing the top of the stairs. "It's okay, really. Sorry you all were disturbed."

"What's going on?" Troy asked.

"The bed frame broke. That was the crash. Sorry you were bothered," Gray sat up.

"There are pillows all over the place, it looks like a massage parlor downstairs..." Troy's voice died off suddenly. "You all can go. It's okay. Nobody's hurt." Troy turned to speak to whoever else was in the living room.

"Massage parlor. Yeah, sure looks that way. It's about time she got massaged," Reed heard Ian say just before the door closed.

Reed wasn't so sure she liked the way he said the word 'massaged.' As if it was a euphemism. Well, maybe... in this case... Oh God. The whole company would know. Her face burned. How could she have forgotten there were other people in the same building?

The door opened again.

"Everything okay?" Roger called out.

"Reed?" Sam's voice floated up the stairs. "Damn. He really does know how to give massages? I thought that was just a come on."

"Oh yeah, he's damn good too," Roger said. "He makes me pay him three hundred bucks for one and it's worth every penny."

"Wow," Sam said. "Troy? Did you find the bodies?"

"I've heard from Gray, but I haven't heard more than a squeak from what I'm guessing is my CFO," Troy said in disgust. "Reed? How could you? You're the respectable one!"

Reed huddled behind Gray and poked him in the hip. "Get rid of them," she whispered. She couldn't tell if Troy could see her or not.

"Everyone is okay," Gray said calmly. "Thanks for checking."

"Reed," Troy said. "One hour and then we need to talk. You hear me?"

Reed poked Gray again.

"Your message will be processed," Gray said.

Reed wanted to slap him for the slow drawl.

"Honestly, Reed, I expected better from you." Troy's irritation was clear. "One hour. We'll meet in the lodge. Sora says we can use the family dining room. Oh, and Gray? You aren't invited to this meeting."

"No problem. I have ranch business to attend to. Thanks for checking."

Reed held her breath until the door shut. "Are they all gone?" she whispered.

"No," Sam's laughing voice carried up the stairs. "Do you two need towels? Sheets? Bandages? Splints?"

"No!" Reed called out.

"Okay." Roger laughed. "Since you're alive, we'll leave you. Just stop wrecking the place, ya hear? Come on, Sam, let's go get some breakfast."

The door shut again and Gray turned to look down at her. "Trouble maker." He peeled back the covers she'd pulled up, and lay down on top of her.

"Oh God." She moaned. "That wasn't supposed to happen." She buried her face against his shoulder.

"We both got caught." He nudged her chin up and grinned at her. "Now there's a penalty to be paid. I seem to recall you started this."

Reed laughed and wrapped her arms around his neck. "What sort of penalty?"

"I think we're going to be late for breakfast."

~ * ~

"Give it up, Troy," Ian said mildly.

Troy didn't appreciate his team looking at him with those smug little looks. Reed was now an hour late, dammit.

"She doesn't need to be here for the technical talk." Sam calmly supported Ian.

"Besides, it's about time she got properly laid. She'll be easier to deal with when it comes time to sort out the money." Ian poured himself another cup of coffee.

"What are you saying?" Troy ignored the amused look on Sam and Dennis's faces and the shocked look on the newest team member's. Stuart. The kid quickly found something to interest him on his empty breakfast plate.

"I'm saying the woman has been a bitch the last three months. As far as I can tell, her massage therapist is crap and she hasn't been laid in at least a year. A woman like her needs it more often than once a quarter." Ian calmly stirred two packets of sugar into the black liquid. "You were certainly more relaxed when you came back from the optics conference a few weeks ago. Don't begrudge the woman a good time. She's earned it. And it will make her fun to be around again."

Troy watched Sam's eyes cut toward the door and he turned to see what had caught her attention. Reed and Gray. Troy nearly boiled over when Gray bent down to kiss Reed before gently pushing her toward the table.

Troy pulled the log-style ladder back chair next to him out from the table and Reed slipped into it after hanging her hat on the back.

"Good morning!" she chirped brightly and accepted the cup of coffee Sam pushed her direction. "Sorry I'm late." Without looking up she reached for the cream pitcher and poured in a healthy dose.

"No problem, Reed." Ian gave her a grin.

Troy grunted when Sam kicked him under the table. If the woman weren't so damn brilliant he'd consider the kick a firing offense.

Reed blinked, then flashed a small shy smile at Ian and returned Dennis's wink before sipping her coffee. Before she had a chance to say anything else, Gray appeared with a plate piled high with sausage, toast and scrambled eggs. He also set down a tall glass of orange juice.

"Good morning folks. Enjoy your day and feel free to use the room until dinner," Gray's hand rested lightly on Reed's back. "Don't forget to drink plenty of water to avoid altitude sickness."

Troy nearly snorted in disgust when Reed

looked up at Gray. He couldn't see the look on her face, but judging by the smirks on Ian and Sam's it was gooey. His guess was confirmed when Gray leaned down to kiss her again, making her sigh.

As Gray left the room, and Reed watched him walk away, Troy cleared his throat.

"Now that we're all here," he said, "perhaps we can get down to business."

"Sure, Troy." Reed turned to her breakfast. "Give me the one minute update?"

"We haven't discussed one damn thing. Well, besides your recent acquisition of a love life, that is."

"I'm a free woman over the age of consent. My love life is no one's business but my own." Amazing how the woman could switch from lovesick to pissy in the blink of an eye.

"Until you wake up the whole damn building and then keep us all waiting while you strut around like an alley cat in heat," Troy snapped.

Sound and movement stopped. *Shit*. Maybe he'd gone too far.

Reed slowly set down her fork and turned to stare at him, her face flushed a hot pink. "Well, excuse me. I'm not the one who missed most of the Amsterdam conference last year because of other *attractions* to be found on the streets. Do you want me to go on?"

Damn, she would have to bring that up. When she brought up that particular barb it felt as if they'd been married twenty years. A flash of fury spiked through him. "This isn't about me, Reed. This is about teamwork. We can't have a team if you're not here," Troy retorted.

"This *is* about you. This is about us covering

your ass for making a bad business decision," she said furiously and tossed down her napkin. "When you're ready to take responsibility for your actions and how they affect the people who work for you, then I'll be willing to sit down and discuss business. My personal life has nothing to do with it."

She stood and knocked her chair over backwards with a crash. Stopping just long enough to swoop down and grab her hat, she walked quickly from the dining room. The pounding of her boots picked up speed, telling of her progress down the stairs to the first floor, through the lobby, across the porch and down the steps.

"Good job, Troy," Sam said quietly.

Troy shot a glare her direction then stood, righted the chair and followed Reed.

~ * ~

Sam heaved a sigh and watched Troy stride from the dining room after Reed. *Troy, Troy, Troy.*

"Anyone know what that was all about?" Ian asked.

"Nope." Sam bit off the single word. She had a suspicion, but wasn't exactly sure. Yeah, Ian was right. Reed had been an uptight bitch the last three months, but it didn't have anything to do with lack of a love life. No, there was something else that had kept Reed at the office sixteen to thirty-six hours at a time. Seven days a week. Reed needed rest, which was the main reason Sam had insisted Troy include her in the retreat. Truth was, Reed didn't really need to be here other than to get some down time to recharge.

"What do we do now?" Stuart asked nervously.

Sam looked at him with amusement. He was the new baby, the ink on his Master's degree barely dry. He didn't understand the company dynamics. Yet.

"We talk about how the hell we're going to design the damn part and bring it in at half the cost of the original budget," Ian said, pushing his empty plate away. "We don't need either one of them for that discussion. Should we save Reed's plate for her?"

Sam glanced at her watch. "Only two hours until lunch. I don't think she'll die of starvation before then. Split it up, boys." She leaned back in her chair and watched while Ian offered Reed's breakfast to the other two men.

A tall dark form filled the doorway and the four remaining at the table looked around to see Gray standing in the doorway. Sam held her sigh. Reed had found herself a hunk this time. The man looked equally good beside the pool, in a suit, or like now, in faded blue jeans and black polo shirt over bulging arms and chest. Cowboy boots gave him the extra swagger that made women stop, drop, and drool. The fact that he couldn't take his eyes off Reed earned him Sam's seal of approval.

"Sam? Ian? What's going on?"

"If we knew that, we wouldn't be here," Ian said.

Sam nearly laughed at the look on Stuart's face as his head nearly snapped swinging from Gray to Ian and back again.

"Stuart," Sam said calmly, "the first thing you need to learn is this is a very small community we belong to. If we haven't worked for the competition we know someone who has or whom the competition has tried to hire away at some point."

"Where's Reed, and better yet, where's Troy?" Gray asked.

"Troy got snotty about Reed being late after making so much noise this morning," Dennis said, spearing another sausage link. "She poked him back. He slashed her, and then she ripped him a new one. That was when she made even more noise by knocking over her chair and taking off. Troy went after her. I suggest you and Troy stop annoying her or y'all won't have much furniture left by the end of the week."

Sam gave Dennis a quelling look and pushed her chair back. "I'd better go make sure Reed doesn't kick the crap out of Troy."

"Would she do that?" Stuart's eyes were round as he asked the question.

"Oh, yeah," Sam drawled. "Youngest of five, three of them brothers. She can kick some heiny."

"I'll go with you."

Sam opened her mouth to protest but the look on Gray's face stopped her. Instead, she nodded. "Let's go."

TWELVE

Gray slowed to a stop when Sam tugged on his arm. Reed paced around one side of the pond in the middle of the main grounds and Troy stood off to the side, watching with arms folded. They weren't speaking at the moment and it looked as if Troy was giving Reed time to cool down. Interesting. What, exactly, had Troy said to piss her off?

It seemed his little Celtic queen had another wrinkle to her quicksilver moods--a red-hot temper to match her hair and passion. He smiled, thinking it was better he found that out when she was furious with someone other than him. Even better when Troy was the object of her fury.

"She's fairly calm for the moment, so let's give them some space," Sam suggested quietly.

So far neither Reed nor Troy had noticed them. Gray looked around and indicated an old tree they could discreetly lean against. Might even hear a thing or two if Reed decided to let loose. Most of the ranch's guests were down at the main corral getting some basic riding lessons from the wranglers.

"So what's going on?" Gray asked. He spoke quietly so as not to draw attention.

Sam grimaced and apparently decided he was trustworthy. "I guess it's no secret to ninety-nine percent of the world that Troy is in love with Reed.

The one percent who hasn't figured it out yet is made up of Reed and anyone who's never met Troy."

"How did they meet?"

"Reed and I met when we shared a house with some other students. Actually, it was in the last year of my doctorate program and the second year of her masters. How an accountant got into a house with a bunch of physicists I'm still not sure, but she answered our ad, Ian and Dennis thought she was cute and we took her in. Boy did she straighten us out. Put us on a housekeeping schedule, set up a household budget and made sure we stuck to it. If she hadn't been so sweet and logical about it, we probably would have kicked her out after the first two weeks. Frankly, we needed her money and weren't too proud to take it."

Gray liked Sam's fond smile.

"The same Ian and Dennis sitting inside inhaling her breakfast?"

"The very same."

"I'm dying to hear about the group dynamics there."

Sam shrugged. "As you very well know, physicists are odd ducks. We just happened to find a flock we liked and so far the fates have been kind about keeping us together. Things have changed a little and we're not all piled into that old house in Albany anymore. Ian got married and Dennis found a girlfriend. Reed and I, not seeing any hope of getting married, bought the house and turned it into girl heaven. She makes it homey, I try to do my part to keep it clean, we both know the best delivery restaurants, and the neighborhood is being reclaimed by young professionals. Dennis and Ian both live only a few blocks away and more people from work are discovering the area. We joke about turning Albany into Spearville someday. A regular company town."

"Except the company offices are down in San Jose."

Sam shrugged. "The commute isn't so bad. I have my Ducati and she has her Lexus. We have our ways of making it useful time."

Gray glanced at Sam and grinned. "I can see you on a Ducati. Black leather and sleek helmet."

Sam laughed low, the sound warm and sexy. "Complete with screaming tunes on the iPod. It's great for relieving stress."

Gray laughed with her. "I bet." He looked back at Reed and saw her still pacing, now throwing murderous glances at Troy who hadn't moved. "So when did you all get hired? And why didn't your résumé cross my desk?"

"Troy had just started the company a year or so earlier, so hiring started just as Reed and I were in the last semester of our programs. Ian got hired first and was talking with Troy over a beer, one evening. Told him about these crazy roommates he had. Troy talked himself into an invite and Ian brought him home. Must have been a Friday night. Reed stomped through the door with a stack of pizzas, movies and a bad attitude. She'd just had a go-around with her advisor and was ready to drop out just three months shy of finishing."

"She doesn't seem like the kind to just up and quit."

Gray wondered at the sideways glance Sam sent him.

"*Au contraire, mon ami.* If things aren't falling into their perfectly ordered slots, she has one of two reactions. She'll bird dog it to death or she'll aim a bazooka at it and destroy it. Not much gray area for our girl and little pity. The world is pretty much black and white to her. It's what keeps Troy out of IRS hell and debtor's prison."

Gray frowned. It didn't fit his picture of Reed at all.

"Give her time to size you up," Sam advised. "She does have a wild streak. When it gets loose...watch out. Come to think of it, I think you released that side of her. Might explain why she's so wound up right now. She's trying to get it back under control."

"I don't want her under control." Gray grinned, thinking of the vixen he'd chased this morning. He nearly laughed out loud. The look on Troy's face had been worth getting caught naked in the loft. There was also no point telling Ree she hadn't been as hidden as she hoped. Troy had definitely seen her little foot sticking out from under the covers.

"I agree, to a certain extent, but right now we've got a girl winding up for what we call a major hissy fit. All her defenses for dealing with work are down right now, and Troy is pushing."

Sam nodded toward the pond, and Gray watched Troy's hands move to his hips as Reed paced past him.

"Okay, so Troy was over drinking beer, Reed came home in a mood. What happened?"

"Troy took one long look at Reed and, I swear to God, you could see the stars and little birds flying around his head." Sam chuckled. "Pretty much how you looked beside the pool when she dropped her sunglasses to give you the eye."

"The earth moved and song poured down from the heavens." Gray laughed at himself. "Troy and I almost always had the same taste in women." Hence, the Tiffany thing.

"Turn about is fair play. Once I'm done with my story I want to hear yours."

Gray shrugged noncommittally. He wasn't eager to talk about that particular lesson. "Go on."

"Well, Reed, being her usual blind self when it comes to men, and pumped up with temper, didn't see it. Still doesn't quite see it to this day. You see, the go around with her advisor was him chasing her around his desk. She was furious. Spent the first hour ranting and raving about lecherous men and how all men were scum, present company excepted--only she didn't quite include Troy in the exception."

"And?"

"Troy was smart enough in those days that he sat back and planned his moves. Only Ree didn't react the way he wanted her to. She saw him as a potential employer from the get-go and held him at arm's length. Friendly, but cool. Frustrated the hell out of Troy."

"So where do the jobs come in?"

"Well, Ian was working there. The company only had five or six people at the time so it was a tight group. Our house became a gathering place. In those days we had space in a warehouse in Berkeley."

"I remember," Gray said.

"Weren't you two partners at one time?"

"For a couple years. I wanted to go one way. He

wanted to go another. We split up." The simple explanation was best for now.

"Right. Anyhow, as the spring semester wound down, Reed started making noises about us needing to look for jobs. Good old Ree." Sam smiled with affection again. "I just nodded, read over the résumé she typed up for me, approved it and let it go. Looked like Greek to me."

Reed had stopped and now faced Troy, hands on her own hips. Delicious hips in tight faded jeans. Her boots gave her a nice authoritative stance with her spread legs. Gray noticed she kept her long sleeve shirt closed over her chest with a couple buttons. The t-shirt she wore underneath had both shocked and excited him when she'd pulled it on this morning.

The picture on the front looked like a pencil drawing of a shirtless, ripped, cowboy brushing the flank of his horse. The caption said something along the lines of 'Every cowgirl's dream,' and though she giggled and blushed while pulling it on, it didn't stop her from comparing the man on the shirt to him.

She'd said he looked better--all that warm skin she could actually touch. Had she not skipped out the door they would've been even later. The fact the lettering had been emphasized by the swell of her breasts hadn't helped much.

Gray was happy she kept the over shirt buttoned while facing down Troy.

Sam's laugh drew Gray's attention back.

"I can't count how many times I've seen this scene."

"They fight often?"

"Often enough. More so these last few

months."

"Why is that?"

"I don't know. She refuses to talk about work at home and I don't understand the details she does let slip." Sam shrugged. "I know it revolves around this project. I keep hearing phrases like 'there has to be a way,' 'keep us afloat just another six months and we'll be set,' and the words 'hostile take-over' have popped up." Sam glanced up at Gray nervously. "I shouldn't have told you that, but it's an indication of how deep the poop goes."

"I can see it from both sides. I meant it when I said I was considering dropping the project. My people have been studying the use of quartz for a low-powered link between the transmitters and the controllers, but it isn't working the way I want it to." Gray ignored the sharp glance Sam gave him.

Yeah, he'd just given her a tidbit. He didn't even stop to think about the reason why. Helping Troy's company go global wasn't his responsibility. Still, apparently it sparked an idea in Sam's head. She tried to hide it but her whole body perked up. Quite nicely, too. He wouldn't be a red-blooded man if he could ignore those lovely nipples and the flush of excitement. Roger better thank him later.

"Okay, so Troy hired you two right out of your degree programs?" Gray brought the story back on track.

"Yeah. He saw Reed fussing around with the résumés and jumped at the chance. He offered us both jobs, and the Monday after graduation we showed up for work." Sam snorted softly. "God, that first year was hell. Neither one of us was prepared for the real world."

"In what way?"

"In my case, I was set to assistant grunt work. At first it was sort of fun, but after being in charge of undergrads and running research, it sucked. There was the whole seniority thing. I wasn't used to Ian now being a rank above me. Eventually we worked it out and as our bidding got better, more projects came through and we settled down. I actually prefer that he be the boss. This way I don't have to deal with administrative junk and I get to concentrate on what I do best.

"Reed had it a little tougher. The old biddy doing Troy's bookkeeping didn't have a clue how to manage the growth. The poor old thing had a nervous breakdown one day. Troy paid for her long rest at a mental hospital and told Reed to straighten out the books." Sam laughed. "We didn't see her for three months, but she was happy as a clam. She got to set things up 'properly' and she slapped the whole company into shape. Troy was thrilled because banks would actually look at him. He finally had decent financials and could see, for once, that he was making money. Everyone else bitched because she made us toe the line. If timesheets were late, we didn't get paid. Man, she's tough about following procedures."

"Most bean counters are," Gray commented. He merely smiled at Sam's sharp look and turned back to see Reed now pointing a finger at Troy's chest. She wasn't speaking loudly enough for him to hear. Still, she was mightily pissed and Troy was getting a good earful.

"I can't believe you called her a bean counter. Don't ever do it to her face."

"Too late."

"And you're alive to tell the tale?" The look Sam gave him was filled with respect. "Wow. She must be in love."

"I keep trying to tell her that."

"The only fantasies she believes in take place between the covers of a book or on the silver screen. Love at first sight doesn't happen in the real world."

"She'll learn. I'm patient."

Sam shook her head. "Good thing. You're going to need every bit of patience and humor you have."

"So, you two have been with Spearman for six years?"

"Plus a few months, but yeah."

"Did they ever date?"

Sam chewed her lip.

"Come on, you can't work that closely with someone without a hint of attraction kicking in. Especially since he seems to adore the ground she walks on."

Sam kicked at a small stone. "You're right. They go out to dinner on occasion, but in Reed's mind he's just one of the boys. One of the housemates. The boss. She almost started seriously dating him at one point, but Troy blew it. Big time."

"Typical. What did he do?"

"The conference in Amsterdam eighteen months ago. She didn't go. She never goes to these things, even though Troy has tried off and on over the years to take her. Well, he'd been between women long enough that when she turned him down, he got over there and... well... got sidetracked, shall we say."

"He wasn't the only one." Gray remembered

telling the conference committee it wasn't a good idea booking the convention near one of the world's most infamous red light districts. Only Bangkok would have been worse. He'd been shouted down. Half the male attendees had barely shown their faces at the lectures.

"Yeah, well, word got back to Reed. See, they'd had an official first date a week before Troy left for the conference. She has this policy of no hanky-panky until at least the fourth date and he got a little put out because he didn't think her policy should include him. After all, they'd been friends and colleagues for years."

"And that probably is making him crazy right about now--the fact she didn't hold me to the four-date rule."

Sam shrugged. "Most likely. But then again, we were in Vegas..."

Gray chuckled. "So I told her."

Reed was back to her folded-arm stance and now Troy waved his hands around.

"What happened when she heard about his conference experience?"

"She told him to blow any dreams of anything beyond a working relationship right out his ear. If he couldn't wait for her, then he wasn't worth her time on a personal level. The fact we lost a big contract to you because of his behavior only added fuel to the fire."

Gray nodded. "You all actually had the better solution to the project but General Skolnick wasn't impressed with Troy's lack of focus. Skolnick had come to the conference solely to award that contract. It was a good one for us, and we were able to take it in a new direction." In fact, it had brought two additional contracts in behind it and was one of his bigger money producers at the moment. It would make even more money when the patent was awarded and they started producing the gadget for sale.

"Yup. Not only did Ian and I let him know it, but once Reed found out we'd lost the contract to you she had a similar reaction to what you see here today." Sam nodded toward Reed now speaking with a cold hard expression on her furious face.

Troy began to noticeably wilt under her verbal punishment. Reed started pacing again, the furious energy only slightly diminished. Was she winding down? Troy held out his hands in a plea for peace. Would she agree to a cease fire?

God, just to watch those jeans wiggle Gray knew, for his part, he'd promise her anything. The only thing better would be to take off that loose over shirt and watch her breasts bounce as she walked. He had a vision of her in chaps and a vest, hat and boots, and nothing else. Swallowing a groan, he shifted against the tree.

"So, the company has been scrambling ever since?" he asked to redirect Sam's attention.

"I think so. We're here to get a fresh perspective on this contract and sort out what might be the make or break deal of the year. I don't know. Those two have been very tight-lipped the last quarter."

"Is that why you and she stopped in Vegas on the way here?"

"Yeah. We've both put in horrible hours over the summer, and Troy was smart enough to at least see that. He sent us on ahead with orders to have some fun. I think he was hoping the trip would wake up Reed's libido and soften her attitude about having sex with him. The Rolex for Christmas didn't do it."

Gray softly snorted. "And the trip didn't work the way he wanted it to. Her libido got woken up, but not for him."

"And it being you only increases his frustration. I don't think he's had sex with a partner since Amsterdam." Sam snickered. "With the possible exception of the optics meeting a few weeks back."

"That's a long stretch for him."

"Yeah."

"So, you've been working with two uptight, frustrated people for a long time. Is it worth it?"

"Most days. Troy's not a total ass, but he got embarrassed by Amsterdam and hasn't been able to turn it around. Making this deal work will go a long way toward repairing his image. If that happens the happy status quo may return. If not," Sam lifted one shoulder, "you may see my résumé yet. You might see Reed's sooner. She hasn't said anything, but I don't think she's been cashing her paychecks for a couple of months. Maybe longer," she added quietly.

"I don't need to see your résumé. The day you leave Spearman, I expect to see you filling out paperwork in my Personnel Department. The offer is open any time you want it."

He glanced over at Sam to see her blink rapidly. Gray grinned. He liked stealing a woman's composure. Some ways were more fun than others, but it was always satisfying.

"I mean it, Sam. I'm impressed by your loyalty,

and your work is highly respected. Come to me with your demands and you'll most likely get whatever you want. Just give me first chance. And don't worry about Reed. I'll take care of her."

"That's the second best offer I've had in a long time," Sam said with a small smile.

"Oh? What was the other?"

Her smile widened and grew dreamy. "Roger offered to teach me how to fly."

THIRTEEN

Reed saw Gray and Sam out of the corner of her eye. Fortunately, Troy didn't. The two held back, so Reed ignored them as much as she could.

"Reed," Troy begged. "Please? We need to work together and having you continually throw my mistakes in my face doesn't help. I know I screwed up, and I know you're the one carrying the brunt of the load by juggling the money. I'm trying to make it easier by getting this product to market. The truth is I'm almost tapped out."

"I know your financial condition," she snapped, scowling at his attempt to be contrite as she began to pace again, hands shoved in the back pockets of her jeans. "You're such a jerk, Troy."

"I know that and I'll go back in there and prostrate myself in apology in front of the others."

"It just pisses me off that I haven't had a paycheck in four months now. Sam has no idea she's paying most of the household expenses. I'm going to have to tell her."

Troy bowed his head. "I'll talk to her."

"No. You haven't taken money out in six months." Reed waved a hand in dismissal. "But Mya's going to be balancing the bank statements while we're gone and she's going to see all those paychecks haven't cleared. It won't be a secret much longer. Especially since we'll have to lay-off someone or ask senior staff to take a pay cut. I don't like either solution."

"Let me guess, Jerry the Rat has your vote as first to go, right?"

Reed felt the evil grin tugging at the corner of her mouth.

"Oh, there's that smile. I knew it was hiding there." Troy bent a little to look at her now hidden face.

Fighting the smile and the urge to snigger, Reed spun and halted just shy of landing a solid punch in Troy's solar plexus. She had the gratification of seeing his face blanch, then redden with fury as he realized she'd stopped. Out of the corner of her eye she saw Sam restrain Gray.

"Shit, Reed," Troy snapped. "I hate it when you do that."

"You earned it, jerk," she said with great satisfaction. Folding her arms across her stomach she stared at him as he folded his arms across his chest. "One of these days I won't pull my punch. Now, are you going to lay off me about Gray?"

"And one day I'll actually take you over my knee and paddle your ass."

Reed narrowed her eyes as her boss glared back at her.

"You just can't get involved with him," Troy insisted.

"I can get involved with whomever I please. You aren't my father, brother, husband or even my uncle or boyfriend. You're my boss. Period. Friend status is in question at the moment."

Damn, she actually wanted to hit him. Then again, hitting him might actually give him hope that she had feelings for him.

"Reed," he said through gritted teeth. "I'm the

best friend you have. I know him. Don't trust him. He'll turn around and stab you in the back and he's only using you to get to me."

"As far as I can tell he thinks about you as little as possible. He doesn't give a damn about your company and would probably only be mildly interested to hear you've practically run it into the ground."

"He wants to know how we're working this project," Troy ground out.

"Baloney. He had the perfect opportunity in Vegas and on the plane and didn't press the issue. He's very much not interested in your business." Reed felt herself blushing and looked away.

"Right. And he'll be the first one to try and make a hostile takeover bid if word gets out we're in trouble."

Reed swung her head back and glared at him through narrowed eyes. "I won't say a word. I haven't said anything to Sam and she's closer to me than anyone else."

"By the way, I didn't sleep much last night. Mind keeping it down tonight?" Troy muttered and ran a hand through his hair. "Shit. Reed, part of this trip was supposed to be you and me hooking up. You're supposed to be sleeping in my bed."

"Fat chance. I already told you that was a dead-end street. I don't sleep with men who visit red-light districts. End of story. I just hope your experience was worth it."

"It wasn't," Troy muttered.

"Tough. Why don't you get back together with Tiffany? Or was her main attraction the fact she was dating Gray?"

Troy's exhalation nearly blew her hat off.

Reed stepped away.

"Would you stop throwing all my mistakes in my face? If I'm not going to get the benefits of matrimony, then I certainly don't have to put up with the abuse."

"Fine. Let's just leave all personal comments out of this week, shall we? Now, I believe you have some groveling to do." Beyond Troy's shoulder she could see Sam had disappeared, but Gray still leaned against the tree. Damn, she had to learn to control her drool. Couldn't be helped--the man was gorgeous. Complete with well worn straw cowboy hat on his black hair and lazy sexy look in his eyes.

"So, are we friends again?"

Reed looked up at Troy's soft tone of voice. Almost lover like. She glared at him. "We're friends if you stop trying to hit on me."

Troy closed his eyes for a moment, then nodded and stuck out his hand.

Reed hesitated then gripped it. "Friends."

Troy lifted her hand as if to kiss it.

Reed ripped her hand from his. "Damn you, Troy. Get your ass back into that meeting and grovel 'til your bellybutton is raw." Men. Couldn't trust them.

"Yes, ma'am," he said, with a smirk that faded when he turned around and saw Gray.

With a slow grin, Gray casually pushed away from the tree. He'd been standing there long enough that he'd begun to feel like part of the trunk. Reed walked toward him with a small smile that reminded him of their romp this morning. She even put a little extra wiggle in her walk and would have walked right by him, leading Troy back to the lodge. Instead he snaked out a hand and caught her arm.

"Whoa there, Nelly," he said, using his best cowboy drawl. He smiled when she readily melted against him.

"Gray." Troy paused beside them. "I'd appreciate it if you'd stop distracting my staff."

"You forget, Troy. Life has a different pace up here. Isn't part of the reason for being here to relax a little?" Gray adjusted Reed's hat so it sat tilted back on her head.

"And find new inspiration."

"That happens when you let things simmer a bit. Let your people enjoy the experience." Just like what he was experiencing by drowning in Reed's eyes. Damn, they looked like forest pools. Deep and mysterious.

"If you don't mind, we're in the middle of a meeting and we need to get back to it. Reed," Troy said, and held out a hand to her.

Gray grinned as Reed told Troy, "I'll be there in just a minute. Go on ahead."

Troy slowly retracted his hand and shoved it in his pocket. "Fine. Just don't keep us waiting any longer than necessary."

Gray stared at Troy for a long moment. "I think she's earned a few minutes to compose herself. She'll be back soon."

Troy hesitated then walked away.

Gray looked down at Reed. She had a wicked twinkle in her eye.

"You do that often?" he asked her.

"What?"

"Don't bat your eyelashes at me. I saw you

sucker punch Troy. I'm amazed he let you get away with it. If it'd been me, you would have been in the pond a second later."

"I didn't actually hit him. I wanted to and he owed me, but I pulled it. He said unkind things about me back there in the dining room. And when I go back he's going to lick my boots in front of the group in apology."

"Next time, if there is one, let me have the pleasure and I'll do it for real. I haven't decked Troy in years and it would feel great."

"Why did you deck him?"

"Doesn't matter. He earned it then, too."

"Has he always been such a jerk?" Reed's head was cocked, her eyes a little sad.

"No, he hasn't. We used to be the best of friends. Until a little bit of green mold crept into his heart." Gray tucked a strand of hair behind her ear. The memory didn't come around often anymore and he wasn't sure he wanted to let it in right now.

"That makes you sad."

Gray nodded. "However, I can't fix what's broken inside him. Only he can do that. I just don't want him to hurt you in the process."

Reed smiled crookedly. "He won't. I'm a big girl, Gray."

"You're a sexy girl." He released the buttons on her shirt. "I want to see how you distort those words again."

"And I want to see you pose like the cowboy. When do I get my second riding lesson?"

Gray bent his head to kiss her. "After lunch."

~ * ~

A few hours later, trying to walk like a normal

person, Reed pretended the slow saunter up the hill was on purpose. Riding a desk and riding a horse were two vastly different life experiences. Come to think of it, she much preferred riding Gray to either.

"What's that grin?" Sam asked suspiciously.

"Nothing. Just thinking about something Gray said last night."

"Gonna share?"

"Nope."

"Slut."

"Look who's talking, strumpet."

Sam threw back her head and laughed. The sound echoed and Reed joined in as they climbed the steps to their lodge.

"Last one in the hot tub is a rotten egg," Reed quipped.

"Better get a long hot shower first. I think you have about a ton of dirt on you. I know I have that much in my hair alone." Sam swept off her hat and slapped it against her leg. A thick cloud of dust gathered in the air, which seemed to be rapidly cooling.

Both women looked up at the sky. What had been tall white clouds building up to thunderheads now looked black and forbidding as they blocked the sun.

"Hmm, storm brewing," Reed said.

"It will blow over fast." Reed and Sam turned to see Kiri with a cleaning bucket in one hand and a stuffed laundry bag in the other. "If you've never been in the mountains for one of our afternoon storms it should be a treat. Hope you don't mind thunder and lightning." She leaned a hip against the porch rail.

"We don't get many thunderstorms where we come from," Reed said. "I don't know if I've ever been in one."

"They get loud, and the rain comes down pretty fierce, but they're over almost as fast as they start." Kiri scanned the darkening sky. "Speaking of, I'd better get to the truck if I don't want to get drenched. Wait until the storm is over before using the hot tub," she told them with a smile then descended the steps with her bucket and bundle. "Oh," she turned back. "Blake will fix the collapsed bed when you're out on the trail."

"Thanks," Reed muttered with a blush.

Kiri gave her a friendly wink and smile, then swung her bundle into the back of the truck, climbed in, and drove off.

"I think we better make a rule that what happens on this retreat stays here," Reed muttered.

"Go get your shower. If the storm freaks you out, let me know and I'll come watch it with you. In fact, let me get cleaned up and I will come to your room. You'll have the better view."

"I'll leave the door unlocked." Reed cast a glance toward the men coming up the hill, and decided escape was the name of the game. Gray wasn't part of the group and she probably wouldn't see him until dinner.

Gray. And his family. Reed didn't know what to think of them. Blake was sweet, as was Jim, Gray's brother-in-law. Kiri's smile and wink outside seemed to indicate she was friendly. The mother and older brother were still unknowns.

Reed kicked off her dusty boots by the door and peeled off her clothes as she headed toward the bathroom. A long hot shower was just the ticket.

~ * ~

Gray stood on the porch of the main lodge, watching Reed and Sam walk up the hill. Their slow stroll didn't fool him. Reed was sore. He'd bet she thought it was from the riding this afternoon. Thinking about the real reason made him grin. A tickle hit the back of his neck and he rubbed at it absently, remembering the previous night.

"Gray?"

He turned in response to his mother's voice behind him.

"Any chance I can get your attention now?"

Ignoring the hint of sarcasm he joined her in the lobby. "Sure, Mom. The office?"

"If you please."

Gray rested an arm on her shoulders as they walked toward the stairs. "She did well this afternoon."

"Yes," Sora agreed. "She has a natural seat. Can you get your mind on business, please? The Stockman's is having their monthly meeting over lunch on Friday, in Avon. You get back from the pack trip Thursday, so you won't have much time to catch up."

"Okay," Gray conceded, and followed his mother up the stairs. "You win. I'll pay attention from now until dinner. I'm dying for a shower, but I'm here, dust, horse sweat and all."

"You smell just like everyone else here," she told him, and led the way into the office.

Gray glanced out the large picture window and noticed the lowering sky. The silver truck pulling away from the upper lodge drew his eye, and he saw Reed and Sam turn into the building. Troy and the others were on their way up the hill at a fair pace as were most of the guests. Good, they'd be indoors. The storm was coming on steadily. The increasing static in the air made the hair on his arms rise and he rubbed the sensation away.

"Looks like we're in for a good gully-washer," he commented.

Sora absently looked out the window while sorting through papers on the desk. "Most likely. It's been a few days since we had one. Today was hot enough it will cool things down nicely. Now, here's the latest roster. You should recognize most of the names."

Gray settled back in an overstuffed leather armchair and took the papers.

His heart just wasn't in it. The names were familiar. Some a little too familiar. Many belonged to his childhood friends and schoolmates. Forcing his mind to the task at hand he looked over the figures for the ranch next.

Why did his mother insist? Dustin had a fine handle on the business.

With the first brilliant flash of light he glanced toward the window, automatically counting until the thunder crashed. Fifteen and to the south. Down the valley. He turned back to the papers flowing steadily from his mother into his hands.

Feeling restless, Gray forced himself to concentrate on the financial reports. The Profit and Loss was acceptable. Personally he'd like to see it just a tad stronger, but overall, year to date, the numbers were solid and comfortable. Cash flow was steady and bookings were full for the rest of the season. A good way to end the year.

The next flash of light illuminated the room. Both Gray and Sora looked up. She reached for the desk lamp and turned it on.

Ten miles. From the north. Long storm front? Probably.

Gray rolled his neck and purposely forced himself to look back down at the monthly statements. "Has this been graphed out?" he asked.

"It has, but not printed." Sora frowned at the window. "I don't think we'd better fire up the computer at the moment."

A flash emphasized her point. When the thunder came eight seconds later the window vibrated ever so slightly.

"Right. That one came from the west. Looks like the storm will move right over us," Gray said. "Been a long time since I was in a good storm."

Sora shrugged with a tiny smile. "One reason I still like being up here."

Gray smiled. His quiet mother loved the wildness of the summer storms. The guests didn't see that side of her, but her family knew.

"Hey," Kiri said from the open door. "Look what we arranged to welcome you home."

Gray returned her grin. Okay, it was no secret he liked the summer storms too.

"I saw you talking to Reed and Sam. What did you say to make her act all shy?"

Kiri laughed. "I just told her the broken bed would be fixed when you all go out on the pack trip. That way Blake isn't banging around at odd hours."

Gray laughed. "Yeah, that would have embarrassed her."

"Do I even want to know how it broke?" Sora asked with resignation.

"Honestly, we just sat down on it and it collapsed." Gray could see that Sora wasn't sure about Reed at all. He was surprised. He would have thought she'd be happy for him.

Kiri laughed. "Right. Good one. Care to tell me why there were pillows all over the place?"

"Okay, so we were having a pillow fight." Gray didn't feel at all repentant or embarrassed.

"Ah, so is that why Reed was moving as if she'd been in the saddle for a week? That little bit of time this afternoon shouldn't be hurting yet."

Gray rested the papers on his lap. "No, she had a huge knot in her shoulder muscle. I worked her over pretty thoroughly with a massage last night."

Kiri's smile had a wicked twist.

"I'm sure she's looking forward to a long soak in the hot tub tonight," Gray said.

"I told them to wait until the storm blows over." Kiri wandered over to the window to watch the wind beginning to whip the trees around. "Good strong winds this time."

"Hmm." Gray set the papers aside to join Kiri at the window. It was comforting to stand with an arm draped over her shoulder. Even more so when she wrapped an arm around his waist. Even then it didn't soothe the nagging worry making the back of his neck itch.

"Welcome home," Kiri murmured and rested her head on his shoulder.

They stood together watching the lightning flashes increase and the wind pick up.

"Wonder what Reed and Sam think of this?" Kiri mused aloud.

"What do you mean?" Gray asked. The itch on the back of his neck increased. He rubbed it absently. Probably a buildup of static electricity.

"Hmm? Oh, Reed said she didn't think she'd ever been in a lightning storm before."

Gray's heart twisted as the thunder crashed louder, the window pane noticeably vibrating as the noise echoed between the ridges. Three miles. The storm was right on top of them. Fear like he'd never known before made his heart hurt. But from what? For what? Reed? In his mind's eye, he was blinded by the flash of a lightning strike just yards in front of him. Passing a hand over his eyes he wanted at once to clear it but to also to see what happened after the strike despite the fear almost blinding him with pain.

"What is it?" Kiri looked up as he pulled away.

"I gotta go." A chill shivered down his spine. Reed. Had to get to Reed. Needed to make sure she was safe. "I'll be back. Have to check on something. Are the keys in the truck?"

"Yes." Kiri's voice followed him as he took the stairs two at a time.

The first splatter of rain drops hit as he cleared the bottom of the steps. For a second, he considered running across the grounds, then jumped in the truck instead. The engine turned over and he pulled around the long dirt road circling the inner grounds. Past the guest cabins and up the hill to the upper lodge at the furthest point from the main house.

Lightning flashed as he slammed the truck into park and shut it off. Barely slowing long enough to slam the door, he raced up the steps to the stairs leading to the second floor, thunder shaking the ground. Close. Just over a mile away. The next strike could be twenty miles away or hit the building.

Trying to rein in the incredible dread squeezing his heart, Gray opened the door to the room as calmly as he could. What had him scared like this? It didn't make sense, but every nerve in his body screamed for him to get to Reed. She was in danger, but why? From what?

Sam stood at the window and jumped when the door slammed open.

"Where's the fire?" she asked.

"Huh?" Gray looked around the room. He knew he didn't make sense and looked like a mad man. "Where's Reed?"

"Oh, she's soaking in the tub..." Sam's voice trailed off.

Gray threw open the bathroom door and watched as Reed rose up from obviously dunking her whole body under water. Shock registered on her face a moment before she recognized him.

"Hey," she said with a softening smile.

For just a moment, a vision of Reed lying in a charred heap before a smoking, lightning-struck tree superseded the scene in front of him. Heart in his throat, Gray reached into the tub and lifted her from the water as white hot light filled the room and the simultaneous crack of thunder rocked the building.

His foot slipped on the slick surface of the floor. Reed's mouth opened, but her shriek was lost in the crashing thunder echoing around them. Like a movie in slow motion, her arms flew around his neck and held tight as the world tipped.

Stunned, for a few seconds Gray wasn't sure

what happened. Ears ringing, he looked at Reed's white face, her mouth still hanging open. Air rushed back into his lungs, his heart kicked into high gear and he crushed her to him.

Ree, Ree, Ree. Her name swam through his head on each madly throbbing pulse of his heart.

Slowly other senses came back. The taste of her mouth, the sound of rain pounding on the roof, the scent of the lavender soap she'd used in the bath, the feel of her water-slick skin in his arms, soaking his shirt, and her wet hair cooling against his skin.

He felt the solid presence of the wall at his back and he let it hold him as he tightened his arms around Reed, kissing her as if the world were ending. Good thing they seemed to be on the floor.

Slowly another sensation penetrated his awareness. Small hands beating on his shoulder and slick legs beginning to flail. Reluctantly he broke the kiss and buried his face against her neck.

"Jesus, Joseph and Mary!" she gasped. "What is going on?"

"Reed," he moaned against her neck. "You're safe."

"Of course I'm safe. Well, except from gorgeous cowboys breaking into my bath and dumping me naked and wet on the floor. Care to explain?"

Gray straightened at her waspish tone. She reached over his head and pulled a towel off the rack.

"You almost got fried." He looked at her, astonished. Didn't she know?

She glared back at him and attempted to cover

herself. He had to admit it wasn't easy with him holding her tight and only one arm free. Loosening his grip, he helped drape the towel around her but didn't let her loose.

"Would you please explain? And may I get back in the tub?"

"Yes, I will explain, but no, you may not get back in the tub."

"Everything okay?" Sam asked tentatively from the door.

"It is now," Gray said. Now that he knew Reed was safe, time began to quickly reassert itself. "Would you close this door and get the other one?" he asked Sam.

"Sure." She gave them a long questioning look and when Reed shrugged, Sam did as he asked.

He heard Troy's voice through the door.

With a sigh he pulled Reed close and rested his forehead against hers. He felt her winding up to speak but another nearby lightning strike changed her mind. Instead she huddled closer in his arms.

"Reed," he murmured against her neck. "I can't remember ever being so terrified." He kissed her tender throat and wasn't sure which of them shook the most.

"Gray, I don't understand. Besides, I'm getting cold."

"Right. Well, as soon as I can stand, I'll let you up. But right now you're not leaving my arms. That was just too damn close a call." He up and pulled down another towel.

He let her sit up enough to wrap the second towel around her. And being a nice guy, he even helped. "You mean to tell me you don't even realize you were in danger?"

"In danger from hypothermia? In danger of being accosted? Dropped on the floor? What?"

"In danger of being electrocuted."

If he weren't deadly serious the look on her face would have been hilarious.

"Look, I stayed out of the hot tub. That's why I used this tub. To be indoors. I'm sore, Gray." She wrapped her arms around his neck again as another crash of thunder shook the building.

Pounding on the bathroom door shook off the dumbfounded feeling he had. "What?" he answered sharply. There was too much going on.

"Everyone okay in there?" Troy asked.

"Fine." Gray snapped. "You don't have to rush up here every time you hear a noise."

Troy's snort was clear through the wood of the door. "If I'd done that, I would have been at your door every thirty minutes last night. I just wait for the really big crashes."

"Well thanks for checking, but Reed's just fine."

"What happened anyway?"

"I hauled her out of the tub just as the lightning hit the building."

"Oh shit."

There was a thump against the door. Gray figured it was Troy's forehead.

"Reed, don't you know you're supposed to stay away from sinks and tubs during a lightning storm?" Troy asked with exasperation.

"And how the hell should I know that?" she snapped. "Go away, Troy. Gray's already chewing me out and I don't need to hear it from you too."

She shifted in Gray's arms, waves of irritation pouring off her.

"Fine," Troy said. "Will you two keep it quiet for at least a night? I'm tired and feeling rather annoyed, and your shenanigans aren't helping."

"We'll try, Troy." Gray nearly laughed at Reed's mouth opening and closing like a guppy. She just couldn't seem to find the right words. He wasn't sure which one of them she wanted to blast most. He found another use for her lips and tongue instead.

When she melted and kissed him back Gray poured out his love for her. As the storm outside faded in intensity the storm inside began heating up. Not sure if they still had company, Gray lay Reed back on the floor, a towel mostly under her, and leaned over her.

"Gray." She gasped as he bit her earlobe. "I don't want to make love on the bathroom floor."

"I'm...not...sure...we're alone." One hand cradled her head, the other sought out her softest curves. He ached for her. Needing to possess her, his hand slipped between her legs and she gasped, body arching up against his. "I need you, Ree." His voice shook with the reaction of fading adrenalin.

"Yes." She moaned and reached for his pants.

What was it about her that all discipline left him? Even as he pumped into her, she was still pushing his jeans off his hips. It took three thrusts for her to pull his shirt up and off with barely a pause. Unable to find purchase on the slick floor, he rolled them over and pulled her hips down tight on him. Fading thunder still crashed and as their releases came upon them, one more flash lit the room, followed by distant thunder several heartbeats later.

Gray forgot to count off the seconds.

Fourteen

The world hovered in suspense for a long moment, then Reed's body crumpled. Sliding with all the substance of a jellyfish, she landed in the secure embrace of Gray's arms, his body a warm bed for her to lie on.

Neither moved, their labored breaths blending with the rain now pattering against the window.

"Reed," Gray's voice rumbled under her cheek. "Woman, you're going to kill me."

A flash of annoyance dulled the pleasure she wallowed in, reminding her of what Gray had interrupted.

Floating in the large claw foot tub had stirred something deep inside. The link had been tenuous at best, a wisp of memory. The memory of a dream? A dream? Or an actual event? Reed hadn't had time to sort it out. One second she was rising from the bottom of the tub like a nymph cavorting in a sylvan pond, the next she was a whale being scooped from the water.

Deliberately, she placed her hands flat on the floor and pushed upward to stare at him. His hands cupping her face and his lazy, sexy smile countered his words, but didn't erase the irritation she felt.

"What is it?" he asked, his expression changing as he took in hers.

"*I'm* going to kill *you*?" She used her best

indignant tone. "Who came rushing in and interrupted whose bath? You nearly gave me a heart attack!" Pushing off him, she stood, legs straddling his waist and looked down with her fists on her hips. "Care to explain what all the histrionics were about? And then before I get my breath back, I get pounced on? Can I get back in the bath *now*?"

Gray cocked his head as if listening, then nodded. "The lightning has moved on." He rose up on his elbows with a grin, his gaze traveling up her body. "In fact, I think I'll join you."

Reed rolled her eyes and stepped over him and back into the water. Swearing under her breath she pulled the plug. "The water's cold."

She purposely didn't look while Gray shucked off his boots and jeans. Scooting forward in the tub, she made room for him to sit behind her. Turning on the water, she adjusted the temperature then put the plug back in. Before she had a chance to debate the merits of adding more lavender-scented bath salt, he pulled her back against his chest. A few moments later she relented and relaxed against him.

Grateful he remained silent for the time being, Reed dropped her head back on his shoulder. So much had happened in such a short time she still wasn't sure about any of it. Gray stroked her wet hair, one arm draped across her collarbones. Idly watching the water level rise, she cleared her mind and tried to sort out the sequence of events.

Shower finished, body aching, Reed had put in the plug and filled the tub, luxuriating in the silky lavender-scented water. A feeling of sleepiness had come over her and she'd drifted with the dreamlike memory that came to her.

Water. Sun-warmed. Green leaves creating dappled shade, birds chirping and singing. A pool. But not like the one surrounding the trysting place. The trees were different, the air hot and dusty. In the dream she rose from the water, hair streaming behind her, rivulets running down her face and throat. Was she alone? She closed her eyes and mentally reached out. Yes. Alone and...anticipating?

"Sweetheart?"

Gray's voice invaded the memory and pushed it away again. She couldn't help the thrum of impatience she felt. "Hmm?"

"Don't you think now would be a good time to turn off the water?"

"Oh." It was nearly at the brim of the tub. Only inch to go at most. "Right." Slowly she leaned forward and closed the taps. Just as slowly, she leaned back.

"Day dreaming?" He spoke softly.

"Trying to remember what I was dreaming about when you barged in."

"Ah. Did you catch it?"

"A pool in a creek. I think I was bathing. To get ready for..."

"Me?" he asked quietly, his lips against her temple melting her frustration. The very gentleness he treated her with obliterated any remaining resistance she felt.

"I didn't get that far, but I think so. I'm not sure if I was asleep or in a trance."

"You were just rising up out of the water. If I hadn't been so terrified I would have stopped to watch longer."

"That's the second time you've used that word. Why were you terrified?"

"You really don't understand?"

"Sorry, no. I don't see what the big deal was."

Both of his arms came around her and he pulled her close, burying his face in the side of her neck.

"Just as I pulled you out of the water a bolt of lightning hit the cabin. There's no way to know for sure, at least no way I want to experiment with, but that energy could have traveled up the pipes and fried you. Just like dropping a live wire in water. Maybe worse. I had a vision of you crumpled and fried to a crackly crisp. It felt like something I'd seen before. Knowing of our past histories, it's possible that in one of our lives..." he voice cracked and trailed off.

"Oh." She chewed her lip while trying to recall what she knew about storm safety, ignoring the picture he painted with a shudder. She'd heard the usual warnings about staying off the phone, getting out of the pool or lake, and turning off the computer, but taking a bath?

"You do know water conducts electricity, right?"

"Of course," she said with scorn.

"Well, these pipes are old enough they're iron. The electricity from lightning hits just one pipe and it connects to all the other pipes and the water running through them. This tub is iron under the enamel. Are you following me here?"

"Oh," she said more quietly. Oh. "And you're saying lightning hit the building?"

"Judging by the way it shook, either a bolt hit the house or the two of us falling on the floor really shook the place up. Again."

Reed giggled and Gray's chuckle could be felt as a rumble against her back.

"We're going to have to stop falling down," Gray said and shifted in the tub. "I'm afraid my ass is going to hurt over that last one."

"And falling with a whale in your arms didn't make the landing any softer," she muttered.

"Reed O'Brien, soon to be Dunbar, what is it with you and these self disparaging remarks? You aren't fat." He hugged her tight. "What is your middle name anyway?"

"Why? So you can use it on me like my mother?" *Ignore the soon-to-be comment.*

"Are you always this cranky?"

"Only when I'm exhausted and sore. So I guess that means yes. Most of the time. Especially the last few months, according to my coworkers."

"What does that mean?"

"I've heard certain words follow me out of meetings and down hallways. I've come across people whispering in the coffee room only to see them turn bright red when I turn the corner. I know what they think of me."

"Reed, what's going on?"

"I can't discuss it with you."

"Does it have something to do with the reason you wanted to punch Troy today?"

"Yes."

"Kiri thinks you have potential as a lightweight boxer, by the way."

"Oh? And what does your mother think?"

"She hasn't decided yet."

"Will I know when she does?"

"Almost certainly."

"That is so comforting. Oh well. It doesn't matter what your family thinks of me." It did, but she wasn't about to confess that little desire. Who wouldn't want to be liked by her boyfriend's family? Why was his mother so cold? How many women had Gray brought home over the years?

Gray pulled her tight. "To a certain extent, you're right. But I want them to love you. Just like I do."

"You don't even know me. You don't know what I like, don't like, what makes me get up in the morning. Do I cry during movies? Do I hog the popcorn? What about the weekends? Do you even know what I like to do? I don't know these things about you, either. How can we even talk about liking each other, much less whether or not we're in love?"

Apparently Gray didn't like her questions. Ignoring the sloshing water, he rolled her over so she lay on top of him. He slid lower in the tub until they were nose to nose, his eyes warm and concerned while she fought to keep hers from crossing.

"Reed, who hurt you?"

Nope. Not answering these questions. She tried to pull away from him. With little effort he held her close, ignoring her struggle.

"I want to know. Who hurt you and how?" he asked again.

"I don't know what you're talking about."

"Reed." He sighed her name and kissed her nose. His forehead against hers felt good. "You're snapping like a dog who's been abused. Lashing out to hurt before you're hurt. It's a protection reflex. Who hurt you? Troy?"

Laughter bubbled up until Reed couldn't hold it in. "Troy? Oh God, no. Not Troy. I've never really been attracted to him. He's okay, just nothing more than a big spoiled baby."

"I won't argue with you there," Gray kissed her nose again. "So, who was it?"

"No one."

"Had to be someone." Gray frowned, and Reed looked away to watch the rain falling outside.

"No one," she repeated. With a tiny sigh she rested her head on Gray's shoulder. Snuggling against his chest, she ran a finger over his collarbone.

"Not any one person," he said slowly, "but everyone who tripped over you to get to Sam or others like her. All the boys who asked you out because everyone else already had dates or they just hoped you'd take off your shirt. Everyone who asked you out because you were just one of the guys. The men who asked you out because a double date with Sam was better than no date. The women who raked you with snotty looks because they were too mean to admit they were jealous of you. The well-meaning relatives who compared you to taller, slimmer cousins and told you you'd be pretty if you just lost a few pounds."

Hot tears pricked at the back of Reed's eyes. "The swim coach who told me to lose ten pounds over the summer by running. The woman in the dressing room who got frustrated because I wear a twelve on top and a ten on the bottom." That had been just last week.

The tears slowly seeped from her eyes. Troy, who was spending the equivalent of one month's salary on this stupid retreat. Troy, who couldn't keep his pants on overseas after just one date with her. Yeah, he was so eager to be with her that, once out of town, he'd run out and found the first whore he could.

That was flattering. Not.

Ian and Dennis who'd never noticed she was a woman until it came time to clean the house they'd shared.

Her brothers who smacked her ass every time they saw her and told her no man wanted a woman with an ass that took up so much of the bed.

Reed angrily wiped the tears from her eyes.

"I'm right, aren't I?" Gray asked softly, his lips on her forehead.

"What does it matter?"

"It matters more than you're willing to admit. It matters to me because all of them, every single one of them, are wrong. But what makes it matter most, is you believe them. They're all wrong, Ree. You're more beautiful than any of them. From what Sam told me, what I know from the dream, your heart is bigger and more giving than you let on. And despite what you may think, I do know you. You cry at movies, happy or sad. You'd give your last dollar to help a friend. As for weekends, I think you either work or collapse in exhaustion if you aren't cleaning the house. You'd have more fun touring wine country or tending a rose garden. I'd say you have a green thumb and make things grow whether it be money or plants. Puppies, kittens and children flock to you and you'll be a great mother."

"You don't know me," she whispered.

"That's the fun. We don't have to know

everything about each other. It's part of the journey. Ten years from now, we'll both be different people. The fun will be growing together. Our hearts already know each other. Our brains need time to catch up. Just think how exciting that will be."

"You're pushing."

"You're right. I got scared when I saw you in the tub. I was terrified I'd lost you as quickly as I'd found you. Please, Reed, give us a chance."

The genuine plea in his voice touched her heart. She wanted him, and she ached for the life he sketched out. Someone to explore with, to be a companion at home. Sharing mundane chores with. A perfect life.

"I'm here, naked, and in a bathtub with you, after having sex, yet again, without a condom. I think I'm giving us a chance. I swear, if I don't miss my next cycle, I'm going on birth control and at the first opportunity we're both getting tested. You're lucky I'm not dragging you to the nearest clinic and dealing with this right now. I'm taking a huge leap of faith here."

Gray laughed and she felt his body relax beneath her. "You're right. Okay, I'll stop pushing."

"Right." It wasn't in his nature to stop pushing. Reed leaned back enough to look him in the eye. "Just kiss me."

He grinned, slow and sexy. "I can do that."

~ * ~

Moisture rose from the ground in steaming tendrils by the time they dressed and went down the hill to dinner. Blinded by the once again brilliant sun, Reed felt like she was back in high school when Gray opened the driver's side door of the truck and helped her climb up. Sitting next to him on the bench seat, she made a joke about going to the drive-in.

"I have a better idea. We'll go watch the stars tonight. There's a nice spot just up the road a bit. I'll have Maria fix us a basket with dessert and a bottle or two of wine, I'll stash a few blankets in the back and we'll go parking."

"Looking for submarine races?" Reed giggled as they pulled up near the lodge.

"Up here we call it hunting for snipe." He waggled his brows then helped her down from the truck. His hand found a way up her skirt and she batted it away.

"Behave," she told him.

"I am. I'm behaving like a man in love. In lust."

Reed rolled her eyes. "Don't you ever get tired?"

"I'll let you know when I do."

"Great. Any time now would be fine."

"I'll work on it." He kissed her neck and wrapped an arm around her waist.

There were two spaces left at a long table where Reed's group sat. Roger looked right at home sitting next to Sam. Gray helped Reed into a chair next to Ian and took the one on the end, far away from Troy. That suited Reed just fine.

After some teasing, Reed decided she and Sam must have been the only people on the face of the earth to not think bathing during a thunderstorm was a bad idea. She took it in stride and was able to tease Ian and Dennis about their attempts to ride. At least she had ammunition. Troy even relaxed over dinner and during dessert struck up a conversation with the group of women from Boulder at the next table. Stuart they still needed to work on. He looked a little nervous.

Since the mood was friendly, Reed talked Gray into joining the group at the camp fire after dinner. He excused himself and promised to meet her by the fire pit. Reed grabbed Ian and Dennis's arms and made them escort her, falling into their old teasing ways. Settling on logs around the growing fire, they were offered cups of coffee in big enameled cups.

"Here ya go, Miss Reed," Ian drawled. "We saved one cream pitcher just for you."

"Nice to know the man remembers." Reed held out her cup and let him turn her coffee a nice light mocha.

"Our Miss Reed, she likes her coffee like she likes her men, light and strong," Dennis teased.

"Strong for sure," she murmured and sipped. "Guess that leaves you two out."

"Oh, that hurts!" Dennis held a hand over his heart. "Ripped it clean out, she did. Never did cut us much slack, did she Ian?"

Ian laughed and draped an arm around Reed's shoulder. "Not this girl. Did us a favor, too. She and Sam turned us into men women actually wanted."

Dennis nodded as he sipped his coffee. "True. Cathy still includes them in her nightly prayers."

"What? For teaching you how to wash dishes or clean the bathroom?" Sam asked.

"Those skills help, but the one Gina values most is laundry. I can wash lingerie and have it look like new. I can even hang up clothes so they never need ironing," Ian said with pride.

"Yeah, but the best one is you iron your own damn shirts," Dennis growled.

"No, you iron your own shirts. I pay the dry cleaners to do it."

"That's cheating!" Dennis cried.

"So, Sam," Roger asked, "which one passed house husband training with the highest score?"

"Ian. He actually got married," Sam declared to the general laughter of the group. "And he found the dry cleaners."

"Am I hearing this right?" Roger asked. "You don't take care of your men?"

"What 'our' men? They were our housemates. Shared the rent, the cooking and the cleaning, but they didn't share our beds," Sam said. "I didn't have time to mollycoddle them and Reed wouldn't let us be pigs. She has this aversion to mice, bugs and odd smells."

Reed rolled her eyes and looked into her coffee cup. Ian's arm around her shoulder was comforting. She'd nearly forgotten what good friends they were.

"How's Gina?" she quietly asked while other conversations picked up around them.

"She's fine."

"Too bad she couldn't come along."

"Nah. She doesn't like altitude or horses. She's happy at home."

"When's the baby due?" Reed smiled when Ian stiffened in surprise.

"How'd you find out?"

"You've been strutting around the building with a rather pleased look on your face. Well, until I come into view." Reed felt her mood deflate, and her shoulders sagged.

A little time away and she could see she'd been just awful to everyone in the office. Short tempered and not prone to lingering for casual conversations. No wonder people had been jumpy and wary around her these past few months. Ian's arm tightening around her shoulder nearly made her burst into tears.

"You've been under a lot of stress. Care to share the burden a little?"

"Can't. Just get this project up and running, okay?" she pleaded with him as she blinked the tears away.

"Actually, Sam received an inspiration this morning that may very well be our ticket to easy street," Ian murmured in her ear.

"Really? That's great." Reed smiled up at Ian. "She never said a word."

"That's because you were too busy beating up Troy." Ian snorted into his coffee cup.

"Yeah, well, he deserved it."

"True, but jeez, do you have to be so hard on the man? Watching you being snatched up by his worst rival? That hurts a guy way down deep."

"There is no 'way down deep' to him," Reed scoffed.

"Okay, you got me there, but if there was, the arrow would be poking in right there." Ian pointed to his own chest with the coffee cup still in his hand. "He's bleeding, Reed."

Yes, he is. In more ways than one. "Well, he'll just have to find a bandage," she said. "So, when? I need time to knit a blanket."

"You have time. We just cleared the first trimester."

"So...February?"

"She can count."

Reed nudged him with her elbow. If she wasn't careful she wouldn't be far behind. Had to do something about that. Maybe she'd ask Kiri where the nearest clinic was.

FIFTEEN

"May I cut in?"

Reed and Ian both turned their heads to see Gray behind them.

"I knew it was too good to last," Ian joked. He kissed Reed on the forehead, then slid over to make room for Gray.

Gray stepped over the log and settled down next to Reed. Missing Ian's body heat she snuggled up close to Gray, who seemed only too happy to wrap his arm around her. She offered him her coffee cup and he peered into it suspiciously in the fading light.

"Would you like some coffee to go with your cream?" he asked.

"Very funny. You could have just said no thank you."

He took the cup before she could completely pull it away, tipped it to his lips and drank.

"Mmm, rich and creamy." Bending his lips to hers he murmured, "Just like you."

Heat burst deep within Reed and blossomed outward, reaching all her extremities like the lightning from the afternoon. A gasp barely escaped her lips before Gray captured it with his mouth, his lips warm and demanding. Gasp turned to moan as his arm tightened around her. *So fast.* How could he do that to her so fast? Mind and body still reeled from forty-eight hours of loving and there seemed to be no end in sight. God help her.

A sharp jab poking her in the side made Reed jump and break the kiss.

"Making out like teenagers. Disgusting, I tell you." Dennis's laughing voice dissipated the last of the fog cloaking Reed's mind.

"They're just jealous," Gray said.

Dennis laughed. "Oh, so they can hear us? About time. We were getting ready to toss a bucket of water on you two."

Friendly laughter echoed around the campfire. Reed looked around, grateful for the fading light. Ranch hands and guests gathered in groups. Without counting, Reed guessed close to twenty people were there and more strolled across the lawn in the gathering dusk. Although she saw mostly adults, there were a few families as well. The teenagers tried to look bored and the younger kids dashed down to help toss wood on the flames.

"So, is the point here to be social?" Reed asked.

"Sure. There will be some singing, maybe even a little dancing. The slow romantic kind."

That could be fun. Reed leaned into Gray's side.

"All right you two, we need to chat before you run off to snog some more."

A woman stood before them, dressed in lime-green jeans with a matching rabbit fur vest over a long sleeved white t-shirt. The words 'Save a Horse, Ride a Cowboy' boldly marched down the arm and Reed tilted her head to make sure she read it right. *Oh. My. God.*

The woman looked at her arm and laughed, the sound rich and throaty. "Don't you just love Big and Rich?"

"Sure do," Gray agreed. "I like their outlook on that particular subject."

Reed ignored Gray and asked the woman, "What may we do for you?"

"Huh?"

"You said you wanted to talk before we go...what was that word again?"

"Oh. Snog. It means to make out."

What was that accent? Not Aussie, but not quite British either. "Where are you from?" Reed let her curiosity override her normal courtesy.

"New Zealand, but all that's beside the point. We need to talk." The woman looked from one to the other. The log was crowded. "You have a choice, either you sit on that stud muffin's lap or I do," she told Reed.

Gray looked at Reed and opened his arms. No question. Reed stood and settled herself on his lap, arm around his neck. His lips on her throat made it even cozier as the woman took Reed's place on the log.

"By the way, the name's Patish...Patri... ah hell, just call me Tish."

"Reed and Gray." Reed extended a hand for shaking.

"Which is which?"

Gray laughed. "She's Reed."

"Gotcha." Tish nodded sharply then peered at their faces. "Okay, here's the thing, you two are putting out major vibrations. You've got pheromones kicking ass beyond what I've ever encountered, not to mention some other cosmic shit going on."

Reed bit her tongue. Apparently Tish had been

drinking and, combined with her accent, the words were a little hard to follow. She wondered what was in the coffee cup that swung around for emphasis.

"Where was I? Oh, yeah. You two." The woman pinned Reed with a look. "Stop fighting your fate. Once you accept your destiny you'll quit shaking up the balance." She turned her sherry-colored eyes on Gray. "Be patient. She'll come around. Hopefully a little sooner, now. Oh, and appreciate her for who she is today. The past is the past. You're both different people now."

Reed stared at the woman with wild curly hair. Twisted corkscrews of deep brunette with auburn highlights tumbled thickly from under a straw cowboy hat, fashionably unfinished on the brim and curled up on the sides. Reed wished she could just stick a hat on her head and look that great. Not to mention the lime jeans fit her form as if tailored. Tish wore her sexuality with easy grace. Even now Dennis eyed her and Reed could see him trying to find a way to strike up a conversation.

"Thank you, Tish," Gray said. "I've been trying to convince her, but it's only been forty-eight hours."

"Well, slow down! You're gonna burn out if you keep blazing this bright. Save some for the wedding, man!" Tish slapped a hand to her head. "Men. Going on like rabbits with even less sense," she muttered.

"Tish!" one of her friends called.

"Hold on, you old bat!" she called back. "Crazy girls. We're up here for a week to get away from men, and what do they want to do? Flirt with the cowboys. Go figure. Silly moos. Anyhow, we'll be here all week and I want to talk to you more when I'm sober. Tonight is fun time." Tish stood and slapped a hand on Gray's shoulder. "So, we good to go, now?" She waited for Reed and Gray to nod. "Good. Smashing. Just ducky. Be good, or rather, be wicked."

"Tish!" another one called out. Another accent, Reed noted. Scottish? Where did these women come from?

"I'm coming. Keep your knickers on," Tish said and was answered with laughter. She turned to Dennis. "You're taken, but," she stepped past him to Stuart, "you aren't. Come with me," she ordered and grabbed his hand.

The last Reed saw of Stuart he was in the middle of the group of forty-something women reported to be from Boulder as Dennis spluttered indignantly.

~ * ~

Gray waltzed Reed out of the circle of firelight. She floated in his arms just like she belonged there. Well, she did. "Come with me," he said quietly in her ear then took her hand and led her away from the campfire.

"Where?"

He resisted the urge to say, *everywhere*. "I want to show you something." He led her back to the main lodge where the truck was still parked. Opening the door he lifted her to the seat. Her serious eyes watched him and he nearly gave in to the desires that'd left him aching since she'd sat on his lap. "Scoot over or pay a penalty," he joked.

"Right." She laughed, but scooted anyway. "I might like your penalty." Taking off her hat, she fluffed her hair.

"Insatiable." He pulled her up against his side when she would have slid to the far side of the truck.

"Look who's talking."

Her little hand rested on his thigh and he wanted to move it higher.

"Where are we going?" she asked as he started up the truck.

Gray drove slowly, the truck bouncing over the road to the pastures. Seldom maintained, the road required four-wheel drive, horse, or foot. "There's a special spot, just over that low ridge ahead."

The headlights flashed briefly on a rise in the road before dipping low again. Gray hated that the road required two hands on the steering wheel. A barbed wire fence hugged the rugged track on the left. Sleepy lows from the cattle drifted through the partially lowered window.

"Smells like cows," Reed commented.

Gray glanced over and in the light of the dashboard saw her wrinkle her little nose. "Cattle, darling, they're called cattle."

"Right. What did Tish call them? Moos. Silly moos."

Gray chuckled and navigated around one particularly deep rut, probably cut by the spring run-off. He'd have to talk to Dustin about that. A little maintenance needed to happen.

"What's out here?" Reed asked him as she craned her neck, trying to peer through the dark. Rapidly fading light made it hard to see beyond the twin beams of light from the front of the truck.

"You'll see."

"Hmm."

The truck eased up over the swell of the small

ridge and then the lights from the ranch disappeared behind them. Just a little further...

A few minutes later, he found the flat area he wanted, turned so the rear of the truck was aimed down the valley and shut off the engine. "We're here."

"We're where?" Reed looked around.

"Okay, so maybe in the dark, from inside the truck, it doesn't look like much. Let's see it from the outside." Gray opened the door and stepped out.

The sharp scent of pine filled the cooling night air. Still warm, the air was soft, a welcome change from the burning heat of the day. He offered her a hand, then closed the door when she stood beside him.

"Now look," he said and pulled her back against his chest.

"I see...a few lights down low. I can't see the ranch buildings, and I can't hear anything other than a slight breeze in the aspens behind us."

"Right. Quiet. Solitude. Peace. Isn't it beautiful?"

"I guess," she sounded dubious. "I'd like to see it in daylight."

"You will."

"I will?"

"At sunrise even."

"What do you mean?"

"Hang on now," he said, then lifted her to sit on the side of the truck.

"Gray! You just can't go flinging me around like a sack of potatoes."

"More like a feather pillow." He grinned up at her. "Swing your legs over."

He braced a foot on the rear wheel then launched himself over the side and into the bed of the truck. "We're gonna watch the stars tonight and count as many shooting ones as we can."

"How cold does it get out here at night?"

"We won't be cold. It's a warm night, but I have sleeping bags and blankets. Careful now." He reached for a box near the tail gate and lifted the lid. A quick rummage produced the battery lantern and switched it on low.

"Oh."

He grinned at the soft exhale that escaped like a breathy sigh. Blake had done well. A filled air-bed was tucked between the wheel wells, and what he recognized as two extra large sleeping bags were zipped together. Bumps under the bags could only be pillows. Another box presumably held more blankets and a tarp just in case a rogue rainstorm rolled through. Not likely. The elements had already erupted in their late afternoon tantrum.

"This looks like a regular love nest," Reed commented.

"Perfect for not only counting stars, but sending them into orbit as well. Go ahead, sit down."

"Don't you mean lie down?"

"Need help with your boots?"

"Sure, why not?"

Reed settled back on the soft bed and lifted a foot. Gray pulled off the boot and held her foot. She lay back and closed her eyes.

"Who knew I could ever like a foot massage?" Her sigh of acceptance made him smile. Having dreamed of this so often, it seemed it was taking longer than expected to break through her defenses, and each little sign thrilled him.

"Other foot," he told her.

With a wicked grin, she dropped one foot and raised the other obediently. She made him want to laugh constantly. His blood felt as if tiny bubbles invigorated him and he let his gaze follow the line of her pale-skinned leg. "Like the view."

"You looking up my skirt again?"

"Every chance I get."

"That's my boy."

"Teasing?" Gray pulled her boot off and dropped it in the bed of the truck.

"I'm feeling relaxed." Strangely enough, Reed realized it was true. It also emphasized even more how uptight she'd been. Time with her friends had helped. It was the most relaxed moment they'd had in months, perhaps years. In truth, she just realized how much she'd missed having Ian and Dennis at the house. The easy camaraderie had been lacking at work. Maybe Troy wasn't such a crackpot for scheduling this trip.

"Make some room for me, huh?"

Reed rolled and scooted around on the air mattress until there was room for Gray to stretch out beside her. He'd removed his boots as well.

"Are you warm enough?" he asked. "We have blankets." He turned off the lantern.

"I'm comfortable. Especially if I do this." She lifted his arm and cuddled against his side, head on his shoulder.

"Hmm." His approval rumbled under her cheek. "This always keeps me warm."

"So. Other than running away from everyone, what are we doing here?" she asked.

"We need some quiet time. Just the two of us. No phones, no walls, no neighbors or anyone else to worry about. Just you and me."

"I like the sound of that. Time to slow down and savor?"

"Exactly."

"Thank you." She heaved a deep sigh. "I feel better already."

"Look up at the sky," he said softly.

Reed shifted until her head was pillowed on his bicep, his arm resting across her body. The night sky held just a trace of deep blue from the fading sunset. Stars dotted the heavens.

"Not much longer and it will be black with only the stars. See?" He pointed toward the west. "There's only a sliver of moon left. Tomorrow there won't be a moon, and the next night you'll see the new moon."

"But the stars," Reed breathed in wonder. "So many..." How easy it was to forget the vast wonder of the heavens when one lived in the city. "I'd forgotten." Just like she'd forgotten so many things. *Like friends.* "I've always had trouble with the constellations. I can pick out the obvious ones like Orion, the Pleiades and the Big Dipper, but I can never find the others."

"I'm not much better, but I've always liked that grouping."

Reed followed his finger.

"Oh look!" she stabbed a finger at the sky. "Is that...?" A tiny point of light flew across the heavens then faded.

"Make a wish...don't tell me."

Reed closed her eyes. *I want to know my dream.*

"Did you wish?"

"Did you?" she asked.

"I did, even though all my dreams have come true. Well, almost."

"Tell me of your dreams. The ones without me in them," she added.

Gray shifted and gathered her in his arms. "Tough to do. All my dreams point to you, or include you, or prepared the way for you."

"Have you lived your whole life, as you said, working toward now?"

"Yes. From the first time I saw you in my dream, you're all I've ever wanted."

A man she hadn't known until two days ago had built his life around her. It was humbling and confusing. "Then why--"

"Why the driving ambition? The drive for wealth?"

"Yes."

"So our life together would be comfortable. I don't want to watch you grow old before your time. I watched my parents struggle and work hard. The ranch is successful now, but when we were young it wasn't. Dude, or guest, ranches weren't my grandfather's dream, so when my dad took over, it wasn't in great shape. We all worked to make it a success, just barely scraping by for years. We weren't poor, exactly. We always had food on the table and a roof, but we didn't have the little luxuries, either. Things slowly improved and about fifteen years ago it started to show a profit. Even now, the ranch is hard work. Not like it was, but the family still all pitches in. Except me. I don't pull my weight here."

"You work hard elsewhere."

Gray shrugged. "The family doesn't see it that way, but they're doing well enough without me."

There was an odd note in his voice. She recognized it. "You miss them, don't you?" Most likely because she had the same feeling about her friends.

"I guess I do. Which leads us back to here."

"What's unique about here? You mean this very spot where we are right now?"

"Yes."

Reed rested in his arms. This spot meant something special to him. She could wait. Just being with him was enough. Too much had happened in too short a time.

Gray cuddled her close and kissed her hair.

"This spot...this is where..."

Reed hugged him when his words faltered.

He tried again. "I once saw a program on TV where a couple had their bedroom on the top floor of the house. They'd remodeled the attic. They liked the outdoors and, on nights when it was too hot to sleep indoors, they could slide their bed out onto a balcony. The bed was on rails and they could just roll it out to the porch and lie like this and stare at the stars. That image has been with me a long time."

"You want to build a house here?"

"You're fast. Yes. I want us to build a house here. A home. But I didn't know--don't know--if you'd like it here. I could build the businesses and get the jet and acquire condos and other homes, but this one just felt like going too far. I have a vision, but I want it to be your vision too. Does that make sense?"

"This is close to your home. Your roots. You

want it to be perfect."

"Yes. And without you it won't be."

Reed rubbed her head against his shoulder. "The dream. Your dream, my dream. How does it all come together? What does it mean?"

"I know what I want it to mean," Gray said with a smile Reed could feel. "What do you want it to mean?"

"I don't know. I need time Gray."

"I know."

They lay staring at the sky for a long time, the sky darkening to black velvet with diamonds scattered across it. Night sounds came to them. The hoot of an owl, the scurry of small animals through the brush, a breeze swishing aspen leaves together.

"It's so beautiful," Reed said quietly.

"I'd hoped you'd think so. I brought a bottle of wine. Would you like some?"

"Sure."

"But first, it's been too long," Gray said, and turned to face her.

His hand, large and warm cupped her head, his fingers threading into her hair. Wanting to touch him, she raised a hand to his smooth cheek. He'd shaved after their bath together. Remembering the intimacy of cuddling in the water, she smiled just before his lips brushed over hers. So light. A delicious shiver slowly worked its way down her body, warmth pooling in her center.

"Gray," she softly begged.

With infinite tenderness, he kissed her, long and sweet. Comforting warmth slowly infused Reed's body, so different from the fast and furious heat, no less welcome. Gray's hand traveled through her hair, down her neck, back, waist to hip, coming to rest on the rounded curve of her backside. Breaking the kiss with a sigh and a nibble, he eased back.

"So beautiful," he whispered.

"You can't see me in the dark." She stroked his cheek.

Gray leaned back. "Oh yes I can. Such pale skin, luminescent in the night. You glow."

"Must be from growing up in Livermore. We lived just a mile away from the Lab."

"Very funny. Most of the true radiation work was done in Nevada and in the Pacific." He pressed a kiss on her nose and leaned across her. "I think you'll like this." Twisting slightly, he reached into a basket behind her.

"What is it?"

Glass clinked against glass.

"You'll have to taste. A special vintage."

The airbed shifted when he sat up, and she saw the glint of starlight reflect off a bottle. He also had a glass which he handed to her. Reed rose up on an elbow and watched while he pulled the cork and poured the liquid.

"Okay, sit up now." He took the glass from her so it wouldn't spill. "We're going to do this right."

"And what is right?"

"Was last night your first experience with tantric sex?"

"Yes." She blushed at the memory. As close as she'd ever come to a spiritual experience, the residual good feelings in all probability contributed to the peace she felt at the moment.

He crossed his legs. "Now, come sit, facing me, legs around me."

She sat in the well made by his crossed legs and his arm held her close. So strong. It seemed he used little effort to hold her.

"We're doing this backwards. In the dream you offer me the cup."

She heard the teasing tone of his voice and smiled. "Actually, I taste it before you show up."

"Well. I never suspected." Gray held the glass to her lips and slowly tipped it.

Reed inhaled the bouquet and her heart beat picked up speed. A tiny buzz, warm and exciting, stroked the back of her neck. The liquid touched her tongue, and she sipped.

Gray lowered the glass and let her roll the wine around on her tongue.

Reed held it against the roof of her mouth and absorbed the flavor. The tingle grew stronger as she swallowed.

"Mmm, this tastes good and--I can't place it...but it's familiar somehow. May I have another sip?"

"Of course." Gray tipped the glass again, his eyes watching her, waiting for her opinion. Something told her it was very important to him.

Reed took a bigger sip and savored the wine. Rich, full, a hint of raspberry, a note of chocolate. Trying to catch a memory, she closed her eyes. Not only did the wine taste familiar, the pose felt the same. It was as if the last time she'd tasted it, Gray held her just this way--the tingle on the back of her neck grew to surround her body.

Swallowing the wine, it hit her. "The dream."

"Yes." Triumph in his voice, his next question followed, sounding as eager as a schoolboy's. "Do you like it?"

"How? I mean, yes, it's wonderful, but where?" Reed opened her eyes to see the gleam of Gray's teeth as he smiled at her.

"Hold this." He handed her the wineglass, reached behind him and switched on the lamp. In the low light, he picked up the wine bottle and held it so she could see the label.

Reed's heart flipped over. It was the dream. As if the artist had caught the two of them, from the waist up, in their shady green glade. Painted in watercolors, it held a dream-like quality, capturing the very moment at which he wrapped an arm around her waist and she held the golden goblet up to him, his hand over hers. Pure romance, She couldn't imagine how anyone had captured the image so perfectly.

"Oh." The word came out of her on a long breath. All other words failed her.

Gray leaned forward and lightly kissed her.

"I couldn't find just the right wine anywhere. I searched. From France to Australia. The closest I came was California. Paso Robles. With a little blending and a superior winemaker this is as close as I can get."

"You... you...made this?" Reed stared up at him then peered at the label. *Clocha Lomhara.* "I've never heard of the winery."

"Privately owned. Very select clientele. Not mass produced. Only about one hundred and forty cases a year."

"You own the winery? Just to make this wine?" Just because of the dream? The very thought made her dizzy as her heartbeat kicked into overdrive.

"Just to make this wine. It's only been the last few years it started tasting right. This bottling is the best so far. You like it?"

"I love it. Wow. I can't believe you bought a winery just to make so few cases." Reed took a long drink. The wine was heady, like velvet on her tongue. It would go great with the finest chocolate or the best cut of steak. "It's fabulous. I'm stunned at the lengths you went to." For her. For them. She could only stare at him in amazement. Either he was insane, or he had supreme confidence in their bond.

Men had brought her bottles of fine wine before, but they'd never made it for her. Much less bought a winery specifically to do so. The lengths this man was willing to go to, just to win her over, were astounding. And yet he didn't seem one bit deranged.

She gulped, trying to clear the lump suddenly lodging in her throat. Tears of wonder stung the corners of her eyes.

Gray filled the glass again and set the bottle down. He took the glass from Reed and drank.

"Mmm." He let the liquid slide down his throat. "Only you taste better."

Bending his lips to hers, he found the wine on their lips as sweet as his memory of the dream.

Reed slid her arms around his neck, clinging to him, trembling. "I just can't believe--"

"Believe. It's how much I believe in the dream. Believe with me." The emotion suddenly clogging his throat made it hard to speak, made him want to pour out his every hope and desire, confess the complete depths of his love for her. He also knew when to pull back in negotiations and let things simmer. She was coming around and he had faith she'd find her way to him. As she'd done before. As he'd done before.

"Oh Gray," she said and kissed him back. "I want, more than anything, to believe."

Gray tipped the glass of wine to her lips and watched as she sipped, their gazes locked on each other. Impatient to be in her, a part of her, he drained the glass and set it aside. Mellow and content, yet craving more, he settled her extra securely on his lap, arms wrapped around her back. Her little feet crossed behind him and her arms held tight to his shoulders. The wine, her kiss, her touch, all together at last. With the stars overhead, the world was perfect.

Seeking her skin, he tugged her shirt from the waistband of her skirt until he felt the warmth of her. Unable to stop himself, he kissed and nibbled on the soft sweet skin her neck, breathing in her scent, filling his senses as much as he could with every part of her.

"Isn't this position better naked?" Reed asked him.

Progress. Pleased, he nipped her earlobe. "Much."

"Well?"

Oh, torturing her would be so much fun. Teaching her more Tantra even more fun. "Patience."

"He's been trying to get my clothes off since the moment we met, and now he says 'patience'," Reed grumbled.

She was too precious, and all his. With a smile against her throat he reminded her, "Tonight is for savoring."

"Yes." She melted against him, testing his resolve to go slowly. At least this time he had a handful of condoms. Good thing Blake was prepared. That should please Reed even more.

One hand supporting her back, he slowly unbuttoned her over shirt with the other. Though she squirmed and groaned from time to time, she fell in with his plan. By the time she'd managed to drag his shirt off over his head, only her bra remained on top. White, it enhanced the glow of her skin, luminous in the clear mountain night.

Starlight reflected in her eyes and Gray found himself remembering what seemed like a thousand lifetimes with her. The Celtic forest, Rome, France, Spain... The dream specters all swirled together, but one fact was clear--they'd found each other over and over again.

Wanting more of everything...her, her body, visions of their lives together...Gray unhooked her bra and watched as she shrugged the garment away. Physical closeness seemed to be the key, and if not, well at least it provided other benefits. So far, it was the only time she completely opened to him and all their outside concerns disappeared.

"Reed..." Gray touched a finger to her collarbone and traced the line. "You're exquisite. Always have been, always will be."

"Just kiss me," she whispered, her hand resting against his cheek. "Kiss me and make me stop thinking."

The warmth of her breasts crushed against his chest felt like searing brands. If it meant being together like this...she leaned into him and pressed her lips to his. The taste of her drove all thought from his mind. An addict, craving what only she could provide, he released the fastenings on her skirt and laid her back on the soft bed. Love and instinct drove him to worship her with lips and hands.

Though he'd already touched each tiny patch of skin, he began the journey again, seeking out this hollow where a kiss made her sigh, that curve where a suckle made her moan, the crest of her breast, the sweet berry of her nipple where a long lick followed by the swirl of his tongue made her writhe.

Four hands tugged at unwanted garments. Two soft hands guided and conveyed orders. One soft, sweet voice cried out his name over and over again. Two bodies melded into the mysteries of the universe and became a single entity.

His queen. His love. His destiny. All bundled up in one glorious woman.

Sixteen

Held close to Gray's heart, Reed woke, dreamily wondering for a moment where she was and what had woken her. A chirp, as if in inquiry, came from nearby. She slowly opened her eyes and in the soft gray light before dawn, saw a bird perched on the side of the truck.

Tiny, it could have fit in the palm of her hand. Mostly white, it had black feathers on the top of its head, like a cap. Sharp black eyes considered the scene, the little head cocked. Reed stared back at the mini inquisitor when it chirped, as if asking a question.

Reed had the maddest urge to reach out a hand and see if it would perch on her finger. Like Mary Poppins. A small snort of laughter escaped and the bird shook its feathers as if offended. Quick wings spread and, in a wink, it disappeared.

Morning. The sun must have just cleared the unseen eastern horizon. It still had to climb high enough to crest the mountains, but the sky was lightening steadily. Reed inhaled the combination of Gray's warm scent and the land around them.

Sharp pine, dry dust, sweet grass, and even the lingering scent of cows. Cattle. No exhaust or pollution. Reed drew the clean air deep and pushed her cold nose under the flannel-lined sleeping bag. Cool now, it would warm up quickly enough. But dry. No dew. Even better. And strangely familiar. Had she once crossed the plains in a Conestoga wagon? Another dream or a memory?

Problem. Reed almost groaned at her body's demands. Leaving the warm nest was not what she wanted to do. Knowing there was no way she could slide out of Gray's arms, the sleeping bag, or the bed of the truck without waking him, Reed kissed his neck. Sleepily responding, he held her closer. Her lips teased his ear and he smiled.

"Gray," she whispered. "I need to get up for a minute."

"Hmm?"

"Let me up, please. I promise to come back." *And warm my cold body on your hot one.* She grinned at the thought.

His arms reluctantly loosened. "Wear your boots," he mumbled.

"Why?"

"Rattlesnakes."

Great. Reed lowered the zipper on her side of the nest and eased into the cool air. Already the promise of the day's heat could be felt. Not uncomfortable, but she did reach for Gray's shirt. It was big enough the tails covered her to mid-thigh, and it buttoned across her chest with room to spare. Even better.

Considering her options for getting out of the truck, she sat on the side and tugged her boots on. Over the wheel looked like her best choice if she didn't want to make a lot of racket lowering the tailgate. But first, she opened the lid of one box and found the extra blankets they hadn't needed. Stepping carefully to the other side of the truck she found more practical items. Toilet paper and wet wipes. A man who was prepared. Maybe he was worth keeping.

Romance was great, and no one had ever done anything more romantic than buying a winery to make wine just for her, but basics were, well, just basics. She tore off a length of the toilet paper and swung herself over the side of the truck as gently as she could.

"You okay?" Gray's question was followed with a yawn.

"Yes," she answered, and hurried into the trees.

Climbing out of the truck was easy, she realized a few minutes later. Getting back in was another trick. Hands on hips, she circled it looking for options. There were running boards, but only to get into the cab. There was the bumper but it was still fairly high for her short legs. How had Gray done it the night before?

The small hairs on the back of her neck prickled and Reed froze. Her back was to the road they'd driven in on last night and somehow, she just knew, someone was there. The birds had quieted, but not fallen entirely silent. She hadn't heard a sound, had she? She listened. A soft snort from a horse and the jingle of reins.

"Gray, I think we have a visitor." She didn't want to turn around. Even more embarrassment was sure to follow. Folding the shirt tight about her, she hoped it covered her rear. What a sight she must make, standing there in her boots, Gray's shirt and her hair sticking out at all angles. But with the shirt so short, there was no way she'd try and climb up over the wheel on this side of the truck. Pretending this happened every day, she casually walked around to the far side of the truck before turning around.

Once she was shielded, the horse moved forward at a slow walk. Blake. Gray's brother had just seen her nearly naked.

Peeking over the truck, she watched as Blake rode closer and tipped his hat.

"Mornin'," he said pleasantly as if seeing nothing unusual.

"Good morning," she answered.

"Blake." Gray could be heard shifting and Reed saw his head rise. "What are you doing here?"

"Wake up call with coffee," Blake said and tossed a thermos onto the bed.

"Reed?" Gray looked around and saw her standing outside the truck.

She gave him a tight smile and he stretched to look over the side. His quick grin made her smile relax a little.

"Need help getting back in?"

"In a minute." She nodded toward Blake.

Gray turned back to his brother. "You still here?"

Blake snorted. "You're welcome."

Reed didn't see the complete nonverbal communication, but she figured the brothers had been through similar routines before.

"We'll be back," Gray looked back at Reed with awakening heat in his eyes, "sometime this morning. In time for breakfast, at least."

Blake shook his head and tipped his hat to Reed again, this time with a wink. "See y'all back at the ranch." Pulling gently on the reins, he turned the horse and left at the same slow walk he'd come in on.

"Been waiting all his life to say that line?" Reed asked.

"Yup. Turn around." Gray reached over the side of the truck and lifted her up by the armpits.

Once Reed sat on the side of the truck he steadied her, then helped her turn to the east. Instead of diving back into bed, he sat beside her, an arm around her waist.

"Aren't you cold?" Not that she really minded him being naked.

"Not a bit." His grin made her blush. "You?"

"Me? Cold? Oh, no, not at all." Not with her hormones sending out wild messages.

He chuckled and kissed her cheek. "We'll get to that in a bit. Look around."

The eastern sky, clear of all clouds, was beginning to lighten from a deep blue. To the left, a mountain rose, decorated with aspen and a few scrub pines fading to lichen-covered rock and low shrubs. To the south, a ledge opened up, a meadow covered in wildflowers, gently sloping down to the wider valley below. To the west, the night sky retreated, a few stars hanging on above the mountains closing off the side of the valley.

"It's beautiful out here. And not one siren or horn blaring."

"Just a few birds and the cattle. Did you hear the owl last night?"

"I did." She leaned against him, head on his shoulder. "And the little bird this morning. He had a cute little black cap on his head."

"Blackcap Chickadee. If you're patient, you can get them to take seed from your hand."

"Really?"

"Um hmm. Cute little things."

"I want to try that. Have any seed?"

"It takes time. You have to put out a bird feeder and train them to come to you."

"Oh."

"As soon as we start building you can put out a feeder."

"Cool." Reed paused and hung her head with a sigh. "You're doing it again."

"Hmm?"

"Talking about the future as if we're already married."

"It's a natural conclusion. I'm not letting you get away. I'll let you get used to the idea, but you aren't getting rid of me, lady. You're stuck with me." Gray slid an arm under her legs.

Squeaking in protest, Reed nonetheless threw her arms around his neck. "I swear, one of these times you're going to throw out a disk or rip a muscle. You can't just keep throwing me around."

He merely grinned and lowered her down to the bed. "You're not heavy. Try lifting a cow sometime."

"Well, when you put it like that..." She tightened her arms up around his neck as he lay down beside her again.

"So, what do you think of my little corner of paradise now?"

"I like it. As long as the relatives don't make a habit of dropping by before sun up. Lord, what will Blake say? I was on the other side of the truck so I know he saw my outfit."

"He won't say anything if he knows what's good for him. I have a few secrets he'd like me to keep. Aren't you glad you wore my shirt? You look very cute in it, by the way. You look even cuter out of it." He kissed her and started releasing the buttons.

"What about my boots?" She gasped when his lips moved to her throat, following the opened shirt.

"They're cute too."

~ * ~

The clear sky was noticeably lighter when Gray dropped Reed off near their room.

"I'll see you down at breakfast. I have to get the camping gear put away," he told her, though he was reluctant to leave her even that long.

"Sure you don't need help?"

"I got it. Dress for riding." He kissed her until she melted against him. "Don't be long."

"Hmm?"

"Getting dressed," he reminded her.

"Oh. Right. Brains. Why do you steal my brains? I actually have good ones, or did until I met you."

He loved it when she couldn't think about anything other than him. The lines on her face softened and her eyes promised erotic delights as much as a safe home to return to. "I know you do. Wear the camisole. I want to see you in tight jeans and the camisole."

"You just want to think about the words printed on it."

"I want to see if it's true."

"Does this mean there'll be tequila on the menu tonight?"

"We know wine works." He kissed her nose. *What a blush.* He loved doing that to her.

"Gray, what are we doing?"

He also loved the feel of her fingers in his hair,

combing, soothing, possessing. "We're being silly and making lots of love. We're swimming in endorphins."

"Right. Got it."

The look on Reed's face was perfect dreaminess. A look he wanted to see on her always. Gray cupped her face with both hands and kissed her long and lingeringly. Three nights. Only three nights together. So many more to live for.

"Aren't they so cute?"

Gray felt Reed stiffen, then sigh and pull away, breaking the kiss. Looking up he saw Reed's coworkers standing on the porch of the lodge. Sam had spoken, Roger's arm around her shoulder, a silly look on her face. Funny, that look was similar to Reed's. Roger looked a little twitter-pated himself.

"And where were our little lovebirds all night?" Ian asked.

"Looks to me like they went parking and fell asleep." Dennis sipped from his coffee cup.

Troy snorted in disgust and strolled down the steps. "Anybody else ready for breakfast?"

"Get some sleep last night, Troy?" Reed turned and glared at him. "You should have had plenty of peace and quiet."

Troy stopped and glared over his shoulder at the burst of laughter from their co-workers.

"I just discovered you two only covered other noises. No, I didn't get much sleep," he growled and stalked off toward the main lodge.

"What's his problem?" Reed squeezed Gray's hand and stepped away.

He felt the loss of her immediately, but knew it was for the best. There was work to be done.

"The kiwi gal blew him off," Sam explained.

Gray laughed with them and climbed back in the truck. "See you down at the lodge."

Driving slowly, he circled down to a storage shed and started unloading the camping gear. Blake joined him a few minutes later from the main lodge.

"I take it everything worked out well," Blake casually commented.

"Like you haven't done the same at least three times already this summer."

"That's why I know what to pack." Blake grinned as he lifted the plastic box holding the blankets from the tail gate and carried it inside the building.

Gray unzipped the sleeping bags. "Where do these get hung out to air?"

"There's a line inside. Hand me one."

Working together, they soon had everything stowed away.

"I need the truck," Blake told him. "Mom wants to see you anyway."

"About anything in particular?"

"Seems you ran out on some business yesterday."

"Ah. Yes." He really did need to concentrate on the ranch. Or at least give a good impression of it. "Do you think I'm crazy?" Now why was he asking his little brother that question?

"About her? Sure you are. I don't know her well, but I like her. She's a lot more genuine than some of the others you've dated."

And since he was going for broke, "I plan to marry her. Soon."

"Is that why you went out there?"

Gray glanced in the direction of his parcel. "I'm starting to get a vision of the house. I want her to be a part of planning and building it."

Blake's hand landed on his shoulder and squeezed. "Your dreams haven't been wrong yet. You've always been on course."

"Except when it came to Troy." Gray shook off the little cloud of doom.

"No, you knew. You just gave him the benefit of the doubt. You do that. You believe people are better than they are and you treat them that way. Sometimes they let you down."

"Such wise words from a little squirt." Gray turned and grinned at his brother.

"Well, if you need advice on women, just be sure you talk to me first. I fall in love all the time. At least once a week. I know all about heartbreak."

"I'll keep that in mind. You might consider taking a break and meditating to see if you can find clues that will lead you to the right one."

"I might." Blake laughed and climbed into the truck.

Gray slapped the side of the vehicle and waited until he pulled away. With a glance up the hill, Gray stuck his hands in his pockets and strolled toward the lodge. He could grab one of Dustin's shirts and worry about his shower later. Then again, the thought of Reed wearing his shirt, just a little while ago, was very sexy. Maybe he wouldn't change.

Seventeen

"Good morning, Mom," Gray said. He found her in the office with a cup of coffee.

"Good morning," she said, barely glancing up from the computer.

"Sorry I ran out of here yesterday."

"I'm sure you had a good reason."

"I told Blake about the lightning strike near the upper lodge. He's going to look into it to see if there's any damage."

Ah, that got her attention. His mother looked up at him, an inscrutable expression on her face.

"I'm not sure if it actually hit the building or just next to it." Gray helped himself to a cup of coffee.

"What's the rest of the story?"

"Hmm?"

"I assume you had some sort of intuition. What sent you running?"

"Oh. That. Turns out Reed was in the bathtub. I got her out just as the bolt hit."

She sat back in the chair. "So that's it? That's all? Is she that stupid?"

Gray narrowed his eyes and Sora looked down.

"She didn't grow up around electrical storms. She knew the basics, just hadn't thought about the tub and sink connection."

Sora shrugged. "Just common sense."

"Sure it is, if you live in the state with the

second highest number of lightning strikes. Not if you live in an area that rarely sees such storms. I'm sure she knows far more about earthquake safety than you're even aware of."

"Fine. I'm sorry."

Not much of an apology, but it would do for now. "So. We were looking at the financials. I didn't see any problems. The ranch is running comfortably well in the black. What do you want from me?"

"Is it too much to ask for you to pay attention to your family for more than five minutes at a time?"

"I'm here."

"Until breakfast? Until her riding lesson? Until when, Gray?"

"I'm here. And she'll be family soon so I'd appreciate it if you'd make an effort to get to know her."

"Really? How can you be sure?"

Gray gave her a long level stare.

"Right. The dream."

"She's coming to accept it. She's had the dream, more than once now. It's meant to be."

"Is that why you took her out to your parcel?"

"Remember how I told you I couldn't visualize plans for a house?"

"Yes."

"Last night I began to see the outline. It feels right."

Sora stared at him for a long moment before reaching for her coffee again. "I have you believing in dreams come to life, and Blake who doesn't seem concerned beyond the next one-week love affair. I need some focus from my sons."

"Why? Things are stable and working well."

"Dustin and I have been talking about expanding the resort side. Taking it more upscale."

"Why? Business is good."

"You're the businessman. Think."

Gray glanced out the window. Reed's red hair couldn't be missed. She was on her way down the hill with the group from work.

"If you marry this woman, will you build the house and live here?"

"Hmm?" Gray turned back to his mother.

"Will you live here after you marry?" she repeated with a touch of impatience.

"That's my plan, but I think she should have a say in it. She has a career. People count on her."

"Troy."

"That part doesn't thrill me. We have to work through it."

"What does she do?"

"She's his Financial Officer. The head bean counter."

"Is she any good?"

"So I've heard."

"Maybe she'll have a place here after all," Sora said and waved him toward the door. "Go on, get your breakfast."

"Sure thing. See you later."

~ * ~

Gray found Dustin on crutches, slowly navigating down the stairs.

"And just what do you think you're doing hauling your sorry ass out of bed?" Gray asked quietly. Didn't need Mom more upset.

"I'm tired of layin' around. There's nothin' on TV, I can't concentrate on a book long enough to read more than a paragraph and I want to meet your woman."

Dustin paused on the stairs. Gray assumed it was to rest. Dustin made it seem like he did it to stare at Gray.

"She'll arrive in just a minute or two. I assume you're heading for the dining room?"

"Yes. I want some real breakfast and not the stupid porridge they keep bringin' me."

Gray almost asked him if he needed help, then bit his tongue. Despite the sweat popping out on his upper lip, Dustin wouldn't accept any aid.

Except for the dark hair, Dustin took after their father, a good, solid, Midwestern rancher type. An inch taller than Gray, he was also a few inches wider and all solid muscle from working just as hard as the ranch hands. Stern looking, he could play the slow-talking cowboy to perfection. Anyone who assumed the mind was just as slow found themselves sadly mistaken. And if a mule was stubborn... Gray shook his head. Dustin had more patience and more stubbornness than most men he knew.

Casually keeping in front of his brother, Gray kept pace with him down the stairs. Reed's laugh made both men look around as her entourage walked through the front door.

God she looked great. Was she wearing...? Hey, that was one of his shirts. He narrowed his eyes and she pulled the top away a little to show the neckline of the black camisole under the faded long sleeve denim shirt.

"First peep show of the morning?" Dustin muttered in his ear.

"Nope, but one of the better ones so far," Gray

said with a grin and closed the distance to wrap his arms around Reed and lift her for a kiss.

"He's making us all look bad," Ian complained. "Gina sees that and I'm toast."

"Then you should make an effort to sweep her off her feet more often." Dennis laughed.

"Before she gets much bigger, too," Sam added.

Gray set Reed down and smiled into her dreamy eyes.

"I hope you don't mind me borrowing another shirt. None of mine would, well, button properly," she said.

"I like the idea of your skin touching the cloth that touches me. Very sexy," he murmured in her ear.

"Anybody else feel like we've just entered a time warp and gone back to high school?"

"Just because you're jealous, Dennis, is no reason to be rude," Reed told him with her little nose stuck up in the air.

Gray kissed it and made her smile.

"Yeah, well I need more coffee before I can deal with all the sugar floating around," Dennis said with disgust and sauntered into the dining room.

"You two coming in?" Sam asked.

"I want to meet Dustin first. You go on ahead," Reed told them.

Gray smiled. Guess it didn't take many brains to figure out who the guy on crutches was.

"Dustin, I'd like you to meet Reed O'Brien," he said, and led Reed the few steps to where Dustin leaned against a wall.

"Pleased to meet you, Reed." Dustin shook the hand she presented.

"How's the injury doing?" She nodded at his legs.

"Just a scratch. The nurses are a worse pain." Still, Dustin looked around and spoke quietly.

"I understand. I don't know about you, but I'm starving. Are you joining us for breakfast?" Reed asked.

"That's my plan. Gray, go get us a table for two. I want to talk with this lady." Dustin waved for Reed to precede him into the dining room.

"I'll make that a table for three," Gray said and took Reed's hand to lead her in.

Reed sweetly fussed and helped Dustin settle his leg on a chair while Gray served up plates. He shared a tolerant smile with Kiri who shook her head and served up coffee and juice. Rachel would be along soon to hen peck her husband back to bed. The show would be fun.

"How are you enjoying the ranch?" Dustin asked Reed, as Gray set down a plate for him.

"So far so good. I'm a tad nervous about the pack trip though," she said quietly.

Gray set her plate down and she smiled up at him. "Thanks."

He kissed her, then went back for his food. Eager to hear why she was nervous he tossed eggs and sausage on his plate.

"The pack trip is no big deal," Dustin was telling her when Gray sat down. "You just sit on your horse and watch the scenery. The horses know the trail better than the wranglers."

"So tell me more about the ranch. I know there's more to it than letting tourists play Wild West," Reed said, as she cut into her sausages.

"We run around four hundred head of cattle

and have about sixty horses."

"Really? I didn't see that many horses in the stables. Where are the rest?"

"Some are out enjoying the pastures. We rotate them week to week or as needed."

"Tell me more," Reed said.

Gray watched while she drew out his normally quiet brother. Leaning on arms folded on the table she asked questions, nudging Dustin when he faltered. By the time they relaxed over coffee, Reed knew more about the workings of the ranch than most guests--everything from beef sales to using the helicopter to help with roundups.

"All right," Rachel said from behind Gray, making all three at the table jump. "You've had your fun, now back upstairs."

"Rachel, have you met Reed yet?" Gray said to his sister-in-law.

"No, haven't had the pleasure." Rachel smiled and extended a hand.

"Pleased to meet you. Sorry for keeping him from his rest." Reed returned the handshake and nodded at Dustin.

"It's a sign he's getting better. The conversation did him good, but now it's time to head back." Rachel gave him stern look.

"Nothing like getting nagged to death," Dustin muttered, but Gray caught the sly wink he sent Reed.

"Well, if I know men, you look tough and you'll complain all the way back to your bed, but the minute she walks out the door you'll be sleeping like a baby," Reed said.

Rachel laughed and Dustin frowned. Gray bit his lip, but a snicker still crept out. Reed had his brother pegged.

"Yeah, you cackle all you want, Gray," Dustin growled. "You'll get nagged too. Then we'll see who has the last laugh." Dustin heaved himself up onto his crutches. "Come by and visit me anytime, Reed. I'm sure you'll get tired of Mr. Charming sooner or later."

"Thanks. I'll make it a point," she assured him.

Gray leaned back and wrapped an arm around Reed's shoulder. They watched while Rachel chased a slow-moving Dustin out of the dining room and listened as she nudged him up the stairs.

"He was starting to look a bit peaked," Reed said and finished her coffee.

"Yeah, but it's the happiest he's looked since we arrived. It's been driving him crazy being confined to bed."

"I bet. I imagine he's all over the ranch all day long."

"He is. Ready for more riding lessons?"

"The horse kind?"

Gray smiled at the green-eyed sultry gaze directed at him. He leaned forward and unbuttoned the over shirt she wore until he could see the words printed on the camisole underneath.

"I wore it," she said.

"I want to see you not wearing it." He kissed her. "But I guess I'll have to wait. I don't suppose you could find one that says 'Wine makes my clothes fall off', eh?"

"I didn't notice one in the store."

"What are you going to do about sun protection today?"

"Gloves, your shirt, my hat, and yes, just the

barest amount of sunscreen on what's exposed." She didn't look happy about it.

"Good. Not that I don't like the freckles you picked up yesterday," he kissed her nose, "but I don't want to see you burned." He buttoned up the shirt again, all the way to the collar. "Shall we go find you a horse before the crowd gets there?"

"Lead on, Rowdy."

~ * ~

"How am I supposed to choose one?" Reed looked at the horses tied to the rail. She'd already tried four and none seemed like a good match. The old mare they'd had her on the day before was too docile and too old to make the pack trip. Reed had glared at Gray when he told her the horse was often used to teach youngsters and nervous adults.

"Maybe the horse should choose you. Walk the line and talk to each one."

Reed looked closely to see if he was joking. He looked sincere, so she shrugged and approached the first horse.

"This one is a gelding," Gray told her. "We call him Jack."

Gray had already given her the story of the American Quarter Horse and his knowledge of the bloodlines had made her eyes glaze over. Luckily he'd noticed and now stuck to nicknames.

Jack looked nice enough, but he was large and tried to nip her shoulder.

"Jack can be on the cranky side," Gray said and pushed the horse's head away.

"Next." Reed ducked under Jack's head and moved on.

"This is Mary," Gray introduced her to the horse. "Mary is a good solid riding horse. Doesn't spook easily."

"She's a pretty girl." Reed stroked her nose, but Mary turned away. "Playing shy or is she not interested?"

"Might be playing shy. Let's move on." Gray followed her to the next horse.

Reed saw him glance down the line of nearly twenty horses. He didn't sigh, exactly, but she had a feeling he thought maybe she was too picky. Gray had tried to put her on another gelding that seemed even less interested in moving than the mare the day before. Not the most experienced rider, Reed felt she could handle one with just a touch more spirit.

Halfway down the line Reed passed on a bay mare and came face to nose with a palomino gelding with a pale gold body and white mane and tail. Reed gave a small gasp of appreciation as the large brown eyes stared at her. She raised a hand and he dipped his head for her caress.

"Oh, he's beautiful," she said in awe.

Nickering softly, the horse looked for a treat in her other hand.

"That's right, Casanova." Gray chuckled. "You've captured another pretty maiden."

Reed laughed when the horse swished his tail as if irritated by Gray's comment. She ran her hands down the smooth coat and Casanova seemed to hug her, his head over her shoulder.

"Before we wed you two," Gray said dryly, "let's see how you do in the saddle." He untied the line and backed Casanova out into the corral, as the wranglers helped the other guests coming to the corral to choose mounts.

Reed let him help her up and adjust the

stirrups for her shorter legs.

"Cass," Gray held the halter and spoke to the horse, "this is my girl. You treat her well or we'll have words. Understand?"

Casanova snorted but nodded.

"Glad we understand each other." Gray patted his neck and came around to look up at Reed. "He also answers to Cass and sometimes needs a firm hand. Don't let him boss you around."

"Yes, sir." She grinned when he shook his head and stepped back, his expression hidden by the brim of his hat.

"Start with a walk," Gray told her.

Reed knew the routine. First, a walk around the large corral. When they circled back to Gray, he nodded. Trot next. Cass eased into the trot and let Reed get a feel for the movement before picking up the pace. By the time they completed the first circuit Reed felt comfortable and they completed a second circuit easily. Slowing to a walk, she steered Cass back to Gray.

"Looked good. How did that feel?" he asked.

Reed leaned forward and patted Cass's neck. "Wonderful. I think we're going to be good friends, aren't we Cass?"

She laughed when Gray blew out an exasperated breath.

"Damn horse. Don't think you can steal my woman."

Reed laughed when Cass snorted and pawed the ground. "Can we go for a real road test?"

Gray glanced at his watch and nodded. "Not too far, then we'll come back for lunch."

"Can Sam come with us?" Reed watched her friend circling the corral, looking bored with her mount's easy trot. Roger was off tinkering with the helicopter and Sam hadn't been invited to play. Troy was helping Stuart get comfortable in the saddle by talking him through the motions of riding. Ian and Dennis joked with a couple wranglers and some other guests.

"Sure. Go tell her while I get mounted."

Reed urged Cass forward and let him walk her over to Sam who pulled up her mare, a beautiful bay named Daisy.

"Well you found a pretty boy." Sam nodded with a grin.

"Casanova, meet Sam. I suppose you already know Daisy." Reed smiled when he nickered in greeting and Daisy replied. "Gray is taking me out for a less restricted ride and we want you to join us. We might get to gallop. Want to come?"

"Sure I won't be in the way?" Sam raised a brow.

"I invited you, didn't I?"

"Okay. Just had to tease. Yes, I'd love to."

"Ready?"

Reed and Sam both turned to see Gray on a large black horse. Reed lowered her sunglasses and looked him over carefully. Maybe Sam had the right idea. Cowboys could be pretty hot looking. Especially when they were also businessmen who were comfortable wearing suits made for the boardroom.

But right now, seeing Gray in his faded jeans, scuffed boots, a blue cotton shirt with the sleeves rolled to show strong forearms, and what she was sure was a custom made hat, Reed felt lightheaded and desperately wanted him to haul her off her horse and into his arms. Yup, she could appreciate both sides of his personalities. Boardroom or stables, she'd take him in either place. When his dark eyes fell on her, she quickly pushed her sunglasses back in place.

Gray nudged his horse over close to Reed and leaned sideways to speak quietly. "Look at me like that one more time and we leave Sam in the dust. I know how to make a bed in the forest, perfect for what I want to do to you right now."

As if to emphasize his point he shifted in the saddle and Reed looked down. Biting her lip she turned away, positive a flaming blush covered her entire body.

Reed cleared her throat. "Guess we should get going, huh?"

Gray laughed and led the way to the gate. One of the wranglers opened it for them and they rode through.

Reed tipped her hat to the ranch hand as she rode past and he tipped his hat back with a friendly wink.

EIGHTEEN

"Quite a woman."

Gray lifted the lunch tray from Dustin's lap and set it on a table before settling in an armchair. He stretched out his legs and rested them on a leather covered footstool.

Dustin eased his leg and leaned back against the pillows of the bed.

"She's pretty special," Gray agreed. The only thing he needed now was a blade of grass to chew on, a cigar and whiskey, or to tip his hat over his eyes for siesta. The long nights were catching up with him.

"So what's she doing with you?"

"Very funny. I'm just damn lucky I found her."

"And to think, if you hadn't stopped in Vegas you still would have met her."

"It's meant to be," Gray replied. He wasn't going to let Dustin annoy him.

"And she works for Troy. Not just any employee either, but his head bean counter. The woman with the keys to the vault. How is that going to work out?"

"She'll soon be too busy to work." Gray smiled with smug satisfaction. The rate they kept going, it was just a matter of weeks before she turned up pregnant. Might even already be pregnant, despite the condoms they'd used last night. The thought made his grin widen.

"What?" Dustin asked.

"Oh, just thinking. What's on your mind?"

"We need to talk business."

"Why? You and Mom have it under control. The ranch is operating with a comfortable profit margin, or rather, you're able to pay good salaries. You have employee loyalty and things run smoothly. Why would you want to change anything?"

"Some believe we should add a few cabins, for one, upgrade some equipment for another, not to mention others want to up our luxury rating."

"The equipment I can see. But why add cabins? Maybe one more, but the attraction is keeping the place small and the guest numbers limited. People come here to be rustic, so redecorate, buy new sheets, but don't change it. This is a special place. Leave it as is with the possible exception of getting better internet service. Oh, and re-grade the pasture road."

Dustin snorted and reached for his coffee cup. "I'm afraid you and I are the only ones who see it that way. The other shareholders are all set to outvote us."

Gray mulled the information. The ranch had been set up as a family corporation since the early sixties. His father had taken over as president when his grandfather lost the will to run the ranch. When Gray's father had died ten years ago, after running the ranch for nearly thirty years, the family had placed the burden on Dustin's shoulder. Gray had already been involved in his own business ventures and Dustin knew the ranch better. Other than providing business advice when asked, Gray was content to let Dustin do as he saw fit.

Currently there were five stockholders--Gray, his mother and three siblings. Gray and his siblings had each gained their shares upon reaching their eighteenth birthdays. Sora had inherited her husband's shares and often served as the swing vote when the other four were divided. Dustin's eldest son would turn eighteen in two years and everyone would turn over a portion of their shares to him. The same as would happen as each child gained their majority. So far it had been a good system. Rarely were sides taken, and all divisions over minor issues were usually settled by coin toss.

"I see we need to have a family meeting. Is this why Mom has been shoving financials under my nose since I arrived?"

"Yup, and why she's annoyed you've all but ignored her." Dustin winked.

"How do the spouses feel?" Even though Rachel and Jim weren't stockholders their voices carried weight.

"They're staying out of it, but Rachel agrees, and I get the feeling Jim sides with the others as well, to a certain extent."

So the family wanted to modernize. Cater to upper-scale clientele. Could mean more money, but the charm would be lost. Was money the real issue? "Instead of changing the place, use the profit to invest in outside stocks, hire more staff, let the others take more supervisory roles and let the kids do more of the work. They need to learn how to run the place anyway."

"Remember how excited you were when Dad said those words to us?"

Gray grimaced. He was the one who'd run as far and as fast as he could from the ranch. "Right. Still, I had a different path to follow."

"This still about the dream?"

"More than ever. Reed has had the dream too." Gray calmly raised his eyes to Dustin's and found his brother staring at him.

"I see. So, you really meant it when you said it was meant to be."

Gray nodded. "She's everything I've worked my whole life for."

"And now you've found her, what happens next?"

"We get married and live happily ever after," Gray said and lounged back in the chair with his hands folded across his stomach.

Dustin threw his head back and howled with laughter. "You always were the dreamer."

"I don't think following my dream has been such a bad thing. I've made a name for myself, built a small empire and can now afford to retire to a life of leisure, maintain what I have or continue to build. Depends on what Reed wants from life."

"What if she wants to keep working for Troy?"

"Maybe for a while, but not long term. My plan is to knock her up then settle her down where the air is fresh and the stress is low. With luck she'll want to be a stay-at-home-mom."

"Have you discussed this with her?"

"Not quite in those terms, but we're working on it."

"As in you're trying to knock her up and then you'll tell her your plan?"

"Works for me." Sounded better every time he

heard it.

"I wouldn't recommend it," Dustin said quietly.

"Oh?"

"Even though things turned out well in the end, Rachel wasn't real thrilled with that approach. Seems there were a few things she wanted to do before she had kids and got tied down."

"And upgrading the ranch would allow her to experience some of those things now the kids are older?"

Dustin shrugged and looked out the sliding glass door that led to the upper balcony. "She doesn't complain, but I'm sure the thought has crossed her mind."

Apparently, Dustin had married another Sora. Gray didn't want to see Rachel harden the way his mother had. A woman had as much right to her dreams as a man. "Would it help if I based here for a while so you could get away more?"

Dustin looked back at Gray, an odd light in his eyes. "Maybe. If you marry will you come back here?"

"I was thinking about moving the company to the Boulder area. Less expensive to operate and live there than where we are. Better opportunities for the kids of the employees, less stress on the parents, closer recreational opportunities all around."

"And closer to home."

"I showed Reed the parcel, told her I wanted to build a house there. She wants to feed the chickadees." Gray grinned. "But she also said I'm rushing her and making assumptions about the future. I think she's melting, but she says she needs more time. Thinks we need to get to know each other better."

"Yeah, Blake told me you spent the night out there."

Gray lifted a brow.

"He didn't say anything else." Dustin chuckled. "Well, other than Reed has nice legs."

"I'll kill him." Gray repeated the ages-old threat without heat.

"So, what are you going to do about Troy?"

"Nothing. Get Reed to quit as soon as she's resolved whatever bind he's gotten his company into and then wash my hands of him."

"You said that when he took Tiffany."

Gray shrugged. "Can't hold a grudge forever. Never did see where his beef was with me anyway. He's the one raised with the silver spoon and all the advantages. He's finally working for the first time in his life and even then he's still riding on the family fortune."

"He's jealous of you."

"Why? He's got the looks, the money, the brains, the women... He has it all. He was born with it all."

"Except a loving family. At the end of the day, who is there for him? Not his parents, they hardly remember he's alive. No siblings, and his cousins are losers who want to suck him dry. Who does he have to fall back on when the world is at his throat? You were his best friend, closer to him than anyone else. You brought him here and he learned what family could be like. Then he screwed up, and now all he has is his company."

"Which is why I let slip, to his top scientist, the key component needed to make his current project succeed. I gave him, in essence, the one thing he needs to take his company global and make me look like pauper. It's a fair exchange for Reed."

"Mom tells me he's in love with Reed."

"Shows he's smart and has good taste in women, but too bad. She's meant for me. He'll have to find another one." Gray lifted a shoulder at Dustin's frown. "He's had six years to win her over. He screwed up with her too. I don't feel guilty about making her mine."

"What's it been? Seven, eight years?"

Gray nodded. "Thereabouts." He leaned his head back against the chair. Troy had been his best friend from day one at college. Roommates, they were both math and physics students. Troy had talked him into pledging to the same House, and they'd worked in lockstep all the way through their doctorates, graduating in near record time at the age of twenty-six. Constantly pushing and challenging each other, they'd made it a friendly competition. Until the summer after their bachelor's degrees when Gray had brought Troy home. That was when the competition took on an edge.

Troy had come home with him for Thanksgiving and spring breaks and, frankly, Gray couldn't understand Troy's fascination with the ranch, but in the spirit of their brotherly competition, the two had worked hard that break.

Troy had caught on quickly to the life of a ranch hand and over the summer they'd both gained muscle and built physiques as they built one of the guest cabins and led trail rides. The following summer they'd graduated to pack trips and teaching rodeo basics to the guests. Gray was better, but Troy didn't do badly. Gray put it down to having been raised on a ranch and didn't think anything of it.

They didn't work any other summers because they wanted to finish their doctorates, but still, the Dunbar family had adopted Troy.

The next logical step had been to find jobs until they had a feel for the market. Young brains, they'd been cocky and arrogant as they'd joined a research lab working with lasers.

Troy made a few enemies with his attitude, but Gray had been laid back and soaked up what he could. A year later, inspiration had hit Gray like the proverbial bolt of lightning. Seeing their chance, Troy had provided the funding and Gray the basic structure, and working together, they'd perfected their invention.

And then Troy had gone and patented it under his name. Not the company name and not as a co-inventor with Gray. His excuse had been that another company was on the verge of claiming the patent and Gray hadn't been available to fill out the paperwork. Snowed in by a blizzard after coming home to help one winter, Gray hadn't been able to refute the rationalization. But the incident had left its mark.

In fact, it had been the final act required to bring into focus all the petty things Gray had ignored for years. The minor digs, the tiny put downs. Each trivial betrayal that on its own hadn't meant anything, but put together the picture, he'd finally acknowledged, wasn't pretty.

Gray had packed up his office and the next day started his own company with his latest idea. One he'd come up with during the blizzard and hadn't told Troy about. Within a year, he and Troy had become fierce competitors. Except Gray had always done all he could to ignore Troy's business and move further away from competing with him.

Their companies eventually worked enough different contracts that the animosity had cooled and things were at least civil between them. Still, Gray essentially ignored Troy and went about his own business. He'd even tried to get General Skolnick to deal with Ian at the Amsterdam conference, knowing Troy would blame him for stealing the contract. Instead, the General had insisted on working with him and Gray had seen the potential. By then, stealing business from Troy had seemed like a good trade for Tiffany's defection the year before.

Yet here Troy was, once again in Gray's life. Why? Why did he have to be Reed's employer?

"So why is he here?" Dustin asked.

"I have no idea." Gray heaved a heavy sigh. "They told me it was a team-building thing. To work out their latest contract. Sam dropped a hint about money troubles, I dropped a hint about how to make the system work. Now all I need is for Troy run with it, drop Reed, and go back to minding his own business. If he takes the solution I gave Sam, he can take his company global within the year."

"Why don't you take the idea and run with it?"

Gray shrugged. "It's a good idea, but I do enough global business. Also, while my people are good, Troy actually has the better brains in his outfit. I've casually tried to lure them from time to time but he's got loyalty. I respect that. His core group, the ones here now, with the exception of the baby physicist they brought along, were together before Troy came along. A tight family-like unit."

"A tight, family-like unit," Dustin repeated.

Gray recalled Sam's words. *Boy did she straighten us out. Put us on a housekeeping schedule, set up a household budget and made sure we stuck to it.* "And Reed is the mother figure," he said slowly. Of course. She even had the rounded figure of the proverbial fertility goddesses found around the world. She held the purse strings. She was making the sacrifice of her salary, if Sam's suspicions were correct.

"Instant family," Dustin summed up Gray's thoughts. "Marry Reed and they'd stay together forever. Troy would have his instant family."

Gray nodded. "The one thing lacking in his life. Brothers and sisters. Close, loving siblings."

"So...he brought them here because this is where he discovered the power of family? By having them here he fuses them into a cohesive unit for all time?"

Gray leaned forward, planting his feet on the floor, elbows on knees, head in hands. "And I thought I had dreams."

"Yeah, except your dream and his seem to revolve around the same woman."

"But for different reasons. And he's had his chance. She's mine. That's why I'm going on the pack trip. To keep an eye on her. He stole my first patent. He won't steal her."

"But what happens when the week is up and they leave? We need you here for at least a month. I might be able to attend some of the stock sale, but I can't do it all. The doctor wanted me off my feet for two months. I won't do that either, but two weeks is pushing it."

"I know." Gray scrubbed his face with his hands. "I'll figure it out before Saturday. Beyond the power of true love, I just don't have the answer right now. My main focus is imprinting myself on Reed's senses, and it's working. She isn't ready to say the words, but she loves me and she's learning to believe in the dream. I'll do my best not to let you and the family down. I just don't know how it's all going to fall together yet. I suppose I'd always envisioned having more time to concentrate on her."

"Just don't forget what he's capable of if he's feeling desperate."

"Right."

"So, what do we do about those who want to modernize and upgrade?" Dustin asked.

"Ah, the original topic. How clever of you to remember it."

Dustin shrugged. "I knew you had to talk the other out first. Now maybe we can get you to concentrate on us for a few minutes."

Gray threw back his head and laughed. "Actually, I have an idea. Get someone famous up here and let them gush over the real life ranch experience. That ought to convince the radicals to cool their jets."

"And who are you going to drag up here?"

"I don't know. Bill Gates? Warren Buffet? Jimmy Buffet? We'll find someone. Entice a few movie moguls up here and offer up the place to film a movie, only make it a winter one so we don't cut into the summer tourist trade."

"Brilliant. Start selling the idea to your

glamour friends. Invite Spielberg and Lucas up for a week."

Gray ignored Dustin's sarcasm. "I'll get my people working on it. Just make sure Kiri handles the arrangements."

"Why?"

"Because she's cuter than you."

"No problem. Now, where did Rachel hide the whiskey?"

Nineteen

"There's my pretty boy," Reed cooed while brushing down Cass. She smiled to herself when she heard Gray's small noise of disgust. Apparently Cass heard it too, because he nudged her with his head. "Yes, sweetheart, I'll see if I can find you a treat. There, did I miss anything?" She gave his mane one last stroke, and Cass shook his head. "I'm sure I saw some apples in the food packs. I'll be right back."

"You're going to spoil him rotten," Gray said as he took the brush from her and passed the grooming tools to Hank. Everyone else had long since finished grooming their mounts.

"I am allowed to give him an apple, aren't I?"

"Yes," Gray reluctantly agreed. "Let's go raid the larder."

Arm around Gray's waist, Reed hooked her thumb in a belt loop. She hung on as much to be close to him as she did to stand up straight. Six hours in the saddle, even moving slow and with frequent stops, had made for a long day, and it was only four in the afternoon. Casting a glance at the sky she saw clouds starting to block out the sun.

"Time for the afternoon squall?" she asked.

"Looks like it. Let's get those animals fed. It will help them stay quiet if this storm is as noisy as yesterday's."

Reed paused and looked at the sky with a

touch of apprehension. "What do we do when a storm happens out here?"

"Jim and Hank will stay close to the horses to keep them calm. I'll stay with you in the tent to keep you relaxed."

Gray's lecherous smile chased away Reed's shiver of fear and filled her with a very familiar warm gooey feeling. She loved that feeling.

"That takes care of me, but what about the others?"

"Troy is experienced enough he can look out for them. Plus Jerry is here as well."

Reed shook her head with a grin and urged him on to the food box.

By the time Reed finished feeding and fawning over Cass, Gray's horse was nudging her for attention. Dark Moon didn't like being left out even though Gray petted and fed him as well.

"Oh, you're another pretty one." Reed stroked the black and though he tossed his head, he moved closer for her caresses.

"Enough," Gray groaned with a short laugh. "Time for you to pet me." He wrapped an arm around her and pulled her away from the picket line strung between trees where the horses were tied. "Besides, time to get in the tent. Unless you want to get soaked."

"In the tent is good."

Gray paused and looked into one of the two large white canvas tents. "This is the full one."

Jim had asked Troy to gather their group together and camp chairs were set up inside. The four women from Boulder had joined the trek so there were nine guests, and three wranglers counting Gray. There was also a camp manager who apparently stayed on. Not the largest group, it was comfortable. With the exception of Jim and Hank, everyone was gathered in one tent to ride out the storm blowing in.

"Guess the friendly thing would be to join the others," Gray said with a scowl.

"Yes, it would." Reed knew he wanted to cuddle up with her in the other tent. Not an unattractive idea, but not part of the team, and no guarantee they'd stay alone. She let go of him and stepped into the crowded shelter.

"Okay, now a few simple instructions," Jerry, the camp manager was saying. "Do not touch the canvas of the tent, otherwise it'll leak. We have coffee and snacks. We have a guitar and several decks of cards. We can play poker and have a sing along. These little weather disturbances generally blow over pretty fast and then we'll set about making dinner and get down to some serious lazing around the campfire."

Reed ignored Troy's tight-lipped glare and sat down on a stack of blankets Gray had arranged. She'd have preferred to lie down on one of the cots and take a nap, but that seemed almost as unfriendly as retreating to the other tent. Gray sat behind her and gave her something to lean against, his arms and bent legs loosely embracing her. Drowsily listening to the conversations as people settled in, Reed rested, wrapped in Gray's warmth.

The realization she'd fallen asleep came when her body jerked and Gray's arms tightened around her.

"Shh, it's okay." Gray's voice was soothing in her ear. "You fell asleep."

"How long was I out?" Reed rubbed her eyes and reached for her neck. Thunder echoed off the mountains and she heard heavy rain falling on the canvas. The air had cooled enough that she shivered in Gray's arms.

Gentle hands pushed hers away and massaged her neck. "About thirty minutes. The storm is right over us and moving fast. It'll be gone in another fifteen."

"Hmm." Reed tipped her head to let him ease the crick. "Don't think I've fallen asleep sitting up before."

"Um." Sam crouched in front of her with a cup of coffee. "I caught you sleeping in front of your computer just a week ago."

"Oh. Yeah." Reed gave her a sheepish grin. "I guess you did."

"You all might want to consider a cessation on the recreational gymnastics tonight and get some sleep." Sam sat down next to them. "Just a suggestion, of course."

"Well, since the tents are gender segregated..." Reed inhaled the aroma of the hot coffee.

"Powdered cream," Sam said absently.

"It works," Reed replied. Real was better, but she'd take what she could get. She wasn't that proud.

Gray shifted behind her. "Actually, I was thinking we could bed down by the fire."

Reed rested her head against his shoulder and leaned back to look at him. He merely smiled at her and she shrugged. She wasn't awake enough to think about it right now. Sounded good, but she was sure she could come up with a few questions when given a chance to mull it over.

"I didn't know Troy could play guitar." Reed glanced over to see most of those in the tent gathered near Troy while he picked out tunes. She recognized an old camping favorite and the women from Boulder sang along. Dennis, Ian and Stuart played poker with Tish and howled through the choruses. Lanterns had been lit to combat the darkness of the low storm clouds.

"Hmm." Gray made the sound absently. "He learned in college. Must have kept it up."

"How did you meet Troy?" Sam asked.

"Freshman-year roommates. We had the same major and, well, we just clicked. Almost like clones."

"So you two were close," Reed said. They wouldn't be such bitter rivals unless they'd been close once. Not the way Troy swore when saying Gray's name. A small part of her felt guilty for being with Gray, but wasn't she allowed a personal life, too? She liked Gray. A lot. *Really a lot.* No one had ever paid as much attention to her and her pleasure before. How could she not like a guy who made sure she had great orgasms?

Reed's head bounced when Gray shrugged.

"Almost like brothers in some ways. So, what do you think about sleeping out by the fire tonight?" he asked.

"And he doesn't want to talk about Troy," Sam murmured and gave Gray a sympathetic smile.

Reed shrugged. She supposed she'd hear about it sooner or later. Considering her own problems with Troy and her growing feelings for Gray she'd rather put it off until later as well. Adding fuel to her anger with Troy probably wasn't a good idea at the moment.

Instead she addressed Gray's question. "If it's dry, I have no problem sleeping outside. Is the temperature likely to reach the dew point tonight?"

"I suppose anything is possible."

A flash of light illuminated the tent and everyone held their breath, all counting off the seconds until the thunder broke. Ten.

"The storm seems to be moving on," Sam said.

A horse neighed outside and Reed sat up. It sounded like Cass.

"Relax. Jim keeping an eye on things. The horses are all used to these storms." Gray pulled her back against him. "Besides, you're keeping me warm."

Reed thought it was the other way around as the music and conversation picked up again. Rain still pounded on the canvas overhead and she relaxed into the comfort of his arms.

Sam looked longingly at the embrace, and Reed set aside the coffee cup. "Come here," she said.

Sam scooted into Reed's open embrace and Reed laughed at the picture they must make. Gray with two women wrapped in his arms. Reed laid her head against Sam's and rocked her gently.

"Oh that is just so not fair," Dennis complained and pointed at the group.

Sam stuck out her tongue. "You're just jealous I get to cuddle up with Reed and you don't." She tipped her head back and kissed Reed's cheek.

"If it weren't for the evidence of Reed and Sam's new boyfriends I'd have questions about those two," Ian said with a wink.

Reed and Sam just answered with blinding

grins. The joke was so old it was an automatic response.

Troy looked at Reed and Sam, then back to Ian. "You lived with them for how many years and you can't answer that question definitively?"

"Who can figure out women?" Ian returned to the cards in his hand. "I raise you a nickel and call," he told Dennis.

"Playing for high stakes again, I see." Reed stretched, trying to see Ian's cards.

"I left my poker chips at home. Want to join us and let me make you poor?" Ian asked.

"Thanks, but I'm already broke enough," Reed said.

Troy's pick tripped and he hit a few sour notes at the same time Dennis and Ian looked up from their cards. Troy kept on playing as if nothing had happened, but Reed felt a subtle shift in the tent. Sam tensed in her arms and Troy's shoulders looked a little stiff. Another sour note and he stopped playing.

"Here." Troy passed the guitar to Jerry. "I think the temperature's dropped enough my fingers aren't working anymore."

Reed saw Ian's eyes narrow before she looked away. Her comment had been a mistake. She'd always played poker and never complained about being short on money. It was a well known fact she was always up to taking Ian and Dennis' money, even one nickel at a time. She held her own enough that she'd never cried poor to avoid playing.

"How long has it been since you deposited a paycheck?" Sam asked quietly.

"About a week," Reed said casually.

"That was mine you deposited. I'm talking about one with your name on it."

"Oh." Reed tried to decide how to answer.

"That long, eh?" Sam murmured. "Babe, you can't lie to me. I just heard your heart jump to double speed and you're starting to wheeze."

Reed glanced at Sam's concerned eyes then looked away. "We'll talk, but not here, not now."

Sam grasped her arm and gently squeezed. "I'm there for you, you know that."

"I know," Reed whispered, as both Sam and Gray rested their heads against hers.

Troy stood and paced the tent, glancing out the door flaps. He turned back and Reed watched his gaze seek hers out.

"Reed, any chance I can speak with you?"

"Sure. Shoot."

"Privately?"

Reed considered his expression and the warmth of being cocooned. "I'm rather comfortable at the moment. How about later?"

Troy compressed his lips in what she recognized as annoyance. He ran his hand through his hair. "Fine." The single word was uttered sharply and designed to spark guilt in her.

Reed started to move automatically in response only to be held back by Gray and Sam.

Gray's lips were close to her ear, his breath warm as he spoke quietly. "Don't. He expects you to leap up and soothe him. Don't do it."

Reed knew he was right. It was just a habitual response, as programmed as her regular calendar updates. With effort, she relaxed and forced herself to listen to the banter and Jerry strumming the guitar.

~ * ~

Reed lay in Gray's arms, their sleeping bags side by side with their feet to the dying fire. Suspecting midnight had come and gone, she didn't know exactly how late it was. Her watch wrist was pinned down inside her bag, the other across Gray's chest, rising and falling with his steady breathing.

Tired. So very tired. She should have fallen asleep immediately, despite the hard ground, when they bedded down shortly after eleven. Morning would come early, and with a body already sore from riding, she needed to get some rest. Gray had done his best to create a cushion out of a couple of extra sleeping bags, but it wasn't her Serta Perfect Sleeper. She just couldn't relax enough.

If it wasn't the memory of Troy's annoyance or Sam's question about the money keeping her awake, it was Ian and Dennis practically tiptoeing around her, unsure of how to take her declaration of being short on funds.

When she was finally able to tune out those images and memories enough to start drifting off, an owl would hoot, a horse would stamp, or some rodent would scurry through the underbrush. Tired enough to get past all those distractions, she did drift off once, only to have the dream start up immediately. Only it wasn't the lovely dream. It was Gray's black eyes staring back at her in anguish, as if she'd betrayed him or cut him to the quick. Gray turning his back on her. Soul-ripping agony jarred her awake with a pounding heart and tears in her eyes.

Gray slept on. Oblivious to it all.

To be fair, he had to be exhausted as well. Three nights with little sleep, working not only to be with her, but to deal with family demands as well, had taken its toll on him. The guilt of the extra burden she placed on him added to her melancholy.

Shifting a little, she tried to get more comfortable. How many rocks could work their way up through the ground in a few hours?

"What's up," Gray mumbled.

"I need to get up," she whispered.

"Why?"

The question was barely intelligible through his yawn.

"Little girl's tree visit."

"Wan' me go with?"

"No, I won't get lost."

"Boots," he reminded her with a sigh.

"Yes." No point in arguing. Didn't want to get her socks dirty anyway.

Gray let her go and she unzipped her bag as quietly as possible. Jim slept across the fire from them, his head pillowed on a saddle just like in a western film.

Reed pulled on her boots and grabbed her fleece pullover. The nice thing about sleeping in your clothes--dressing was quick and easy. The bad thing--it was uncomfortable. Jeans weren't made for sleeping in.

Finding the communal roll, Reed pulled her tiny Maglite from her pullover pocket and found the trail to the convenience trees. Boys down the hill, girls up hill, a discreet distance from the camp. Cass nickered softly as she passed by and she patted his nose. Dark Moon demanded his pat as well and she was allowed to wander down the path.

Not really needing to go, Reed kept on the trail, her light easily picking out the path until she reached another clearing, this one smaller with a large rock just a tad off center. She couldn't hear the night sounds from the camp and settled on the flat top of the rock to think. A quick look at her watch showed the time to be just shy of one-thirty. Turning off the flashlight, she looked to the skies, hands buried deep in the center pocket of her pullover. As her eyes adjusted, the stars came into focus and filled the moonless sky. Dark moon night, Gray had said. Perfect name for the black horse, for the night was surely as dark as he was.

Contemplating the stars, she felt insignificant against the vastness of the universe spread across the inkiness pressing down. And yet, the sky felt close enough to touch.

The night she and Gray had spent in the back of the truck, she'd thought of how people adored diamonds because they resembled the stars. She'd always thought diamonds too cold but now, looking at the stars, she reassessed her view. Wearing diamonds and black velvet would be a reminder of that one heavenly night with Gray.

Gray. And the dreams. What did it all mean? There was no point denying she was drawn to him as she'd never been drawn to anyone else. Being with him felt as natural as hanging with Sam. He was one of her people. Like Ian and Dennis. Chosen family. Lesser still was Troy. Troy was the boss, forever doomed to remain just outside the inner circle. That and he'd hurt her once.

What Troy didn't know, and she'd never

confessed to, was she hadn't planned to make him wait for that fourth date. While he was in Amsterdam, she'd laid her plans carefully. The right hotel suite had been booked, a secluded table reserved at a dark romantic restaurant and a proper limo arranged to carry her to meet him at the airport. A full makeover and body pampering had been part of the treat.

If Troy wanted her, then she'd give him her best, a proper seduction to go with his hot kisses. He'd never made it a secret he found her attractive, but since he was the boss, she'd kept her mild crush on him quiet. Not even Sam had known about it. After all, what wasn't there to like?

Troy was handsome, witty, and rich. He also respected her intelligence and relied on her to keep the company solvent. Only a dead woman would have been immune to his flirting. Nevertheless, he'd been the boss which meant hands off. Until his invitation for a date had come on the heels of yet another disappointment in the dating department.

Returning from the spa, she'd paused to check her email before catching a nap in preparation for a long night. Sam's email with the news of Troy's behavior and its consequences for the company had arrived while she was out. Reed made one more run that day. The full length red fox coat she'd bought to wear to the airport was returned to the furrier before Troy's plane touched down.

The snap of a twig made her jump and she turned toward the path. Heart pounding, she twisted her light on again and aimed it toward the hulking shape emerging from the trees.

TWENTY

"Troy!" Reed's tiny flashlight picked out her boss's familiar form approaching from the trail, and she turned off the light. "Don't scare me like that!"

"Don't avoid me and I won't have to stalk you in the middle of the night."

"You nearly gave me a heart attack." Reed sank back on the rock and tried to catch her breath. They'd climbed another thousand feet in altitude today. Tomorrow, Jim promised, they'd go down five hundred.

"What are you doing here?" she asked him.

"Making sure you don't fall over a cliff in the dark. You shouldn't be out here alone."

"Why? Is a bear going to eat me? Please. I'd welcome it."

"Going all dark on me, Reed?"

Damn, he would have to bring up her periodic bouts of depression. In some respects he knew her too well. Troy sat down beside her and she moved over to put more space between them.

"You don't need to sit so close," she told him.

"Reed, how long are you going to punish me?"

"For what?" Reed jerked her face away when Troy stroked a finger down her cheek.

"You know for what."

"It's over. There is no chance of us. Done. Died before it got started." *Thank God Sam had sent the email*. Others had followed from Ian and Dennis confirming the disaster.

"Was there ever a chance?"

"There was a small one until you made one critical decision. Actually, a whole string of them. One visit to the red light district, out and back in the dead of night, and no one, least of all me, would ever have known. To spend most of the week there? Sorry. I don't buy the 'poor me I made one bad decision' cry. Sell it to the next gal to hear about your adventures."

Troy lifted her hand and held it when she would have pulled it away.

"Sam told me you looked like shit when she got home from the airport. Like you'd been crying for hours. She said you spent the weekend in bed staring at the ceiling."

"So? Allergy season. The mold was killing me and the antihistamines knocked me out."

"There is no mold in your house. It wouldn't dare think of growing there."

"Stop trying to sweet talk me." Reed pulled her hand away.

"She also told me she found a note with the name of a limo company, a restaurant and a hotel crumpled up in the trash. You had reservations for the night I came home."

"So? I was meeting an old boyfriend."

"Only you were at home."

"He canceled on me." Reed turned away from Troy and pulled her knees up under her chin.

"You canceled. You did it because of what you heard. Someone told you."

"More than one someone told me. If you're going to screw around you need to be more discreet."

"We'd only had one date you considered official," Troy said roughly. "I left in agony from that date. You don't know how hard it is for a man!"

"And you don't know how hard it is for a woman. I kept my thong on." Reed righteously pointed at her sternum.

"It's not like you had guys lined up around the block," he muttered.

Reed drew in her breath sharply then froze.

"Aw shit, Reed. I'm sorry. No, why should I be sorry for telling the truth? Everyone knows I want you and they stayed away."

"Is that the truth? Or did you just feel sorry for me? Poor Reed, couldn't get laid if she stood on a street corner giving it away." She climbed off the rock and paced, eyes searching the blackness looking for a trail, any trail. As long as it was away from Troy. Turning on her heel, the last thing she expected was to bump into him. Strong hands gripped her shoulders as she started to fall backwards. A gasp of surprise escaped and he lowered his mouth to hers, cutting off her building scream.

More angry than scared, Reed tried to push away from him but he held her tight, his mouth insistent against hers, his tongue wet against her lips. He held her arms until she quit struggling, then he slid his hands down to her waist and drew her close against him. Reed's heart pounded as he softened the kiss, urging her mouth to open more to him.

No! This wasn't right and she didn't want it. Troy took her whimper as encouragement and deepened the kiss, his tongue sweeping inside to stroke the inside of her mouth. She pushed harder against his chest and he released her mouth, moving to kiss her cheek.

"I don't want you," he told her with shortened breath, "because I think you're easy. If anyone knows you aren't easy, it's me. I want you because I love you. Have loved you ever since the first moment I saw you."

Heart hammering in her chest, Reed held as still as she could. "Let me go," she told him with a shaky voice.

Troy made a noise in his throat, but released her.

"I mean it. You came through that door with flashing eyes and color high on your cheeks." He reached to touch her face. "Your hair was tumbling down from the bun you can never keep tidy and I lost my heart. You stole my breath away."

Reed stepped two paces back. "I don't believe you."

"Why not? I could barely wait for you to finish your degree and then I didn't give you a chance to interview with anyone else. I gave you the career you'd studied for and since then I've given you every consideration at work. The biggest office-- with your own bathroom and sofa no less, always top of the line equipment and programs. You have the highest salary for your position and field. I give you the best. I bend over backwards to keep you happy. For crying out loud, Reed, it took five years for you to agree to go on a real date with me. Five long years."

Reed stared at him, doing her best not to let her jaw drop. When she found her voice, she spoke slowly and quietly, as if her life depended on the clarity of her words. "You...bend over backwards...to keep me happy? You do this because you love me? And not because I earn it?"

Troy opened his mouth, but she cut him off with a raised hand.

"I want to be perfectly clear about this," she said calmly. "You hired me, and made me your top executive officer, not because of my skills but, rather, because you believe yourself in love with me? Am I hearing this correctly? Because if I am," she spoke a little faster over his attempt to speak, "then my loyalty and eighteen-hour days have been wasted on the wrong person. I'd ask you to convince me otherwise, but honestly, I don't know how you can at this point. You certainly didn't prove it to me by keeping your pants on for just one more week. I can't trust you. And without trust, there's...nothing."

She stood there, staring at him in the dark, seeing his face veiled in shadows, his blue eyes and expression hidden from her.

"I...I don't know what to say to you..." she said. "I...guess...I resign." Needing distance from him, she stepped back. "You'll have my letter of resignation when you...return. I'll stay long enough to see this...situation...through to the end." Another step back and she stood against a tree.

"Ree," Troy stepped close, confining her against the rough trunk.

"No! You don't get to call me Ree." She tried to duck under the arms trapping her.

Troy grabbed her upper arms again. "Ree, I'll find a way to prove myself to you. I do love you."

Reed tried to twist away from him but the bark

and branches ensnared her as much as Troy did. Disbelieving, she was powerless to stop him as he lowered his mouth until his lips touched hers. Shutting him out, she held her mouth closed against his kiss. His hand cupped her cheek, thumb brushing over her chin. Soft lips brushed hers, teasing, gently testing.

"Give me another chance," Troy murmured.

She clamped her lips tighter, refusing to give him an opening.

He tipped her head back as he pressed his body against hers, his thigh insistent between hers.

The tree at her back held her tight and she did her best not to respond. Now wasn't the time to fight, better to wait until he loosened his grip, and she relaxed as though softening to him. Reed felt his other hand release the tree and glide down her body to grasp her waist. She whimpered. Too far from camp, there was no way Gray, or anyone else, would hear her call out.

Troy's thumb slowly began to exert pressure on her chin. Raising her hands to his chest to push him away didn't dissuade him one bit and he pulled her closer. She'd bite him if she had to.

The next thing she knew, she was free. One moment Troy was about to force her surrender to the kiss, the next he was gone. She shook as she drew air into her lungs.

It took a moment to take in what happened.

A roar. A black shadow throwing another one across the clearing.

"Damn you, Troy!"

Gray. Reed slumped in relief. Gray was here. Shaking, her legs gave out and she slid to the ground, gasping for air to stop her head from spinning.

"Spearman!" Gray growled again. "What the hell do you think you're doing?"

"Claiming the woman I've been taking care of for the last six years. I saw her first." Troy struggled to his feet and stood facing Gray with his hands clenched at his sides. "So back off."

"Oh, there's an intelligent statement." Gray folded his arms across his chest and snorted in disgust. "So what happens now? We brawl over her? Or would you rather choose dueling pistols at dawn?"

"Why do you get the best of everything? Why is it so bloody effortless for you?"

"Oh lord, Troy." Gray forcefully blew out his exasperation. "Are you still singing that same old song? Take responsibility for your actions and earn your rewards the way I do. Work for them. That's how things come to me. I study, plan, set goals and then I work to see I reach them. It isn't easy, but it is generally a simple process."

"Very funny."

"Why do you expect things to land in your lap? Rewards don't come to you just because you reach out your hand. They don't appear because you want them to. You have to work for them."

"Well, I worked for Reed. I didn't just dream her up. I've spent the last six years working for her, nurturing her, building the company for our future together. I've invested everything I have, everything that I am, in that plan. What have you done for her?"

"My whole life has been focused on searching for her. You've known that from the first year. You knew from the first moment you saw her that she was the one meant to be with me."

Gray stared at Troy a few feet away, both of them breathing hard in the thin air. Troy was just as angry as he was. Everything boiled down to this one moment. He could hear Reed behind him, gasping to catch her breath. What would Troy have done to her? Would he have raped her?

"Reed? Are you all right?" Gray asked, his voice more harsh than he intended.

"Y...yes. I'm fine. Good timing."

Gray ground his teeth together. Had she not strayed away in the first place they wouldn't be in this situation now. He drew in a deep breath and slowly released it. No, maybe not now, but this situation would have come up eventually. Better to deal with it now.

"Catch your breath. We'll go back in a minute," he said more gently.

"Reed, you don't believe all this mystic talk, do you?" Troy asked.

"I don't know what to believe," she replied, the words spoken with great weariness.

"She knows where she belongs. She's just leading me on a chase," Gray said. *And what a chase.* He grinned in the dark.

There was scrabbling behind him. Reed standing up, he decided.

"Excuse me?" The indignant tone of her voice sent a warning. What had her upset now? Must be the situation he'd just rescued her from. A near rape was enough to upset anyone. Even him.

"What?" Gray answered her.

"Excuse me? I know where I belong and I'm just leading you on a chase?" Her voice rose in pitch with each statement.

Maybe his choice of words hadn't been the best. "Reed, that's not exactly what I meant. Can we talk about this back at the camp site?"

Ignoring his plea, she pressed on. "Then what, exactly, did you mean?"

Maybe she wanted to have this out here and now, but he didn't. Hoping to placate her, he softened his tone a little more. "Ree, we'll talk about it back at camp."

"I think not," she snapped out. "I don't *belong* to either of you. I belong to me. And the sooner the two of you recognize that, the sooner we'll all be able to have reasonable conversations."

Gray turned in time to be blinded by her powerful little flashlight aimed directly in his eyes. He heard Troy yell out a curse and guessed she'd nailed him as well.

Gray threw up an arm to block the light, but the damage was done.

"Damn it, Reed! Why'd you do that?" Troy yelled.

"Because you're both idiots. Do you realize how much alike you are? Egotistical, self-righteous, pig headed...swine. I've had it with both of you!"

She turned toward the trail, her little light pointing the way, and ran off, leaving the two of them to blink away the temporary blindness.

Listening to her boots running down the trail, Gray turned to Troy. "Good job, asshole."

"Same to you, dickhead."

~ * ~

Reed ran down the trail, tears blurring her vision already hampered by the night. She tripped once and nearly fell. Catching herself, she didn't let up until she reached camp, where the horses nickered as she startled them. Once she reached the edge of the circle cast by firelight she stopped to catch her breath.

"Everything okay?"

Reed jumped. "Jim? Jeez, you scared me."

"I scared you?"

Even with his low tone she could still hear his disbelief.

"Sorry." As if it would calm her heart down, she patted her chest.

"As long as you're okay, all's forgiven."

"I...I'm fine."

Jim stood and picked up another log to lay on the dying fire. He moved with a calm that seemed many years wiser than the two men she'd just left. At most he could only be a year or two older than them. Might even be a year younger.

"So, what did you do with the two boys?"

Reed grimaced and looked over her shoulder toward the trail. "I aimed my flashlight in their eyes." She looked down and turned off the little light.

"Served them both right, I'm sure." Jim's chuckle was reassuring. "So, what's the game plan now?"

Reed looked around the campsite. "Girls' tent?" She pointed to the one on the left.

Jim nodded.

"I guess I'm moving in there for the rest of the night." Footsteps could be heard coming back down the trail. "And I guess I'm going now." She bent, scooped up her sleeping bag, and ducked under the canvas door flap.

Hearing Jim move in front of the tent entrance brought a sigh of relief. Not wanting to wake anyone by stumbling around looking for a cot, she spread out the sleeping bag on the ground and sat down on it. She wouldn't be able to sleep anyway so the hard ground didn't matter.

Listening carefully, she could hear a quiet conversation take place out by the fire where Jim told both Troy and Gray to leave well enough alone for the night. Reed pulled her legs up against her chest, arms hugging them close. The sound of footsteps pacing around the fire and horses shifting at the picket lines were muffled. Quiet slowly descended and Reed huddled on the sleeping bag. She let her head drop to her knees and stared at the canvas wall where shadows cast by the fire danced. What was she going to do now?

Turning the events and conversations of the last few days over in her mind, Reed found no easy answers. Circles, dreams, words, magical lovemaking--the images and sensations all left her more confused than ever.

Outside the night sounds subsided and the fire slowly died down again. Inside the tent she heard Sam's soft snore and smiled. Another woman mumbled in her sleep and a cot creaked under shifting weight. Was that Jim snoring just outside?

Easing her tight muscles, Reed straightened her legs and stretched to let the blood flow again. Hoping to see the time, she pushed aside the flap of canvas that served as the door. There was just enough light left from the fire to read the watch. *Fifteen thousand dollars for a watch and it doesn't even glow in the dark, much less have a light. What good is it?* At least he'd bought her a plain style and not the diamond encrusted ones she'd seen on the website. Three forty-five on

Wednesday, the eighteenth of August. Good to know the date, she snorted. And no sleep in sight. She opened the flap a little more and looked around.

Gray's sleeping bag was empty, his body nowhere to be seen. Where could he be? Jim was stretched out, sound asleep. Troy, presumably, was back in the other tent. Lowering the flap, she sat back and considered her options.

The morning was going to be awkward, not to mention the next two full days before returning to the ranch. And then, how to make quiet arrangements to leave early?

She'd have to find a way to Denver, and without a car that would be difficult. It wasn't as if she could ask Blake to run her down to the airport. Then again, Mrs. Dunbar might even offer to drive Reed down herself.

Keeping the light aimed low, Reed turned on her flashlight and looked for her gear. In a corner near the front she saw her hat and saddlebags with a change of clothes. She crawled over and dug out her gloves. Her fleece and boots were already on...and she knew where Cass's saddle was. She sat back on her heels and reviewed her plan. It would work. Cass knew his way. And she was good at being quiet; her brothers had taught her that. Did she dare?

TWENTY-ONE

"She's gone to sleep in the tent," Jim said.

Gray stared at his brother-in-law standing in front of the women's tent as if guarding a room full of virgins.

"I don't need to know what's going on," Jim said, arms folded across his chest, legs braced apart. "I just know she's upset and if you two insist on pushing the issue now, the whole camp will wake up and we'll have a regular mess. So, settle down and let it rest for the night. Whether or not you sleep is up to you."

Gray watched Troy pace as if trying to figure out a way to get past Jim. No, Gray knew his sister's husband well enough to know Jim wouldn't move. Reed was safe enough for tonight. He glared at Troy who paced a half circle around the fire.

"Fine," Gray said. "You stand guard. I'm going to meditate."

Troy snorted but didn't say anything. Gray watched him stalk into the other tent. Jim relaxed and settled down on the log he'd been standing near, his calm eyes watched Gray as he turned away with a shrug.

Retracing his steps, Gray returned to the clearing, the walk calming him with each step. Forcing his anger and frustration aside, he began his mantra, seeking his center. Funny, the language didn't matter, yoga or the shaman roots of the Cheyenne, the process was nearly the same.

In the clearing he found a flat spot on the rock and settled himself. Simply crossing his legs and resting his hands on his thighs worked fine for relaxing. Form didn't matter, clearing the mind did.

Listening to the music of slumbering nature, Gray cleared his mind and settled into a comfortable meditative state. This time it came faster than recent meditations. The last few months it had been hard to reach. He cleared his mind and settled in again.

The dream came to him on a swirl of mist. Were the mists the veil of time? He'd often wondered, but never seriously enough to contemplate it further.

Riding his black stallion, tall and proud, he approached the leafy bower where his love waited. Passing the deep pool, his heart leaped. Around the boulder and past a large oak tree...and there it was, the small stream from the spring inside, dancing in the sunlight streaming through the high canopy of the dense trees. The spring was one of many that fed the deep pool where his love bathed him. Where he knew she'd bathed earlier to be ready for him. Always fresh and clean, always ready for him in every way.

A lance of sunlight broke through an opening in the canopy and shone on the leafy twigs bent and woven into a living shelter. He saw her outline, the long white dress and the glint of red gold from where the shaft of sunlight touched her hair. His chest tightened and his blood shifted, his body growing hard in anticipation of her embrace.

Reining his horse to a stop, he swung down from the saddle. With a quiet word he patted the strong neck, then ducked to enter the shelter. Servants would come to care for his steed.

Liadan waited, as he knew she would, a circlet of small white flowers resting on her unbound hair, her large green eyes luminous with a warm welcome, a goblet of wine ready to refresh him. Reaching out with both hands he gathered her and the cup to him. Soft, willing and supple, her curved body, barely hidden by the diaphanous gown, warmed him as she pressed against his battle hardened frame. The hours spent training to hone his skills and muscles were worth it when she ran her hands over him, seeking out each plane and defined muscle beneath skin bronzed by hours training in only a loin cloth.

Eyes on hers, he savored the wine, rich and fortifying. Wanting to see her lips stained red, he offered her a drink, holding the goblet to her lips. Her expression, never shifting from his face, was equally as intoxicating as the wine. Impatient to taste her kiss, he drained the goblet and let the heavy gold drop to the mossy ground as if it were no more than a wooden cup.

Slowly he lowered his head, her rapid pulse and breath telling him she hungered for him as much he did her. He smiled when her hands reached for him, and breathed in her gasp of need an instant before their lips touched.

Sweet, so unbearably sweet she tasted! Unable to hold back, his tongue invaded her mouth, claiming his prize for being victorious. Unafraid and bold, she pressed back and took from him, giving of herself with each stroke of her tongue.

Knees weak with his need, he slid the gown from her shoulders, pushing it to her waist where he released the girdle of gold just long enough for the gown to pool at her feet. He refastened the chains around her waist--they would make it all the better to hold her when taking her from behind--then lifted her in his arms, never once breaking their kiss. From behind was only one position they'd enjoy this night. He grinned in anticipation and helped when her hands reached for his clothes.

Clothing removed and weapons set aside, he took a moment to drink in her lush beauty with his eyes. The expression of desire and her delicate white hand reaching for him sent him to the bed of moss and leaves as much as her succulent breasts and the glistening treasure where her soft thighs met.

Rising up to meet him, she opened her legs, welcoming him into the cradle of her body. Eager, but still in control, he rested his hard shaft against her, the scent of her arousal stirring him even more. Taking her mouth, his hands slid under her shoulders and up into her hair. Hair that smelled of wildflowers and felt like clouds of dandelion fluff. Ravenous, the heat of the kiss consumed them both, her sexy whimpers making desire coil tight within him.

Her fingers combed his shoulder-length hair, pulling the strip of rawhide holding it out of the way. She loved to feel his hair, she'd told him. She didn't like it bound and wanted him to grow it longer. Fingernails against his scalp sent heat down his spine. Unable to hold back the first rush of need, he shifted his hips, his length caressing her nether lips. Her hands tightened around his head and she tilted her hips until he was poised to enter her. His control hung by a thread as she growled with impatience, conveying her demand he take her.

Always ready to please his queen, he plunged into her. Her shout of triumph fired his blood as their souls merged.

~ * ~

Gray drifted in his trance, reliving the loving in the dream recently revealed to him. He felt his heart swell and expand with each union, until she led him by the glow of fireflies to the pool where she tended his body, kissing each wound and scar, healing now after the battles he'd fought for her.

"*Carrick.*" Her rock solid hero, her warrior, Liadan called him, as she personally tended to him. Washing, oiling and massaging him, feeding him tender morsels of meat and sweets brought by silent servants. Then more wine, more loving. The night was spent in voluptuous pleasure until they drifted into sated sleep just as the light of dawn began to color the sky.

The dream shifted and once again he stood at the entrance of the tiny bower. His hands held her hips and he watched her face while she straightened his tunic and adjusted his belt. Sadness slowed her hands and her eyes avoided his. Still dressed in only her gold jewelry, she'd never looked more beautiful to him. He raised a hand to stroke her cheek, using the back of his fingers, not wanting to hurt her with battle roughened skin. She had enough of those marks on skin as pale as fresh cream. Marks of love.

Apparently satisfied with his apparel, she

grasped his hand and held it to her cheek. A single tear, sparkling like a diamond as a ray of morning sunlight touched it, slid to his finger and rested there. Her sad eyes rose to his as he lifted his hand and kissed the tear, licking the salty treasure from his lips.

"*Liadan,*" he whispered her name.

He gathered her up in his arms, her large, soft breasts pressed against him, and he kissed her, all his longing and love pouring from him. She carried his marks upon her body, had his seed taken root inside? Would she have a present for him the next time he returned? The battle cries echoed in his ears and he felt the pull of duty dragging him away from her. She clung to him, her tears flowing silently and he tasted the salt in their kiss.

The neigh of his horse broke the spell and he reluctantly pulled away, her sad eyes belying the brave smile she gave him.

"Come back soon," she whispered. "*Carrick,* my love, my hero."

"I swear," he whispered and kissed her again. Turning, he ducked to exit the private bower and mounted his horse. Soon he'd return for good, but first he had business to see to.

She stood in the entrance, the morning sun glinting off her hair and jewelry. No halfhearted waves or hysterics from her. His queen stood tall and proud as she watched him ride off to battle. Touching a finger to his brow in salute, he turned his horse and after a few paces urged his mount into a trot. Just before disappearing into the trees he turned to look back at his love one last time.

Expecting to see her standing on the boulder

over the pool as he'd seen her before, he wasn't disappointed. And yet, the sight chilled his blood for she didn't stand alone as she had previously.

His breath stopped in his chest and dizziness assaulted him. Still close enough to see faces and expressions clearly, despite the blond hair there was no doubt who stood with his arms wrapped around the gold-clad body of his love. Pain, deep and searing, tore into him, far more devastating than any sword or spear.

Tears slipping down her cheeks, *Liadan*, Reed, leaned back into the arms of a man wearing a circlet of gold upon his brow.

~ * ~

Gasping, Gray jolted awake as his meditative state vaporized. The pain of the vision was a physical pain in reality, as excruciating as if a knife had pierced his back.

Had the dream been treacherous from the start? Had he been set up for heartbreak of the cruelest kind? Reed. He needed to see Reed, had to talk to her, hold her.

Shaking his head to clear it in the cool morning air, he saw the light beginning to rise. Barely noticing his stiff muscles, he loped down the trail back to camp. The morning sounds of horses stirring reached him, then the scent of coffee and bacon. Picking up speed he burst into the clearing to see his companions quietly eating breakfast while Jerry and Hank assembled gear near the horses.

"Where's Reed?" he asked, looking around but not seeing her.

"Good question." Jim stood on the far side of the fire pit calmly shoveling scrambled eggs into his mouth.

"What do you mean?" Gray looked around.

Accusing eyes from Sam, Ian and Dennis stared back at him.

"Where's Troy?" he asked.

"Another good question," Jim said and bit into a piece of bacon.

Gray turned to look at the horses. Casanova was missing, as was the bay gelding Troy had ridden.

"Talk to me," he ordered Jim.

"Might as well grab a cup of coffee and some breakfast," Jim said calmly.

Panic gripped his heart. "There's no time to eat."

"There's time," Jim said. "If you're going chasing after her, you'll need fuel."

"What do you mean 'if'?"

"Get some food and I'll tell you."

Gray felt a presence at his elbow. Tish stood there with a plate and a cup, her sherry eyes unfathomable.

"He's right, mate," she said. "Eat."

Gray sank onto a log and set down the coffee cup beside him. "Talk to me."

"Well," Jim drawled. "Somewhere around four this morning Reed saddled up her horse and moseyed on out of here. Back down the trail judging from the tracks we found."

"Reed by herself? Or with Troy?"

"Troy woke me about five-thirty wanting to know where Reed was. Anyhow, when he saw Cass was gone, Troy saddled up and took off after her. He's only been gone about twenty minutes."

Gray glanced at his watch. Six-fifteen. "Why

didn't you come get me?"

"One, I didn't know exactly where you were. Two, it was dark. Better to wait for daylight. If she fell off Cass and he kept heading for the barn you could pass her without ever knowing it."

Gray picked up the coffee cup and washed down a mouthful of eggs. He glanced back and saw Dark Moon was off to the side, ready to be saddled first.

"Why did you let Troy leave?" Gray asked.

"Fat chance of me stopping him, but he does know the trails. Not much I could do."

Gray grunted. Jim's logic was sound. The only flaw was no one coming to find him. No, Jim was sound there as well. No one knew where he'd been and, since he'd been sitting still in the dark, they could have walked right past him. The sky was just now showing the beginning signs of pink. Gray finished eating and stood, swallowing the last of his coffee.

"Where are you going?" Jim asked, standing in front of him.

"I'm going after her." It should be obvious.

"We're all going back," Jim said.

Gray frowned. "There's no reason. Keep on with the trip."

Jim gave him a long look. "The group already decided. Spearman's people are missing one third of their team, their two top company officers, and the Boulder ladies don't want to miss the fun."

"Fine, then turn everyone around and head back. Have you radioed the ranch?"

"Not yet. That's next. My plan is to ask Sora to send up the helicopter to see if they can find Reed. Cass may know the terrain, but Reed doesn't and might get lost if she doesn't trust Cass."

Gray nodded. "Good thinking. Don't let me stop you." He turned toward the tent to grab the rest of his gear.

"Just so's we're all not rushing off blindly, I think you should wait for helicopter confirmation. That way if she's off the trail you'll know it ahead of time."

Gray stopped and turned back to glare at Jim. "Then I suggest you get on the radio and see if you can raise someone. I'll wait an hour, no longer, helicopter sighting or not. That will give Roger time to get in the air and scope out the lower part of the trail."

He met Jim's stare without flinching until Jim nodded. Gray picked up his coffee cup and went for a refill.

~ * ~

Gray hovered at Jim's shoulder. Radio contact had been made, but the connection wasn't clear. Until Roger called from the air with a clear line of sight they wouldn't be sure the message was completely understood. At least Sora had released the chopper. Right now they waited for Roger to call back.

The group was ready to leave and the game plan was as organized as they could make it. Gray would go ahead at a faster speed once he knew how far Reed had made it, and the others would follow at a safer pace. Once they left the camp, Gray would only have a tiny, short-range radio for communications. Jerry had the base unit that reached to the ranch. Gray could already see one area where updating things for the ranch was critical. Damn the luxury items, the safety gear needed improvement and communications equipment was paramount.

Dammit, Reed! Why did you have to take off?

Gray whirled when the radio crackled to life.

"Base camp one, this is the whirly bird."

"Whirly bird, base camp one here," Jim's calm voice smoothly replied. Gray wanted to rip the mic from his hand, but Jim's steady gaze stopped him.

"It's a fine beautiful morning. Now, what is it we're searching for?" Roger's cheerful voice crackled crisply over the radio.

"Keep an eye out for Cass with Reed on his back, heading back to the ranch. We believe."

"You believe?"

"The tracks show her moving that direction and as long as she lets Cass follow his head, she'll be fine."

"Roger, we read you. One rogue redhead on a palomino."

Gray grabbed the handset. "We?"

"Madame Sora is along for the ride serving as spotter. Her far-sight is better than anyone else's, plus she can use the binoculars while I concentrate on flying this bucket of bolts."

Gray's head fell backward and he stared at the sky. *Great. Just great. Mom would probably prefer Reed to ride off a cliff.* She hadn't made one effort to get to know Reed, in the little time there'd been.

"Just find her, Roger," Gray said into the handset.

"Aye, aye, boss. Anyone, or anything, else we should keep an eye out for?"

"Spearman went after her about forty-five minutes ago."

"What are you still doing there?"

"Waiting for you to tell me where she is."

"Smart man."

"Jim's suggestion."

"Ah, that Jim has a calm head on his shoulders. Do I want to know why Reed took off?"

"Save the chit chat and start following the trail. She has a good two and a half hour head start but would have been moving slow in darkness. I don't know if she would have picked up speed with daylight."

"Okie dokie, we're following the trail from the ranch out, looking for one palomino with a small redhead on his back. What colors is she wearing?"

"Tan hat, jeans, charcoal fleece jacket."

"Ah, nice colors for blending into the landscape."

Gray grit his teeth at Roger's cheerful tone. He also knew it was Roger's way of covering stress. Then again, it was also how Roger spoke when he was relaxed. Roger pretty much had one mood-- cocky. Most days it suited Gray just fine. Not today.

TWENTY-TWO

Reed heard the helicopter before she saw it. The sound brought back the memory of a search for a lost boy when she was younger. Her whole family had been camping out in the Sierra Nevada at a lakeside campground, with a couple extra kids along as usual. Boy Scouts from her father's troop. The same troop all three of her brothers belonged to.

The boy, eight-year-old Andrew, had wandered away from his family's tent in the night. He'd headed for the latrine and gotten lost on the way back. He'd spent the night wandering around the woods. At daylight his parents had found him missing, and the rangers had launched a search. Reed's father, hearing of the search, had volunteered his scouts.

They'd spent most of a day hiking through the woods, the boys traveling single file and calling out the kid's name, a helicopter flying overhead with a loudspeaker calling for him to come out. All had proved fruitless. Until Reed's brother, Kurt, the youngest of the three, bringing up the rear, stepped around a tree to find Andrew standing in the middle of the trail.

"Hey, kid," eleven-year-old Kurt had said. "Your name Andrew?"

The kid had nodded.

"Why have you been hiding? Haven't you

heard us calling for you? Didn't you see the helicopter?"

Andrew had nodded. "I was scared. I was afraid I was in trouble."

Kurt had called out for their father. Andrew was safe.

What Reed remembered, and put into use now, was that Andrew had seen the helicopter overhead, but by stepping under the trees, the helicopter hadn't seen him. She steered Cass under the trees and waited until the helicopter moved on.

Pausing to sip from the water bottle she'd grabbed at camp, she also shed the fleece jacket, tying the arms about her waist. She wore a long sleeved, light blue, cotton shirt over a white tank top and sport bra. Tugging her gloves into place and settling her hat on her head, she watched the helicopter fly on, then started Cass walking again.

"There's my pretty boy," she said and patted his neck. "Let's head for the ranch, good-looking. You know the trail and I recognize the landscape so we're doing good. But we still have a long way to go."

Cass nickered in reply.

Reed glanced at her watch. Five after eight. They'd been walking nearly four hours now. They couldn't be all that far from the ranch, could they?

Sunrise had been gorgeous and the birds cheerful as they flew about. The peace and steady rhythm of Cass's hooves had been soothing as the light came up.

The first hour, in the dark, had been hair-raising. She'd had to place all her trust in Cass and, as far as she could tell, he'd done quite well.

Now that the sun was up, she could pick up speed on the flat portions of the trail. They'd be after her by now. Or rather Gray would. The rest of the campers would go on without her. She wasn't needed for Troy's group.

Troy's group. The thought brought a new sob to her throat.

"It's okay, Cass, baby," Reed said and stroked his mane. He didn't like her crying. "Just get me back to the ranch. Here's a flat spot, let's kick up the speed a bit." She gave him the direction with her knees as Gray had taught her.

Gray. Another sob choked her.

Forcing thoughts of the men and her co-workers from her mind she concentrated on the rocking motion of the canter.

"Am I doing it right, Cass?" she asked. She felt silly talking to the horse but he seemed to understand her. He snorted as if in agreement and kept his gait even.

The breeze coming up the trail felt good in her face. She could already feel the heat rising and if the wind blew, it would keep the temperature comfortable. With the sound of Cass's hooves and the breeze blowing through the trees, Reed let her mind wander.

She'd verbally resigned. Okay. It was a good time to cut her losses. If Troy didn't get the new gadget up and working soon she wouldn't see a paycheck anyway. His comment that he'd invested everything in the business was true. Sure, there was still money his family hadn't turned over to him yet so he'd be okay in the long run, but for now he didn't have much left. Even with both of them not cashing their paychecks, funds were extremely limited and the banks were no longer willing to loan the company money.

At best, without layoffs or pay cuts, they only had two months' reserves on hand. The clock was ticking and time was short. With a working, marketable gadget in stock and patents pending, they could get the loans they needed to launch the marketing campaign and then move the company global. Research had shown there was an immediate market for the gizmo that would link wind, solar and traditional power sources and work them to the most advantageous effect for both commercial and private use.

Two months. Could Sam pull it off?

Then again, Reed reminded herself, she'd resigned. No longer her concern. Except, she'd promised to hang on until the situation was resolved, one way or another. Did she have two months of reserves left? She'd been avoiding dissecting her own finances and now she let the numbers roll in her mind's eye. The blessing and curse of a photographic memory.

Adding numbers as she rode, Reed considered her options. There was no way around it. Her liquid savings were shot. Either Sam carried the household expenses or Reed would have to cash in some of her retirement account. That hurt. Lean on Sam, who would happily carry her without question, or pay the absurd taxes?

Reed dashed away the tear of self pity that leaked down her cheek and counted the rhythm of the gait, letting it soothe her. When she got home was soon enough to decide.

Home. What was she going to do about home? If the company went belly up then Sam would also be looking for a new job. Sam would have no problem. Gray said her reputation was solid. But who would want a CFO who'd let a company fall apart? No, her chances weren't so good. She'd be lucky to get hired as an accounting clerk. Entry level.

The cloud of doom she'd been fighting off for months settled over her, falling across her shoulders like a shawl of ice. No longer allowing her denial, darkness closed around her and she no longer heard the birds, or noticed the sun shining on the waving meadows of grass and wildflowers. Relaxing her body she didn't even notice when Cass slowed to a walk again. She was so deep in her circle of misery she didn't see, hear or notice anything around her. All she could see as she stared blankly through dark glasses was the long black hole of her future. She could see no light.

~ * ~

"Gray," Sam said quietly as she grabbed his arm.

"What?" He'd just gathered Dark Moon's reins. The helicopter was taking off again. They'd seen Troy, but they hadn't seen Reed. Roger would head back, put the chopper down near Troy and talk to him. Roger had thought to bring CB walkie-talkies along and Gray carried one. As long as they had line of sight and weren't more than a couple miles apart Roger wouldn't have to land to communicate with Gray.

Sam's eyes looked pinched with worry as she spoke. "When you find her, be gentle."

"What are you talking about?"

"She has bouts of depression. She's been under stress and she's about ripe for an episode."

Gray lowered the foot he'd raised to slide into the stirrup. "Explain."

"The money thing. She hasn't said a word but she's been working long, long hours, sleeping in her office and keeping quiet when the subject of money comes up. I've only seen her this stressed a few times. Usually a day or two spent in bed with trashy novels is plenty to straighten her out again. She holes up. She doesn't eat unless I throw chocolate or food at her, drinks water if it's handy, gets up only to go to the bathroom and not to shower. She hibernates. At home it works. Out here? I don't know. Please, treat her gently."

Gray grasped Sam's hand. "I'll be gentle."

"Are you sure? You looked pretty upset and mad when you came rushing back to camp."

Gray saw the deepening worry in Sam's eyes. "I had a disturbing vision while meditating. I won't let it cloud my judgment when I find her."

Sam nodded and stepped back.

"I will find her, Sam. And she'll be safe. I promise."

"I believe you. She's growing to love you, but she just isn't ready to believe you really love her. It doesn't seem believable to her that anyone could love her. Especially so fast."

"I'll keep that in mind too. I have to convince her I've been in love with her for all time. She's seen the proof of it whether she wants to believe it or not."

"Go find her, then. What are you doing sitting around here?"

Gray returned her weak smile with one that held more confidence than he felt. He had even more reason to find Reed now. Swinging up on

Dark Moon he urged the horse forward, breaking into a trot a few yards past the camp boundary. Farther down the trail they eased into a lope.

"Find Reed and Cass, Moonie. Find my girl," Gray said to the horse. "We need to ride like the wind, buddy."

Dark Moon answered with a snort, a shake of his head, and effortlessly surged forward.

~ * ~

Reed shook herself. How long had Cass been standing still? She looked around to get her bearings. Trees to the left, meadow to the right, small stream cutting across the trail. Cass was drinking and Reed realized it was hot.

Taking hold of the reins, she turned Cass's head to the left. "Let's find some shade and rest, sweetheart." The sun was pretty high in the sky. Her watch said nine-fifty.

Amazed at Cass's intelligence, Reed was pleased when he readily turned into the trees, following the stream. Ducking under branches and around bushes, they followed the water for fifteen or twenty minutes off the trail to where it widened into a small pool, not much larger than a courtyard fountain and just as shallow. Plenty large enough to provide cool moisture to a deeply shaded clearing under some spruce, and screened by aspen.

Reed swung off Cass's back and found a branch to loop the reins over. He could drink and there was green grass for him. She dunked her bandana in the stream and wiped her hot face and neck. Gauging the sun, she chose the deepest shade she could find and sat, resting against a tree trunk.

"I don't know what else to do for you, Cass.

Can you stand there or do I need to take the saddle off? I'd rather leave it on because it's a little heavy for me to sling around. Do you mind?"

Cass lowered his head and snorted softly against her cheek.

"You're so sweet." Reed stroked his nose. "I need to rest for a little bit. Didn't get much sleep last night." And no coffee this morning.

Cass nudged her again, then stood beside her.

Reed untied the jacket from around her waist and rolled it up to make a pillow. "I'm gonna lie down for a little bit. Wake me up if I fall asleep, 'kay?"

She smiled when horse lips touched her cheek and she wiggled down into the leaves covering the ground. Just a little rest was all she needed.

~ * ~

Troy slowed his horse to a walk and pulled off his hat to wipe his forehead. The curse of the mountains was the thinner atmosphere. Being out in the sun could get plenty hot. Late morning didn't help. Fortunately, stepping into shade provided instant relief. He settled the worn brown hat back on his head and caught the sound of a trickling stream up ahead. Maybe he'd see clues to Reed's progress there.

He cast his gaze on the ground and started searching for tracks. Gray's father had taught him what to look for those distant years ago. The two summers Troy had spent here learning to wrangle had been the best of his life. How could Gray stay away? Why had Gray sought out the business world?

Troy would gladly give it all up to trade places. At one point, he'd fancied himself in love with Kiri and dreamed of marrying her and living here. Kiri had been one of the very few women in his life he'd never conquered.

Acknowledging at last what he'd ignored for years, Troy knew his dream to live the simple life was most likely the root of the animosity between him and Gray. On one level, he stood in awe of the man to whom everything came with such ease.

Gray had always been just one point better whether it was acing the exams, catching the concept, or developing the idea or strategy. How was it that a mountain troll with no breeding or social training could get the upper hand on a Spearman?

Troy's own family had the connections, the money and a blue-blooded genealogy that traced back to at least three European royal families. He'd been sent to the best boarding schools and pledged to the best fraternity. He'd taken on Gray, his freshman roommate, and because of Troy, Gray had been accepted as well. Then why was it Gray had been the more popular and better liked?

What was the line from *Count of Monte Cristo*? "I'm not supposed to want to be you!" Troy identified all too well with that sentiment. He'd gladly give up his birthright to be Gray. The man had it all and he came from dirt and mixed blood. God surely had a sick sense of humor.

Troy stopped his mount a few feet from the stream crossing the trail. They'd stopped here the previous day and let the horses drink. He could see the hoof prints heading up the hill. What he was looking for were fresher ones heading down the trail.

In the distance he heard the distinctive sound

of a chopper approaching. It wasn't close enough that they'd see him yet.

There were tracks all right, faint in the dust. Drips of water on the ground were quickly drying in the hot sun. Made an hour ago? Half an hour? He stared at the ground on the far side of the stream. No more tracks. He looked back at the near side. More tracks, but they turned sideways.

A nicker from his horse made him hold his breath, listening. An answering one? From the trees? Hard to tell with the chopper growing steadily closer.

Reed had rested in the shade here the day before, ducking out of the sun each chance she'd had. Unlike Sam and the other ladies who stripped down to tank tops or sports bras to catch the rays, Reed hid, swathed in her long sleeved shirts and gloves, hat firmly in place.

He mounted his horse and followed the tracks heading up the stream, away from the main trail. It was worth checking and, with the rattlesnakes and spiders in this area, better to check out any possibility.

Beautiful Reed. So pale and mysterious looking, like a queen from an ancient Scots or Irish tribe. A little more generous in curves than the women he usually dated, she had an earthy appeal that spoke to the peasant in his soul. He'd seen enough of Gray's obsession to understand his rival's desire for Reed. Enough to appreciate it, for once.

Gray was right. The moment Troy had laid eyes on Reed he'd known who she was. What Troy hadn't expected was to fall in love with her in that very same moment. Already not on speaking terms with Gray, he hadn't felt honor bound to introduce the two. No, this time, he'd told himself, he wanted something just for himself, something not touched by Gray. Reed was his and Troy had carefully kept her away from any functions Gray might have attended.

Sure he'd invited her to conventions, but he knew she'd never accept. It'd been a game he'd played in his mind. The same as she'd played holding him at arm's length, refusing to see his invitations to dinner or lunch as anything more than business. Five long years it had taken him to wear her down. Five years to get her to accept an official date.

There, the nicker was a little louder and his horse answered with a whinny. Troy ducked under a thick branch. It was logical Reed would have pulled off to rest. If she'd left camp around four, then she hadn't slept all night. How many times had he seen Reed working with little sleep? Far too many times in recent months. And if he hadn't seen it for himself, Sam's worried gaze following Reed would have told him.

Following the stream, Troy thought about their first date. The most nerve-wracking date of his life. Never had so much been riding on one evening. For the first time in his life, he hadn't known exactly how the date would end. Dates were always made when he knew for sure he wouldn't be alone at the end of the night. Not with Reed.

Dark romantic restaurant, dark romantic movie with Reed cuddled up under his arm. When she'd cried at the happy ending, he'd kissed the tears from her cheeks and ended with sweet kisses on her lips. Sweet kisses that had quickly turned hot and left them both breathless. How had she managed to say goodnight to him on the front porch? She'd closed the door on him, leaving him hard and aching, heart pounding, his last sight of her those passion-glazed eyes. A date hadn't left him that frustrated since high school.

Time, she'd told him breathlessly, she needed time. She never slept with anyone on the first date. His argument that they knew each other better than that had fallen on deaf ears. Her answer had been clear--if he didn't like her standards he could look elsewhere for a bed partner. If he wanted more from her, he'd have to show a little control.

Five years it had taken him to get a kiss and a cuddle. Five years to touch a bare inch of her skin, feel her body pressed against his, and taste her lips. If that wasn't the supreme demonstration of control, he didn't know what was. And it had taken only one week to lose the tiny foothold he'd gained.

He ducked under another branch and saw hoof prints in the soft ground near the base of another tree. She'd come this way. Relief made him release the breath he hadn't realized he held. The bay he rode, Kravitz, snorted and was answered by another horse only a few yards ahead. Troy guided the horse around a clump of aspen and there they were, the palomino standing guard over Reed as she slept.

Lying on her side, head pillowed on a hand, the horse stood so his front legs braced her. The folded jacket a few feet above her seemed to indicate she'd rolled in her sleep and had her horse not stopped her she would have rolled into the stream.

Troy slowly dismounted, speaking low and soothingly to the horse. "Good boy," he told Reed's mount. "You did well looking after your rider." He gave the horse a pat of approval. "I've got her now, let me catch her." Troy kept a hand on the horse's chest so the palomino would know where Troy was at all times. Didn't need the animal to take fright now and stomp the two of them.

Troy lay down next to Reed and pulled her into his arms. Rolling slowly, he pulled her across his body until she lay uphill from him, her head pillowed on his shoulder. With a sigh she melted against his body and he closed his eyes.

Reed. In his arms again. It was all he could do to not pounce on her. Slowly he picked leaves, pine needles and tiny twigs from her hair. In sleep she looked so peaceful, a smile curving her lips as he stroked her face.

"*Carrick*," her dreamy voice said. "My hero, my love." She sighed, a tear spilling from her now sad face.

Troy dried the tear with his thumb and frowned.

Her smile faded and anguish marred her features. "*My love, don't hate me*," she choked on her whisper, as if her heart were breaking.

A sob tore from her throat and her eyes popped open. Troy watched as she froze, stared at him with glazed eyes for a long moment. With a blink she flinched, then screeched and tried to pull away from him.

"*Cillian!*" she gasped.

"Reed! You were dreaming. It's me, Troy," he said desperately as she continued to stare at him, an expression of horror on her face.

"Who's...*Keelyan*?" Where had that name come from? It almost sounded like that Irish beer.

She drew in deep breaths, her body quivering. Pulling away from him, he watched as she struggled to sit up.

"Troy," she gasped. "What are you doing here?"

She looked around in confusion until her eyes lighted on her horse.

"Cass." She squeaked with relief.

Troy sat up. "Great, you're relieved to see the horse but not me?"

"Seems to me you're one of two people I'm mad at," she snapped. "What the hell were you doing lying down beside me?"

"When I found you, you'd rolled, so the horse was keeping you from continuing down into the stream. I'd just pulled you away from his hooves."

Reed looked up at her horse and Troy wanted to shoot the beast.

"Oh Cass! You angel," she cooed.

Pushing to her feet, she stepped right over Troy to wrap her arms around the horse's neck.

"You darling! That earned you an extra large, hero serving of oats when we reach the barn. Did you get a good rest, my pretty boy? Enough grass? Water? Are you set to go?"

"Reed," Troy said with exasperation.

"Are you still here, Troy?"

She stepped away from the horse and brushed dirt and leaves from her clothes. Looking over her shoulder she must have decided it wasn't good enough because she began to unbutton her shirt. She slipped it from her shoulders and shook it vigorously. Right over where Troy sat.

"Dammit, Reed!" he snarled and stood.

She stood there, hands on her hips and glared at him.

"You're not gone yet?"

"No, and I'm not leaving you alone. I'll guide you back to the ranch, but first we're going to get a few things straight."

Reed bent to retrieve her jacket and shook it out as well.

Troy's eyes were glued to her impressive tits jiggling with each flap of the cloth.

"What we're going to get straight is I'm not some toy to be tossed around between a couple of overgrown adolescents."

"I never said you were."

"Then quit staring at my chest! You do that every time I walk into the same room as you. It's the first thing you notice about me."

Troy's gaze flew to her eyes and he saw flames snapping in the clear depths. "Damn it, Reed, that isn't true." Still, she did have a nice rack. He stepped forward and curled one hand around the back of her neck, the other around her waist. He pulled her close, the feel of her breasts like heaven against his chest. Taking advantage of her open mouth, he bent his head to kiss her, his hand gliding from her waist up to brush a thumb against the side of her breast. One second of heaven.

Her hands forced him away and, before he could gauge her reaction, one of those little hands connected with his cheek, leaving behind a stinging imprint.

"You don't have the right to touch me!" she snarled at him.

Troy stepped back, shook his head and rubbed

his cheek. Guess that approach wouldn't work. Dazed, he watched her pull on her shirt again, hiding the tight tank top beneath it. "Why do you do that?"

"Do what?" She bent to pick up her hat and shook out her hair before tucking it up under the crown of the tan Stetson.

"Hide under loose long-sleeved shirts."

"Sun protection. Duh."

"Is that all?" Troy stepped close and pulled another twig from her hair. "Reed, please, we need to talk."

"Really?" She stepped away from him. "Is that what you called it when you were trying to force yourself on me last night? And just now?"

Troy let his hand fall with a sigh. "All I wanted was to kiss you. Like we kissed on our one and only date. Remember those kisses? How you kissed me back?"

"Your words--our only date. That was your chance, bud."

Reed untangled Cass's reins from the branch and pulled the horse around to head back down the stream, effectively pushing Troy away from her.

"Who is *Carrick*?" Troy gave the name the accent he'd heard her use.

She froze but didn't look back over her shoulder. "*Carrick*? I don't know what you're talking about."

"Reed, you're a horrible liar." He walked around until he could see her face. "You said the name as if speaking to your lover. And then you asked him not to hate you and you cried. That's what woke you, a sob." Troy watched her face pale and she closed her eyes, a crease of anxiety between her brows. He moved closer, the body of her horse between them.

"What did you dream about, Reed? And what was the name you called me when you woke up?"

"I don't know what you're talking about. Now move or I won't be responsible for your black eye."

Troy stepped back and picked up the reins to his horse. "I'll take you back."

"Thanks, but I was doing just fine on my own."

Troy paused when he saw the horses' ears twitch and Reed looked to the sky. The helicopter was on its way back.

"Damn," she swore. "Is that them looking for me?"

"Yes."

"Then I'll wait until they fly on."

"Won't do much good. Roger's flying and it looked like Sora has a pair of binoculars."

"I dodged them the first time."

"Gray is doubtless hot on our tail as well. Roger landed a while back and told me Gray now has a radio so they can coordinate air and ground searches. Just what is your plan anyway?"

Reed chewed her lip.

Troy wanted to give her something else to chew on instead.

"My plan was to get back to the ranch and get someone to drive me down to where I could catch a bus to Denver and out to the airport."

Troy exhaled noisily.

"Dumb plan?" she asked

"Extremely. Not like you at all."

"Thanks. I think." Reed gripped the saddle horn and with a bounce swung up onto her horse.

"Getting better every time," she muttered to herself. "Thanks for holding still, Cass."

"Do you always talk to your horse?" Troy moved forward and grabbed the palomino's bridle.

"He's my friend. What are you doing?"

"Leading you back to the trail."

"I can find my own way," she snapped.

Troy felt something hard against his shoulder and then he stumbled. The bridle was ripped from his hand, and as he straightened, Reed kneed her mount forward.

"Did you just kick me?" he called after her.

"No. Tempting, but no. I just nudged you." Her voice floated back to him.

Cursing under his breath Troy mounted the bay and followed the swaying branches marking her passage.

TWENTY-THREE

Reed paused where the trees ended beside the trail at the edge of the meadow. Bright sunlight struck her eyes and she fumbled for her sunglasses, shoving them into place. Better.

The helicopter was loud and near enough she could see Roger's blond head and a darker one. Gray.

"I thought you said Gray's mother was with Roger?" she asked Troy.

"She was. Must have traded off. I bet they saw me heading upstream."

"Well, you go out there and tell them you didn't find me."

"Right."

Reed glared at him and had the mad urge to whip him with the leather reins. *Not very ladylike.*

"Get that look of bloodlust out of your eye."

He hadn't even looked at her and he still knew what she was thinking. Reed grinned when Troy moved his horse off to the side, out of range.

"Afraid of me?"

"Frankly? Yes, a little. You've already punched me in the stomach and kicked me in the shoulder this week."

"I *almost* punched you and then nudged you. I didn't kick you. I only nudged you. With my foot."

"Your brothers never should have taught you how to fight."

"You should have learned." Reed watched the helicopter lower until it landed in the meadow a hundred yards away. "Besides, my sister taught me how to kick."

Damn, that was Gray jumping out of the cockpit. Men. Too many men. She was surrounded by men. When she got home she was grabbing her mother, sister, Sam, and any girlfriend she could reach, and they were holing up. Chick flicks around the clock. Wine, chocolate and daiquiris. No, *margaritas*. Just tell the guys they were daiquiris so they'd stay away. *Good plan.*

What was Gray's plan? The helicopter blades were winding down. Okay, that confident were they? Now, how to disable Troy so she could kick Cass into a gallop? Maybe, just maybe, she could get back to the ranch and lock herself in her room. Gray's room. She'd moved into his room. Possession. If she got back there first she could kick him out. Reed glanced at her watch. How long had she slept? Noon? Already?

"I see you still wear it," Troy said.

She glanced at him. "It's the only one I have that works. I still think you spent too much." Almost three month's salary for Stuart. Six months minimum expenses for her. Wonder how much she could get for it?

"Gray's coming. What's your plan?" Troy asked.

"You stay here and talk to him. I'm leaving." Reed dug her heels into Cass's sides. "Come on, baby," she urged him and he charged from the trees.

The next thing she knew, she lay on the ground looking up at the underside of Cass's head.

Backward. Pain radiated through her body as she tried to take a breath. Gasping, she fought and finally a shuddering breath rushed into her burning lungs and her eyes watered, the pain making her want to cry. Before she could move, Gray, Troy, Cass and Kravitz stared down at her.

"Ree!"

She blinked through tears to see Gray's face directly over hers as he knelt beside her.

"*Liadan*, my love, are you all right?"

The name... She blinked. From the dream... "*Carrick*," she whispered and closed her eyes.

"Tell me if anything hurts, anything at all, okay?"

She felt Gray's hands gently probe her neck then down her arms. She flinched when his hands passed over her ribs, but her hips and legs seemed fine. Before he carefully lifted her to a sitting position, he made sure all her limbs moved and then ran his hands down her back. Pain from the left side of her ribcage made her moan.

"I'm sorry, baby, I didn't think Cass'd stop that fast. I was only trying to call him to me," Gray said.

"What?" Reed still had trouble drawing breath.

"Cass stopped because of my whistle. He wasn't supposed to stop, he was supposed to change course and come to me."

"Oh." A horse who responded to whistles. *Traitor*.

"Think you can stand?" Gray waited for her slight nod. "Come on, let's stand you up."

Troy crouched on her other side, his hands gently closing around her arm to help.

"What did you do to her?" Roger's voice

carried across the distance.

Reed watched Gray's face, his eyes scrutinizing, watching her for any reaction.

"Tell me if anything hurts. Here we go," he said.

Reed felt both Gray and Troy's hands tighten on her arms and press against her back. Gray's hand rested on her waist, just below the pain on her left. She folded a leg and they eased her to her feet.

"Did I land on a boulder?" she asked.

"A small rock," Troy confirmed.

She had the impression the two men shared a glance over her head.

Slowly they let her weight settle on her legs and she stood, blinking, in the bright sunlight, gasping for breath as she bit back tears of pain.

"Hat?" she asked.

"Right here." Roger's voice was closer.

Her hat was pressed onto her head.

"Sunglasses?" he offered.

"Please." Single words were all she could manage.

Roger's face swam into view then darkened as he slid the glasses onto her face.

"Ree?" Gray asked from her side.

"Yes?"

"Do you think you can walk?"

"Walk?"

"Jeez, Gray, think you knocked her around enough?" Troy asked sarcastically.

Reed barely heard them. Her ears were ringing, her back continued to hurt on the left, and she felt dizzy.

"The damn horse wasn't supposed to stop like

that."

Reed heard a snort from Cass. "Traitor," she muttered and felt his nose at her back. "Who fed you an apple last night? Who brushed you until your coat shone? Who promised you extra oats?"

Cass whinnied pitifully and gently nudged her again.

"Males. Can't trust a single one of 'em. Next time I'll find a mare to ride."

Gray coughed. "I think you just hurt his feelings."

"Right. He's the one who dumped me and I hurt his feelings." Reed tried to shake off the arms holding her. They tightened instead.

"Into the shade with you," Gray said.

They slowly escorted her under the trees.

Reed closed her eyes and leaned against the tree in front of her. Shaking her arms loose from the men, she wrapped them around the sturdy trunk. Now she was a tree hugger. Living near Berkeley she'd been accused of it often enough.

"Roger, did you grab that bottle of water?" Gray asked.

"Right here."

"Reed? When was the last time you ate or drank?" Gray asked.

"I... I...can't...remember."

"Roger, food?"

"Protein bar. Hey, Spearman, that looks like a boot print on your back." Roger laughed.

"So what?"

"Reed? Did you do that to him? That's a pretty small boot print. Why did you boot his shoulder?"

"I was too high up to kick his ass."

Roger hooted with laughter and even Gray

chuckled. Reed heard a wrapper ripping.

"All right, think you can turn around and sit down? You need to eat this and drink at least a bottle of water."

Reed looked at Gray. Why was her brain not functioning? Food. Her eyes focused on the chocolate-covered bar Gray held out to her.

"Take a bite, then we're going to sit you down."

Doing as he said was easier than arguing. Besides, her stomach growled loud enough for everyone to hear. Undoubtedly it had been heard up and down the valley. Reed let the men help her sit with her back against the tree. Man, she was going to be sore. The pain in her back eased to a dull throb.

"You owe me a few massages," she told Gray when she swallowed the bite.

"At least once a day. Maybe even twice."

He crouched beside her and held out a large-mouthed plastic water bottle.

Reed didn't argue when he tipped it to her lips, but drank deeply. Cool. It tasted so good. Sitting in the shade, she slowly ate the protein bar and drank the entire bottle of water as Gray shoved each one in her face.

Gray. She was mad at him, wasn't she? Why was she mad at him? He must be furious with her...but why? It frustrated her when she couldn't remember.

Reed heard horses moving and male voices. Roger and Troy must be taking care of the animals. She rested her head back against the tree.

"Reed? Are you really okay?" Gray asked with a worried tone in his voice. His hand gently rested over her ribs and she winced.

"I think so. Just let me take a break. The pain is easing."

Strong arms lifted her and she found herself cradled in Gray's arms, sitting on his lap. She rested her head against his shoulder.

"What was the name you called me?" she asked him.

"*Liadan.*"

"Pretty. What does it mean?"

"I don't know, but I intend to look it up as soon as I get near a computer with internet. You called me *Carrick*. Did you have the dream again?"

"I...I think so. I remember you...leaving...and my heart breaking."

"I dreamed of you last night, crying as I left, but so brave and proud. Then I turned back to look one more time and..."

"I wasn't alone, was I?" she said sadly.

"No."

She nuzzled his neck. "*Cillian.* Troy?"

"He had his arms around you and you leaned into him."

"He held my arms, behind me. I had no choice."

"What was his hold over you?"

"I don't know. I woke up too soon."

"Reed." Gray's quiet voice cracked. "I need to know..."

"I don't know. Don't ask me now. I'm thinking. I promise. I'm thinking."

"Okay. Let's get back to the ranch and take it easy. Neither of us has slept well." Gray's head rested against hers and she felt him sigh. "I love you so much," he murmured. "I just can't bear the thought of losing you."

"That is so like you, Gray." Troy's voice broke into their quiet moment.

Reed felt Gray slump then stiffen, his jaw tighten, then he relaxed again. "Troy, this isn't about you. This is about Reed and me."

"I'm involved here. I knew her first and I was making progress with her until you showed up. Besides, she works for me."

Reed held up her hand, silencing both men. "I don't want to hear another argument, even another word, between you two. The last argument is the reason why I left camp in the first place. Keep it up and I'll leave again, taking both horses with me and leave you two to duke it out over who gets to ride with Roger. Now, Gray, please let me up. I'm feeling better."

"Maybe," Roger said with a sly smile, "I'll run off with the pretty maiden and leave the boys to the horses."

Reed smiled and accepted the hand he offered. Moving slowly, with Gray's hand supporting her from underneath, she stood and tested her balance. Good, brain function seemed to be returning though drawing in a deep breath was difficult.

She rolled her head slowly and felt her spine creak. "Maybe I can talk you into flying Sam and me back to California?"

"Only if these two get obnoxious again." Roger gave her a wide grin.

Reed tucked her arm through his. "Roger, we need to talk. I need an impartial, objective perspective. How long have you known these hooligans?" She glared at Gray and Troy when they both spluttered.

Roger's chuckle was warm in her ear. "You want the dirt? From an outsider's view?"

"I figure you're about as impartial a spectator as I'm likely to find. How and when did you meet them?"

"Well, now, it all goes back to college," Roger drawled.

"Maybe you shouldn't tell the story in front of us," Gray returned the drawl.

"Painful to hear?" Reed asked.

Gray shrugged. "He might be more objective without us listening in."

"Then," Roger said, "I suggest you two find somewhere else to be. Sora should be along soon and the others aren't all that far behind her. Why don't you take the horses and ride back up the trail to assure them everything is okay?"

Roger shifted his arm to curl around Reed's shoulder and she leaned against him. She merely grinned when both Gray and Troy stared at her. With a shrug they went to get the horses.

~ * ~

"And so, that is how they came to part the ways," Roger finished the narrative.

Reed sat quietly thinking about the two men. Troy acting like a spoiled baby--again. Gray not acting much better, but still taking the higher road. She moaned and Roger's hands gently kneaded her shoulders.

"You've had a rough few days," he said.

"How about several rough months? Though I do have to say getting thrown off a horse beats just about everything." She grimaced as he worked the muscles beginning to tighten.

While talking, Roger had apparently noticed

334

her squirming on the hard ground. He'd picked up her jacket, folded it, and placed it over his crossed legs. Too tired and too sore, she'd barely squeaked when he'd picked her up and settled her on his lap, back against his chest. Damn if he didn't make a good armchair. She shamelessly rested against him, letting his soothing voice wash over her.

The story he'd told her allowed for the balance of her sympathy to swing to Gray, but he wasn't wholly blameless for the falling out.

"So, what you're saying," Reed mused, "and I think I've felt this, is that they're far more alike than either one wants to admit."

She felt Roger's rumble of amused agreement through her back as his hands gripped and released her shoulders.

"Yep, that they are. They're both okay until it comes to the other. The split hurt them equally and even though Gray has been able to channel his energies into building his business and diversifying, they really aren't all that different in their goals. Troy just narrowed his focus down to one company. Gray spread out."

"And both business models have their strengths and weaknesses."

"Exactly."

"Any chance of getting them to remerge their companies?"

Roger's hearty laugh rang out. "I don't see it happening."

Reed smiled when he wrapped his arms around her and gave her a hug.

"You're a mighty nice armful." Roger rested his chin lightly on her head. "How's the spine feeling?"

"Not broken, the ribs are a bit sore, but a few hours in a hot tub would be great."

"That and a massage."

"Yes." She melted against Roger.

"I don't get those kinds of massages from Gray."

"Glad to hear it." She giggled. "Does he really charge you three hundred dollars?"

"Sure he does. And since I charge him the same we mostly stay even. Although we prefer a certain massage therapist back in California. We only work on each other when we can't get back there."

Reed laughed. "What led the two of you to study massage?"

"Gray had a feeling you'd be an uptight business type, or a very active sporty type. Either way he figured knowing how to ease your aches and pains would be a good way to break the ice. That was the original thought. Then we ran into these gals from Golden and they taught us the ways of the Tantra. Gray was already dabbling with Shamanism because of the dream and Tantra led to a whole chapter of Eastern Philosophy. He became a regular student of the Kama Sutra, and mystic healing. He's obsessed with the healing properties of gemstones, but none of his studies quite carry over into giving up meat and drinking strange herbs. He's also studied Celtic ways as well."

Reed laughed quietly. "Believes in balancing the ch'i?"

She felt Roger pause then his chuckle joined hers. "Something like that."

They sat for a time, Reed lightly dozing and

enjoying Roger's friendly embrace. It was nice to sit with a man who wasn't trying to feel her up or look down her blouse. Their breathing matched and she felt herself beginning to slip into a trance.

Not wanting to drift off, she asked, "What about Sam. Where does she fit into your life?"

"Ah, now there's a rare beauty of a woman."

"I'm glad you can speak of her with reverence while holding me in your arms," Reed said teasingly.

"Oh, you're a nice armful all right and I'm quite happy with you there. You're welcome to cuddle anytime Sam doesn't want to, but she's...wow. She floors me, Reed. I know you're used to guys using you to get to her..."

"You didn't use me and you're not using me now." She smiled when he gently kissed the top of her head.

"Will you help me, Reed? I've never fallen head over heels before, but she...she just takes my breath away. Brains like I've never encountered mixed with humor and a sharp wit. And love for her friends... it's awe inspiring. She's been worried about you."

"I know. I adore her and didn't want her to worry."

"But she knows you well."

"Yes."

"I think I'm in love, Reed."

"I haven't had much time to talk to her, but I'll find out and make sure she tells you, okay?"

"Thanks." Roger laughed. "I feel like I'm back in high school. Does she like, you know, really like me?"

Reed laughed with him. "I think she does."

"Oh good. I can work with that."

"So tell me about you, Roger, just so I can sing your praises to her."

"A man's favorite subject. Himself. I just might fall in love with you, too."

Reed laughed softly. "In the beginning, Roger-- what is your last name?"

"Do I have to confess?"

"You do."

Sigh. "Fink."

"Roger Fink?"

"No laughing now."

"Okay, Mr. Fink, tell me your life story. You were born...?"

"To Frank and Freda Fink, of Stockton, California. Determined to break away from my small town life and small name, I got good grades and found myself attending the University of Colorado at Boulder. There, one day, I met these two bozos...."

Reed smiled and relaxed as he spun his tale.

~ * ~

"Well isn't this cozy?"

Reed struggled to open her eyes. When had she fallen asleep? Why did that voice scare her? Mrs. Bartles?

"Not happy with two men panting after her, she needs a third?"

"Now, Sora," a warm male voice said then yawned. "Don't misinterpret what you see."

Sora? Reed's eyes fluttered open and saw a woman on large black horse staring down at her. She blinked heavily, her head ached and vision was a little blurry. *Sunglasses must be dirty.*

"Um," Reed started to speak then covered her

own yawn. She started to move to stand but strong arms held her down when a tiny groan slipped out.

"How are those aches, Reed?" the man asked her.

"I...I don't know. Until I move...was I asleep?" The words felt difficult, her voice a little gruff. Where was she? Oh, the man looked a little familiar. Cute, too.

He lifted her left arm and glanced at her wrist. "Nice watch," he murmured. "Oh, I'd say about twenty, maybe thirty minutes," he said a little louder. "Sora, are the others far behind you?"

"I don't know. Maybe an hour, maybe less." The older woman shrugged and swung down from her horse.

"Roger?" Was that his name? It seemed right. "I...could you help me stand up? Please?"

"Feeling stiff?"

"A little." *About as stiff as a board. Don't whine.* Would the nurse give her some aspirin?

Reed kept up her inner pep talk while Roger lifted first under her armpits and then under her very sore butt. The pain in her side made her moan.

"Um, Reed?"

"What?" she replied miserably.

"It isn't working. I think you're too stiff."

Reed didn't answer. She couldn't. Muscles that had tightened up while she rested refused to budge and the pain was nearly blinding. Eyelids closed tight held back the tears forming. Not only was her body hurting, so was her head and her side.

"You're a desk jockey, aren't you?" he asked.

"Mmm," she murmured noncommittally. What

was a desk jockey? Sounded boring.

"Rumor has it you've been putting in long days and sleeping on the sofa in your office trying to keep Troy's head above water."

She lifted a shoulder and let it drop. *Office? Troy?* Oh yeah, she knew a Troy.

"All work and no play." Roger made a tsking sound.

"Makes for a very out-of-shape Reed."

"Let's try this another way." Roger turned her in his arms and slid an arm under her legs.

"Arms around my neck," he told her, his eyes crinkling in concern at her grimace. "Reed?"

"Yeah, let's try this." She couldn't hold back the whimper as Roger lifted her arm over his head.

Roger pulled her sunglasses off and looked in her eyes. "I don't think you're okay, babe. What day is today?"

"Um." Reed felt her heart leap. Her head hurt, but surely she knew the answer to this simple question. After all, her watch told her what day it was every time she looked at it. "Um, Sunday?"

"How do you spell 'willow'?" a woman asked.

Reed looked at the women crouching next to her. Twins? She didn't remember meeting twins.

"Willow? W-h-e-l--no, um... w-h-i...?" Reed frowned. "What does spelling have to do with anything?"

"How does your head feel?" Roger asked.

"I have a little headache," she muttered.

"Okay, up we go," Roger said as he stood, gently lifting her in his arms. "Sora, I'm flying her straight to the hospital in Vail."

"Good idea." The other woman frowned and Reed had the feeling she'd screwed up somehow.

"No," she protested. "I just need to rest. If you call my mom and she'll come pick me up. She gets off work at four so if I can wait in the nurse's office until then..." So tired, maybe if she could sleep a little. "Oh, and can you get my calculus homework from Janie?"

TWENTY-FOUR

Gray watched the helicopter taking off from the meadow with a frown. Roger was supposed to wait for them. He reached for the walkie talkie he still carried.

"Whirly bird, this is big boss, come in," he spoke into the handset.

"Hey there, big boss, I'll be with you in a minute." Gray noticed Roger's voice was unusually tense and his stomach clenched. What was wrong?

He strained to listen while Roger spoke over another radio, but it didn't make sense. ETA thirty minutes? Where was he going?

"Whirly bird here, big boss. I'm heading into Vail with a special package."

"Come again?"

"Small redhead is showing signs of concussion and possible cracked ribs. We're headed for the hospital. Blake is heading up the trail in a truck to get you, so pick up the pace and you'll meet up with him sooner."

"I'm not that far behind you, pick me up so I can go with you." His eyes were glued to the helicopter as it gained altitude and headed down the valley.

"No time. I don't want to waste a minute. She's unconscious. I'll tell the hospital to expect you."

"Roger!"

"See you at the hospital, Gray." Roger's voice

crackled out.

"Shit!" Gray leaned over the palomino's neck. "Run, Cass, run like the wind."

~ * ~

Gray stared at the paper cup for a moment before following the line of the hand and arm up to the face of the person holding it out to him. Roger's face was grim as Gray sat up and took the coffee.

"She's going to be okay," his friend assured him.

Gray grunted and sipped the bitter black liquid. "How long did they think the surgery would take?"

Roger glanced at the watch stretched around his wrist.

Gray watched as he slipped the feminine gold band off over his hand, handed it to him and pulled a chain of twisted gold from his pocket. Reed's necklace and watch. The Rolex from Troy. The necklace from him. Roger had taken the jewelry from the nurse who'd prepped Reed for the emergency surgery needed to look for unexplained internal bleeding.

Gray took the small watch and looked at it. Three ten. Roger had met him at the door of the Emergency entrance an hour ago as Reed was being wheeled into surgery.

"They think two hours. They weren't sure what they'd find."

Gray nodded and sipped the coffee again.

Blake's hand landed on his shoulder in an attempt to offer comfort. He didn't shake his brother off. A small commotion at the door of the waiting room caught his eye and he looked up to see Sam and Troy rush through, followed by Sora.

Rising to his feet, Gray handed the coffee to Blake. His eyes met Sam's and she hesitated just a moment before moving into his arms. Not sure who was doing the comforting, he held Reed's closest friend and felt tears clogging his throat as Sam clung to him.

"She's tough, Gray," Sam whispered. "She'll be just fine."

So, she was comforting him. He almost laughed. "I know. I just feel so guilty. It's all my fault."

"Shh, don't say that." Sam pulled away to look him in the eye. "It was an accident. It was a miracle she didn't fall sooner, running off the way she did."

Sam's fingers gripped his arms until he nodded.

"I think you have the information Admissions needs," Gray told her gruffly.

Sam nodded. "Yeah, I'll get her checked in properly. What's the word?"

"They're looking for internal bleeding. She's been in surgery about an hour."

Sam's grip tightened.

Roger squeezed his shoulder. "I'll help Sam."

When Roger and Sam stepped away Gray looked at his mother. For a long moment he couldn't read the expression on her face, and then it softened, her dark eyes recognizing his pain as only a mother could. He opened his arms to her and she moved into his embrace. Biting his lip, he blinked back the moisture in his eyes. Why did this happen to Reed?

"What's the word?" Troy's rough voice broke

the quiet.

Gray looked over his mother's head toward the other man. "Concussion, undetermined possible internal bleeding and cracked ribs," he answered shortly.

Troy sank into a nearby chair, his face more pale and haggard than Gray ever remembered seeing it before.

"They expect her to be good as new in a few weeks," Gray added.

Troy nodded, his face bleak.

Gray's mother stepped back and pulled him down into a chair. "I know this isn't a good time, but you two need to talk."

Gray didn't like the way she eyed both him and Troy.

"Mom, you're right, this isn't a good time." He leaned his head back against the wall. "I don't have anything to say to Troy right now."

"Well I have something to say to both of you," his mother said. "This silly feud of yours has gone on long enough. If you can't do it for the sake of the friends you once were, you need put it aside for Reed's sake. She will need peace of mind to heal quickly and you two fighting over her will hinder her recovery."

Gray glanced toward Troy who sat bent over, elbows resting on his knees, hands dangling between his legs. Did the feud matter? Sure, Troy had filed the first patent, but Gray had moved on and filed patents for better inventions. The original one was already obsolete and had only achieved modest success. The real question was, had he stayed with Troy, would he be as successful as he was now? Would he have expanded as globally as he had? Perhaps not. Had Troy done him a favor in the long run? Gray thought about the contract he'd picked up in Amsterdam. Troy's mistake there had more than compensated for the original invention. Were they even? Did it matter anymore?

"You think it's just that easy, Mom?" Gray turned his gaze to the white ceiling tiles.

"You two were close as brothers once, which is why this feud has hurt you both so deeply. If you didn't care, your fight wouldn't be so bitter. It's time to let bygones be bygones and start fresh."

Gray nearly laughed. How many times had he heard the words as a child? "We're not children fighting over chores anymore. This is business."

"Yes, you two are adults now. All the more reason to stop this childish behavior."

Gray lowered his head. His gaze met Troy's, noting the blue eyes looking back at him were filled with pain. Maybe the other man really did care for Reed. But the dream said she belonged to him, not Troy.

"Gray." Troy started to speak, then paused to clear his throat. "I know you don't believe me, but I swear, I'm sorry. I did not intend to steal the work."

Troy met his eyes, and for the first time, Gray believed him. He gave Troy a short nod and relief showed in the blue eyes. "It's forgotten," he said and leaned forward to rest his elbows on his knees. "We've both moved beyond it, anyway. Now we need to settle the situation with Reed."

Troy nodded. "I know you've dreamed of her, but I've been close to her. I've taken care of her. I'm in love with her, Gray. I can't...I don't think I make it without her."

Gray stared into the tortured eyes he'd once known almost as well as he knew the eyes that stared back at him in the mirror. "I understand your infatuation, but the dream says she belongs to me. She's my soul mate, not yours."

Troy leaned back with a snort of exasperation. "The damned dream. Gray, this is the real world."

"Yes," his mother interrupted. "It is the real world and Reed is a woman who can make up her own mind. Nobody doubts you both love her. But she should have a say in this. It's her future in question here."

Gray stared at Troy and saw the new part of the dream from just this morning. Reed, dressed in chains of gold with a man like Troy behind her, holding her hands. The smile of pure triumph on his face at odds with the tears of misery running down Reed's face. Cillian and Liadan. How did the puzzle fit together? What was the hold Cillian had over her? How did Troy fit in? Had Cillian-Troy always been the thorn in their sides?

A sharp elbow dug into his side and Gray glanced at his mother. "What? Nothing is going to happen until she's well. She can convalesce at the ranch. However long it takes. You want me at the ranch anyway, so I'll stay and look after her."

"But can you lay off her all that time?" Troy asked. "Can you leave her alone while she heals? I need her in the office. I can't do without her expertise."

"Why is that Troy? Doesn't she have staff that can fill in for her for a few weeks?"

"Yes, she has competent staff, but right now she's needed for a particularly sticky situation."

"And why is that, Troy?" Gray stared at him.

Troy shrugged it off. "It's business."

"Well, I'm no expert on concussions, but between the surgery and the head injury, she won't be competent to work for a few weeks at least."

"Thanks to whom?" Troy pinned him with an accusing stare.

"It was an accident," Gray ground out. "You have no idea how guilty I feel. The damn horse wasn't supposed to stop like that."

"Cass?"

Gray glanced at his mother and nodded. "I whistled for him to change direction and instead he stopped cold. That's how she went over his head."

He wondered at his mother's reaction when she closed her eyes and raised her folded hands as if praying. "Nobody told you."

"Told me what?"

"Jamie has been working with Cass. Trick riding. The whistle we use to call the other horses, he's trained Cass to stop with."

"Great. Is Cass the only one?" Gray watched as she nodded sadly. "What other training has Jamie messed with?" He hadn't had a chance to do more than greet his sixteen-year-old nephew.

"He had Dustin's approval, and mine."

"Then why was Cass in the lineup?" he asked.

"It was an oversight." She shook her head sadly. "Jamie's been filling in for Dustin, so he wasn't down at the stables the last few days. One of the hands must have saddled up Cass without thinking."

"And he and Reed picked each other for riding

partners," Gray finished the thought. Leave it to Reed to pick one of the best horses on the ranch. The thought made him grin. Only the best for his love. He wrapped his hand around her watch. "Well, it should make for an interesting rematch when she's well enough."

"Yes." His mother agreed. "Yes, it should."

"You never answered my question, Gray," Troy reminded him. "Will you be able to leave her alone to make her own decision?"

"Can you?"

"Boys."

"Yes, Mother."

"Yes, Sora."

"Let's get her well first, shall we?"

~ * ~

Gray paced the waiting room, his hand wrapped around her watch. As it ticked in his hand, he hoped her heart still beat. It seemed an eternity before Sam and Roger returned and settled into side by side chairs. It seemed like two eternities before a doctor dressed in scrubs appeared, his eyes searching the waiting room.

"Who is here for Ms. O'Brien?"

"We all are." Gray's hand swept the room.

"I'm Doctor Santori. Her surgery went well. We found only a small bleeder and a cracked rib."

"She went over a horse's head. We think she landed on a rock," Gray explained.

The doctor nodded. "Well, she's going to be sore. Other than the rib, no broken bones, but I'm concerned about the concussion. Head over heels off a horse explains the head injury. We did a CT-Scan and didn't find significant swelling, but it's still early. Apparently she wasn't coherent before she passed out."

Gray caught Roger's nod.

"So, what's her prognosis?" Gray asked as Sam stood and walked over beside him.

"She'll be here for at least five days. After that..." The doctor shrugged. "She'll need another three to five weeks but should make a full recovery. We'll know better in a few days, but I don't anticipate any complications." The doctor's eyes glanced around the room and fell on Sam.

"I'm her roommate, so that makes me the closest to her at the moment," Sam told the doctor even though she looked at Gray before looking at Troy. "I also know how to contact her family."

"When can we see her?" Gray wanted to know.

"She's resting comfortably in Recovery. She'll be there about an hour and then we'll move her to a room. I'll have a nurse tell you when she's settled. You might as well get something to eat, take a walk, or sort out who you want to stay with her tonight. Judging by the crowd here, I assume you won't let her stay alone." The doctor's mouth lifted in a crooked smile. "I wish all my patients had support like this. The nurses will grumble, but Ms. O'Brien will heal faster with people who care for her at her side."

Gray nodded shortly and extended his hand. "Thank you, Doctor."

"Doctor?" Sam spoke up. "Is there any chance you can put her in Intensive Care for the first forty eight hours or so?"

Gray and the doctor both looked at her with questions.

"I was planning on overnight, but why longer?"

"I'll stay with her, but she doesn't need outside

issues bothering her. I'm stepping in as her guardian at the moment and I want her visitor list restricted, at least until she's awake and mentally functioning. She's had something of a rather stressful time these past few months, more so specifically in the last twenty-four hours, and I just want to make sure she has complete rest."

"Sam..." Gray said with the doctor's confused eyes on him. Out of the corner of his eye he saw Troy stand, a look of protest on his face.

"No. Gray, Troy. Neither one of you needs to be near her right now. You two have upset her enough. I won't have you agitating her further. If it weren't for the two of you, we wouldn't be here now," Sam said, glaring daggers at the two men.

Dr. Santori's voice was soothing when he answered. "She'll be in the ICU overnight and then depending on how she's doing, we'll make the decision in the morning, but I see no reason why she can't be moved to a private room with restricted access."

"Thank you," Sam said.

"Sam," Gray tried again.

"No!" The force of her rejection made him step back a little. "She wouldn't have taken off like that unless she was fed up with both of you. I talked with Jim this morning and I know you both had a hand in whatever upset her. I won't let either of you push your agendas. Now, I need to call her mother and let her family know what's happened. Her mother will also have a better medical history for her. You all might as well clear out and go home." Sam held out her hand. "I'll take her jewelry as well."

Gray looked at the watch in his hand for a long

moment before he handed it over with a small nod. "I'll get a room at the nearest hotel. Roger has my cell number. Call me if anything at all comes up."

Sam pursed her lips but nodded as she slipped the watch over her hand and settled it on her wrist. "I'll need a few things from the ranch."

"I'll get them for you," Roger said.

"Doctor." Sam shook his hand. "Thank you."

Gray noticed Roger's frown when the doctor held Sam's hand just a second too long.

"I'll check in on her after she's settled in her room," he assured Sam, then left the waiting room.

"Sam, I want to see her," Gray said.

Sam shook her head. "No. Not until her head is clear. This isn't about what you and Troy need, this is about what she needs. If she wakes up and asks for you, I'll call. That's the best I can offer right now."

Gray's heart constricted in his chest as Sam turned away from him to speak to Roger.

"In addition to my suitcase, I'm sure Reed would like a few of her toiletries and her cell phone. Might as well bring her purse and a change of clothing for when she gets out. I need both laptops as well."

Roger nodded. "We'll get it all together and have it here tonight.

"Do you think her mother will want to come out?" Gray asked.

Sam turned back to him and nodded. "Most likely."

"I'll make the arrangements."

TWENTY-FIVE

Sweet blackness. Images floated through it, but soft comforting blackness held her cradled it its arms. Each time her body tried to wake, her mind pulled her back to the plane of no pain. Waking hurt too much.

Carrick. His strong body warm against hers in the pool, his face smiling down at her like the sun. The sun of her world. Strong arms holding her, her body cradling him, his flesh her pillow, her flesh his bed--the images of their love brought joy to her dreams. Then the pain began to creep in.

Her stomach, no, her side... like a knife wound, it burned. Her hands, bound and chained, unable to move as Cillian held her and made her shame known. Now her love knew her dreaded secret, the hold Cillian had over her. Why she and Carrick could never truly be together. She was already wed, bound to Cillian, Carrick's king. And she, she was the prize Cillian offered up to Carrick for his loyalty. Chattel. The prize loaned out to Cillian's greatest warrior. No more than a bargaining chip, a toy, a whore.

She fought against the painful vision of Carrick's anger and hurt as he learned of her betrayal.

"Don't hate me, my love. Forgive me. I had no choice!" she sobbed as Cillian held her.

Because Carrick was away fighting from one

battle to the next he did not know of Cillian's attempts to claim her. Carrick returned to the clan only when she sent a messenger to inform him of her desires. Messages sent only when he sent word of his victories to the stronghold. Only in Carrick's arms did she ever forget the one night Cillian had succeeded in bedding her and making her wed him.

All illusions were destroyed. And why? Because she carried a child. She didn't know which man it belonged to, though Cillian was convinced it was his. Either way, no longer would Carrick be allowed to dream she belonged only to him. No longer could she dream of living only in his arms. The tears streaming down her face washed away all hope of ever seeing her love again, for Cillian had sworn to see him dead once their final enemy was vanquished. One battle left and his life would be forfeit, win or lose.

"No!" she moaned, pulling against Cillian's hold. "No! Carrick! Run!" He was coming toward her, fury in his black eyes. "Carrick! Flee!" Sobs tore from her throat as she struggled against Cillian's grasp.

Carrick had to flee. He couldn't save her. Cillian already had her prison prepared. The prison where she'd linger while the child grew, the prison where she'd live out the rest of her days, producing one child after the next to satisfy her king and clan in the peace secured by the prowess of her true love.

He was to be sacrificed as a peace offering to the god of war, and she, Liadan, was to become nothing more than a brood mare to produce fine strong children who would produce more fine strong children to rebuild the clan. A new generation to fulfill Cillian's dream of supremacy over all the tribes.

"What is this?" Carrick's harsh voice rang out as he looked down from his horse.

"This is your queen, warrior. The reason you fight." Cillian's silky voice filled the glen. "Your victories have ensured the safety of your clan. Defeat the usurpers to the south and your clan will reign over all others. You've done the bidding of your queen most satisfactorily."

"And who are you to trap her this way?"

"I am but your king, warrior. You think you fought for her approval? No, my paladin. You fought to secure the future of her offspring. Even now she carries the first of my heirs, your future monarch. You fight for the future of your clan. One last battle, warrior, and then you will have earned your leisure for all time. A single victory and a life of ease for evermore is yours."

"She bears your fruit?"

Liadan closed her eyes in shame at the break in his voice. How she wished it was his child growing within her womb. A child with warm brown eyes instead of cold blue. A child who would grow to be valorous and not deceitful, to be a leader fair and beloved instead of one envied and feared. Tears ran unchecked down her cheeks as she opened her eyes to look into the deep wells showing the pain of her true love. The hurt of her betrayal.

"My love--"

Cruel hands twisted her arms behind her back, cutting off her plea for mercy and forgiveness.

"Nay, *my* love," Cillian murmured in her ear. "You are mine." He pulled on her arms making her quivering breasts thrust out more. Bands had been secured around her arms and chains from the bands were attached to the collar around her neck. Chains had been added to her girdle.

Well and truly shackled, Liadan knew the chains would remain in place to remind her that her body was his to command. Tears continued to silently flow as Carrick stared down at her. There was naught she could do.

"Return to your battlefield, General," Cillian ordered Carrick. "Send me word of your next victory and I'll reward you well. Mayhap I'll give her to you when I grow tired of her." Cillian's shrug pulled on her arms.

Shamed and seeing no hope, Liadan lowered her eyes and watched her tears fall upon the earth. She had no say, no hope, no dreams. No reason to live.

"No!" Carrick roared, and the sound of steel rang in the glen as he drew his sword.

~ * ~

"Reed!"

"No!" Her throat was tight with tears.

"Reed, honey, please wake up!" Sam's pleading voice broke through the thick blanket of black hovering over her. "Reed, please. Wake up for me. Reed, it's me, Sam. Sammiekins."

Reed felt a tiny smile touch her lips and she calmed immediately. Sammiekins. The silly pet name for her best friend.

"Sammiekins," she whispered. Her throat was sore and still tight with tears. Her eyes stung from the salty drops.

"Oh, Reed." A happy squeak from Sam made her smile a little more. "Come on, honey, you need to wake up. Talk to me, babe. Otherwise the doctors will think you're in a coma."

"Sammie-ow!" She moaned.

"We know, honey. You hurt, but you have to wake up. We need to know your brains aren't scrambled. The nurse won't give you more pain medication if you don't wake up enough to talk to us. Oh, and Troy needs to know your passwords for payroll."

"Troy knows the damn passwords. He picked them out." Reed tried to growl around her sore throat. "Head," she gasped, and squeezed her eyes tight, "ache."

"I know it hurts, babe." Sam's voice and soft hand soothed her. "Drink a little water. That will ease your throat."

Reed tried to shake her head.

"Okay, a few ice chips instead. Just suck on them and let them melt in your mouth."

The ice felt cool, and the melting water eased her swallowing.

"What do you remember?" Sam asked.

"Did Mom pick me up from school? Homework assignment. Call Janie. Oh and tell Troy, I didn't cash my check. Mya will know."

"Mom is on the way to be with you. Gray sent Roger to fly her out."

"Gray." Reed sighed. Gray...she smiled. "Hands." She needed his magic hands. He could ease the pains in her body.

"Gray isn't allowed in just now. You need to rest and get well."

"Gray." Reed protested. "Need, Gray."

"You want Gray?" A tinge of surprise? Regret? What was Sam thinking?

357

"Massage." Oh yeah, massage by those magic hands. "Magic."

Reed heard a deep sigh. "Yes, babe. I'll let Gray know you want him."

"Gray." Reed felt her heart skip a beat. "Hands..."

Sweet blackness engulfed her. No more pain. Only sweet dreams of black eyes. Hot black eyes and hot, gentle hands.

~ * ~

Reed's head throbbed with a dull ache but her stomach was growling and stabbing hunger pangs hurt worse than her head. Her whole body throbbed with dulled pain. She felt as if she'd wrestled with grizzlies and lost.

Unable to bear the thought of moving more than her fingers, she flexed them a little. Her hips hurt from lying in one position too long and she wanted to roll on her side. But her side hurt. Something warm wrapped around her hand and lifted it to warm lips. A kiss. She smiled. Who didn't like kisses?

"Yes, sweetheart, I'm here." A husky male voice spoke from her right side.

"Hmm?" A machine bleeped nearby and the sound of air moving made her aware of something lying across her upper lip. Was there something stuck up her nose? She turned her head to dislodge it.

"It's just a little oxygen, Reed. A little air to make sure you breathe easier."

"Why?" Her voice cracked around a dry throat.

"Water? Open your mouth, I have a straw here for you."

Reed wrapped her lips around the plastic tube

and drew in cold water. She swallowed eagerly hoping it would wash away the terrible metallic taste in her mouth. A few swallows and she felt exhausted. Opening her mouth, she let the straw go and a few drops of cold water dripped on her chin.

"Oh! Sorry, sweetheart." A warm thumb wiped up the drops. "Better?"

"Thanks." She relaxed against the pillow. "Sleepy. No, hungry." Her stomach rolled over again.

"The doctor will be pleased to hear that." The warm voice sounded pleased as well. "Ah, here's the nurse."

The air pressure changed and she heard the soft swish of a door.

"And is our Miss O'Brien awake this evening?" A soft but cheerful voice interrupted. Female.

"She's working at it." A large warm hand gently squeezed hers.

"Food," Reed muttered.

"Ah, so it's food she wants," the nurse said approvingly. "Let me see what I can find. I'll go get that right now then check your vitals while Mr. Handsome feeds you, hmm?"

"Hmm," Reed replied and opened her eyes. The room was dim but she could still make out the man standing beside the bed. "Gray."

"I'm here, Ree." He looked tired, but still smiled at her and lifted her hand to kiss it. "And so very happy to see you awake."

"Day?"

"It's Friday night. You had your accident the day before yesterday."

"Accident?"

"You don't remember?"

"Hurt?"

"You got tossed off Cass. You needed surgery for internal bleeding and you bumped your head."

The bed beside her slowly dipped.

"Oh." She frowned, trying to remember. Four faces staring down at her. Two with large hairy noses. Horses. "Casanova?"

"Yes. I didn't know he'd been trained to stop on a whistle. I'm so sorry. I never meant for you to get hurt."

She pried her eyes open to see the anguished look on his face. "S'okay. I know you didn't mean it."

Gray held her hand to his cheek and she felt warm dampness. Was he crying?

She brushed her finger over his cheek and he bent to kiss her palm.

"I'll make it up to you, I swear," he whispered.

"Accidents...happen." Her stomach growled again. Louder than before, she could almost swear she heard it echo in the room.

"More water?"

"Please." She sipped from the straw then let it go. The water tasted so good on her raw throat. "Sam?"

"She just took your mom back to the hotel to get some sleep. They were here all last night and most of today. It's about nine now."

"Mom?"

"Roger hopped in the plane and brought your Mom back."

The door swished open again and light footsteps followed.

"I have some very nice lime gelatin here," the

cheerful voice said. "Get that down, keep it down, and we'll consider upping you to grown-up food in a couple hours."

Warm soft hands placed a cuff around her left bicep. "I bet you'd like to sit up a little. Don't want any sore spots from lying still too long."

Reed nodded. "Yes. Want to move."

"Well, we'll move in baby steps here. Sing out if something hurts."

The head of the bed rose a few inches. "Better?"

"More?"

"Yes, ma'am."

Reed could hear the smile. The bed rose a few more inches.

"There, let's try that for a little bit."

She opened her eyes again and saw a pretty young woman with dark-rimmed glasses.

"I'm Kathy," the woman said.

"Hi."

A warm hand gently squeezed her arm and a warm smile lit up Kathy's face. "I do believe you are going to be just fine. Now try some of this delicious green wiggly stuff while I get your blood pressure, okay?"

Reed nodded and looked toward Gray who held a spoon out for her.

"Open up, beautiful."

She stared into his smiling eyes as the cuff tightened around her arm. The first spoonful of Jell-O was cool and tasted of lime. It slid easily down her throat and she opened her mouth for more. That seemed to please Gray immensely. How hurt was she, really? The next spoonful followed the first. The cuff ratcheted down until it deflated completely.

"Good pressure, there," Kathy commented, making a note on a clipboard then reached for her wrist.

Another spoonful of the gelatin.

"Itch." Reed turned her head away from the next spoonful.

"Where?" Gray lowered the spoon.

"Left shoulder." She tried to wiggle as if to get away from it.

"Ah, that would be the defibrillator patch," Kathy said. "Sorry, can't take it off yet."

"It really itches," Reed heard herself whine. The itching sensation felt like it went bone deep and threatened to consume her whole body. Once started, the itch took over.

"I'll see if we can add some antihistamine to your next med dose," the other woman told her.

A gentle knock sounded on the door before it slowly swung open.

"Reed? Honey?"

"Mom." Tears stung the back of her eyes.

Gray stood up and made room for Mom to sit on the edge of the bed.

"They called to say you were awake, honey." Soft lips and the scent of Chanel No. 5 invaded her senses.

"Mommy." Tears leaked. Home.

"I'm here, honey."

TWENTY-SIX

"When do I get to break out?" Reed groused. She flipped the TV off in disgust. Sunday evening programming sucked. The episode of *House* was a repeat.

"My, we are cranky, now aren't we?"

Reed directed a glare at her mother sitting in a chair calmly knitting.

"Sure you don't want a ball of yarn and a crochet hook? That would keep your hands busy."

"No, I don't want to crochet," she muttered.

"Then why don't you try to sleep?"

Reed blew out a sigh. Maybe she could sleep a little more. "When did the doctor say I could get out of here?"

"Day after tomorrow."

Reed leaned back against her pillows. The incision from her surgery hurt. At least they'd pull the staples first. That was good news. The concussion was still a pain. Even now her head throbbed with a dull ache. Tylenol helped, but didn't completely erase the discomfort. The rib hurt when she coughed or sneezed despite the tight bandaging. What frustrated her even more was how weak she felt. One little trip to the bathroom and she was dripping in sweat and needed a nap. It was the altitude, right?

"What has you so agitated?" Emerald green eyes continued to gaze at her with a deep calmness. "Are you going to tell me about your dreams?"

"Dreams? What dreams?" Reed looked away.

"The ones you mutter your way through every time you nod off. You still talk in your sleep, dearest."

Reed fingered the jade pendant around her neck. Gray had put it back on her sometime after her surgery. As far as she could tell, the Celtic dream had blossomed into Technicolor since he'd given the stone disk to her. She had vague recollections of it, and others with similar themes from over the years, but she'd never remembered them in daylight. Now she couldn't escape them, sleeping or waking.

"Do you believe in dreams, Mom?"

"Sure I do." She frowned at the look on Reed's face. "Not the right answer?"

"I don't know," Reed muttered. "Gray seems to think it proves we're soul mates. If Troy has ever had a similar dream he's never admitted it."

"I know Troy is out of the running, so now we have Gray. Handsome, charming, successful and madly in love with you. He's obviously brilliant. What's the problem?"

"I don't know. I was seriously falling in love with him last week...and then..."

"And then something led into you bolting in the middle of the night and ultimately resulted in your accident and subsequent hospitalization."

"Right. And since then he's had to deal with family business." Only making it to the hospital at the end of the day. "We haven't had a chance to talk." Or cuddle. He'd been distant. Charming, but holding her at arm's length.

Reed glanced at the clock. He should arrive with dinner in the next hour. Hospital food being horrible as usual, Maria, the cook at the ranch took it upon herself to send along a basket with food for however many people were hovering in Reed's room. Since Troy and company had left yesterday, they were down to three now. Her, Mom, and Gray.

"Yes, well he rushed home to help his family, and here I am to help with my family."

"Thanks for coming, Mom. I do appreciate the company. I just hate being laid up."

"I know, honey. Besides, I'm looking forward to spending the next week at the ranch. I've never been to a dude ranch before."

Reed glanced at her mom only to see her eyes twinkling mischievously. "Not so different from Ernie and Cora's ranch. Just larger, with more people wandering around. And they have a gift shop. And a saloon and dining room."

"Right. Not so different."

Reed lapsed into silence and thought about the visit from Troy and the others. They'd stopped on their way back down to the airport in Denver. Troy and Sam had both asked for time alone with her. Ian, Dennis and Stuart had settled for a brief group visit, Ian and Dennis planting big, noisy kisses on her cheeks.

The return of their easy affection had brought tears to her eyes. She'd been far too cranky with them and missed their friendship terribly. She was so glad to have it back. They'd laughed at her when she'd promised to be nicer, but they'd promised to be nicer too.

Sam had been encouraging as well, promising

Reed she had the solution to the invention problem. All she needed was two weeks in the lab and things would be better. Sam had even laughed when Reed confessed how much she'd been supporting the household.

"Don't worry about it, baggage," Sam had said. "You've kept me from being laid off and my salary whole. We'll work it out later. I can carry the house for as long as needed."

Sam's gentle hug had sent the previously gathering tears spilling over as they'd laughed together. "You just get well and don't let those two bozos jerk you around," Sam ordered.

"Yes, ma'am."

Troy's visit had been tougher. He'd sat on the side of the bed, very close to Reed's hip and held her hand.

"Reed, don't make any snap decisions, please," he'd pleaded with her.

"Troy, it just isn't there between us. I like you fine. Most of the time anyway," she said trying to tease but it had fallen flat. "You and Gray want instant answers. I don't have any right now."

Troy had then cupped her cheek tenderly and stared into her eyes. "Reed, I really do love you. I want you by my side."

"Troy, please.

"You're right. I hate that I have to leave now. But, the good news is, I think Sam is onto something big. We'll know in a couple weeks. Ian, Dennis and I are going to closet ourselves in the lab with her. If we can't find the solution, it doesn't exist. If we weren't on to something big, I wouldn't leave..."

Cutting off his wandering thoughts she'd given

him a big smile of encouragement. "No problem stands a chance against that dream team of brains."

Troy's answering smile had been wistful. "It'll be late when I get home so I'll call tomorrow morning, okay?"

"Fine, Troy. That works for me."

She hadn't been able to stop him when he'd leaned forward and softly kissed her. Nice. Pleasant even. Just no fireworks or jumping hormones.

Then Gray had arrived and his kiss had sent her hormones into high sizzle.

"That was a big sigh," her mother commented. "Troy or Gray?"

"Gray," Reed admitted quietly.

"Carrick in your dream?"

"Yes."

"So what's the problem?"

"In the dream, he kills Cillian. Troy."

"That's a problem. What do you think it means in this world?"

"Gray annihilates Troy's business? Puts him, his company and all his employees into bankruptcy? Or he scores a hostile take-over. I'm not sure which is the worse scenario."

"Have you discussed this with Gray?"

"No. Both of them made me promise not to worry over it until the concussion healed. They seem to have reached a truce, so there's some good news. Hell, even Gray's mother is being nice to me."

"Why shouldn't she?" Reed's mom looked up with a raised brow. "She strikes me as being a very capable and caring woman."

"Never would have guessed it by her initial reaction to me," Reed grumbled.

"Everybody is allowed a second chance. It seems you both get one."

"Maybe."

"Either start crocheting something or take a nap. You're sliding into a black hole you have no business going into."

"Yes, Mom." Reed pulled the blanket up and closed her eyes. Gray would wake her up.

~ * ~

"What are you going to do, warrior?" Cillian's sneer whistled past her ear.

He stood with one arm around her, while the other held her wrists together behind her back. The bracelets and arm bands cut into her skin and she bit her lip to keep from crying out. Carrick's eyes held a murderous glare directed at Cillian. She didn't want to distract him. Cillian's guards stood nearby, ready to kill Carrick if need be.

Hoping to fade from the scene, she lowered her gaze and willed herself into a trance. The same trance she used when Cillian wrapped his bindings and chains around her body. So far she'd frustrated him by not responding to his lovemaking. Sex. Mating at its most basic and crude. Rutting. Not love, nothing like the love she shared with Carrick.

Cillian's soft hand flattened over her womb. So different from Carrick's strong, rough hands. "Have a care, warrior, here rests your future king. Hurt her, hurt the child, and you lose your future and your very life. There are things far worse than death."

Liadan controlled the flinch when the chains

around her tightened. She heard Carrick's sharp intake of breath.

"What if I hurt you instead?" Carrick's voice was low and carried a dangerous note to her ears.

"Foolish. A dozen arrows are aimed at you this very moment. Your best recourse is to turn your mighty steed around and rejoin your troops. Bring me word of your victory and I may grant you a fortnight in her bower. Accomplish it soon and she may not be too fat to plow properly."

The chains loosened and hung against her body again. Cillian's hand stroked her skin, stopping to glide over a tender breast before moving to her hair.

"Is she not beautiful? Is she not worth fighting for? The issue she produces will be fair indeed. Strong and intelligent. Our clan will be mighty, and your victory will ensure the child she bears will rule. Fail, and you will be hauled back here in chains and spend your life watching her submit to me while another fights for her honor and the right to use her as you have."

Cillian wrapped her hair around his hand then jerked backward, forcing her from her trance, making her eyes pop open. Carrick's stare chilled her.

"Bring peace and victory to our clan and you will be rewarded with lands and women as fair as Liadan." Cillian's gaze bored into him and the promise rang with arrogance.

Liadan could only wonder if he truly meant to keep his word. It mattered little as she knew Cillian would never let her spend another night in Carrick's arms. Last night had been their farewell, grudgingly granted by Cillian only because he felt sure the child was his.

But what if he were wrong?

What if the child was born with dark eyes instead of blue? Would Cillian let the child live and raise it as his own anyway? Or would the child be banished or, worse yet, killed to hide the shame it being another man's child?

She stared at Carrick and tried to convey her love for him, only for him, with just her eyes. He stared at her hard, then flicked his gaze over Cillian. With a sharp nod, he turned his horse and galloped away.

Cillian pulled on the chains. "Well done, my queen." His biting sneer of her title made her shiver. "Time for your reward."

~ * ~

"Reed."

The softly spoken sound of her name made her jump.

"I'm here, Ree."

Gray. His voice came from next to her ear and she relaxed against his body.

"Shh, it's okay, sweetheart." His lips brushed her cheek and his fingers soothed her wrinkled forehead. "No need to cry, my love."

"Oh Gray. You have to end this war with Troy. You just have to." She turned her face into the crook of his neck.

"Already in the process. We'll work it out when you're well and strong. Until then a truce has been declared."

"Oh good." With a small grunt, she shifted in his arms. The antiseptic smells of the hospital were faint against the more pleasing scent of him. Now all she needed was to get rid of the pain in her side and her head.

"Careful now." He gently pulled her against his body, his arm holding her secure even as she pillowed her cheek on his shoulder.

The hospital bed was a tight fit for two, but they made it work. She didn't sleep well without him there and she knew the reclining chair was uncomfortable for him. This was only slightly better but at least they were together. The nurse even admitted she slept better in his arms than she did alone.

"You okay?" he asked. "Do you need more morphine?"

"No, God no. No more morphine." Just the thought of it made her skin feel hot and itchy. "I hate that stuff."

"You're almost off it anyway," Gray yawned.

"And I'm keeping you awake again."

"S'okay," he said quietly and kissed her forehead.

"No, it's not okay. You're exhausted, and no wonder, running back and forth between here and the ranch. Then not getting a good night's sleep in a comfortable bed."

"I get to hold you. That makes it all worthwhile." He yawned again. "'Sides, only one more night and then you come home."

Home. Home to him. The ranch to her. She chewed her lip. Could it ever be home to her? Sure, she loved the little plot of land where he wanted to build a house, but could she live in such isolation? And what if Sora never liked her? Would he have to travel often for business? The private jet seemed to indicate he traveled a lot. Would she be left alone week after week?

"What's wrong?"

His question startled her. She thought he'd fallen asleep again.

"Nothing."

"Stop trying to fool me. You're heart is racing a mile a minute. If I didn't know better I'd think you'd just made wild love to me."

"I'd like to try..." She kissed his neck.

"Not now. You're not healed enough." He turned to capture her lips in a kiss.

Long and sweet, his tongue teased hers into a dance. She moaned against his mouth and he slowly eased back, foiling her plans to heat it up.

"Easy there." He protested. "I will not be responsible for your staples ripping out. Don't worry, I'll still be hungry and waiting for you."

"I'm hungry now," she growled and tried to nip his lower lip.

"Then I guess I'd better see if the leftovers are still good. Lasagna or chocolate cake?"

"Cock."

"Such language! Better watch your mouth, young lady."

"Fuck me," she moaned against his lips.

"I promise." He groaned. "The minute the doctor gives the all clear signal, I'll be on you."

"I want you in me. Now," she muttered against his neck. To emphasize her point she ran her hand down over his chest. The shirt had to go. "Besides, it must be uncomfortable sleeping in your jeans night after night."

She reached for the button on his pants and his hand stopped her.

"You're killing me," he growled. "Now what's this all about? You were sweetly sleeping just a few minutes ago until you started whimpering. Was it the dream?"

The dream.

"How far did the dream go tonight?" he pressed.

"Uh... the usual."

"Which is? You haven't said anything in a few days."

"Uh, well... oh jeez, here I am, keeping you up again. Go to sleep. You've been looking awfully tired lately. I'm being selfish again."

"Reed." He heaved a heavy sigh. "You have got to be the very worst liar I've ever come across."

"I think I'm insulted."

"You shouldn't be. But the point here is, you shouldn't even try to lie to me. I can read you too easily."

"Somehow that just doesn't seem at all fair," she grumbled.

"Stop stalling and tell me about what you've dreamed lately," he said and kissed her nose.

"You... you...ride off."

"And leave you trembling in Cillian's arms? More chains? After he tells me you're carrying his child?"

"Yes," she whispered.

"What you don't know is my plan."

"And?"

"While you're there, all I can think about is how I've already won the war. My next plan is to lead my army against Cillian to steal you away. That's why I leave."

"Oh...I thought you were disgusted and angry."

"I was, but not with you." He pulled her close, lips against her forehead. "Never with you."

"Wait a minute... you'd already won the war?"

"Um hmm."

"Then why? Why were you leaving?"

"Because you dressed me and shoved me out the door?"

"What?" Reed leaned back and looked up at him.

"That's the way it always worked. One glorious night and then after breakfast you send me on my way."

"And even though you'd beaten all the enemies, you were just going to leave, right?"

"I was going to come back once I sent the army home."

"Oh."

"Sleep, my love, it will all work out. I promise to not actually lop his head off. Well, not in this world."

TWENTY-SEVEN

Leaning back in Carrick's arms, Liadan focused her will on pushing. A labor pain gripped her stomach and she gritted her teeth.

"That's it, my love," Carrick crooned in her ear and had the pain not been so great she would have laughed. He didn't sound the least bit confident, but at least he was still there. He was the only one still there.

The labor pains had started two nights before. Determined to discover the true father of the child in a safe place, she'd risen and left their bed. Thankful it was deep night and the village slept, she'd meant to steal away and deliver the child by herself. If it resembled Cillian in any way, she had vague thoughts of leaving the child with a family far from the village, with the witch hiding in the woods, or possibly, as a last resort, drowning it. Or maybe a passing traveler could be persuaded to carry it to the monks their enclave, a three day ride to the north.

If the child was Cillian's, the product of a union she hadn't wanted, the child's father was dead anyway. Dead by Carrick's sword in an honorable battle.

Now rightful and beloved queen to Carrick, she wanted no reminders of Cillian in the form of a child which should have been Carrick's by rite of love. She didn't want Carrick to see his enemy each time he looked at the unfortunate child and be constantly reminded of that horrible day he vanquished Cillian and rescued her.

Not that he'd said anything at all about the child's parentage, one way or the other, but she'd caught the thoughtful and speculative looks of servants and villagers alike. A sense of waiting hovered over everything.

Of course Carrick had woken with the first stirring. Knowing her desire to be rid of the discomforts of pregnancy, he'd gathered a bundle of clothing and food, then lifted her onto his horse. He'd brought her to a small hunting hut far from the village, sheltered in trees a stone's throw from the sea. Though his eyes looked oddly sad, he didn't argue with her about her chosen location.

Hours later with only the rising sun as a witness and no one around to hear, she let out a scream as the baby's head passed. It felt as if her pelvis were being ripped apart.

"Oh Morrigan!" Carrick prayed to the goddess. "Liadan? Tell me what to do!"

"Take... pull the babe," she panted.

Carrick laid her back on the bed of moss he'd made for them then moved to her feet. "I see it!"

"Pull it out!" She grunted as another contraction squeezed her body. Thankfully Carrick had the presence of mind to follow whatever instinct lived in man. She felt the small body slide from hers and she fell back, sweat pouring off her naked skin as she panted with the exertion. Exhausted from the long hours of laboring, she had no strength left. Let Carrick deal with the child and after-birth for now.

"'Tis a boy," he told her, a note of wonder in his

voice as the babe let out a wail.

"If it looks like Cillian, I don't want to know. If the hair is blond, just wrap it up and do something with it. A few miles yonder is a family with a passel of bairns. They won't notice one more especially if he's left with a handful of coin."

Carrick didn't answer, but she felt his censure in his silence. The child's wails grew stronger and she listened to the rustling of cloth. Presumably Carrick was cleaning and caring for the newborn.

"He's got a red, scrunched up face. I think he has your chin." Carrick laughed softly as the bairn continued to wail in protest at the rudeness of the cold world.

"A weak chin for a male. Please, Carrick, if it isn't yours, I don't want to know. If it is from Cillian, take it away. I care not what you do with it."

"You can't mean that!" Carrick sounded angry and she lifted an eyelid to look at him. "This child had no choice. He's innocent and was thrust into the world. The sins of the father are not the sins of the child. He's the only one innocent in this play."

"Aye, he is. But if I look into his face and see his father, I don't think I can live with myself. It isn't his fault and it isn't fair, but his father treated not only me, but many people cruelly. What if the child has his father's nature? I don't want the village tainted with his blood ever again. Ridding ourselves of the child will purge the tribe once and for all. If you won't give him away then toss him into the sea," she said wearily.

An unearthly light filled the hut and she heard Carrick's soft intake of air. Lifting her eyelid again she saw a woman standing over the bed, assessing the situation with a cool eye.

"Yes?" Liadan was too tired to be gracious.

"You would kill the child?" the dark haired woman asked.

"Only if it is not Carrick's and the family down the road will not take him. I won't ask our people to raise Cillian's son and ask them to accept him as their future king. I can't risk his nature being the same as his father's."

"This is not his father?" The goddess indicated Carrick holding the swaddled and now silent babe.

"If the child has blond hair, then no. His father is dead."

"So this could be Cillian's child." The woman nodded to herself. "Although his nature is sweeter than his sire's it could very well be brave Carrick's child."

"How do you know? Who are you?"

"Do you not recognize me then?" The woman smirked.

"Morrigan?" Liadan asked. It must be.

"Oh Liadan and Carrick, you pray to me often enough. Yes, I am Morrigan. I will take the child and raise him. I have a spot he can fill in this world. One that will wash away his father's cruelties. Give him to me," she ordered Carrick, arms outstretched.

"No." Carrick held the child to his chest. "He has a head of dark hair. Possibly red, it's hard to tell in this light and wet as he still is, but it matters not. I claim him. The child is mine."

"How can you be sure the child is yours?" Liadan said. "What if the hair color lightens once the child is properly washed? We won't know by eye color for months yet. If Morrigan wants him, let her take him. He'll be raised where there's never a question of his parentage."

"There will be no question. I won't allow it. I claim the child as mine," Carrick stated firmly. "If he chooses to serve the goddess later, I'll let him go with my blessings, but I won't send him off to the arms of a stranger. Regardless of his sire, he needs his own mother."

Inside a knot loosened and Liadan felt her heart swell, her eyes burned with tears of exhaustion. Who was she to argue with Carrick? If she felt a sense of relief, well that was for her heart to know.

Morrigan gazed down at Carrick then nodded before looking toward Liadan. "I know your true heart and know you do not truly wish death on this child. You seek to spare your people pain and protect the child from the hatred they would shower upon him. Cillian was a good seed turned rancid. Regardless of his sire, in this child the good returns. This child and your future children will carry forth your lessons of love, allowing peace to rule for a time. This beginning is a fresh start. Rule your people well and with mercy such as you show this child."

A feeling of great weariness settled on Liadan and her eyes closed. All she heard was a rush of wind blowing through the trees around the hut. A small bundle was tucked into her arms and larger, stronger arms wrapped around her. A tiny mouth found and latched onto her breast, while other lips kissed away the single hot tear easing down her cheek.

~ * ~

"Gray, please, don't make me do this!" Reed

clutched at his arm. He ignored her and gently pushed her hat down on her head.

"You have to. You can't live up here and be afraid of horses. You need to climb back on. Jamie is waiting with him in the corral." Gray slid his arm around her waist and all but pushed her out the door of the cabin.

Reed looked over her shoulder. "Mom, help me out, here!"

"He's right. You need to see Cass."

When Mom took her other arm, Reed knew she was sunk. There was no getting past the determined combination of Gray and Mom. They were gentle, but nonetheless firm, as they slowly escorted her down the wooden steps toward the stables and corral. Even at this distance she could see Cass's big brown eyes watching her, his tail flicking idly. He didn't have a saddle on, just a halter with lead rope.

Reed had only returned to the ranch this morning, not quite a week since the accident. Gray had let her sleep after lunch and now the long shadows of afternoon were cooling the mountain air.

"I can't ride him yet. I just got my staples pulled."

"You're right, but you can feed him an apple and pet him," Gray said. "We'll get you up on him in a few days. Right now we need the two of you to make friends again."

What Gray didn't say was that she needed to make friends with Cass again. The horse had only been responding to his training, and for as little time as they'd been partnered, Cass wouldn't have missed Reed. Gray was simply worried about Reed and her future at the ranch, and he wanted her to feel better about the horse.

"No hesitation, Reed. You need to walk right up to him and treat him just the way you did at the camp. Talk to him as if there's nothing wrong," Gray coached.

"Right. Have an apple handy?"

"In my pocket. I've got three already cut up to make it easier. Just baby him the way you have from the start."

Sucking in a deep breath she nodded. He was right. Didn't make it easier to do. "Okay, you two can release me. I don't need to look like a prisoner approaching the gallows."

Quiet laughter accompanied her release and she eased into a casual walk. Loose sweats replaced her jeans and one of Gray's shirts covered her arms. For once she wanted to shed the concealing clothes and wear shorts and a tank top. Maybe she'd reconsider her views on the sun. Another time.

A ranch hand opened the gate when she approached the corral, and she gave him smile.

"There's my boy, Cass," she said softly and the horse turned his head to look at her. Reminding herself she wasn't riding today, Reed reached out a hand to him.

The big horse must have caught a hint of her nervousness or the scent of the hospital on her because he snorted and tried to turn away but she caught his halter. "No, you don't get away that easy, sweetie. I've missed you, and now I want some lovin'." She stroked his neck, her hand firm against his coat. "We brought you a little treat." She held out her hand and Gray gave her the bag with the apple pieces. Cass nudged her arm and she laughed. "Yeah, you only want to see me because I have food. I'd always heard the way to a man's heart was through his stomach. I just didn't realize it worked with horses too."

Gray glanced at his nephew and Jamie nodded with a small smile. It was going to be fine. He relaxed enough to smile and step back a little to lean against the fence rails. Reed was quickly relaxing as she fell into talking with the horse. She was the one who'd been hurt, but the males around her were the ones who needed the reassurance.

Even now Cass became putty in her hands as she held a slice of apple for him. The big nose nudged her looking for the next one but she shook her head.

By the time she finished feeding Cass, her face was pale and lines of pain made her eyes looked pinched, but she'd made a good return to reconnecting with the horse. A few more days like this and they'd get her up in the saddle for a gentle ride.

"Well, Cass," Gray stepped forward to pet the horse, "you fell for one of the oldest tricks in the book. A pretty girl." He shook his head with a mock sigh and laughed when Cass snorted. "Yeah, I'm with you, buddy. I'll eat anything she wants to feed me from those pretty little hands too." For a long moment he stared into Reed's eyes and considered lifting her onto the horse's bare back. It would be an easy way to get her back to the cabin. Then he remembered the bright pink of her scar. No, too soon.

Patting Cass's neck he gently pulled Reed

away. "Okay old boy, this pretty lady needs to find her own stall and dinner for the night. She'll come see you again tomorrow and in a day or two she'll be ready for another ride." How much Cass truly understood, Gray decided he'd never know, but the big head bobbed as if nodding and the brown eyes looked amused.

"Sweet baby." Reed stepped away from him and kissed Cass. "To bed for me, I think."

"Yes, ma'am," Gray drawled, and reeled her back into his arms.

Letting Gray turn her from the corral, Reed saw Sora next to her mother, leaning against the rails, chin resting on folded arms. Mother Dunbar was still a great unknown. Every other member of Gray's family had been warm and welcoming, many of them taking time to visit her at the hospital at least once.

Dustin had stayed for an afternoon after seeing his doctor and they'd traded commiserations about their injuries. Everyone agreed he had the more impressive scar. Sora had sent a pair of moccasins to replace the hospital slippers and a soft robe, but otherwise had remained aloof. Someone had to look after the ranch, after all.

"Mrs. Dunbar--"

"Sora," she replied shortly with a small smile. "Dinner is ready if you feel up to joining me. We have the family dining room to ourselves tonight."

Reed glanced up at Gray, and he lifted a brow. It was entirely up to her. She turned back to his mother and nodded. "Thank you. I'd like that very much."

"Gray, drive her up." Sora pushed away from the fence and tossed her head toward the truck behind her. "Walking down the hill is one thing. Up is another while you're recuperating."

"Thanks."

"I'll walk with you," Reed's mother said to Gray's. "I've been sitting for days and stretching feels good."

Bemused, Reed let Gray tug her over to the truck while the two women strolled toward the lodge, talking like old friends.

"Come on," Gray said. "Up in the truck with you."

"I'm not an invalid," Reed grumbled but let him boost her up anyway. She liked the feeling of his hand on her bottom.

"For now you're convalescing, so enjoy the attention."

He patted her gently and she grunted in response. If his chuckle was any indication, he ignored her before pulling her up under his arm for the short ride to the lodge.

"Not nervous are you?" Gray asked her.

"A little. It's the first time your mother has spoken to me. The abrupt invitation to dinner is a little daunting."

"Mom's okay. In fact, she's the one who made Troy and me back off and leave you alone at the hospital. Well, her and Sam."

Reed watched the grimace cross his face. "Sam really barred you from my room?"

"For a whole twenty-four hours," he grumbled then grinned. "But you asked for me so she couldn't very well keep me away."

"So do I get the full story behind you and Troy?"

"You don't remember? Roger told you all about

it."

"When?" Frowning she tried to remember but so much was missing.

"He told you right after the fall. While Troy and I went back to get the rest of the group. You two practically ordered us away."

Gray stopped the truck near the lodge and turned it off. There was a gray, fuzzy spot on her memory as she tried to bring back the afternoon.

"I remember a man talking, being held, Mrs. Bartles from high school...and then everything is blank."

"Mrs. Bartles? From high school?"

"Your mom kind of reminds me of her," Reed said simply. There was no way she was going to tell Gray what a dragon Mrs. Bartles had been.

"Is that good or bad?"

"Oh look, they're waiting for us." She nudged him in the shoulder.

"Think I'm going to let you out of this truck before you answer my question?" His eyes sparkled as he teased her.

"Yes, because our mothers are staring at us, wondering what is going on. Let's go." She shoved a little harder.

"Fine. I'll make you answer later." Helping her from the truck, he pulled her close and kissed her nose before turning to join the older women.

Delicious smells teased Reed's senses as soon as they stepped into the lobby and her stomach reacted immediately. It was an hour before the guests would eat. Gray's arm around her shoulders guided her to the stairs.

"There's a dumb waiter that will send food up. Rather handy," he commented.

She could only agree as the food was waiting for them when they arrived in the dining room. Gray lifted trays from the cabinet in the wall while Sora poured water and iced tea. The long table, more than large enough for Gray's extended family, held four place settings at one end. Reed gingerly sat in the seat Gray nodded her to. What could Sora want?

The first several minutes were taken up with general conversation as food was passed. Reed inhaled the aroma of the perfectly cooked steak. Just as good as the food that had been sent to the hospital to make up for the plain breakfast and dull lunch offerings.

"Sora, thanks for sending food each night." Reed decided it was time to move forward.

The older woman smiled. "Dustin complained loudly enough when he was there. Cafeteria food is as bad as what they serve the patients. I'm just glad you enjoyed it."

"The nurses enjoyed the extra desserts." Not to mention they enjoyed Gray delivering the desserts. More than one nurse and volunteer had gazed after him with lust in their eyes.

Reed had to agree, he was more delicious than the food. Glancing at him, she found him watching her and she blushed when he winked back. Could he read her thoughts? Clearing her throat she turned back to Sora. "The ranch didn't have to pick up my hospital bill. My insurance will cover it."

Sora waved the comment aside. "They get plenty of business from us each year. Don't worry about it."

"How much business did they get when Gray

was a kid?" Reed asked.

Sora's laugh took Reed by surprise. It lit up the older woman's face, transforming her into a truly beautiful woman. "It's a toss-up as to who spent more time in the ER. Actually, hands down, I have." She grinned. "Only I wasn't the patient. I was the one holding hands."

"Here's your chance." Reed held back her giggle. "You get to tell me every naughty thing Gray did as a child."

"No, no, no!" he protested loudly.

"Oh yes, yes, yes!" Reed laughed. He actually blushed. Rather cute, really.

"Fine, but just keep in mind your mother is here as well. Seems to me, she might have a few stories to tell." Gray settled an arm around her shoulders.

"Nope, I was the good child. No good stories there." She glared at her mother choking on her glass of water.

"Now really, Reed." Rhona coughed while Sora patted her on the back. "No fair telling tales while I'm drinking."

A burning flush raced across Reed's face. Mothers. Who needed 'em? With a heavy sigh she sank back into her chair and stared at her plate. She'd really put her foot in it this time.

~ * ~

"Enough!" Reed held her stomach an hour later. "I can't laugh anymore. It hurts too much."

"You asked for it," Gray reminded her.

"I know, I know. I'm sorry. I should have waited a week." The hand pressed against her healing incision didn't help much and she couldn't reach her rib even though it was still taped.

"Ah, he's a good boy," Sora said with a soft smile. "The memories have been fun."

"I agree," Rhona added. "Big families always provide the most adventure."

No kidding. Reed had learned more about Gray in an hour than she'd discovered in a week and a half.

"Troy called today," Sora said, drawing their attention.

"Oh?" Gray sipped from his coffee.

"Seems to think his gadget will be ready for testing this weekend. Wants to bring it here for the shake-down."

"That was fast," Gray muttered.

"No kidding. Sam's idea must have been just the ticket." Reed gave him a curious look. What did he know about it?

Gray shrugged. "Must have. Well. We should get you back to bed. You're looking a little peaked there." Funny how his kisses could convince her of almost anything.

~ * ~

"What are you doing?" Reed's soft voice made him jump and Gray looked over his shoulder as he stretched to cover the surprise.

The lamp on the table next to him created a warm glow in the dark living room of the small cabin.

"Just reading over some papers for the ranch."

"Anything exciting?"

She looked exciting wearing a long cotton gown with the shawl her mother had knit around her shoulders. Like a farmwife from another century...another life. Unable to resist, he leaned back as she wrapped her arms around his neck from behind.

He wanted nothing more than to wrap her up in his arms. Ranch business be damned. "Oh yeah, expense reports, cash flow, and don't forget the really exciting one, the profit and loss statement. Then for the big finish, there's the projections worksheet."

"Mmm, lucky you. Learning anything?"

"The ranch is doing a good steady business. Some of the stockholders want to upgrade. It could be done, but I'd feel better with a little more cash set aside." Soft hair tickled his cheek and reminded him of it brushing over his body.

"So...generating more cash is a priority?"

"If those who want to upgrade prevail."

"You don't want to upgrade?"

"Not as much as they want to." He leaned back and nuzzled her neck. "Umm, you smell good. What are you doing awake? Did the light disturb you?"

"I was about to ask you the same question. It's the middle of the night."

Shuffling the papers, he set them aside. Fatigue immediately set in. "What time is it?"

"One in the morning. Why are you up reading these now?"

"Family meeting tomorrow."

"Ah. Should I leave you to it? Or lure you into my bed?" she whispered in his ear. No sense in waking her mother in the second bedroom.

"I think you've already shot my concentration to hell." Her lips on his earlobe were mighty effective. "You're very good at convincing me to go to bed." A bed would be great. Hers even better. Had it really been more than a week since he'd slept in a proper bed? The last two nights had been spent on the sofa. An attempt to keep his hands off her as promised.

Warm fingers moved down the neck of his shirt and a streak of fire continued down his body. One small turn of his head and his lips found hers. God she tasted so good. Toothpaste mint had faded leaving behind just her, sweet and tender. Smelled even better. Warmed flowers, and even warmer woman.

Tempted to pull her over the back of the sofa and into his arms, he resisted. Popping open her incision would not be a good thing right now. A middle of the night trip back to the hospital was not on his list. Reluctantly he broke the kiss and buried his face in her hair when she dropped her head to his shoulder.

"So, you're coming to bed?"

"No place else I want to be. Ever. As long as you're there."

TWENTY-EIGHT

Footsteps behind her on the deck made Reed turn around.

"Surprise," Troy said with a smile. "Here, these are for you."

Daisies, looking a little worse for the wear of traveling, were thrust into her hands.

"Thanks," she said, and lifted the flowers to hide the lack of a welcoming smile on her face. Discussions with Troy had been kept short this past week. Mya had a good grip on the accounting department and Reed was content to let her handle it. Not that there was much to do other than assure Mya the outstanding checks wouldn't be cashed unexpectedly. "They're pretty." She lifted her head from the flowers and looked at Troy. There was an air of excitement about him she hadn't seen in some time. It was slightly tempered with an odd hesitancy. Nervous to see her again?

"You look much better, Reed. From the last time I saw you, that is. More like yourself."

Anticipating his step forward to hug her, she stepped back and almost laughed. Just as if they were on a dance floor, they moved in unison. The hurt on Troy's face kept her amusement in check.

"You seem happy, Troy. Is the gizmo working?"

"Funny, it was such a simple thing. One little piece and everything fell into place. Sam's idea is absolutely brilliant. So simple we'd overlooked it completely. But there it was and now we have a product to test. If it works we have a customer waiting for it and they're willing to be our beta test. By this time next year all our money woes will be behind us. Maybe even sooner."

"That's great, Troy, really great." Reed gave him a smile. It really was good news. But standing on the porch of the lodge made that world seem a million miles away. Two weeks ago she might would have jumped into Troy's arms and kissed him over the news. Now she was just pleased for him and Sam. The whole team had worked so hard on this...thing.

"You just got in?" Of all the stupid things to say. Of course he'd just arrived. She'd watched the car pull up.

"Yeah. Sam and the guys will be here tomorrow. I wanted you to myself tonight."

"I see." A gulp didn't quite ease the lump in her throat.

"You did leave dinner tonight open for me, didn't you?"

"I...I guess I can do that. I didn't know for sure when you'd be in..." With a sigh she admitted, "I'm sorry, I'm sure you told me but I just can't seem to hang onto details like that. I can't even remember what day it is." She sank onto a bench and looked at the flowers in her hands. "You know me, without my day-planner at the ready I'm lost."

Troy sat beside her, picked up her hand and tapped on the crystal of her watch. "Your watch tells you what day it is," he said softly.

Despite all Gray's assurances the ranch was safe and she didn't need to, she still wore the watch. Unless she could lock it up, she didn't like leaving it lying around. "I know, but it has no meaning. Friday. So? My only task is to get dressed and show up for meals. And even if I forget about the meals they still appear wherever I am. They're determined to feed me here." The rueful grin came easily. What felt strange was not caring what day it was. Twisting her hand to look at the watch, she contemplated removing it and giving it back to Troy.

"Don't." The harsh tone in Troy's voice made her look up sharply.

"What?"

"Keep it." Troy set her hand down on her leg. "I have a feeling which way you'll go, but just the same, I don't want the watch back. I don't care if you toss it into a safe deposit box and replace it with a Timex, but I just can't take it back. It's yours with no strings attached."

Reed nodded. His pride couldn't take so deep a rejection. So much of Troy was wrapped up in that watch, it would be the ultimate insult to give it back to him. Fine. Gray probably had half a dozen vaults. It could go in one of those.

Troy drew in a deep breath and looked toward the mountains rising up behind the ranch. "Where's Gray?"

"They're having a ranch meeting of sorts. They're upstairs in the family dining room. I don't expect them to break for a least another hour."

"Care to walk me to my room?" The old light-hearted Troy was back. Great.

"Um..." She bit her lip. Alone in a room with a bed was not her idea of a way to spend quality time with Troy right now.

"I won't jump on you, I promise. On my honor as a gentleman." He even held up two fingers in the old Cub Scout salute.

Looking into his eyes, Reed determined he seemed sincere enough--his blue eyes were clear of mischief. "Well...as long as you keep your hands to yourself."

A shadow briefly crossed his face but he nodded. "I've got the same studio as before. Where are you staying?"

"W... I've got the small cabin over there." She pointed off to the left of the lodge. It was the closest and the smallest. Mom had left this morning so she and Gray had moved to a place with only one bedroom. Nestled under fir trees, it suited them just fine. They had a perfect view of the sunrise.

"Let's go for a stroll. Jamie said he'd get my gear to the room."

"Did you bring the gizmo with you?" Holding the flowers, she ignored the hand he held out to her.

"Only a few bits. Sam's finishing the polishing of the back-up quartz pieces today and she'll bring the more sensitive instruments with her tomorrow. She and Ian should be here by two or so. They're coming by chartered jet to keep from bouncing things around too much."

"Wow. This must be big."

"It is, Reed. It is so big..."

She gave him sharp glance. The words were right but the tone wasn't. Troy was looking around the ranch and taking in the atmosphere. A couple of wranglers were by the pond with a half dozen guests. Fly fishing lessons. Troy took her elbow and steered her off to the side of the trail when some riders on horseback passed on their way to the stables. Back from a lunchtime ride into the forest. Laughter came from the pool area where it seemed a game of water polo was underway. A couple of the younger wranglers were there playing lifeguard.

"How are you and Cass getting along?" The change of subject was abrupt. Troy trying to find neutral, comfortable, ground for conversation.

"Ah, me and Cass, we be mates," Reed said with genuine warmth. "I visit with him each day, but I'm really still too sore to ride." She covered her taped ribs briefly. Nothing but time would heal the cracked one and the surgical incision was still too raw. "Gray barely lets me out of the cabin, so riding is a few weeks away. Not to mention I tire easily, so we're taking it slow."

"Good." Troy still held her elbow. "Feel up to detouring by the stables?"

"Sure." As long as they kept their walk to a stroll she could handle a little more exercise than Gray had been allowing her. "You don't seem overly excited about the invention."

"Oh, I am. It's just...well..." Troy steered her around a horse offering in their path, "I'm really wondering if I'm cut out for the business world. Being up here again seems to have opened up something inside me that yearns for the simple life. Know what I mean?"

Reed laughed softly. "Yeah, I do. That could explain why I didn't remember what day it was. I can't seem to dredge up any enthusiasm for bank statements or financial reports. Gray was going over some numbers for the ranch last night and for once I couldn't dig up enough curiosity to read over his shoulder."

"You? Not grab them out of his hands and give him a full analysis after only five minutes reading the numbers?" The teasing sarcastic tone made her laugh.

"Yeah, me. I was happy to see the papers tossed aside." Better not explain that one further. "So, if you're no longer thrilled with the world of lasers, optics and the gizmos they belong to, what do you want to do?"

"I've been wondering if Gray would be willing to buy me out so I could get a ranch of my own. Whenever Sam kicked me out of the lab I did some searching. I haven't found any likely ranches yet, but there are some regions that interest me. Of course, I'm most familiar with this spread but that doesn't mean I couldn't do well in Arizona or Wyoming either. Not to mention, Colorado is a good sized state. There's room for more than one guest ranch in this market."

"Sam kicked you out of the lab?"

"Yeah. Seems I've lost my touch. I had a hard time concentrating on the job at hand. Good thing she has Ian and Dennis. Stuart is also going to be an asset once he loses his baby teeth. He did contribute a couple innovative ideas that helped pull it together better. This thing is so simple it's ridiculous. We'd been over engineering it." The shake of his head was rueful.

"Simple is best."

"Ah, but it isn't any fun if it isn't complicated with bells and whistles."

"Boys and their toys." Reed scoffed and watched a wrangler help a young teen boy pull a fish from the pond.

"Absolutely."

"So. You want to give up all that for all this?" She indicated the ranch with a wave.

"Nuts, huh?"

"Nah, I don't think so. Trading crowded freeways and smog for fresh air and wide open spaces? You're not crazy at all. It just won't make money hand over fist."

"It could with the right crowd. Remember I told you about my friend with the kid who wants to do films?"

"Yeah. Buster somebody."

"Buddy Franklin, but yeah, he's the one. Anyhow, Buddy's kid is coming up here tomorrow as well. He's got an idea for a cowboy romance and is looking for a good location. He goes back down to LA in a couple weeks and for his senior films project he has to do a short. He's looking to film in October. I told him how beautiful it was up here in the fall so he wants to look it over."

They stopped at the corral and Troy folded his arms on the rail, resting his chin on top. His hat sat back on his head and the denim jacket he wore blended right into the background. For a moment Reed could only stare. Troy looked as if he belonged here as much as Gray or the wranglers giving riding lessons on the other side of the rails.

"Look at that kid swinging the rope. Bet he gets the calf."

Reed turned her attention back to the corral and watched a young teen follow a calf running from the chute. With a cowboy yell he swung his lariat and caught the back legs of the calf. Whooping with excitement, his dad shot a video from the side. Once the calf was released he turned back to his fans with a wide grin.

"Not bad. A tad clumsy, but not bad at all."

"You really do like it here, don't you?"

"The two summers I worked here were the best of my life. I really liked working with the guests. Since I was raised by myself, it was my first experience around kids. Don't know that I could deal with them all the time, but most of them were really great."

"Yeah, but I bet you liked the older daughters better." She cast him a sideways glance.

Troy actually looked a little abashed. "Well, yeah. I was just barely a man at the time, of course girls were on my mind."

She watched his face as his eyes followed a young woman try next.

"She's going to miss," he predicted.

He was right.

"And there's Mike to help her fix what she did wrong. I can see you doing that twenty years ago."

"Eighteen," Troy muttered.

"Oh Troy, don't get all touchy about your age like a woman."

"Very funny. Truth is, I never meant to go so long without getting married."

"I didn't think you were the marrying kind." His dates had never seemed like anything more than trophy wife material. She'd always expected him to marry one of them. Any would have done. In her mind they were all interchangeable. "Why didn't you marry Tiffany?"

"You're kidding, right?" Troy turned to her with a look of disbelief. "I was waiting for you to wake up and realize I was sitting there worshipping you."

"Then why did you steal ol' Tiffy from Gray?"

"I was hoping to make him mad and you jealous."

"And it didn't work."

"Exactly. Gray was glad to dump her on me, and you just shrugged your shoulders and dove back into the books."

"So is that why I got the watch when you broke up with her?"

"The watch was to get you to meetings on time."

"And to help me remember what day of the week it is."

"Right. That didn't seem to work out right either."

"Sorry."

"Don't be. If you weren't late for meetings then you wouldn't be you. The thing is, when you're late for a meeting I know it's because you were working up until the last minute to get the details right. When anyone else is late it's because they stopped in the coffee room and got caught up in a gossip session. That's why you got the watch. You wouldn't take any other gifts from me and this way I could say it was job related to help you perform better."

Troy's look was a little more affectionate than she was prepared to deal with and she turned away feeling the burn of a flush across her cheeks. If she tilted her head just right the brim of her hat hid her face from him.

"Reed, if I hadn't screwed up in Amsterdam, would there really have been a chance for us? Or was it doomed from the beginning?"

She closed her eyes at the quiet agony in his voice. "I think we were doomed. Not to make you feel any more guilty than you already do but, you see, because I know how impulsive you are, I wasn't going to make you wait for the fourth date. I...I had everything set up to meet you at the airport. I was going to be bold and shock your socks off. And then I started getting emails."

Her heart twisted as Troy hung his head and scuffed the dirt with his boot.

"It wasn't just about your activities in Amsterdam, Troy. That was merely a sharp illustration of who you are. You're used to getting what you want, when you want it." She laid a hand on his arm and he froze. Just as softly she lifted it away. "If you'd managed to restrain yourself then, you wouldn't have been able to later. It's who you are. I don't want to be your mother, going around after you and cleaning up all your messes. That is who I would have turned into by being closer to you. It's who I am now when I'm with you. At least it's only related to business. I didn't want it to be my personal life as well."

"Things have changed, though."

"Yes, you've had to learn to do without these past several months but, honestly Troy, your idea of having to do without means flying first class instead of chartering a private jet. Maybe even using an upgrade coupon to get that seat rather than just booking it straight. You haven't made it all the way down to economy class and you don't live off macaroni and cheese. You give a thousand dollars to charity instead of ten thousand. You're still living in another world."

Troy stared across the corral for a while. "What

do Gray's dreams have to do with you?"

"You know about the dreams?" Was there anyone who didn't know?

"He talked about them in college. Especially the one that he said seemed to be in ancient Celtic times. He mentioned others... Middle Ages, settling the West... I don't remember all of them. We did a little research with some of the details he remembered and those were just a couple of the time periods we came up with." Troy kicked at the fence post. "So, what do they mean to you?"

"I've been having the same dreams. As they grow clearer, I realize I've been having these dreams all my life." She paused to let the implication sink in. Hell, she was still letting it settle in for herself.

Gray had found her. He'd been right from the very beginning. They'd been together before and were meant to be together again. For all time, if she understood correctly. At least it was what she wanted to believe. Gray was her future...all her futures.

Before Troy could respond, a horse stopped on the other side of the rail and made her look up. Jim sat on Cass's back. "You here to ride?" he asked her.

Shaking her head she playfully pushed Cass's nose away when he tried to eat her flowers. "No, a few more days yet." Jim knew that, but he liked to tease her anyway. In his own way, he made it clear he wouldn't let her be afraid of riding.

"Hey, Troy," he greeted the other man.

"How's things, Jim?"

"Other than trying to keep Cass from getting too spoiled by his newest girlfriend, things are just about the same as they always are. You going to ride this afternoon?"

"If I do, I can saddle up for myself. Mainly just want a chance to talk to Reed before the crowds arrive again. Also, I want to talk with you about where the best place to set up the equipment."

"What do you need? And how much gear?"

Reed tuned out while they discussed terrain and gear boxes. Instead she plucked petals from one of the daisies and fed them to Cass, taking time to stroke his nose. After a time she became aware the men had stopped talking and seemed to be looking at her expectantly.

"I'm sorry, I wasn't listening," she said.

Troy shook his head. "Reed, really, this does concern you to some small extent." He rested a hand on her shoulder and dropped his gaze to the ground for a moment then looked up at her with sad smile. "Don't worry about it. You don't really need to be involved with the testing." He turned back to Jim. "We'll want to leave as early as possible Sunday morning and should have enough gear and food for two or three nights. That ought to give us a pretty good feeling for how it will work and allow us time to build a shelter for it. Then we can come back down and monitor from here for the rest of the week."

"Sounds very doable to me. I'll tell the bosses when they come out of their meeting."

"Don't they usually wait for the end of the season to hold the yearly meeting?" Troy asked.

"Yup, but since Gray's been absent for a couple years they figured it was now or wait he shows up again," Jim said.

"What's to discuss? Other than upgrading the

internet access you have a sweet thing going here. Don't change a thing."

"Had a feeling you'd be on the anti-development side of things." Reed could hear the grin in Jim's voice and looked up.

"What's there to develop other than a slightly more aggressive advertising campaign?" Troy looked around. "I wouldn't change a stick."

"Well, some folks want to hire an educated marketing genius for a GM and then let him run things. Sora wants to step back for a change. Dustin wants a little time off, or rather his wife does and he wants to make her happy. Gray's the next logical person to run the place but his other business concerns keep him away too much. We've already seen that. Kiri can do the marketing, but she doesn't want to run the whole thing. We still have young kids so she doesn't want to be away from home promoting the place and Blake, well Blake has no business sense at all."

"So, hire Troy to run the ranch," Reed said.

The two men fell silent, both staring at her as if she'd said the world ended yesterday and they hadn't noticed. "Seriously," she continued. "Troy was just telling me he wanted to sell the company to Gray and buy himself a spread like this one. Simple. He wants out of the laser business, you want a General Manager who loves the place like family, who knows it like family. Where else can you find someone with those qualities?"

Both men still stared at her and she shook her head. "Can't you think outside of the box for once? It's a simple matter. So simple it seems ludicrous, but just stop and think for a minute. You won't earn a six figure income again until you bring up the profitability of the ranch, but by selling Gray the majority ownership of your company you'll have cash assets again and if you maintain stock you'll see profit from the latest gadget you're here to test."

On a roll, she had the undivided attention of both men. "You won't need the big income but you will have meaningful and soul-satisfying work, which is more important than money. And if you do bring up the profitability of the ranch, then you can negotiate appropriate compensation with the family corporation. Too bad you can't marry or get adopted into it, but somehow I think Kiri is very happy with Jim so tough luck on you." She softened her teasing with a hand on Troy's arm.

An odd light had been growing in his eye while she talked and now Cass danced a little, presumably responding to a touch of reaction from Jim. If she had to guess, she'd say both men liked the idea.

"Anyhow..." She returned to petting Cass's nose. "It isn't my decision to make and they've most likely come up with a better solution already."

The silence held for a minute, then Jim swung down from the horse. Slinging the reins over the rail he waved for Reed and Troy to follow him. He met them at the gate then took Reed's arm and pointed them in the direction of the lodge.

"Reed, honey, your idea is so damned outrageous I think the family needs to hear it," Jim said with a note of glee in his voice.

"Oh, wait, no..." She dug in her heels and pulled him to a stop. Troy nearly ran into her he'd been following so close. "Jim, I didn't mean it. It's a silly idea. Knowing how Gray and Troy get along..." She gave up when Jim tugged on her arm again.

"Darlin', your idea is the best I've heard yet. Troy has the social connections to work the marketing campaign and maybe word will filter down to a movie making type who will want to use the place for a film and then we can do some basic upgrades without draining the cash reserves and over leveraging ourselves hoping the remodeling will bring in more upscale clients. Does that make sense?"

"Well, Troy was just telling me there's a film student coming up tomorrow to scout out locations for his senior short film."

Jim stopped and wrapped her in a hug, lifting her from the ground and swung her around.

"Whoa there!" she screeched. "Ow!" Jim set her down and she reached up, trying to keep her hat on and not drop her flowers at the same time she tried to catch her breath. The hat lost and flew off as Jim bent and kissed her cheek.

"Sorry about the ribs, but you're brilliant. Gorgeous and with the brains of Einstein all in one package. Gray better marry you soon or I just might!" Jim crowed.

Reed slapped his chest to make him release his grip on her waist. "You're already married to the prettiest girl on the mountain. I won't tell her what you said." She took her hat from Troy and slapped the dust off it against her jeans clad leg.

Jamming it back on her head she turned away from the lodge. The man was nuts. The whole family was nuts. It had to be the thin air.

Jim grabbed her arm again. "Oh no, you're

coming with me. Grab her arm, Troy. Upstairs we go."

"Troy, you could help me out here," she grumbled when he grabbed her arm.

"Unfortunately, you've reached into my heart and pulled out most of my dreams. The only one you missed was you marrying me," he said and gave her a silly grin. "I'm rather curious to see if this will fly."

Reed was out of breath when they reached the top of the stairs and stopped in front of the closed door of the private dining room.

"You're both crazy!" she gasped. "I'm not marching in there with any kind of proposition. You like the idea so damn much, Jim, you lay it out." She turned and found herself held tight against Jim while he pounded on the door.

Hand still in mid air poised for the third knock, the door swung open and Jim nearly knocked on Blake's nose.

"Hey! What's goin' on out here?" Blake stopped Jim's fist with a deft catch and stepped back to let them in.

Gray rose when he saw Reed pressed against Jim. His look turned bemused when Jim thrust her into Gray's arms. Feeling out of place she tried to avoid his eyes but his finger tipped her head up. "What's up, sweetheart?"

"Jim has this crazy notion that I thought of something brilliant. Stupid is more like it."

"What's this?" Sora asked, her eyes moving from Reed to Troy to Jim and back again.

"We were just chatting down by the corral and Reed came up with the most brilliant plan I've heard yet for bringing this place into the new millennium," Jim said, his usual slow drawl missing at the moment. She couldn't help noticing how the family stared at him in amazement.

"Well then, let's hear it because we aren't getting anywhere at the moment," Dustin said and leaned back in his chair at the head of the table. "We're just going around in circles here and no one is happy. If Jim is this excited it must be good."

Reed gulped and wondered yet again, just what had she gotten herself into?

TWENTY-NINE

"And that's all there is to it, really," Reed concluded quietly. The room had gone dead silent. Through the open window they heard the neigh of a horse and a singing bird, but not one person in the dining room breathed. Still standing, she shifted on her booted feet and snuck a glance toward the door where Jamie and a few of his cousins hovered.

This concerned them too. It was their future. Other than the balcony, there was no escape from the room so she held her ground and looked at the floor. Her boots needed polishing.

She needed air. The next thing she knew Gray had her pinned in a tight hug and everyone spoke at once. Only a squeak could make it out because he held her so tight. Slapping his shoulder made him loosen his grip.

"Oh darlin', sweet, sweet Ree. You're incredible," Gray whispered in her ear as he fought to regain control of his business face. "I love you so much."

"What? It isn't that big a deal." She pushed away.

"Oh yes, it is," Dustin contradicted her. "Sit down everyone. Jamie, shut the door, but all of you come in. You can't vote about it, but I want to hear your opinions." He waved the kids into the room. The littlest ones were down the hall with one of the maids.

"First of all, I want to hear from Troy. Is this something you'd seriously consider?" Dustin asked.

Chairs scraped into place then silence fell again. Reed sat on Gray's lap where he'd pulled her and Troy sat next to them and answered the question.

"Actually, yes. I very much want to consider it. However, a large part of my decision is based on whether or not Gray wants to buy the company and how he'd integrate it into his. I think negotiations need to start there. First and foremost, I want my people taken care of."

Gray nodded. "I think we can come to an agreement. I've been thinking about moving my operations to the Boulder area, and it would be a good time to merge."

Reed watched as Troy cocked his head and nodded thoughtfully. "I hadn't thought about relocating... though somehow I think everyone might be rather pleased with the idea. And if I retain some stock, I'd be close enough to pop down from time to time just to keep my hand in."

She was pleased when Gray nodded in agreement and indulged in a small sigh of relief. Gray gave her a small squeeze to show he'd felt it, but didn't look at her.

"Okay, so Troy's open to the idea. Now, what does the family have to say?" Dustin turned to his mother.

"Troy knows us." Sora spoke slowly. "He knows the ranch and the operations, knows how to handle horses and guests and, as Reed said, he has the social and business network to help spread our name. He also knows those people and what they're looking for in a vacation experience. I think it would be a good match. I am concerned about the compensation package and the other expenses we're looking at. Before we commit one way or the other I'd like to discuss his vision for moving forward."

Dustin's eyes swung to Troy who nodded.

"A reasonable request and one I expect will take time to formulate," Dustin continued. "We need a new business plan anyway and this a good place to begin discussions so we all have a clear picture. Kiri?" He directed the discussion to his sister next and Reed saw her nod as well.

"I can work with Troy. He loves the ranch. I see no problem moving forward."

Dustin nodded and looked to Blake next.

"I'm cool with it."

Dustin scowled but accepted the short answer. "Troy, I know this is off the cuff, but do you have a very high-level vision you're willing to talk about right now? We're in a stalemate at the moment between those who want to make this place upscale and those who want to do basic modernization but retain the charm."

With all eyes on him, Troy nodded slowly and Reed was relieved he didn't look nervous. In fact, he exuded the cool business head she admired.

"I can see both sides and both have their points. The current room situation is just about right. Maybe one more cabin and you could make it the top of the line in luxury, a real honeymoon spot, but I think that would be all, as far as adding rooms. The basic decorating scheme is fine but looking a little worn. Replace a few items and everything will look and feel fresh. Up the luxury just a touch, but keep it simple. Folks are here for a break. We want them to relax and feel comfortable. Update internet and cell access to attract the business conferences as well as the Sundance or Hollywood set. Sell the ambiance." Troy stood and paced to the glass door leading to the balcony.

"Yeah, I think we can accommodate both sides of the debate. Keep it family friendly during the summers, and in the fall and winter you can bring in the movie makers." Troy turned back to the room. "I can see it. What it will mean for all of you is a chance to get away. You've all been here all your lives, day in and day out, season after season. You've put your hearts and souls into it and that isn't to be discounted one bit. I can see you deserve a break every now and then. The worry is making sure things continue to run as you'd run them and still have a chance to take off and travel. I know Rachel's always wanted to go on a long cruise. Dustin could take her. He retains the position of CEO, but I become his right-hand man. With quarterly meetings we keep the corporation on track and things running smoothly."

"But are you sure the movie people will come?" Kiri asked.

Reed bit her lip to keep from smiling and earned a curious glance from Gray. She just shook her head and wrapped her arms tighter around his neck while Troy answered.

"Kiri." The grin was evident in Troy's voice. "They're arriving tomorrow."

The look on Kiri's face was priceless. "What?"

"Well, not exactly Hollywood, but the UCLA

Film Department. We have a student coming to scout out the area for his senior project. He's the son of a friend and has just finished a summer internship with a big name Hollywood production company. He has a cowboy script and I suggested he at least check out the area."

"Oh!" Kiri's jaw dropped and her eyes sparkled.

Reed imagined Kiri could see a director looking like a modern day John Huston or John Ford striding across the compound in her imagination. They might never reach that level of recognition, but it was a start. She knew Troy also had connections to the Sundance Film Festival. The potential was out there.

"So, Gray, what do you think?" Dustin directed the next question to him.

"I think there are enough possibilities to look at the situation. I'm in favor of serious discussion."

Reed wanted to smack him. Discussion? It was perfect. He'd be free to take care of his other business interests without having to bear the responsibility of the ranch, too. Not to mention he'd get to hire Sam, Ian and Dennis. And her.

The thought made her forget her resolve to keep a poker face, and she frowned. But she'd resigned. Did she want to work for Gray? Would he want to hire her? Or did he still want to marry her and would she want to work after getting married? Would he want her to work, or not?

Married? Work after getting married? Oh Lord. Had she already accepted in her mind? In her heart? Yes. If he really wanted to marry her she'd say yes in a heartbeat. That much she knew was right. The rest would work itself out.

"Reed?"

Gray's soft voice made her look at him. "Hmm?"

"What's wrong?"

A glance around the table revealed all eyes on her. "Oh, um, nothing. Sounds like a good idea all around." She put a smile on her face even though it felt stiff and forced.

"You think you'd like to live in Boulder?" he asked her.

"I...I don't know. I've never been to Boulder."

"Rumor is it's a lot like living in Berkeley."

"I don't live in Berkeley. I live in Albany."

Gray held her close with a chuckle. "You're being obtuse. Do you want to live in Boulder, and here, with me?"

"What?"

"I'm asking you to marry me. I wasn't going to press the issue so soon, but none of these plans will mean a thing if you don't want to live here with me. If you're not with me I might as well give Troy all my companies and come home to the ranch. I built all those businesses to make your life easier. If you don't want me, then I don't need them anymore."

Dark eyes stared deeply into hers and it felt as if he could read her very soul. A wave of dizziness made her cling tighter to his shoulders and if there was a sound in the room she couldn't hear it. Every atom of blood was suddenly rushing past her ears, downing out all but the sound of her heartbeat.

"I..." she swallowed to try and clear the lump in her throat. All at once she understood. The last part of the dream suddenly made sense. The baby represented a new life and a new way of doing things. Carrick had been right to hold firm all along.

Troy would do more good at the ranch. That was where his heart lay. Gray could merge the companies and bring new prosperity to all the employees. Troy would bring new growth to the ranch. Both sides would grow and bring happiness to many people.

"The idea has possibilities," she answered softly, using his own words. If there was ever a time she wanted to shout out to the world her love for him, this was it, but their love went to a far deeper, more personal level. A love that had crossed centuries and lives...with more to come.

"And build a house here as well?"

"As long as I can feed the chickadees. If they won't feed from my hand it's a deal breaker." She couldn't hide her teasing smile.

"If I have to staple them to your hand, they'll eat from it. Just like Cass. Just like me." His forehead rested against hers and for a moment they breathed in unison. "I want your help designing the house, I want your help with the merger and you can choose whether or not you want to continue working. Or Mom has said she could use your help with the books. You'll be part of the family so it only seems fair you should carry your share of the load."

"Just like you carry your share." She looked at him with a raised brow before nodding. "Okay, you talked me into it. Yes, I'll marry you."

Gray's hand shook ever so slightly when he cupped her cheek and locked his gaze with hers. "I promise I'll make you happy."

"You've already made me happy."

"Then I'll keep you happy," he said with a touch of well-earned arrogance.

"I love you, Gray." She cupped his cheek with her hand. The feeling was there between them, but she'd never said the words.

"I love you, Reed." The gleam in his eyes showed every ounce of his feelings for her. A gleam she recognized from several lifetimes. A slight dizziness assaulted her as memories flooded her.

A small sob from Gray's sister brought Reed's focus back to the present. Judging by the silent anticipation, she guessed the whole room could feel the very truth of those words as deeply as she did.

"I promise," Gray said softly, "I'll keep you happy for all time."

Impatiently Troy tipped his head back and groaned to the ceiling. "Oh just shut up and kiss her already."

"Smart man," Gray said with a grin and pressed his lips to hers.

The End

DEDICATION
To my two true heroes, my husband and son.

ACKNOWLEDGMENTS

Although most of my stories are set in Alaska, this one comes from five years spent in Colorado.

The setting is loosely based on the Black Mountain Guest Ranch in McCoy, CO. The very kind people there sent me a DVD from which I imagined the ranch. If you're looking at such a vacation be sure to check them out. www.blackmtnranch.com

I thank the massage community in general for providing great descriptions of massage techniques on their individual websites. I personally benefited from the skills of a wonderful massage therapist in CO, who has my eternal gratitude for the time spent under her healing hands at a time when my back wasn't happy. I've since found a new therapist back home in Alaska and I pout when she's overbooked.

For details on the Yoni Massage and the Lingam Massage, neither of which any of my therapists have ever provided--in case you were wondering--go to: www.whitelotuseast.com.

For the re-edit, my eternal thanks go out to Carlee Winn, Lizbeth Selvig, and Sandy Shacklett. Thank you for taking on the role of beta reader. Again. And again.

As for some of the characters, a few are based on real people. You know who you are, though names have been changed to protect the suspects. Well, as much as the thin veils can protect you. My lips are sealed. Okay, application of enough tequila might change that, but until then, I hope you enjoy this book and check back for more.

ABOUT THE AUTHOR

Morgan is an everyday kind of woman--a wife and mother like many others. These days she's also a semi-empty nester with her one and only attending university. There isn't much that makes her stand out from the crowd, with the possible exception of her imagination.

Inside her mind live characters who look normal, if almost a little boring, on the outside. Inside they have passions and hungers that would shock their preachers and next door neighbors.

Kinky? Maybe. Twisted? Warped? Definitely-- but in a fun way. Bloodsport is not her style. Leather and lace? Oh yeah. A sexy stare-down, a thorough tongue lashing, bubbles and petting. Champagne and hot tubs. Morgan lives for decadent luxury and love. Ripped abs, smooth warm skin, and tight butts on her heroes a must. Strong arms on strong men with lusty appetites.

Let your inhibitions go and step into Morgan's world. Erotic adventure often mixed with danger-laced action keeps the pages turning.

http://morganqoreilly.com
Romance for All Your Moods